TIME
ON MY
HANDS

TIME
ON MY
HANDS
GIORGIO
VASTA

faber and faber

TRANSLATED FROM THE ITALIAN BY JONATHAN HUNT

Originally published in Italy in 2008 by Minimum Fax as *Il tempo materiale*
First published in the US in 2013 by Faber and Faber, Inc.
First published in the UK in 2013
by Faber and Faber Limited
Bloomsbury House
74-77 Great Russell Street
London WC1B 3DA

Printed and bound by CPI Group (UK) Ltd, Croydon CR0 4YY

A CIP record for this book is available from the British Library

This book has been selected to receive financial assistance from English PEN's "PEN
Translates!" programme, supported by Arts Council England. English PEN exists to
promote literature and our understanding of it, to uphold writers' freedoms around the
world, to campaign against the persecution and imprisonment of writers for stating
their views, and to promote the friendly co-operation of writers and the free exchange
of ideas. www.englishpen.org

ISBN 978-0-571-27220-4

FSC
www.fsc.org
MIX
Paper from
responsible sources
FSC® C101712

10 9 8 7 6 5 4 3 2 1

TIME
ON MY
HANDS

There was the sky. There was water, there were roots. There was religion, there was matter, there was home. There were bees, there were magnolias, animals, fire. There was the city, there was the temperature of the air that changed in your breath. There was light, there were bodies, organs, bread. There were years, molecules, there was blood; and there were dogs, stars, climbing plants.

And there was thirst. Names.

There were names.

There was me.

NIMBUS

(JANUARY 8, 1978)

I was eleven years old and lived among cats ravaged by rhinotracheitis and mange. They were warped skeletons with a bit
of skin on them; infected: if you touched them you could die.
Every afternoon String went to feed them at the end of the
garden opposite our apartment; sometimes I went with her.
They came toward us slowly, their bodies angled askew, and
looked at us with eyes that were drops of water and mud.
Among the dying I'd grown attached to the worst, the one that
sat at the end of the asphalted paths, sunken in the abyss; he
heard our footsteps and moved his head slowly, like a blind
man following a song, his sooty-black coat reduced to fluff on
his flaking skin, one leg hanging loose among the others. He'd
been lame ever since he was a kitten; now he was full grown, a
natural cripple.

String put the saucepan down on a low wall that formed the
base of a pale green railing. While her back was turned, I

touched the railing with my tongue to taste the chlorine of the old paint and rust, then turned away and swallowed. I took a spoon and scooped up a little heap of *ditalini* with meat sauce. I carried it over to the cripple, crouched down beside him, and let him smell it. He pushed his scabby face forward, his nose blurring in the steam; then he picked up a lump of black meat between two teeth and started gnawing at it. String gestured to me not to touch him, told me to pour it all out and step back. I made a little volcano with the *ditalini*; the cripple listened to it with his nose, then went on tenaciously biting the lump, filtering each mouthful through the gaps between his teeth, twisting his head to destroy and swallow, turning nutriment into blood. When he'd finished he lay down with his muzzle on the ground in front of the little wet volcano, the idol to be worshipped. He was no longer hungry; his breath hissed out from the fan of his ribs. I touched him with the tip of the spoon; he didn't move, but emitted a pigeon-like whirr from his neck. He could still manage a yawn; he opened his mouth and ate air. Then he sank back into a stupor, his head in the midst of a patch of light.

Behind me I heard the last scrapes of ladle against saucepan. For years, at this time of day, down in the gardens, String had ladled food out of her saucepan with a vigorous movement of shoulder, arm, and hand, making little heaps of pasta on the ground. Then she'd click her tongue to call the cats and look around to see if they were happy, if they had enough to eat, as they staggered in toward the food from all directions. Then she'd walk home, encrusted ladle in one hand, saucepan in the other: her sword and shield.

Now she'd finished and had sat down on a bench to rest. I checked that she wasn't looking, then took a piece of barbed wire out of the pocket of my windbreaker and pressed the spikes into the bare patches on the cripple's back. Each time the skin dimpled in for a moment, then slowly flattened out again.

He never moved, except for a slight twitch of the head. I'd increase the pressure and he'd shudder, have a brief fit of nerves, an outburst of bewildered indignation that lasted a few seconds before fading away, then settle back into his former pensive pose.

"Let's go," said String.

I got up, put the barbed wire in my pocket, and walked off. There was a harsh cry behind me. I turned around and saw the cripple standing on all four legs, taking one step, then another. At every movement his head lolled forward, recoiled, and vibrated. He turned a complete circle, then meowed again disgustedly.

"He's gone mad," said String behind me. "Cats often do when they go blind."

I said nothing and watched him walk in ever faster circles. I felt the sun on my cheek.

"He does it every day," she added, "after he's eaten."

The cripple walked blindly on, stiff with cold, inhaling mucous. He turned another circle, meowing harshly; then he stopped, shrank, lay down, and nodded his head again, to say yes, yes, that's the way it should be.

String set off toward our home—number 130, Via Sciuti. I turned and followed her. The asphalt was metallic in the low sun; at every step, I felt I was sinking.

●

Later I went out on to the balcony and looked for the cripple at the end of the gardens. From that distance he was a dark rock that other cats kept clear of, making wide detours to avoid going anywhere near it.

In the sky the sun had become a dry lung; it coexisted with the moon and the rarefied dusk that was beginning to seep into cracks in the road surface, into pools of oil leaked from car engines, into squiggly skid marks, into saplings supported by broomsticks.

The day before, a boy had gone over to a car that had parked down there. Speaking in dialect, he'd asked the owner for money; the man had refused and told him to go away. The boy had pointed to the car, asked again and stood waiting. When the man had put the key into the door to lock it, the boy had pulled up a broomstick supporting a nearby sapling and smashed the headlights and windows. Then he'd thrown away the broomstick, bent down, and bitten one of the tires, his teeth going right through the tread and puncturing the inner tube. Finally, his face smeared with engine grease, he'd attacked the man and bitten his cheeks and forehead.

I heard the sound of harp music from the living room and went inside to watch *Intervallo*. It was intended as a brief respite, a patch to cover the hiatus between programs. I found it hypnotic.

The humpback bridge at Apecchio, the Visso Valley strewn with pale houses. San Ginesio, Gratteri, Pozza di Fassa. The facades of Sutri, the white fountain of Matelica. Ten seconds per picture postcard, then a fade-out and a new picture. The eternal rustic, pastoral Italy built of gray, hand-hewn rocks, stonewalls adorned with ivy and moss, inhabited only by Oscans and Etruscans, a simple, rural world whose dead slept in village graveyards, with graveled paths between tombs, crunching footsteps and a smell of gladioli, cypress berries mingling with the gravel, a clear sky, roses. Ghosts of the land-scape, deluders of the national self-image. The picturesque, the local, the premodern, the authentic. A beautiful semiliterate Italy, too honest to need a knowledge of grammar.

Until a year ago we'd had *Carosello* too, an X-ray picture of joy. Now we were left with *Intervallo*, a slow merry-go-round of nostalgia, a Nativity scene confected by television.

The news came on. They talked about Rome, an ambush the day before on Via Acca Larentia. Some shots had been fired, two members of the escort had been killed, and a policeman had wounded one of the attackers. The picture showed a body covered with a white sheet. The faces of the dead were young and pale, their features whirls against the light.

On television Rome was an animal. Viewed from above, the shape of the houses and streets was a stone backbone, a mineral animal. It contained the dead and generated them, or perhaps attracted them. At any rate, only in Rome did people die. So I took the Roman dead, picking them up one by one out of Via Acca Larentia and all the other streets, and put them into the nonexistent Italy. I laid one on the pebble beach under the bridge at Apecchio, hung another from the battlements of Caccamo castle, left a third to float in the waters of Civitanova Marche, and lodged another, fittingly, between the rocks of the necropolis at Pantalica. I gave the rest of Italy back its dead.

String came in and told me supper was nearly ready.

"Have I ever been to Rome?" I asked her.

"We went there just after you were born," she replied.

"Have I ever been there since?"

"No, you haven't. Neither have I."

"Can I go there?"

"Why do you want to?"

I didn't have a clear answer to this, so I said nothing.

"Not on your own," she said.

"Can *we* go there?" I said, changing tack.

She stared at the television screen, put one finger to her lips, and nibbled at the cuticles.

"Maybe," she said.

"When?"

"Perhaps at Easter."

String continued to stare at the screen without turning toward me.

"Have I ever been to Apecchio?" I asked.

"No," she said. "I've never heard of it. Where is it?"

"It doesn't matter," I said.

"Do you want to go there?"

"No."

"Why do you want to go to Rome?" she asked again.

"Because of the dead," I said unguardedly.

"What?" she asked, turning to look at me, the tip of her ring finger between her teeth.

"Because I'm curious," I said.

•

By the time Stone got home, Cotton and I were already in bed—not under the covers, but sitting on top; he in his pajamas, I in my daytime clothes. Our beds stood end to end along one wall of the bedroom, fitting neatly into the space. They were identical; Cotton and I were far from identical: I was fully evolved, he was a microscopic amoeba; I was arbitrary, he was democratic and flexible.

While Stone had his dinner in the kitchen, Cotton and I listened to the radio, poking our fingers through the thick wool bedspread and clenching our fists to feel the pleasure of constriction.

Stone came into the bedroom, his lips still wet with food. He turned off the radio, took a book from the shelf, and sat down between us. It was a big book, with a stiff, smooth, enamel-like cover. The cover illustration showed a thin, fair-haired boy clothed in animal skins except for his bare chest, playing a wooden harp and gazing raptly into the distance, a wild-eyed sheep at his feet. In the background Christ could be seen entering Jerusalem, surrounded by a white-robed, adoring crowd. Above the illustration, in capital letters, was the title THE GREAT-EST STORY EVER TOLD. A graphic synthesis of spirituality as conceived by the Edizioni Paoline—gentle admonition, mildly stern sentimentality, compassionate naïveté: pastel religion.

The keystones of my bold young atheism.

Stone had been reading the Bible to us since before we'd

been able to read for ourselves. He didn't do it out of religious conviction, or out of a desire to supplement the catechism, or a general respect for the holy scriptures, but just out of habit, a reluctance to let anything go to waste: because of the sheer inertia that governed our family life. But he read badly, paying little attention to the meaning of the text and with an uneven delivery marked by exaggeratedly open vowels. While Cotton lay on his bed with his feet toward the pillow, I adopted my own listening position, sitting up straight, with the back of my head against the wall, arms folded and legs crossed: uncomfortable but resolute, I was creating my atheist halo.

One evening, while Stone was reading, Cotton had drawn my attention to the part of the wall I was leaning against. I'd turned around and seen, at the level of my head, an oval circle, blue in the middle and fading outward to a peachy color before blending with the white of the plaster. I'd created this halo by the pressure of my occiput, through the slow corrosion of listening. When I rested my head against the wall in the evening, I was making my own halo—or rather, my nimbus: *nimbused* was the word the scriptures used to describe a haloed saint, and nimbus—"small cloud," "circle of hazy light"—perfectly encapsulated my own natural supernatural circumfusion.

The previous evening we'd read about the prophet Jonah, who spent three days in the belly of a whale and came out full of the word. This evening we were going to read about Ezekiel, the prophet of splendor. He wore a bright, powerful, blue tunic with a yellow shawl on his head; his beard and eyebrows were white. Ezekiel was a seer, a creator of images, a pure, insane old man. I was a pure insane *young* man who yearned to go out into the world to preach, be full of the word like Jonah and visionary like Ezekiel, to express my desire for language, that fever of the throat.

A few months earlier I'd been doing my oral exam at the end of my final year at elementary school. I'd had the exhilarating sense of telling a story that regenerated itself and regenerated me. The floor of the classroom around me was flooded with light. Gugliotta, Chiri, D'Avenia, and my other classmates sat quietly at their desks, listening. I had my precious little pack of picture cards in my back pocket—Beppe Furino's black face was squashed against my buttock. I felt I could go on forever, that language was an epidemic from which there was no point in trying to escape. I'd talked on and on, there in the sunlight with the others watching me, expatiating on science and geography, joyously crossing borders, ranging from subject to subject. Finally the teacher had smiled, put her hand on my chest to stop me, and said: "You're mythopoetic."

I'd gone back to my seat with the pleasurable and disturbing sensation of her thin fingers still on my ribs. As one of my classmates took my place at the teacher's desk and struggled to answer the first question, I'd whispered to Chiri and D'Avenia, "What does it mean?" Neither of them knew. Later, when I got home, I'd looked it up. *Mythopoetic.* "Word-making: said of one who generates words." I'd felt pleased, gratified, and moved; recognized.

Now, as Stone read us Bible stories, I was showing my mythopoetic powers by turning reality into words. I'd learned technical terms by reading the encyclopedia *Il Modulo,* and the *Ricerche* workbooks published in weekly installments by Edizioni Salvadeo: slim, pale yellow volumes accompanied by sheets of color photographs. On the back of each photograph was a text describing it and providing background information, using precise terminology. Each number was devoted to a particular subject: animals, history, the sky and the weather, the sea, science and technology, tropical plants. You cut out the pictures with scissors and stuck one edge into the workbook so that you could flip the photograph over and read the text on the back; once you'd glued them all in, you played with them, sticky-fingered, for the rest of the day.

As Cotton's head drooped over the pages and mangled sentences issued from Stone's mouth, I worked at my nimbus, focusing on my old toy basket with its cylindrical shape and protruding strands of wicker, on the lacquered bookcase with its various shades of white, on a Scrooge McDuck doll dressed in a peeling rubber bathrobe, on a red Bambi that had faded to a shameful pink, on a picture of a curly-headed little boy holding a pretty flower in his hands and smiling at me.

As I pressed the back of my head against the wall my brain was dizzy with words, with flashing sentences. I stuck to my task, naming a coatrack with jackets on it, a green felt cowboy's hat suitable for the bad guy in a Western film, a miner's helmet with a smashed lamp, the flame-colored veins on the door, scattered knots in the wood, and a ten-centimeter groove near the handle that I'd made a few days before with my piece of barbed wire.

The riot of language built up till I could no longer contain it.

"No!" I said, jerking my head away from the wall. It didn't seem like a word, more like the opening chord of a symphony.

Cotton woke up and peered at me in mild, placid bemusement. Stone stopped reading.

"What's the matter?" he asked.

"Nothing," I said. "There was one bit I didn't understand for a moment."

He looked at me thoughtfully, then read on: "To show that God has the power to restore life to the dead, the Prophet told this story: *The Lord set me down on a field strewn with bones and asked me: 'Do you believe that these bones can come back to life? Then bend over them and prophesy with these words: "Behold, I will infuse you with the spirit and you shall live."'* In the vision the Prophet obeyed, and behold, bones joined together with bones, sinews linked them together, flesh grew, skin spread over it, and the spirit entered the bodies, and they became men."

I moved closer, craning my neck toward the open book. There was a picture of a plain, scattered with white, contorted skeletons. In the background the tiny figure of Ezekiel stood on a blood-colored mountain. I put the Roman dead around him too; I spread them out over the plain and covered them with white sheets. But Ezekiel prophesied, and they slipped out from under the sheets, got to their feet, dusted themselves off, and walked away.

Stone put the book down and went to get a pack of cigarettes he'd left on the desk. Cotton slipped under the bedclothes, switched off his bedside lamp and fell asleep. Stone lit an MS and stood there motionless, in his brown pants and brown sweater, with his forearm diagonally across his chest and his elbow in the palm of his other hand, bringing the cigarette to his mouth, then pulling it away, his fingers slowly caressing his cheek under his big black-rimmed glasses.

When he left the bedroom I got undressed, put on my matted powder-blue wool pajamas, slipped under the covers, and switched off the lamp on my bedside table.

I was too hot. I threw off the sheets and blankets and pushed them down to the end of the bed. Then I lowered my pants and underpants to my ankles and rolled my pajama top up to my neck to feel the cool air on my skin.

In the darkness, in silence broken only by Cotton's gentle breathing, I tensed my jaws, stiffened my throat, and pushed the spasm into my chest and abdomen. I held my arms away from my sides, bent my wrists like beaks, and twisted my legs at an angle, the knees pointing outward. I felt hungry for air, crippled and bitten. As I'd done every night for the past few weeks, I acted out the mythical infection, rehearsing and simulating, imagining tetanus turning to body inside me.

Then I collapsed into sleep, at the start of it all and exhausted.

THE GOD OF INFECTIONS

(FEBRUARY 7, 1978)

Two months earlier, in December, I'd gone in our white 127 with String, Stone, and Cotton to a country area outside Palermo, on the road to Messina. Stone was on a professional assignment to survey some fields. Once we'd gotten out of the car, I dug the tips of my sneakers into the crumbly brown earth to make holes in it. Then I looked up and saw, thirty meters away, a single thread of barbed wire separating two fields. It ran along horizontal and taut about a meter above the ground, held up by gray wooden posts. Black and interspersed with spiky knots, it was a handwritten line on a page. I walked toward it. I touched it: it felt hard and grim. It swayed in the wind. A few short lengths of rusty wire lay among the clods of earth at the base of a post. I picked up two of them: one was bunched up, the other slightly curved. I knocked them together to shake off the earth. They were beautiful—reddish, the color of dried blood. I turned around. In the distance

Stone was talking to String, and Cotton was leaning against the car reading a comic. They too were thin and knotty. I hid the two pieces of barbed wire in my jacket pocket and walked back toward them.

In the car I thought about tetanus, the god of infections. I thought about my fear of tetanus, and how String was constantly telling me not to touch anything or go near anyone. It was always: stay here, keep back, walk on this side. She'd glare at me if I petted a dog because it might bite my hand. There was rabies, foam and madness in every dog, and there was rust in every piece of iron, and among the grains of rust there was the psychopathic bacterium, a microorganism that hated us, a monster, a subverter, and iron was everywhere. Rust devoured things and bodies; there was rust on cutlery and in the meat we ate; it got into our mouths, disintegrated inside us, in our saliva, and in our stomachs, filling us, populating us, becoming legion beneath our skin.

With my cheek against the window and my hand in my pocket, I pressed a spike against my palm till it hurt; then I reduced the pressure, zipped up my pocket, and took the evening lights in my eyes. Later I listened to Stone reading, my head in my nimbus. When he went away I turned off the lamp on my bedside table, where I'd hidden the two pieces of barbed wire. I waited for Cotton to go to sleep, then pulled down my pants, and pulled up my pajama top, and for the first time, acted out the spasms, my longing for infection, half-naked in the dark.

.

On February 7 there was no school, as it was Carnival time. I was at home in the morning, but felt restless because I was looking forward to the afternoon and the explosion of evening. I mooned about for a while, then went out, and walked along Via Sciuti in the direction of Via Notarbartolo. But even walking didn't lessen the itchy hives on my stomach.

From time to time, especially in summer, String got hives—she *suffered* from hives, as they say; but she enjoyed her suffering. She reveled in it. Her arms and legs—especially the insides of her thighs—were covered with big red blotches, and she'd wear light sundresses so her skin could breathe and to reduce the itching. She'd take all her clothes out of the closet and lay them on her bed one by one; she'd examine them, finger them, judge them, classify them. She'd inspect every shelf in the fridge, separating the different kinds of food from one another, calm, stern, and implacable, imagining that she was restoring some meaning to the world by her tidiness. She took packs of tablets out of the medicine cabinet, read their information leaflets, phoned her doctor brother, and took notes in a 1973 diary. Then she'd sit disconsolately glowing, holding her arms away from her body, muttering about pinworms and endocrine disorders, in the grip of her personal spasms. String was allergic to herself, to her own breathing, to being in the world, to living with me, Stone, and Cotton. And by her constant struggle against her obsession she'd passed it on to me.

I turned left into Via Nunzio Morello. A little way past the corner, beyond the church of San Michele, there was a stationery shop, run by somebody else who had spasms. But in his case it wasn't tetanus or hives; it was more likely brain damage. He moved jerkily and spoke in animal grunts: I looked at his fleshy tongue and its purple frenulum. I'd been to the shop on Via Nunzio Morello so many times I thought *he* was Nunzio Morello—that that was his name.

He was behind the counter when I went in. Usually I came to buy decals, but not today. I looked at him and pointed to a jar. He swiveled in reptilian fashion, picked up the jar, and placed it on the counter. Then, breathing hard, he unscrewed the lid. I dipped in my hand, rummaged about, and took out a small, sky-blue, marbled rubber ball. I put some coins on the counter and went out.

I walked fast and restlessly, feeling the germs in my veins. I stopped behind the newsstand in front of the church and squeezed the ball in my fist. It was hard and compact and felt reassuring in my palm. It was the perfect gift for later, when I'd be torn between my fear of going up to her and speaking to her—breaking my resolution only to imagine her from afar—and my yearning to do so.

When I reached the building where I lived, I continued walking, and turned left. I came to the pet shop on Via Cilea, went in, and called out a greeting. The shop was full of pedigree cats, eyeless black poodles, cocker spaniel puppies that trampled on their own ears, a few chicks, and some fearsome canaries. I went over to the fish tank and watched the fish swim about in subaqueous blue. In the glass I saw my features dissolve in swarming bubbles gently expelled by an oxygenator; my hair was shot through with tiny torpedoes of light. My hair was thick and strong—light brown with occasional flecks of blond, a few tufts slicked down over my forehead, and a rudimentary parting created by Stone in the morning before I went to school. I used to sniff his hand as it held my head to comb my hair, noting his thick skin and the rich smell of red brick that made me feel nauseous.

Suddenly the pressure of the oxygenator increased, turning my face into a liquid cloud. I called out a goodbye, left the shop, and walked on through the February streets, among a winter detritus of dry bougainvillea, reddish corymbs heaped up to rot at the sides of the pavement in puddles. I stepped out, measuring time with space, but felt as if I was standing still, so I walked faster and faster, in the direction of the school, till eventually I was running, the little ball in my fist, my heart pounding in my chest, my elbows smashing into the air behind me, my knees lifting powerfully. I ran, bit and swallowed the wind, and felt invincible. When I stopped to get my breath back, I looked around: on one side of Piazza De

Saliba was my school, on the other the immense square. The previous day I'd raced Scarmiglia here. His full name was Dario Scarmiglia, but everyone called him just plain Scarmiglia. He was a dark-haired boy with a lean intellect. He didn't say much, and what he did say was never encouraging. We were in the same class; he worked hard and got good marks, but his interests weren't limited to schoolwork, and he took a keen interest in what was going on in the world outside. Like me, he was dour and ideological.

We'd agreed to race from the school gate to the other side of the square. It was our way of organizing our relationship, satisfying our rivalry, settling our hierarchy. We'd be helping the world to write the rules of the game. A hundred meters away, on the other side of the square, looking small despite his bulk, stood our referee, Massimo Bocca. To me, again, he was just Bocca; and I pronounced the *Bo-* with my lips open wide. A fat globe of flesh, Bocca was in my class too. Scarmiglia, Bocca, and me. Lucid, aloof, and hostile. Three eleven-year-old newspaper readers, television news fans—with a special interest in political news. Focused and abrasive, critical and somber, anomalous preadolescents.

Bocca was going to start us off by flapping his arms in the distance. As we stood there, leaning forward, one leg bent and the other ready to drive forward, Scarmiglia and I waited for his signal. I could see him out of the corner of my eye: concentrated, his lips parted. Bocca sliced the air three times, and we sprinted forward, running so close we could hear each other's breathing, our bodies similar, a twinship of bone and muscle structure. Almost at once my throat went loose and I felt an urge to laugh, and Scarmiglia drew two meters ahead. I put on a spurt and caught up with him again. But I couldn't stop looking at him, running both my race and his. All at once I remembered how, not long before, on the way home from school, he'd told me that people in Africa kept sharks as pets, like we do with dogs, and that every African house on the coast had an underwater paddock delimited by long wooden stakes to stop the baby sharks swimming off and getting lost in the ocean. He'd told me all this in a very serious tone, as he always did, and I hadn't doubted a word of it. Then, the next day, trying to reproduce his tone, I'd told the same story to some of our classmates; they'd laughed in my face. Now, in the middle of the race, I burst out laughing as I remembered the sharks and my embarrassment, and slowed down to a halt. Scarmiglia duly reached Bocca, ran past him, and turned around, panting, to look at me. When I finally reached the finish line, at a walking pace, with tears in my eyes and my face still distorted with laughter, Scarmiglia came toward me glaring, said "Dickhead!" and stomped off.

Piazza De Saliba was empty now. I turned around, walked back down Via Cilea, and stopped outside the pet shop again. I looked at my reflection in the window—my stiff wool sweater, my thin shirt collar, my rough cotton belt with its painted metal buckle adorned with a picture of a little car, my blue cord pants with patches over the rips, and my green and brown sneakers.

I played with the little ball again, bouncing it idly against the glass, bombarding my own face. The animals in their cages—blank cocker spaniels, irritable poodles, fidgeting canaries—turned to gaze at me disapprovingly. Finally the shopkeeper stuck his head out the door and told me to pack it up. Rubbing the ball ruefully between my hands, I headed for home, under a sky heavy with low black clouds that made every street a burrow. I turned down Via Nunzio Morello again. When I went into the stationery shop, Nunzio Morello was reading a magazine on the counter, slapping rhythmically through the pages with his oar-like hand, twisting his lips, and grunting with concentration. Without saying a word I put the little ball down beside the open magazine; it ran along the cracks in the wood, wandering aimlessly, then came to a pensive stop. I pointed at the shelf where the decals were kept: yet again a collector's cravings had won out over lukewarm good intentions. My usual spinelessness.

Making grotesque movements in the air, Nunzio Morello passed me the battlefield cards, transparent leaves showing pictures of warriors, then picked up the ball, and returned it to its jar; I watched as the blue dropped down among the other colors and my gift disappeared. Then, humiliated by my change of mind, I went home.

•

In the afternoon I took some photographs out of the cabinet drawers. They were almost all from the last two years. Some of them I'd taken myself with a Polaroid 1000. I liked the hiss of the card as it came out of the camera. Then you'd wait for it to dry, blowing on it to speed up the process, and the picture would emerge, but never become crisp, always stopping before it reached that stage. The image would be pallid—jaundice yellow or bottle green—and the faces always sickly, always distorted.

I looked at one that had been taken on my birthday a couple of years earlier. It showed a wan-looking Chiri, Gugliotta, and D'Avenia in equally wan afternoon light. I was with them, wrinkling my nose, and String's head was just visible too. There was cake with strawberries and crème pâtissière, a blue-and-white carton of Fabia water, some red plastic cups, and little pictures on walls. We wore brown sweaters or scruffy sweatshirts, and were making the cuckold sign behind someone's head, giving a thumbs-up or a V for victory sign. People were smiling; Gugliotta's arm, with a patch on the elbow of his sweater, was around D'Avenia's neck, and D'Avenia was choking and laughing, his eyes red, his pupils on fire.

We were all ironic in that Polaroid. I didn't like irony. In fact, I hated it. So did Scarmiglia and Bocca. It was becoming all too common, this new Italian irony that shone on every face and in every sentence. It was waging a daily war against ideology, devouring its head. In a few years' time there'd be no ideology left at all. Irony would be our sole resource, our defeat, and our straitjacket. We'd all be the same—ironico-cynical and coolly detached, expert at timing a quip and delivering it in a throwaway manner. We'd all be simultaneously involved and detached, observant and corrupt, resigned.

Using a spike of my barbed wire I disfigured all of us—Chiri, Gugliotta, D'Avenia, myself, and String—poking out eyes and lengthening mouths. For I was an ideological, focused, intense little boy, a non-ironic, anti-ironic, refractory little boy—a non–little boy.

I checked the time, put my two pieces of barbed wire into my jacket pocket, and went out. After walking along Via Sciuti as far as the crossroads with Via Principe di Paternò, I continued straight ahead and turned right onto Viale Piemonte. The gardens of Villa Sperlinga were already crowded. It was still early, so I decided to stay near the sandy paths, the yellow flower beds, the ponds, the tall palm trees, and the mastic bushes. There was a merry-go-round in this part of the park, with no music. I'd often ridden on it when I was small. Hunched over a blue-gray Dumbo, I'd whirled around, emulsifying elation and anguish, nightmare and excitement, in the total silence of Sunday afternoon, while String and Stone digested their lunch and watched me.

Now the merry-go-round operator was taking people's money and handing out plastic tokens in exchange from inside his cubicle, while the merry-go-round circled lopsidedly by the force of inertia, carrying three-year-old children, all in winter coats and red knitted helmet caps. At first they'd protest, raising their arms in vain, then they'd meekly submit to their destiny of riding around and around.

There was a pony at Villa Sperlinga that you could ride for five hundred lire. Arabesqued yellow, with highlights and a fringed mane, it trudged shabbily along through the dust, led on a rope by two dialect-speaking little boys. Now and then it would shake its head and neigh gutturally. This pony was a heroin addict. There were lots of cavities in the trunks and among the roots of the trees of Villa Sperlinga, and in those cavities were hidden little pouches of heroin. During the pony's breaks from work, when the boys left it free to graze while they went off to smoke a cigarette, it would go up to a tree and rub its back against the trunk. If it smelled an acidulous scent, it would seek out the cavity and forage inside. Once it found a bag, it would tear it open, lick up the wonderful heroin, scattering much of it around, over the trunk and streams of ants. On its next ride, with three toddlers on its back, it would trot along merrily, with miotic pupils, whinnying shrilly.

Some boys sitting in a circle on the lawn quarreling noticed the pony's behavior and grew curious. One of them got up, his blue flared pants flapping, and walked toward a tree. He was followed by a dog that darted back and forth across the park, with a long shaggy coat and legs like stings, its narrow body taking the wind like a sail, changing its wavelike shape as it ran sideways, slicing the area of a flower bed, eager and pointlessly mercurial, with no origin and no purpose and therefore, like every aimless animal, furiously swift.

Meanwhile the boy, having searched with eyes and fingers, had found nothing and turned back, disgruntled. He'd been hoping to turn the Host, the taste of which lingered in his mouth after ten years of prone communions, into heroin and then the heroin back into the Host again, compacting it in a microscopic Italian alchemical process that involved transforming Catholic rite into pathological social trend, white tunic into bushy sideburns, conversion and reconversion, and so on.

When the boy sat down again, the dog entered the circle, looked around, panted, and whined two or three times. The boy mouthed a command and made a gesture; the dog came toward him, dropped down, and lay there, its head flat between its paws, its muzzle rhomboidal.

I left, walked back along Via Principe di Paterno, and went on to Via Libertà. I crossed the street, keeping the Statue behind me and looking for a turn to the left. I found one—Via Ugdulena, Scarmiglia's home. His parents were holding a Carnival party that afternoon. He resented the whole idea. So did I, but at the same time I couldn't wait for it.

I buzzed at the intercom, the door opened, and behind the "Who is it?" was a hubbub of noises, voices, and blowing wind. I got into the elevator and looked at myself in the mirror. I pulled my shirt collar out of the neck of my sweater; it made me look more haphazard, more real. I stepped out of the elevator, sniffed, and rang the bell. The door opened. I put my jacket down on something and threaded my way through bodies into the mist of the party, into the phantasmagoria where all was steam and corrosion and tears in eyes. There were clothes, Carnival decorations, mirrors, lighted chandeliers. We were all eleven-year-olds; nobody smoked, we all smoked. I didn't greet anyone, people greeted me. I looked for cigarettes between fingers; they weren't there, I knew they were there. There was blood in my fingers, an itch, my fingers attached to my hand, my hand to my wrist. I walked and looked around and felt myself split up into segments, into limbs. I ran a check on them all to keep myself together.

I spotted Scarmiglia sitting alone on the living room floor in front of the television. I went in to join him. Behind him was a table, on it a brown orangeade bottle with its tapering neck and undetachable label; an oval tray of small rust-colored fried *calzoni*, their little bodies dimpled by fingertips; a round tray of minipizzas piled up in a pyramid, which had been excavated and devoured, leaving a metal void in the middle of the tray exposed to the yellow light that flooded down from the chandelier on the ceiling. There were also some chips in a white porcelain salad bowl, and a sprinkling of crumbs on the tablecloth and carpet, trailing out toward the living room.

I sat down beside Scarmiglia and looked at him. His anger about the race seemed to have subsided; he was focused on watching television. *Space: 1999* was on. Maya was speaking to Commander Koenig. Maya was a beautiful, liquid, metamorph woman with dotted eyebrows. In an emergency—or just for fun—she could turn into a bird, a beaver, an alligator, or a puma. A swift, grayish-green smell swarmed over her.

Scarmiglia handed me his plastic cup of water. I took it, held it for a moment, examined it, and put it down beside me. He told me Bocca had a fever and wasn't coming. Then he said there was a new program on after this one. A bald statement, providing minimum information. He was trying to pique my curiosity, but I was looking around the room, watching bright stars sparkle around heads, hands, noses, and cheeks, which touched unself-consciously, unseductively.

Finally I gave in.

"What is this new program?" I asked.

"A cartoon," he replied, continuing to stare at the screen. "A Japanese cartoon."

"What's so special about that?"

"The newspaper says it's important."

"Is it funny?"

"You mean is it ironic?"

Scarmiglia and I shared the same obsessions.

"Well, is it ironic?" I asked.

He grimaced and looked at five cowboys, all carrying silver-handled pistols in low-slung holsters and wearing crimson vests and sequined hats.

A little farther away, three musketeers were absorbed in

conversation. They all had green and red tabards with a silver cross in the middle, fake boots made of cloth held in place beneath their shoes by an elastic band, and bent plastic swords.

Scarmiglia studied them sourly. He and I were the only ones there not in fancy dress.

"No, it's not ironic," he said, turning his gaze toward four brigands in black hats like atomic mushroom clouds who were swapping cigarette cards.

"It makes you cry," he added.

I looked at him quizzically.

"It's about a little orphan girl," he said. "I saw a photograph in the paper: it showed her, a mountain, and a meadow."

An introverted Zorro had sat down on the floor a short distance away. His shirt was actually dark blue, but he was trying to brazen it out, trusting in the dim light and a thin Spanish mustachio drawn on his upper lip with burned cork. Alone, blank, and isolated from his surroundings, he nibbled at the charred edge of a minipizza and drained his cup of orangeade.

"Why should that make you cry?" I asked.

"Isn't that how it works?"

"What?"

"Little girls," he said.

I was beginning to get irritated; I knew that was just what he wanted, but I couldn't help it.

"What do you mean?"

"Little girls make you cry."

As he said this he looked at three little nineteenth-century ladies with tulle dresses and parasols who were talking among themselves, their ectoplasmic cheeks rouged with felt-tip pens at home by their aunts.

I told myself that he was right, but he wasn't. Scarmiglia knew; what he didn't know he deduced, the rest he guessed, and used.

I saw nine light-blue fairies approach with conical hats

draped in ragged white gauze, and flared dresses spangled with
stars: all alike, they formed a huge sky-blue cloud that envel-
oped the rest of the party. Their magic wands lay on a chair by
the wall behind me; the next chair was heaped with coats and
jackets. I got to my feet, picked up one of the coats, and lay it
over the magic wands. Then, after looking around, I sat on the
coat. I heard stars crack with the sound of eggs hatching. I despised the very word *stars*. Holding on to the sides of the chair
I moved about, pressing down, and it seemed as though fragments of stars were coming out of my anus. Then I got up, didn't
touch anything else, and sat down beside Scarmiglia again.

"She's just arrived," he said without looking at me. "She
went into the kitchen with her friends."

I sat with my elbows on my knees and my head bowed. I felt
my breathing grow irregular. I bit the edge of my hand, got to
my feet, and pushed my way through the milling bodies. The
eye sockets on everyone's faces were calloused, like those of
gorillas: forty baby gorillas in Carnival costumes. Finally I
reached the kitchen—and I don't know what happened. Suddenly I was deaf, and the world had receded: it was a ghost, a
skeleton. I stood in the doorway and looked. There, between
an open wall-cupboard and the white bubble of the fridge, motionless in a chorus of innumerable fairies, was one who was
here and was ancient and was future and was sacred melancholy
and burning and involution, collapse of language, harmony,
and barbarism, clarity and mystery, shadow, chaos and fusion,
magma, nourishment, ash. The Creole girl's body was red and
black. It was full of lions and tigers, of nocturnal forest sounds—
rustles, crackles, and drips (I looked at her from the doorway,
and there were lightbulbs above us, shadows below us; the
floor was green). Deep inside her body was an orderly, clean
silence, free of incrustations, smudges, or stains; a present, mobile, gentle, soft silence (she looked at a puffy-faced fairy and
listened to her speaking; she was dressed—I don't know how

she was dressed, not in Carnival costume: she was red and black). No words came out of this silence, but sometimes a laugh, with a wonderful festive gusto (the puffy-faced fairy had finished speaking, and she was laughing and her laughter was almost triumphant. The hostess, an earnest woman with an ivy-leaf brooch on her dress, saw me standing in the doorway and asked me something; I answered her: water). Her hair was alive. Each strand was a demon (the hostess gave me some water, as her son had done before; the tumbler was of ground glass, still warm from the dishwasher, purified: I could drink from it). The Creole girl never spoke; she just listened attentively to the swollen fairy and another who'd just arrived: always looking into their eyes, listening with her eyes, her head bent slightly on one side (the hostess poured out the water; I brought the tumbler to my lips and drank slowly, touching the glass rim with my nose: the water tingled). She made a gesture with her right hand, which was not a small hand and was dark, with a little pale patch on the back whose shape reminded me of something. I was struck by the gesture, which was silken and proud, and the little pale patch, which was beautiful and alarmed me.

As I drank I looked around each side of the semicircular glass and remembered something that had happened a few months earlier, at the beginning of the school year. Everyone was in the entrance hall, waiting to go home. The light of Palermo was so transparent you could see the progressive changes in its structure, corpuscular matter aggregating and collapsing above us through the effects of gravitational acceleration, a snowfall of particles in mid-September. Among the crowd I caught sight of the Creole girl. She was sitting alone on a step, her textbooks beside her and an open notebook on her knees, her right hand holding it still, the index finger of her left hand following the writing and then, as a thought formed in her head, lingering on the cut between pages.

Just then, perhaps attracted by the little pale patch, a mosquito that had been floating in the sun had glided down onto the still hand without the Creole girl noticing, and begun sucking at the white of her skin. I stepped forward in astonishment and alarm; the Creole girl looked up toward me, the mosquito broke away from her hand, and with a quick snatch I caught it in my right fist, without clenching too tightly. I didn't say anything; I looked at the girl, turned around, and went home, taking care not to squeeze my hand shut.

I walked home holding my arm away from my side. I could feel a movement on my palm. When I got to my room I opened my fist slightly, keeping my fingers together, and blocking the end with my other hand: the movement was still there: the mosquito was alive. Then, with my left hand, I picked up a small translucent plastic box and gradually maneuvered it in. Then I sat down and looked at it.

It was dark yellow. Its six legs were hinged to the plastic floor, its wings open and its halteres closed, its head raised toward me, the sheath of its stylet still, in bewilderment and rancor. It must have spawned from an aquatic larva floating in a green saucer under some flowerpot, wet with water drained out of a plant, one of those great ficuses that soar up from the balconies of Palermitan apartment buildings in the Libertà district. After feeding on plankton it had flown away, mated in flight, promiscuously, in a swarm of males, and absorbed human liquid, drawing protein from it. Then, all of a sudden, probably attracted by her epidermic substance, the carbon dioxide around her body, and the small pale gleam on her dark skin, it had landed on the Creole girl's hand. Now it was there in front of me, in its transparent capsule, with its huge mandible, slowly rubbing its front legs against its pointed stylet, with her blood inside it, a drop of the Creole girl's blood, a particle of her biology. I fell in love with it. I looked at it with a tenderness to which the mosquito responded by turning its back, but I wanted to take care of it, to guard it as one guards a reliquary containing a piece of a saint, worship it like a tabernacle insect; I wanted to keep it and the red globule it contained segregated, while ensuring its nutrition and life.

I looked in *Il Modulo*, but it didn't have an entry on mosquitoes, I looked in *Fanciulle operose*, one of String's old school books, but drew another blank. So I took a bit of lettuce and put it into the box, but the mosquito turned its back and ignored it all day long. I broke up some bread, both the crust and the soft part, dropped it into the box and waited another day, but again nothing happened. I was no more successful with instant coffee powder, Alka-Seltzer, or a tiny piece of cutlet.

Days passed without the mosquito eating anything. It stood motionless, in an antalgic position to control the pain of starvation. I was at my wit's end. I brought a speck of my own feces on the tip of a ballpoint pen from the bathroom: even that was no good. So, in desperation, terrified that it would die, I got a plastic bag, coaxed the mosquito into it, and put my bare arm inside; then I tied off the bag with a knot at my elbow, using my other hand and my teeth, and tenderly offered it my skin and my capillaries, so that it could inject its anticoagulant saliva into them and suck and feed, mingling my blood with that of the Creole girl. It would be a kind of insemination in its abdomen, in its spermatheca, two blood drops caught in a ruby-black coagulum, creating an emotional zygote, love enclosed in the body of a sinister, spiteful insect.

I spent the whole afternoon with my arm in the plastic bag, walking backward and forward in the apartment, more withdrawn than usual. In the evening I locked myself in the bathroom and opened the bag. There were several big red lumps on my arm, and the mosquito's body lay in a white crinkle at the bottom, folded and stiff, its antennae drooping, its threadlike legs shriveled, its stylet lifeless, having died of anger and grief after taking its revenge, my blood drying inside that of the Creole girl.

With tears in my eyes I picked up its body between my finger and thumb and threw it in the sink. I turned on the faucet to wash it down the drain but the body swirled around in the water and stopped at a dry point on the ceramic. The water caught it again and it swirled around again, then stopped again, this time inside the spiral of water, at another hydrophobic point. I pushed and blew, then finally picked up the body by one of its wings, and dropped it straight down the drain to get rid of it, to dispatch the blood, and was left looking at my bitten arm.

Now the Creole girl was drinking water herself; she listened, making a slow gesture with her head; her hair moved and demons appeared among the black. Just then I bit the tumbler, breaking the glass. I took the tumbler away from my mouth and tasted blood. The Creole girl turned toward me. The chorus of ladies and fairies turned too. Her face expressed puzzlement and curiosity. The hostess took the tumbler out of my hand and told me not to swallow. She searched inside my mouth and removed the broken glass. Then she made me put my head back, dampened a cloth, and dabbed my lips. I wondered why she was making me put my head back; it wasn't as if my nose was bleeding. I'd rather have held my head up and looked at the people who were looking at me, not at this ivy-leaf brooch, which seemed to grow bigger and bigger. But all right, I'd hold it back. While the light from the chandelier flooded my eyes I thought that the ideological little boy, the nimbused boy, the focused, intense, anti-ironic, refractory, non–little boy—in short, me—was standing here with a damp cloth over his mouth, eyes looking at him and confusion all around. This was not what was supposed to happen. I straightened up my head and ran out of the kitchen with the hostess calling after me. I reached the front door, found my jacket, searched in the pocket, and came back into the apartment. I passed Scarmiglia, still sitting on the floor in front of the television. I saw yellow, red, and blue on the screen; a little girl walking in her bare feet and some white goats, a swing and some music; but the little girl was pink, she was not Creole: she was worthless. Out of the corner of my eye I saw the fairies clustered around the wreckage of their stars in consternation and grief, open-mouthed and on the verge of tears, Zorro crouching beside the chair peering sleuth-like at a shattered wand, and a little boy dressed as a chick, with a bright yellow tuft on his head, his eyes full of despair.

When I entered the kitchen the Creole girl was sitting on a chair by the table. She was so beautiful, the black of her hair against the pale tiles, her reddish skin, and a sudden, touching pallor. I wished I could explain to her, say something, get the glass and words out of my mouth, abandon my usual haughty reserve, and hear her speak for the first time, hear her voice, after asking her what her name was and how old she was, but I looked at her with thirsty eyes and said nothing, putting it off for another day.

As everyone around us stood quite still, with a silent gesture as quick as a switchblade I produced my two pieces of barbed wire, offering them to her like a bunch of eccentric flowers. She gazed at me, and I looked at myself through her eyes: two prickly stems sprouting from a tensed fist, standing out dry and arrogant against my face, still a little damp redness on my lip, feverish eyes full of trust and dismay. Then her brown hand with the pale patch moved, stretched out toward mine, and with thumb and forefinger took the curved piece out of my fist, which opened, and at that moment, as light turned to darkness outside and inside, my heart was flooded with life and happiness.

DAWNS

On the evening of March 24 we boarded the train for Rome, the mineral animal, the city of the dead. Easter was in two days' time, and we'd be spending it in Rome. The trip would take all night, and we'd arrive in the morning. I felt cynical and excited; I touched my scar with my tongue.

There were six seats in the compartment, but we had it all to ourselves. Above each seat was an Italian landscape painted on a rectangular sheet of glass—rural scenery and crumbling walls: more picture postcards, more national mystifications. Someone had scrawled on the pictures with a felt-tip pen, putting genitals on walls and in country scenery.

I slept on the top bunk, next to the luggage space. I fell in love with the yellow light housed in a niche at the end of the bed. You turned it on with a little white lever shaped like a thin pear; when I pressed the tip, at first it resisted, then there was a loud click.

As the train traveled from west to east, with the dark sea on the left, I read an *Alan Ford* comic; I liked Bob Rock but found Sir Oliver disturbing. After a while String got up, drew the curtain halfway across, and said something, and we turned out the light. I waited ten minutes till the breathing established a rhythm. I rolled over onto my stomach, turned the light on again, and instantly cupped my hands around it. I lay still for a few seconds; the light within my finger-grotto turned orange. I studied the backs of my hands, the shapes of the phalanges, the dark-pink contrast of the nails against the fingertips. I examined my bones too; I felt shapeless. Then part of the time I read, turning the pages slowly, savoring the paper's vibrations; and part of the time I rested my head on the comic, my ear against the drawings, and closed my eyes. During the stops in stations I turned off the light and looked outside. On the platforms there were men with little carts or cigarette-girl-like harnesses. They sold hot coffee that they kept in large thermoses. I saw the arms of sleepless travelers reach out to take the little plastic cups and pay by stretching downward just as the train was leaving, hot black drops spurting onto fingers.

As soon as the train left the station, I turned on the light again, and screened it. I put my lips to my knuckles and felt as though I was drinking light. I thought about coffee. It was edgy and disturbing, liquid smoke. I knew what it looked like and smelled like, but had never drunk it. Every afternoon, at home, when Stone made it, I'd watch and listen to the gurgle it made as it rose; I stood riveted in front of the espresso maker, stunned by such rancor.

By the time I raised my head again from the comic, hours had passed. I turned off the light, sat up, rested my back against the suitcases, and watched the landscape outside grow with each passing second. In the depths of this early light, which seen from the moving train remained limpid and intact, still unspent by the bodies that would soon move through it, shredding it into

countless fragments, was the Creole girl. In the days after the
gift I'd decided that what had happened between us had been a
wedding. The exchange of barbed wire instead of rings: she'd
accepted the piece of wire and recompensed me with the movement of her arm and fingers, her beauty. But at school, since
then, there had been only silent gestures of the eyes, a tremor,
mine and hers, of the crystalline lens; nothing more.

By nine o'clock we were ready to break camp—bunks
folded back, sheets and blankets under seats. There was dust in
eyes and foulness on breath. Dazed skin, faces with supplemen-
tary features imprinted by pillow creases. We peered at each
other suspiciously.

The train was running late. At Aversa station Stone bought
some coffee through the window. String took my water bottle
out of her bag; the water came out tamely, each sip ran puppy-
like into my tired mouth. Meanwhile Cotton read *Topolino*,
but his head lolled sideways and forward, as if his neck were
broken. The dark yellow end of a piece of bread protruded
from his closed fist. Cotton was four years younger than me
and a moderate—solid without aggression, silent without hos-
tility. By day he ate only bread; in the evening, fruit: like a
canary or a hamster. On the rare occasions when he ate meat,
he'd strip off the sinew and fat and other white parts by a process of hacking and gnawing. Once, a few months before, he'd
rammed the handle of a plastic tennis racket, one of those used
with a foam-rubber ball, into his mouth. The capillaries around
his mouth had split, but he hadn't noticed because it didn't
hurt. String had seen him calmly enter the kitchen, his mouth
ringed by this corolla of unbleeding blood, take a piece of
bread, and leave. She hadn't known what to think, whether to
laugh or scream. I'd sat him down in an armchair, got out my
camera, and taken his picture. It showed Cotton, his feet not
reaching the floor, his red-rimmed mouth half-open, and a
white patch of calcium on one of his upper incisors. In his

hand, resting on his lap, was the usual half-eaten piece of bread.

At Latina station, a man and a woman got on and came into our compartment. We made room for them, and they sat down side by side: he next to the window, she on the middle seat; I was beside her, by the door; String, Stone, and Cotton opposite us.

They were young, and both wore denim jackets and battered blue jeans. He had curly black hair, sideburns, and a mustache, she curly blond hair and a red-and-purple scarf. Their expressions were tense, as if they smelled evil. Neither of them spoke: she stared straight ahead—at String, or into the void; he'd taken off his jacket, removing a comic book from one of its pockets, and was now reading, but listlessly, gazing out of the window from time to time and despising what he saw, the world outside, the day taking on its definitive shape, so vast and so pointless.

We were similar, the man and I. The woman and I were similar too. Same stock, same temperament. Glass-eaters. Grim and dangerous, with narrowed eyes that saw into the distance, zeroing in on the tiniest specks. If anyone had come into the compartment at that moment, he'd have thought they were my parents, that I was their son. And those three sitting opposite us? God knows—they were already here when we got on.

At Rome Ostiense, my new family got to their feet and left without a word. The man picked up his jacket from the seat, but left the comic book behind. I walked across, picked it up, and returned to my place. I wasn't particularly interested, just mildly curious, whiling away the time till we arrived in Rome. But I felt sad at being deserted by my extemporaneous feral family, so I took the comic book as their legacy to me: I opened it and sank in.

At first I could see only physiognomies, indecipherable situations. Then the seconds stopped flowing by and merged like droplets of oil on the surface of water. Coalescence, it's called.

The pamphlet turned out to be a deplorable and wonderful example of the comic-book porn of my youth: two pictures per page, four per double-page spread, like in *Diabolik* or *Kriminal*. When I went with Scarmiglia and Bocca to our urban porn-nests, I always found, along with magazines illustrated with photographs, the comic-book kind, such as *Jacula, Cosmine, Lucifera,* and *Jolanka*. They were less stylish than the ones that showed real bodies but more arbitrary in the imagination, more subversive, because drawn bodies can do anything.

I moved across to the middle seat, where I had no one on either side, and String, Stone, and Cotton in the distance, facing me. Outside, the countryside was tearing itself threadlike out of itself. I put on my disgruntled expression again, tucked my elbows in tight against my sides, like a good little boy doing his reading, with the Catholic good manners that turn the Host into heroin, heroin into the Host, prayer into porn, porn into prayer. I read and became confused.

In the center of the picture was a naked, mustachioed man leaning back in a low chair beside a double bed, holding his penis in his hands—both hands, such was its size—and watching a younger, fair-haired man coupling with a beast-woman repeatedly portrayed on this and other pages as a nymphomaniac queen, sex goddess, inexhaustible source of orgasm and limitless fount of lust, with a vaginal cavity of indescribable size and voracity, a huge mouth and a magnet-like anal sphincter, a whore and slut with every orifice agape, powerful and disturbing in the depiction of her legs and breasts and the lustful line of her eyes, as she lay simultaneously prone and supine, twisted around and reclining, bent over and intertwined, penetrated through her navel, her side, her back, her rib cage, and the back of her head, all over her body, which I touched with my fingers, doing my best, out of respect and awe, to avoid the various phalliform rockets and, when they appeared, the oil-like eruptions of sperm, steering my fingertips toward the woman's incredibly white flesh, the opalescences, the outpouring of bright light that turned from opaque to transparent when, as I leafed through the comic, I lifted a page and glimpsed the outline of the picture on the other side, somewhat confused by intrusive lines that showed through from verso to recto, imprinted on the paper by the half-moons of my nails, comma-shaped incisions that segmented the sexual image and dissected the syntax of the coupling into its many component parts.

The train lurched, there was an outburst of sobbing, and suddenly the Creole girl was there, bewildered among the pornoworld pictures. She looked around at the huge penises and cavernous vaginas, uncertain which way to go, then wandered about, a tiny figure among the pen-drawn movements, and eyed them anxiously, she herself nothing more than the faintest of sketches on the paper, always on the point of disappearing. She sat down beside the mustachioed man, looked at him and the penis in his hands, then turned toward the beast-woman and observed the cannibalistic mechanics of the penetration, the astonishing feast that the fair-haired man was making of the impaled woman. The fair-haired man stopped, turned, and peered at her. He stood up, his penis wagging between his legs, and went over to her. Taking her by the arm, he led her to the bed, and pushed her backward onto the woman's body, which expanded to an immense size. He pressed down on the girl's breast, immersing her in the beast-woman's body, sinking her into her quicksands till the girl vanished, to be replaced by a dazzling light.

Meanwhile the train had passed the indeterminate lands of the suburbs and was moving more slowly, as the landscape outside became cloudy and chaotic. It slowed down again and came into Termini station. String and Stone got up and started gathering our luggage; Cotton slept on, crushing his cheek against the armrest, having dropped the empty shell of his

crust of bread on the seat. I stood sideways between the seats
with the comic book in my hands, reluctant to leave it behind,
especially as String and Stone hadn't realized what it was: they
thought it was my usual *Alan Ford*. As I struggled to put on my
windbreaker, I shifted the comic book from one hand to the
other, shielding it with my body. Then I stood at the window
end of the compartment, with my back to everyone, still engrossed in reading. I was a worker friar, jealous of his faith,
stingy with his religion—one who turned his back on the
world, wedged himself into a corner, and forgot about everyone else. I absorbed the things the characters said, their movements, their arrogance, and their leers.

By now our suitcases were blocking the doorway of the
compartment; there was a jolt, a recoil, and the train stopped.
People started filing along the corridor and I slipped into the
line, the comic book in my fist. I'd rolled it up tight to form a
pipe, and as I inched my way forward I felt its tubular shape in
my palm, with the drawn bodies twisting around, coming together, intersecting, and merging, all desperately perfect, yet
bent out of shape. The tube was like my penis when I held it in
my hand, my obsessive, literary, fictional penis, genie's lamp
that I rubbed and implored in my fantasies, begging it to satisfy
all my desires and fears. Sometimes the genie would emerge,
microscopic and liquid, making me feel sick—a nightmare of
broken, liquefied organs trickling out through holes.

I looked out through the windows at the first signs of the
ravenous city that had been exploding in newspapers and on
TV for the past few months, the city crammed with dead bodies, beautiful Red Brigade bodies, and the bright March air
shed a furious light on the man and woman I'd seen on the
train, my new parents, and on their footsteps fleet between
hideouts, frantic in the secret delivery of communiqués, the
constant tingling of the skin, the snatched sex on cots, the animal existence, this tragic Rome in the sun.

I reached the end of the corridor, still clutching the comic book, with the bodies on its pages swamped by continual, motionless ejections of sperm, the Red Brigade women's faces smothered with white, their mouths full of Red Brigade sperm—bitter and fecund, ideological and glorious—their maternal eyes tenderly watching their men die. While Stone and String stooped over the luggage down on the platform, I dropped the comic book on the linoleum and went down the steps to set my foot for the first time on Roman soil, then strolled along, hands in pockets, fingertips pressed against palms. Walking toward the yellow taxi, I kept my eyes on the ground, my forehead furrowed, and felt the world's mouth take me by the scruff of the neck and shake me slowly, ironically. As Stone passed the suitcases to the driver, who stacked them in the trunk, I unscrewed the cap of my water bottle and took a quick succession of sips that flooded down my throat, holding my head back, the bottle perpendicular to my mouth, and the March sun falling between my eyes with a clink of chains; when I pulled the bottle away with a smack, there were tears in my eyes and I didn't dry them.

As I sat in the back by the dirty window, the taxi gliding through the streets, my tears turned cold and hard. Had it been possible, I'd have taken one of those barbed-wire tears and engraved my name on the window. Instead I drew a little penis in the dust with my finger, and above it an open mouth; then I noticed that String was looking in my direction, so I put petals on the penis and rays around the mouth; I also added a tree, a river, and that stupid fence. But my belly was full of lumps.

In Palermo the word for "to have an erection" is *sbrogliare*, to disentangle. The nonerect penis is a lump, a little skein of flesh. Excitement unravels it, reels it out to its full length, disentangles it. But that's a dialect expression, and I didn't speak dialect. I neither spoke it nor thought in it: I merely observed it from the outside, but only after anesthetizing it. Once the dialect words had gone numb, I'd pick them up and examine them: like everything natural they struck me as artificial.

The taxi reached its destination, and I rubbed out the flower and the sun with my arm. Stone got out the suitcases, paid the driver, and said goodbye. String looked for a name by an intercom, and Cotton wandered around. We left the luggage at the home of some friends. There were two of them, husband and wife; their apartment smelled of bread and saliva. Then we went out. During the day, as we traveled around town, I kept my jacket open, lowered my chin, and looked at my chest. I was pigeon-chested; my breastbone stuck out as sharp as a beak, vital, prehensile, lunging at everything. At the Barcaccia I went over to the fountain and drank. I liked the name Barcaccia—it was a rough name, with a dirty past—and I drank, feeling hostile to the water, hostile to the tourists and to this meaningless Easter. I looked around; there were crowds of people but I took out my piece of barbed wire, hid it in my hand, and as I bent forward to drink, gouged out a few centimeters of marble, digging slow and deep, scratching the back of a gargantuan friend. Then I wiped my mouth with the back of my hand, uncouthly, staring through half-closed eyes at a girl with tousled hair who was leaning against an apple-green car. She was probably called Cinzia, or Loredana, as all girls were nowadays. I fell in love with her and stared at her brutishly; she walked away and I didn't mourn her departure. I was godless and knew everything. I had dominion: life was the fruit and I was its core.

We walked around among the women of Rome till the early evening. During dinner, back at the apartment, I didn't speak. I poked about with my fork in the mashed potatoes and dissected the cutlet like an anatomist, spinning out the main course. Our hostess asked me what the matter was, why I didn't join in the conversation. I was vague and evasive. I possessed an indifferent look and a melancholy one; I used them

both. I said there was nothing wrong, my manner hinting at
worlds of sadness. She pressed me, asking if I was in love. She
thought she was being kind, but she was oafish and imbecilic,
and I ignored her, let her evaporate; she persisted, and behind
her, on the yellow wallpaper of the dining room, I saw mouths
with black outlines and breasts like bows, and percussive, wavy
upward movements like the flames of a fire, and I wished the
fire would consume her, reduce her to ash and silence. But I
lowered my forehead and dropped the visions.

After dinner we all watched television in the living room.
String and Stone sat on the sofa with our hosts; Cotton curled
up on the carpet. I remained standing, a gentleman. Then my
legs started to ache, so I got a chair and put it next to the sofa.
Vianello and Mondaini were on; I at once felt an urge, restrained myself, but maneuvered the chair imperceptibly toward the TV set. There were sketches and jokes. Enzo Liberti
was in it. He had a protruding lower lip and a prognathous jaw.
He was short and squat; his body smelled of grocery stores, of
sauces. It was a living smell but a tame and honest one, white
and pink, chaste—the opposite of Gianni Agus when he played
Fracchia's boss, with his white mouth and immaculate hair.
Whenever I sniffed him I smelled starch on his dark jacket, the
way his aftershave seeped into the cloth and remained there,
gently exuding—the odor of dignity, ambiguous and deep.

During a dance routine I said I couldn't see clearly from
where I was, and moved my chair to within a meter and a half
of the television, though keeping to one side so as not to dis-
turb the others. I saw the dancing girls' sweat-craters open up
at various points on the screen; I closed my eyes and the smells
of their bodies blossomed into little corollas and exploded inside my nose and my head. The dance finished, and Sandra
Mondaini came on again. She was wearing a short-sleeved top
and pale baggy pants.

"Have you noticed that Sandra Mondaini has a mole just

under her nose?" I asked, getting up and moving even closer to the screen.

There was no reply from the sofa, only a gesture from String to get out of the way.

"Can't you see it?" I asked excitedly, pointing at the close-up of Sandra Mondaini and pushing my face right up against the screen. I just had time to inhale the smell of a slim, light-weight, well-drained, and ventilated body, tainted only by the merest hint of perfume; then String snapped at me to stop it, not to be a nuisance, that I was a guest here, so I turned around, apologized, and returned to my seat.

The show ended and we went to bed—String, Stone, and Cotton in the guest room, where a cot had been put up along-side the double bed, I in the living room, on the velvety sofa draped with sheets and blankets. String gave me a glass of water, found a lamp and put it on a chair beside the sofa. She switched it on and turned off the main light. Then she said things to me—sensible things that made me feel like a shorn lamb—and went out.

Left to myself, I undressed, put on my pajamas, and got into bed. The cushions of the sofa, which before you touched them looked like blocks of marble, were soft and liquid, and I sank into them. I got up, went over to the window to open the slats of the blinds slightly, slipped back under the sheets, and turned out the light. The glow from the streetlamps sliced through the slats. I pushed off the blankets and listened to the sounds of the apartment—something dripping, brief rustles. Then I got undressed and silently played the epileptic, bending, twisting, turning myself for a few minutes into an eruption of harmoni-ously uncoordinated movements. When I became breathless and felt sweat on my chest and forehead, I stopped and lay there exhausted, my eyes open and my arms shaking, and I thought back to a few evenings ago, when in the dark bed-room, after the Bible reading, I'd been engrossed in my daily reconstruction of the spasms, in cataloguing them, when suddenly I'd heard a creak and felt air moving over me, so I'd switched on my bedside lamp, to see Cotton standing there looking at me. I must have woken him up so he'd got out of bed to come and see what was happening. He didn't do or ask anything; he just looked at my contorted body on the sheets, my grotesque body pleading for infection. He stayed a moment longer, his head on one side; then, without saying a word, he went back to bed, leaving me to stew in my own ridiculousness.

Meanwhile, somewhere in the house someone must have gotten up to go to the bathroom; I heard a shuffle of leather slippers and a faint clump on the floor. I waited till silence fell again and the machinery of the domestic space had completely stopped.

Now, I thought.

I went into the image of the Creole girl—a pause in the devastation, away from the pornoworld that existed inside my head, away from this obscene, blasphemous flesh-eating plant that devoured everything except the Creole flower, my sweetest infection. So, as everything grew smaller and sleep emerged, my life was Creole, my hands were Creole, and my tongue and my closed eyes; my lungs were Creole, Creole the air they silently processed, my heart, which stirred it, and my buried veins and organs.

I turned on my side and rubbed my cheek on the pillow. I felt like crying; I didn't cry.

Then I stopped and slept.

•

When I woke up it was still dark. One arm had fallen asleep. I sat up and shook it; I slapped it gently against my thigh but it hurt, so I rubbed it with my other hand. I lay down again but couldn't get to sleep. I turned to one side, saw the glass on the chair, and took a sip of water. My mouth was wooden. I lay back on the sofa and through the slits in the blinds looked at strips of Rome.

I knew little about the Red Brigades—only what I read, which was next to nothing. I knew people talked about them, and that they had something to do with death. They had something to do with sex too, but nobody talked about the Red Brigades and sex as two related things. Over the past few days I'd seen pictures of Via Fani on television—the dead covered with white sheets, the police inspectors in their wide-ankled pants, the carabinieri, with their dark uniforms and the dazzling flash of their bandoliers, walking among cartridge cases or kneeling down to draw outlines with chalk—and felt an itch that ate at my skin and something in my belly that churned and scraped, a whirling presentiment that opened out on my chest and on the palms of my hands.

Soon, with the first light, the space outside, which was now full and mixed, would grow finer and more geometrical, would become line and perspective, and in the apartments people, still half-asleep, would stretch out a hand toward the body that slept beside them. In the March dawn Rome would be lit up by torched bodies, by fire from arms and mouths, fire that mingled in embraces and dispersed in gleams where brigadist bodies burned, the young, glowing bodies from which I yearned to have been born, and there was a fire in that room too, in the center of my body, where my Creole love burned and the sweetness of this second dawn of my life—and after another sleep, at the new awakening, I lifted the blanket, and in the clear, climbing air of the morning saw at the end of my body, on the tip of the glans—the genie, the genie—a droplet of light.

THE CENTER OF THE EARTH

(APRIL 18, 1978)

I knew nothing about the Creole girl. I was aware of that: it was a conscious choice on my part. I didn't know her name, or how old she was; the same age as me, by the look of her, but in her case the eye and ear were not reliable judges. I did know a few things, though. I knew she'd been at the school since the previous September, that her skin was darker than mine— enamel, honey, ancient oil. I knew her hair was black, and sometimes blue, and that there were demons in it. I didn't know what school she'd attended before, or where she'd lived. I didn't know if she was Italian, I didn't know what language she spoke; I'd never heard her speak, I didn't know what her voice sounded like. In the morning, before school, or at lunch-time, after we came out, I used to watch the car that brought her and picked her up, and try to make out who was inside it—her parents?—but I couldn't see. I couldn't see them just as I couldn't see the other parents, although they existed; they were present and all-pervasive and yet at the same time rarefied, imperceptible. All I saw was a car door open, her dark hand appear and wave goodbye, her head take shape, clear and perfect, the outline of her body form in space, the door close again, her turning and walking toward the gate—where I would be standing—and her steps, one after another, which echoed in my stomach as they approached.

We passed each other and didn't say a word. As she went by I searched on the grainy surface of her schoolbag for a sign—her name written with a felt-tip pen, as most kids did, but it wasn't there; she was nameless. I could have asked one of her classmates, I could have eavesdropped till her name was mentioned, till I heard it enter me and germinate, but I didn't. I wanted her to remain just a phenomenon, for me. A creature unsullied by details, unencumbered with history. Her name was *Creole girl*, just Creole girl, that was all, and when I saw her walk across the schoolyard or in the hallways, when I saw her arrive at school or leave, I heard words migrate from space and time and enter her body. I heard the words *lovely* and *beautiful* sail in an arc through the air, gently pierce her flesh, and disappear into the darkness within her, and I knew I'd never be able to say the words *you're lovely, you're beautiful* to anyone ever again, because the Creole girl and her form had absorbed them, and they belonged to her; to say them to anyone else would be to tell a lie.

•

One day, during our science class, the teacher talked about slugs and snails—gastropods, those little soft blisters that had been coming out of the ground after the rain for the past few days and nibbling leaves. They lay in the spewy earth of flower beds, or clung by their stomachs to the walls at the bottom of railings. Most had a shell, but some did not and were just fingers of solid, gray water. Usually I squashed them but avoided killing them, making a paste of flesh and fragments of shell, so that I could watch them squirm as they died.

When I came out of school that day I stopped by the walls and picked off snails, prying them gently away from the surface. I ran my fingers through the wet leaves in the flower beds under the bushes of Viale delle Alpi and found more snails. I collected dozens of them. I put them in cardboard boxes with a bit of grass, some leaves, and a piece of lettuce, telling String it was part of my science homework. In the afternoon I got some felt-tip pens and took the snails out of the boxes one by one. Their bodies would shrink shyly back into their shells, and I'd be left with a light, sculptured pebble in my hand. I colored the shells—blue, red, green, and black. On some the color faded after a few hours, on others it remained strong and bright. I watched the snails mingle in the box, form flags, disband, and regroup. The next day I put the snails into my jacket pocket and went to school. As I walked I checked them with my fingers; my pocket was wet and gluey. I stopped where the car that brought her pulled in every morning, took out the snails, and lined them up on the pavement. Then I withdrew and waited. As the minutes passed, two snails fell off the curb, slithered on and were crushed by tires. In the brutal roar of the traffic I heard two distinct crunches. I felt them inside me, behind my breastbone—the quick, sharp sound of the words of love being cracked. Two more snails were squashed by the shoes of passersby. A backward step of disgust, of repulsion, scraping the sole to clean off the infection. Other shells—one dark blue, one orange—were spotted and picked up by people I didn't know. I wanted to attack them, make them put the snails back, but instead I watched them walk off looking at the shells in surprise, holding them up against the light like precious stones. By the time the car arrived and the Creole girl said her goodbyes and got out, the chromatic message, whose meaning I didn't even know myself, had disintegrated. Only one red shell was left; it climbed, slow and solitary, up a wall, a retreating blood drop, but she didn't see it and walked on by.

On the way home I collected more snails, teasing them out of the earth with my fingers as I had the day before. Luckily it rained a lot in April—the weather was unleashing all the water it could before the warm season came—and the flower beds were full of snails. Again I took them home, fed them, and preserved them. Then, when I'd finished my homework, I got out my felt-tip pens and took the snails out of the box. I wrote a letter of the alphabet on each shell; the letters formed words and the words made an elementary, tragic sentence. *Who are you?* Just that. One letter in the middle of each cochlea, on the apex. The question mark had a shell of its own. The sentence was a question, but not one of my making; the world would ask the creature a question through me.

Again I watched the alphabetic snails mill around in the box, churning up the question. ROWH?YEAOU. YEWROHU?OA. ?AHWOERUYO. Next morning I took my question to school. I waited till the last moment, when I saw her car coming. Then, in front of my classmates, I took out the snails and arranged them on the ground; I put each of them into one of the squares formed by the little paving stones. Then I stepped back to mingle with the others and watched as the Creole girl said goodbye to the driver of the car, got out, turned around, walked straight past the snails without seeing them, and entered the school. I went disconsolately over to the sentence, bent down, and noticed that I'd put the shells in the wrong order, making a statement instead of a question: *You are who.* The question mark had wandered off: I watched it slither disobediently away toward the road.

I went on like this for days, digging snails out of the earth, cleaning them, writing on them, and forming sentences. I tried to vary the wording but the substance was always the same. As was the inevitable process by which the whole thing broke up in the morning. Some of the letters were killed—run over by cars with excruciating crunches—others were picked up by strangers and taken away; still others slithered off somewhere or other. The few that remained were not noticed.

One day, after I'd been trying for ten days, the Creole girl got out of the car, turned around, slowed down, and stopped. She looked. She contemplated the whitish, winding, translucent trails of varying widths that the snails had left. Shattered shells in dried pulp were dotted all around, a massacre that had passed unseen for days; the despair of words.

She stepped aside, bent down, and looked at the one surviving word *who*, which was gradually breaking up and drifting resignedly away. The word didn't ask and didn't answer; it just was. She picked up the three shells and put them on her palm. Then she crouched down again and looked around. There must be a sender, she seemed to say to herself. An explanation, a meaning. I backed away, mingled with the crowd, and felt, under the skin of my forehead, agitation at the letters that remained and succeeded in conveying a message even as they wandered off. I felt grateful. Then I saw the Creole girl stand up, still holding the snails in her palm, and crane her neck in that characteristic way of hers, looking around for a connection. She was so beautiful, so serene; I heard packs, swarms, flocks of words move from the world toward her; whole dictionaries disappeared into her body, all conceivable language became microscopic matter and found a place within her flesh.

While she looked around in bewilderment and her pulviscular beauty spread through the air like pollen, I walked down the steps into the schoolyard. I walked slowly, pensively, becoming increasingly curved with every meter, like a billhook, like a bramble.

•

On the afternoon of April 18, after having lunch and doing my homework, I went out. The sky was gray and globular: it made you feel sleepy and want to turn back. I took a road to the right, then turned left, which brought me onto Via Libertà. Scarmiglia and Bocca were already waiting for me at the intersection. Silent, our throats full of ash, we walked toward the monster.

The center of Palermo was the Gehenna of fire. Where we weren't supposed to go. We never did go there, either; we had no reason to. I'd been through the area occasionally by car, with Stone, but hadn't seen much—peeling plaster, gashes in walls: a hieroglyphic landscape, the center of the Earth. Bocca's experience was much the same as mine. Scarmiglia had been there a few times with his brothers; to hear him describe those visits was like listening to a spelunker's tale.

When we reached the Quattro Canti we turned left, then left again after Via Roma, going into the market, by butchers' stalls, along narrow streets, down alleyways. The stalls were empty, the shutters down. Demobilization. The air was humid and smelled moldy. A piece of purple-and-red animal liver lay in a corner; it was large and shaped like a flying saucer, its convex surface covered with faultlines and cracks, and small jelly-like whirls where the lattice of veins showed through. Next to the liver was a burst garbage bag, a black animal; white bones blazed out of holes like random legs; one, longer than the others, pointed skyward, stripped of its flesh, an ankylosis walking up the tuff wall of a house. There was another hole, underneath, from which entrails spilled out like fecal matter.

We came out of the market onto Piazza San Domenico. There was a dead dog lying in the middle of Via Roma. Bocca and I stayed on the sidewalk; Scarmiglia went over to the dog. Cars passed but he took no notice. He stood for a minute examining it, then turned toward us and beckoned; we joined him.

"It's alive," he said.

"It looks dead," said Bocca.

"No, it's moving its eyes and making noises," said Scarmiglia.

"It's dying," I said.

I thought of the natural cripple and Christ on the cross. If nobody else had been around I'd have bent over it, touched its stomach with the end of my piece of the barbed wire, pierced it.

"Want to take it?" asked Bocca.

I looked at the body, the back legs crushed and tangled together, the triangular head with its coat ripped open to reveal the white of the skull.

"Move it, I mean," Bocca added.

"Why?" said Scarmiglia. "It'll die anyway."

"Yes, but not here."

"Who cares where it dies," said Scarmiglia. He moved away.

Bocca and I stood for a few seconds longer gazing at the creature as the cars passed by, then we followed Scarmiglia. Just as we were about to go back into the market, Bocca turned around and stopped us. Two boys were standing beside the dog in the middle of the road. They were locals; I couldn't hear what they were saying but I was sure they were speaking dialect. One bent down over the body, tied a rope to a leg, and pulled the dog over to the sidewalk. The other took out some matches, lit them, and threw them on the dog. Nothing happened; people kept walking by. Then one of the matches stayed lit, and the flame spread across the dog's coat. Gray smoke rose from its stomach; a few seconds later, more flames appeared.

"Let's go," said Scarmiglia.

We went back into the half-empty market. I heard a faint trickle and saw little streams of water running along the grooves between the *balate*. Balate are marble slabs—gravestones, the paving of the city center. I walked on tombs, watched water flow onto the walls of houses. It gnawed and bit; it had teeth. If you scratched with your fingers, the house would come away.

Palermitans stood in the narrow streets, among the *catoi*, the tiny inner courtyards. Their speech was guttural, gastric, a constant rasping of words in the throat and stomach. They exclaimed: Palermitan is an exclamative language—whenever something happens, anything at all, Palermitan instantly begins its siege. Often it's a single sentence repeated with different intonations, in dynamic litany, reiterated and intensified, reducing the phenomenon to its primal, authentic nature— that of scandal. But always with a sense of menace, of anger: to a dialectal Palermitan, every event is a horror.

We sat down on the steps of the church of San Francesco, under the rose window. The sky was dark; the air heavy with imminent rain.

"Damn!" I said, and didn't know what else to say.

"Damn what?" Bocca asked.

"It's going to rain," I replied.

They looked at me, puzzled.

"Damn!" I said again.

They said nothing.

"Damn!" I repeated quietly, mortified because I knew I was hopeless at exclamation, a masochist. I used childish, anachronistic expressions; the original emotional impulse was authentic, but at the moment of becoming a word it put on a disguise and out came *Damn!*, the way people in comics say *Great Scott!*, *Great Caesar's ghost!*, or *Leapin' Lizards!* Once or twice, with tears in my eyes for the shame of it, I'd exclaimed *Fiddlesticks!* Even saying *Sugar!*—clinging to the word like a castaway to a piece of flotsam—was humiliating, especially if my adversary said *Shit!*, if he was capable of saying *Shit!*; and since everybody except me *was* capable of saying it, I was left floating among the waves, with a storm of black excrement raining down on me, as I clung to a huge sugar lump that was rapidly disintegrating, grain by grain.

Meanwhile the voice of a street vendor, one of those people who drive around slowly, at walking pace, in little open-topped vans, came from Corso Vittorio Emanuele. He was selling salt. His call describing his wares and stating his price was a perfect, hypnotic hendecasyllable, a commercial and religious incantation: *Four cartons of salt for a thousand lire.* I listened to him. The lira was a neo-realist, working-class currency—Catholic, bourgeois, filmed in black and white.

Suddenly Scarmiglia got up and walked off toward Corso Vittorio Emanuele without a word to us. Three minutes later he came back holding a white pack.

"What did you go and buy salt for?" Bocca asked.

"I didn't buy it, I stole it."

"You stole it?"

"Sure. I walked past the van, stretched out my arm, and stole it."

"What do you need salt for?"

"I don't need it."

"Why did you steal it, then?"

"No reason."

"No reason?"

"No reason."

Scarmiglia reflected a little longer.

"I wanted to feel guilty," he said.

I liked the word *guilty*. I'd never had the courage to *be* guilty myself, so I envied Scarmiglia for his ability to do so. Because that was what it was, an ability: not everyone could be guilty; it had to be your destiny, your vocation.

"What do you mean?" asked Bocca.

"I wanted to do something that other people consider to be wrong, but which was right to me at the time when I did it. No, not right; just something I felt like doing."

"But why salt, of all things?" I asked.

"Because street vendors piss me off."

Scarmiglia had an unsurpassed ability to make me feel lonely; he was also the only person who could give me a sense of belonging.

"Weren't you scared you might get caught?" asked Bocca.

"No."

Bocca looked at him. He believed him; he couldn't not believe him, he *had* to believe him, but he didn't know how to.

"No, I wasn't," repeated Scarmiglia. "Why should I have been?"

"But the people around here . . ." said Bocca. "Can't you see what they're like?" And discreetly, trying not to draw attention to himself, he gestured with his head in a full circle.

It was like being in a house with no roof, with alleyways instead of hallways. Everyone was related, everyone was united. Everyone looked alike and everyone spoke with the same voice; the children sounded just like the old people. There was no difference between stones and skin; skin covered a stone; if you broke a stone, there was flesh inside.

"I can see," said Scarmiglia. "Do you think they might try to harm me?"

Bocca said nothing; he turned toward the people again. They stood in doorways and looked at us. From where we were sitting I could see the inside of a house, its ground-floor shutters open. There was a straw-bottomed chair, a portable radio, a dark, round table, of which I could see only a segment, bare lightbulbs that shed a warm light, onions and garlic on a shelf, a loaf of bread split down the middle. Urban rusticity: an *Intervallo* postcard.

Scarmiglia walked over to an old woman and a man and started talking to them. We couldn't hear what he was saying, but he talked at great length, never pausing to give them a chance to speak. Then he stopped and waited. The woman looked at the man; the man uttered a few monosyllabic words, then fell silent. Scarmiglia took his leave of them with a wave of the hand and came back.

"There you are," he said, smiling.

"What do you mean?" asked Bocca.

"I talked to them."

Bocca grimaced with irritation, unable to follow his train of thought.

"I'm not scared of them," said Scarmiglia. "There's no reason to be: I speak Italian. All three of us do."

"What did you say to them?" I asked.

"I asked them for information. And I used the subjunctive a lot."

His smile grew broader, filling a silent pause. Then he went on.

"To them, words are hammer and nails," he said, "spoons and knives. They only use them for saying things."

"The only language they know is dialect," I said.

"Yes," said Scarmiglia. "They don't understand anything we say in Italian."

Now Bocca had grasped the point and was starting to enjoy the discussion.

"We know the pleasure of language," he said. "Not just the subjunctive: the pleasure of sentences."

While Bocca was speaking I touched the living barbed wire in my jacket pocket.

"To us," said Scarmiglia, "speaking in Italian, using complex sentences, is a way of escaping."

I remembered the schoolmistress telling me ironically yet realistically, almost a year before during the oral exams, that I was mythopoetic. I remembered how happy I'd been when I'd found out what she meant, the pleasure that was to be had from moving about inside words, from spending time in language. Going away by constructing sentences, isolating yourself from others. The consequence of our mode of expression—the subdued tone, the low volume, each word flat, carefully selected, calm yet seditious—was that our classmates didn't recognize us. To them we were abnormal, idiots. And when they heard what we are talking about—our detailed analyses of the political situation and our radical criticisms of the authorities—they'd make sarcastic comments and leave us alone.

"We can leave Palermo," Scarmiglia began, "simply by speaking."

"We're guilty of language," exclaimed Bocca.

"Yes," said Scarmiglia. "Language is our crime."

"Nobody else speaks like us," said Bocca, proudly. "Not today, nowadays," he added in clarification.

"That's not true," said Scarmiglia. "There's one group of people who do."

Bocca waited, his curiosity aroused. He seemed almost sorry that there could be someone else who devoted as much attention to language as we did.

"The Red Brigades," said Scarmiglia. "They speak like us, or at least they write the way we speak. Their communiqués are complex, their sentences long and powerful. They're the only people in Italy who write like that."

Now the air was humid and condensing; it congealed into solid gray, then broke up, and thinned. Above my head a cumulonimbus took on the shape of an anvil. The dark cumulonimbus. The pale nimbus around my head. The language that elected me. The harsh buzz of static electricity. The ions. Leaves and dust beginning to swirl, close to the ground.

While the thunderstorm was gathering, five reddish-brown dogs appeared. The one at the front was missing a leg, and walked with a limp. They ran this way and that, sensing the rain in the air, weaving among the *catoi* children and their mothers, who were bringing out red or light-blue buckets and stiff-bristled brooms, as if they intended to wash the streets when the rain came.

As the first raindrops began to fall, the dogs started fighting. The amputee snapped and snarled ferociously. A cancerous pigeon appeared. Pigeons usually vanished when it started to rain; this one must have lost his way. He hopped, puffed out his breast, cocked his head, and stared at the fighting with one orange eye. He watched the amputee lunge at one of his companions, fall down on his stump, get up again, and return to the fray. The pigeon too was a cripple: one of his cartilaginous reedlike legs was missing its claw. He hopped toward the group of fighting dogs, moving nearer and nearer, and I stood up, wanting to stop him but not knowing how. By now he was only a meter away from the gnashing fangs and tufts of flying fur. One last hop took him into the midst of the dogs. They stopped fighting; the dust, already saturated with moisture, was settling. The amputee looked at the pigeon's clawless leg, then at the other dogs. Anger seeped through his skin, his chest shaken by hard, rhythmic breathing. He looked at the disgusting pigeon again, paused, restraining his anger for a moment longer. Then, with a sudden lunge, he jumped on the pigeon, grabbing him by his teeth. He lifted the pigeon up and shook his head frantically to tear it apart, outspread wings protruding from his mouth.

We walked off down Via della Loggia and along Via Terra delle Mosche, and sat down on the edge of the fountain in Piazza Garrafello, in the middle of a Paleolithic Nativity scene.

The fountain reeked of the muriatic acid that had been used to clean it; the marble was dazzling white. Scarmiglia told us he'd come here one evening not long ago with his brother to buy some octopus. The fishmonger had started cutting the tentacles on the stall. Suddenly, out from the gloom of a *catoio* had come a tortoise-woman, crawling on all fours. The slimy, greenish-black shell on her back was at least a meter in diameter. The market people had been quite unperturbed at her appearance. One man had bent down to give her a strip of raw meat. She'd crawled around for a while, with the meat dangling out of her mouth; then she'd stopped and started chewing it.

By now we were in the thick of the storm; the rain was lashing down with a vicious intensity. We hurried to get to the bus stop on Via Roma, getting splashed with muddy water from passing cars as we walked. As we waited in the bus shelter, Bocca spotted the body of the dead dog we'd seen before lying in the gutter now on the other side of the road. It was burned black; we could still see some smoke rising, and a few last flames being doused by the rain.

We got on the bus: more faces, among gray metal handrails and honey-colored wooden seats covered with key-carved graffiti. We went to the back; I stood by a window that was open at the top to get some air. The surface of Via Roma was paved with square cobblestones, and since the bus's suspension was broken, it was a bumpy ride. The rain beat down even harder outside; inside the bus people held on to one another in unreal solidarity. I kept upright by leaning with my folded arms and chest against the window, getting squirted with rainwater. More people got on at every stop, and I had to move along. I did all I could to avoid touching the handrail; I wedged myself into a corner, but it was no use, still more people got on and pushed against me, so I gripped the handrail hard, disgusted. To take my mind off the smells, the voices, and my hand, I looked out at the wet road, the countless puddles, the double black slits of drains with effluent bubbling over them, and the black water that flooded houses' front yards and *catoi*, submerging the market stalls, the alleys, and the animal liver.

When we arrived on Via Sciuti, two hundred meters from my apartment, I said goodbye to the others and got off. The rain was still teeming down, and I made a dash for it. By the time I reached the doorman's office I was out of breath, my clothes dripping with water and mud, my hair plastered down over my forehead. As I walked up the stairs I sniffed the palm of my hand. It had a sickly sweet, cold smell, a composite of all the hands that had gripped the bus's handrail throughout the day, the sum of all their odors. As I got changed, I was aware that it was the same smell my hands always had. But other people were the infection that I rejected and lacked.

·

That evening I sat alone in the kitchen in my usual place at the head of the table, with my elbows on the table and my fists against my temples. I was tired, my legs and feet were weary from all that walking, my head ached from the rain.

The table was still set. String stood in the doorway with her arms folded, watching me. In front of me was a dish of *stracciatella*—a swamp, a mush of beaten egg, gluey oil, and dying beef. I imagined it scraping gelatinously against the walls of my stomach. The light from the ceiling shone down into the *stracciatella*: I stared dejectedly at the gleams and didn't eat.

On the other side of the table, on the dishwasher, was the portable TV. It was white, enameled, round-cornered, and sensual, with its stiff whisker of an aerial and its extractable carrying handle on top. Lately, with everything that had happened, we'd taken to bringing it into the kitchen in the evening and watching the news over supper. The big black set, impassive whatever scenes it showed, stayed in the living room.

String turned the knob to switch it on, pulled a chair away from the table, and sat down. The newscaster said the Red Brigades had killed Moro today and his body had been dumped in a lake near Rieti. There were shots of men making exploratory dives into the frozen lake. The black-and-white picture started quivering; String got up, adjusted the aerial to stabilize the image, and sat down again. Black forms of divers descended into craters of water, searching inside for Aldo Moro's body, lost in the dark depths. There were upward shots too, of helicopters filming the perforated sheets of ice and murky water.

To my left, below the window, was the utility sink. This was a low, square basin, made of discolored ceramic chips. It was used for discarding the dirty water after washing the floors, draining the hose from the washing machine, and shaking out the tablecloth after lunch and supper. Although the rest of the kitchen was spotless, the floor of the utility sink was always a mess. Crumbs, torn pieces of bread, scraps of lettuce, apple stalks, grains of rice, the odd hair, dry foam, cigarette ash. However much you cleaned it, the residue clung tenaciously: it wasn't so much a residue as a form of pride.

In the morning Crematogastra, our cleaner, would sit on the utility sink when she'd finished work. She was a large old woman with dark skin, a headscarf, and a face like an ant's. Our obese ant. The utility sink was her seat of honor, her throne: she'd wedge her fat bottom between the edges and settle down, brooding over the light as she waited for her son to come to take her home.

When I got home from school I'd go into the kitchen and see her—an enormous cloud. I'd tiptoe in, sit down, and pretend to start drawing. I'd listen to her hiss as she breathed, microscopic geysers emanating from her body. In the room there'd be nothing but her and me, the sound of pencil on paper and the hiss of her breath. Now and then the canary in its cage with its piece of white celery on top of the wall unit would give a surprised chirp. When Crematogastra finally stood up and left the kitchen—slow, moribund, muttering in dialect—I'd get down from my chair and go over to peer into the ceramic square. The inside of the utility sink was full of dazzling light: Crematogastra was the keeper of the family light. She knew the leftovers on the floor of the sink must not be removed but preserved, for they were the solid manure of the light, the filth that fueled it.

On TV people were making statements—Cossiga, Zaccagnini, Fanfani. There was talk of communiqué number seven. Some believed it, some didn't. He was at the bottom of the lake, he wasn't at the bottom of the lake; he was in heaven. One said he refused to believe it, another that he couldn't, another that he dare not.

String got up, took a glass from the cupboard over the sink, and poured some water into it from the bottle on the table. She drank; a snake of skin quivered for a moment before disappearing at the bottom of her throat.

String had a hooked nose, a thin curve of bone; the cartilage at the tip was sharp. Her nose was always pale and transparent. When I moved close, I saw the mingled molecules and caught a smell of bread and milk, bathroom tiles and laundry detergent, cats and damp wool: String sniffed things; she pecked at molecules and stored them away in her glass urn. I had her nose, but mine was wider on the bridge, more ardent and shameless.

"When you've finished, put the plate in the sink and turn on the faucet," she said to me.

"When you've *finished*," she repeated, leaving the kitchen.

The TV showed more interviews, more shots of the ice; then there was talk of Via Gradoli, a broom and water.

Now I should have picked up my spoon, let the soup run into it, and brought it to my mouth. I should have dropped my resistance and just finished it. But instead I got up and looked out of the window, at the evening. Below was a patch of bare earth strewn with garbage bags; at night they caught fire because of cigarettes tossed down from balconies by sleepless people—the blazing insomnias of those years. Rats scurried about among the fires, and when the flames died down they rooted about for scraps of food in the cold embers: sometimes I awoke to the sound of their gnawing and chewing.

I went back to my chair. The TV was showing the lake and the helicopters again. I looked down at the soup, my lake of pale ash: all Italy was searching for Aldo Moro, and Aldo Moro was lying there on the bottom of my plate, his little body curled up like one of those dark caterpillars I used to see in the summer; they'd coil slowly around the thin, trembling, tendon-like green branches that reached out from the shrubs around our house by the sea—a melancholy, larval lepidopteron, dressed in black and disheveled. I looked at the crust of oil and yolk, picked up my spoon, and slid it down from the edge of the plate toward the bottom, with the bowl upward and the convexity rubbing along the surface, searching for an obstacle, an object to make contact with—Aldo Moro lying stiff, his bent arms tight against his sides, his head sunken between his shoulders, his knees against his chest, the distinguished parliamentarian exhibited, flaunted, raised up in his stainless steel cradle and offered as sacrificial food, as a Host to be brought to the mouth and swallowed without a thought, for the whole of Italy to eat the chairman of the Christian Democrats, to take communion, swallowing without chewing, and recognizing as they did the taste of Lent and wheat, of medicine, then looking into each other's eyes to see them bright and unanguished, the full, solid, honorable gaze of the Italian people.

I pushed the chair back, put the damp spoon on my napkin, picked up the plate, and carried it to the utility sink. I leaned over and started pouring out the *stracciatella*, trying to steer the yellow thread of broth down the drain. Any moment now Aldo Moro's body would disappear down the drain, among whisked egg and filaments of beef, slipping down through the pipes into the submerged reticulum, and from there sinking deeper into the world's stone memory, through magmatic basalt on the ocean bed, through marble that had hardened around quartz, through gypsum that had once been sea, vapor, and sediment, and through rocks of fire and sky, till it reached a cocoon of hard glass at the perfect center of the Earth.

I tilted the plate more sharply, but Aldo Moro still didn't fall. I was waiting for him to hit the grid of the drain and bounce sideways on to the ceramic, still curled up in a ball, but he didn't come out, so I straightened up, put the dish to my mouth, and drank; I swallowed the ice-cold liquid and the soft and the hard, the whole list of textures.

I laid the empty plate on the tablecloth. On my lips I felt a thin, grainy yolk that dried instantly in the air, a feeling of weariness. Aldo Moro was lost in the lake, in the plate, in my throat. He was the world-driller, the hole-maker. I was the hole.

String was standing in the kitchen doorway. She turned the knob to switch off the TV. I felt two or three sentences form in my mouth but didn't say them; my mouth was focused on listening to a flavor, which was white and was human and was dismay.

Above us, from the darkness of its cage, the canary said something in its sleep.

SELF-DISFIGUREMENT

(MAY 5-8, 1978)

Today I gouged a four-centimeter line on my desk with a spike of my barbed wire; propping an open book in front of me to conceal my movements, I cut through the hard Formica surface and into the soft wood below. Finally I blackened the cut with a ballpoint. When I'd finished, I surveyed my work; it had taken me three hours.

After recess, just as the class was about to begin, the principal's secretary came in and handed out head lice diaries. We wondered what point there was in distributing them in May, since they were dated 1977–1978 and the school year was nearly over. She said the diaries themselves were not the point; we were to read the information they gave about head lice. There'd been a number of outbreaks in primary and middle schools recently, so preemptive action was necessary.

As she was saying this, Morana—the focus of infection, the plague-spreader—ran his fingers through his hair, which was thick, fine, Scandinavian-blond, and greasy. I looked at his wrist as it bent. You could tell from the color of his skin that he hadn't washed his hands for days. I could see black grime under his fingernails and dark signs of sickness on his face.

Except that Morana always looked like that; he'd been repulsive all year. What I admired about him was the power of his malaise. It was primarily social: incomprehensible family; persistent lateness for school; excuse notes written by his mother in a crabbed, semiliterate hand. Only at a secondary level was it a physical malaise, as if his perennially disheveled appearance was an epitome of his family life and a constant source of pain: a focus of infection, in fact. A malaise so powerful it had prevented his degenerating into caricature, into folklore. For in the class's collective imagination, Morana had seemed destined to become the repulsive victim, the scapegoat, the target of all the cruelty that's inflicted without unkindness or malice, the cruelty people show because they feel irritable or because they just can't resist doing it. Potentially Morana was this: the hapless classmate whom you unrelentingly made to suffer for his isolated existence, and whose tears, when they came, you didn't understand; but his innate repulsiveness, his constant and total marginality, prevented us, without our realizing it, from mobbing and destroying him in that way. Like when a pack of animals isolates a dying member yet respects him: it isolates him because he's dying, but respects him because, by the very fact of dying, he's a millimeter away from discovery.

So when Morana scratched his head, I looked at him and suspected him, but then instantly withdrew my suspicion, knowing that it was ridiculous, because he was always to blame, and therefore invariably innocent.

We put our head lice diaries into our knapsacks and the class went on.

After school I left with Scarmiglia and Bocca. We took the

road that led from Piazza De Saliba to Piazza Strauss. Scarmiglia
and I lived in the same area; Bocca didn't, but he came along
with us anyway to talk. Besides, this area was his realm—the
land of the porn-nests. Narrow alleyways, cars that had been
dumped there decades ago, now full of straw and stripped of
their tires—the dark metal discs of the wheel rims curving angrily in their beds—razor-sharp briars, thickets through which
Bocca, despite his large girth, contrived to squeeze, reaching the
porn-nest and retrieving with his bare hands comic books trans-
fixed by roots that rose up lustfully from the ground, couplings
pierced through the middle by branches with rows of red ants
walking along them, branches which curved toward our chests,
seeking the blood in our veins like divining rods. Each time
Bocca pulled out the sexual flower of the comic—the comet, the
celestial guide that had suddenly crashed down to the ground,
the star half-buried under wire, gravel, and car tires, marking
the exact and terrible spot where our erotic gazes had been
born—he detached one page from another and displayed to our
crackling eyes little castles of limbs, heaps of genitals, expanding
archipelagoes of bodies.

We stopped in Piazzetta Chopin, put our knapsacks on the
ground, and sat down on the wall that bordered the flower bed.

We were surrounded by apartment buildings, all whitish,
all eight stories high, all with brick balconies, their facades
subdivided by timid attempts at darker or lighter bands, but
always at right angles, in square Christian Democrat shapes.
Below them, little gardens that still took my breath away when I
remembered long, monotonous afternoons spent playing pointlessly with bikes, sandboxes, and swings—my mouth against the
rope as I swung, the dusty taste of hemp.

At first we sat in normal postures, but then we tried twisting
our legs into different, more uncomfortable positions. We went
on to the lawn by the flower bed and moved our buttocks,
thighs, and feet around, to look wilder, different. As we talked,

we lay on the ground as if strapped to gynecological chairs: elbows pointing backward, body weight on the sacrum, stomach muscles contracted, legs apart, knees bent and sticking upward. We knew we were viral but we didn't know how.

Scarmiglia said there were already head lice in our class; there'd been talk of it for days in the other classes. Some people had already taken precautions—powder, shampoo. Bocca said that when his mother was small they used to shave children's heads and sprinkle them with DDT to combat head lice. He also made a crack about Morana but I defended him, saying it was nothing to do with him. Sure, he was dirty, but so what? In fact, I thought—though I kept the thought to myself—Morana should have been an example to us, the true viral boy, the incarnation of innocent evil, a rabid dog sprinkled with rust, someone who every day, obstinately and without any capacity for comprehension, lived with infection, absorbed it, and spread it.

Bocca said his family talked of nothing but politics at the moment. At lunchtime his father would bring several newspapers home, not only the *Giornale di Sicilia* but also *La Repubblica* and *L'Unità*. Moro was supposed to die every day but he never did; he was kept alive by words, by negotiations, by breath from the lungs of Andreotti, Fanfani, Craxi, and Zaccagnini, like when you play with a soap bubble and keep it up in the air by puffing and blowing, intensifying your efforts if it drifts dangerously low, steering it away from sharp edges, blowing so hard it goes out of shape.

I didn't mention that I'd eaten Moro, or nearly eaten him, felt his microscopic body fall, curled up and primordial, down through my body and down through the world. Then everything had ended; things had started anew, it had been easier to breathe. But in any case, here in Palermo there wasn't so much pain: in March something had slackened off, lost impetus; it was clear from the conversations over supper—we ate with other bodies as well as our own sitting at the table: we ate with the Red Brigades, with their hungry ghosts—but the tension was high at that point, during the television news and for another hour afterward; then the ghosts would disappear, leaving only a secondhand, peripheral tension.

And yet for the three of us, who could perceive it, there *was* a ferment, an excitement, a need to be ravenous, for something to pick us up and sweep us along, for something to concentrate on. The struggle, for example. Because that was the heart of it. The word *struggle* contained sex, anger, and dream. We tried to say it under our breath, brazenly, and link it to an action. But at that point opaqueness returned—the frosting that separated purpose from its fulfillment.

"Have you thought about what I said about the Red Brigades?" Scarmiglia asked suddenly.

"About their language, you mean?" asked Bocca.

"Yes. And about the fact that they don't stop at language. They act."

"What did you expect us to think?" I asked.

"That what they're doing has a meaning."

"Even if they kill?"

"Do you remember what I said about being guilty?" he asked me, without answering my question.

I nodded.

"Being guilty is a responsibility. The Red Brigades are accepting that responsibility."

"They're making Moro innocent," I said.

"That's true," said Scarmiglia, "that's happening too, but it's inevitable. There are consequences to having the courage to be guilty. One consequence is making Moro into a victim."

"Still," Bocca said quietly, "it's true that they're the only ones who act."

"Yes," said Scarmiglia. "They're not interested in being together just for the sake of forming a group. The Red Brigades *act*. They do things."

While we were talking, I felt the May sun on my skin and heard the crickets around us, a few bees, their spring psychosis.

"The Red Brigades," I said, "are the only people who've understood that a dream without fulfillment is bound to wither."

"Yes, that's true," said Bocca.

Scarmiglia looked at us, but said nothing; I could see he was tempted to smile; he was pleased that we were following his train of thought.

"What the Red Brigades have grasped," he said then, in a very low voice, "is that a dream must be linked to discipline; it must become hard and geometrical, and be projected toward ideology."

Around us the occasional car passed; people in their homes had lunch, passed one another water, bread, feeding in their own ways.

"Toward ideology," he repeated. Then he sat up, arched his back, and touched his hair. He did this for a long time; he rubbed and ruffled, searched in the deepest black, and found another sentence.

"The Red Brigades *feel* all this," he said; "they *are* all this. They lend substance to what is intangible, pith and impulse to what was shell and inertia. They've excised the political gland of an entire nation, and now they're forcing Italy to look at them."

I observed his head cocked to one side, the sensual curve of his shoulders. I could tell that he was moved. Bocca had sat up too and was looking at him.

"What about us?" said Scarmiglia. "Shouldn't we be doing something?"

•

On Saturday, May 6, the newspapers carried the text of communiqué number nine. Its final words were: "We therefore conclude the battle that began on March 16 by carrying out the sentence to which Aldo Moro has been condemned."

In the morning we met at school and before the first class started we discussed it. Now and then a classmate stopped, listened for a moment, called us idiots, and went off. Morana sat at his desk, on his own, in the khaki denim shirt he wore every day; he did nothing: didn't revise his notes, didn't write a word.

Bocca was excited; he repeated what he'd heard his father say, that the meaning of the communiqué was that there was still time, that there *must* still be time, but that they must hurry.

In my opinion, *carrying out*—the term in the communiqué that the newspapers focused on—was, like every gerund, a verb with a belly, a marsupial that held hypotheses and ambiguities in its pouch. Whether the Red Brigades meant the reader to think of hypotheses, and therefore possibilities of salvation—more blowing to keep the soap bubble up in the air—or ambiguities—the bubble is no longer there but it's transparent and we act as though it *is* still there—was impossible to tell.

Scarmiglia listened without saying a word, without nodding. I watched him against the light as he sat on the edge of the desk: pagan, absorbed, and fecund, the founder of a new religion.

After the fifth period, we walked homeward together. Scarmiglia kept silent. Bocca argued, I responded. We discussed the communiqués again, and their language. Bocca was entranced by them; he liked their magniloquence, their precise, ferocious sentences.

I listened to him, thought about it, and realized that although I felt the attraction of their language there was something that bothered me: I was uncomfortable with their callow dogmatism, their puerile magniloquence. And yet I myself was as magniloquent as anyone. I couldn't help but be so, for I knew, as the Red Brigades knew, that magniloquence was the only way of gaining access to the vision, the prophecy of history. True, you made yourself ridiculous, but there was no alternative. if I had to choose between irony and ridicule, I would choose ridicule.

While Bocca talked excitedly, I suddenly changed course, crossed the street, went to the newsstand, and returned with some daily papers.

"We must study them," I said.

Bocca brightened; Scarmiglia nodded.

"That's not enough," he said. "We need a lot more."

We decided to go home to get more papers, all the ones we could find from the past month and a half. We agreed to meet in the early afternoon, in the porn clearing.

The porn clearing was between the street and the back railing of the church of Santa Luisa, a kind of no-man's-land, forty square meters of garbage and random foliage that thickened toward the middle till it became a solid mass of branches and black leaves, a thicket that Bocca faced with a happy smile at the prospect of finding yet more paper porn in the vegetal shrine. There, surrounded by an areola of trampled grass, was a spherical bush about half a meter high. Bristling with hostile little branches and livid leaves, it formed a blue globe that was both a strongbox and an instrument of divination. Bocca was the only one of us who had the physical courage to thrust his arm into the vegetal head and bring out sex.

These incursions, and the plungings-in of arms and lust, were a clearly defined ritual: we went there once or twice a week, either right after school at one o'clock, or in the late afternoon, when we'd done our homework. We did this throughout the winter and straight through June; Scarmiglia and I never went on our own but always with our priest. Bocca would stand by the bush, unbutton his right shirt cuff and push it down with his left hand till it encircled the metacarpal; next, with an effort, he'd put the button back into the buttonhole, so that only a jagged outcrop of hand protruded, a claw large enough to grip the comic book without getting scratched on the back of the hand and the knuckles; then he'd bend down and thrust his arm into the bush. To us, seeing his arm disappear and come back out clutching a porn comic was like watching an eclipse of the sun: momentary darkness followed by joyous light. Finally, Bocca would straighten up, compose himself, smoothing his pants down in dignified fashion; then he'd free his hand from the cuff, pull both his sleeves up, and lay the comic book on top of the bush, while our optical nerves started cracking like whips inside our skulls.

That was what usually happened, at any rate. This time, however, there was no contemplative wonder. This time excitement was replaced by concentration. We had work to do.

Bocca and I went into the bushes, carrying armfuls of newspapers; Scarmiglia would be joining us later. We sat down on the grass and searched for articles that might contain anything of interest to us—claims of responsibility, proclamations, sporadic communiqués.

"I've found a story from 1970," said Bocca, leafing through the newspapers. "The Red Brigades seized the personnel manager of a factory in Sardinia; then they hung a placard around his neck, sat him on a donkey, and led him around the village."

He was enthusiastic. He liked the idea of ridicule—creative punishment. "We ought to do something like that," he said.

He'd torn out several articles containing communiqués that the Red Brigades had written over the years. The newspapers had republished them all after Moro's kidnapping.

"Do you see those sentences?" he asked me, marking columns of articles in pencil. His hands were large and invertebrate. He pointed out photographs and headlines; he was a prospector who'd found a vein of gold.

"I see them."

"It's just like Scarmiglia says: every sentence is a bomb, it explodes."

"Every sentence is a simplification," I said.

Bocca stopped and looked at me.

"What do you mean?"

"Just what I said: it's a simplification. Don't you feel it?"

"Why do you say that?"

"Because the purpose of those sentences is to make a distinction. Like when a teacher divides the blackboard into two halves with chalk to separate the ones who've been good from the ones who've been bad."

He was dismayed, crestfallen; it was as if someone had torn off his clothes to leave him standing before me half-naked.

"You're being unfair," he said.

"No. I'm not. I like those sentences, they're great. But we can't pretend not to understand what they're trying to achieve."

"What *are* they trying to achieve?"

"I told you: they're trying to divide things up, to organize the world."

"Could you do any better?"

"I'm not saying that."

"What *are* you saying, then?"

I didn't answer; there was no sense in going on. Bocca too kept quiet and read to himself, frowning angrily. He'd lost his earlier carnal happiness, his artless enthusiasm. To tell the truth, he was right: at first sight the Red Brigades' language was a mythological animal, a unicorn. Muscular, sanguine, powerful and phallic, with its horn spiraling up on its forehead, sharp and indestructible. A language that rampaged through the text, uprooting and devouring, that expressed anger and transformation. The Red Brigades were always fiery, always apocalyptic. They spoke of "active struggle" and "dislocating structures." They were oracular. The desert fathers had left the sandy wastes of Palestine and come into the city, into the universities and factories, to tell stories, to bear witness, to prophesy and curse.

I felt weary. I reached out into the pile of newspapers and leafed through them for a while; I read: "No further equivocation is possible, and any attempt by the Christian Democrat Party and its government to evade the issue with ambiguous communiqués and underhanded delaying tactics will be interpreted as a sign of cowardice, a sign that they have made a decision (this time clear and definitive) not to give the problem of political prisoners its only possible solution."

As I read I lost concentration and couldn't go forward or back. It was like those times in the swimming pool when suddenly I couldn't breathe, my stomach and legs ached, and I had to stop in the middle and float on my back, like a dead man.

The Red Brigades' sentences floated like dead men. The Red Brigades' sentences *were* dead men. The Red Brigades' sentences built a world shaped like a dead man, while pretending they could imagine the future, the life to come.

The Red Brigades' language, I thought, was a worn-out mythological animal, a broken-down unicorn: its body was emaciated, its blood sludgy, the horn on its head a phoney phallus. It was a language in which opposite impulses coexisted, just as enthusiasm and disillusionment—about that language and about everything else—always coexisted in me.

I heard a rustle in the thicket, and the space rapidly broke up: the noise seemed to be creating light by creeping, thrusting its way through the bushes to where we were. The rustle grew louder, there was a swish of trampled leaves and a crackling of branches, and Scarmiglia appeared. Only he wasn't Scarmiglia—not anymore. Or maybe this was the real Scarmiglia.

His head was shaved bare. His skull bore the marks of the cutting.

He looked at us, smiled, and sat down beside us.

We didn't say anything.

Then Bocca asked if he had head lice. Scarmiglia said no.

"I told my parents a doctor had come to the school," he said, "and found lice and nits in my hair."

So his father had taken scissors and a razor and cut all his hair off. This had all happened an hour ago, as soon as he'd got home from school.

Bocca sat there, stunned, torn-out sheets of newspaper on his lap.

"Does it hurt?"

"Does what hurt?"

"Your head."

"My head?"

"Your hair, I mean."

"I haven't got any hair."

"That's what I mean."

Scarmiglia gave Bocca a look expressing contempt at all his questions; then he relented and smiled indulgently.

"We need to become unrecognizable," he said. "So we can exploit this mundane epidemic to satisfy our desire for an absolute epidemic. After all, it's not only us that feel this desire, but the whole of Italian society."

He gestured toward the newspapers scattered on the grass. He held his fingers tightly together: the skin turned white; there were tiny fragments of hair stuck to it.

"Italy is pervaded by contagion," he went on. "It *wants* to be pervaded by contagion. It's enjoying it, but it can't admit that it is. You can't enjoy violence and crisis. It's not done."

Light filtered through the leafy roof above our heads and turned to shimmering hexagonal shards on the grass; I stretched out my arm, opened my palm, and intercepted one. Scarmiglia looked at me and went on.

"But in fact," he said, "it's all a sham. Italy pretends that it wants extreme heat but what it really wants is just something slightly more than lukewarm. Since March 16 the country has been acting as if it can live with a temperature of forty degrees Celsius, but that's impossible—nobody can live in that kind of heat. The incandescence is a game. The civil indignation, the moral repugnance, are fictions. Indignation was instantly institutionalized; fear was institutionalized."

Scarmiglia stopped and looked at us again, inspecting his two-man army.

"But there's still a temptation," he said, lowering his tone. "The enjoyment of fear is still there; it flows like an underground stream, although people tend to become inured to it. Our civilized instincts are desensitized, our sense of responsibility is very weak. So we resort to these periodic national charades so we can kid ourselves that we're different. This isn't Italy's real temperature. Italy is lukewarm; reality is lukewarm; therefore Italy is real. And it's because of this, as a reaction against all this, that we need to change ourselves beyond all recognition. Because this is the beginning, and we need a new look."

I watched the shards of light dance on his skull as he talked.

"We still look like kids," he resumed. "We don't have a single hair on our chins, not even a bit of fluff. These faces aren't going to frighten anybody."

He paused again, sweat glistening on his cheekbones.

"That's why I've done this," he said. "To disfigure myself."

He was right, I thought; Italy was lukewarm, incapable of taking responsibility for tragedy. It could create tragedy, all right, but then it turned it into farce. Contagion and epidemic were just the kind of thing we needed: another god of infections to impose form on things; or rather, deform things— deform them and mix them together. If it wasn't tetanus, head lice would do, and after the head lice, through them, the struggle would come.

Scarmiglia had stopped talking and folded his arms; he'd spoken and acted; now it was our turn.

In the afternoon I took some ham out of the fridge and went down into the gardens.

The natural cripple had disintegrated. He was lying against the wall, two dark scabs over his eyes, his coat smelly. I crouched beside him; there was dry feces under his body. I hadn't been down for weeks; String had fed the cats on her own. I had no idea how long he'd been in that state.

I took the piece of barbed wire out of my pocket and touched his sticklike front legs with it. I lifted one leg up, pulled the barbed wire away, and the leg fell down again. A small breath rose in the exposed stomach, an infinitesimal mass that swelled the skin, disappeared, then returned, and disappeared again, haphazardly. I stuck a spike into the swelling but there was no reaction. I pressed harder; one of the cripple's legs twitched, nothing more. I pushed the spike further in and pulled it sideways; there was a harder puff, the head rising, the two scabs looking at me. I was about to stand up, but instead I stuck the spike in again, consciously—I needed to see, to know—and kept pressing till a little red dot appeared on the pale belly, among the grains of flaking rust. The dot remained still for a moment, then swelled, rounded, and began to trickle downward. I stood up, looked at the barbed wire, then at the cripple, threw the ham on top of him, and left.

At home I turned on the television; *Buonasera con . . .* was on. I sniffed Renato Rascel; he had a sweet, mild smell of sebum and fatty acids, of cholesterol. As I sniffed I didn't look at the pictures; I stood in front of the TV set with my nose against the glass and smelled only the molecules that were released by the screen and passed into my nostrils and my thoughts. But I did listen, and what I heard was a caricature of our conversation earlier that day. The solidly cynical stanzas, reducing intergeneration conflict to a facile joke, and then the refrain: "We are small but we will grow, and then, comma, you will know. Open parenthesis, count to ten, treat us all like grown-up men." A crude but honest representation of the way we were. We wanted the world to treat us like adults, to take notice of us and respect us, but we couldn't escape from our schoolboy world; we smelled of stagnant water in the stoups of churches, of multiplication tables learned by heart, of clunky rhymes, of perfunctory signs of the cross, and hysterical acts of heroism. We sounded like Renato Rascel; we even smelled like him: we were sebaceous.

I turned off the television and watched the dot in the center disappear. I went into the bathroom. String and Stone were at the pizzeria with Cotton; I could take my time.

I filled the basin with water, got out some nail scissors, and started to cut, but made little progress—the scissors were too small; so I got the big scissors from the kitchen. Now the locks flaked away easily, slowly breaking up in the water. Each snip of the blades took a snapshot of the scene and cut it out: a picture of me on the evening of May 6, 1978, disfiguring myself.

I went on for forty minutes, cutting all the hair I could reach, forcing the handle rings of the scissors shut when I encountered a thicker and tougher lock of hair, then bending my head forward and shaking the cuttings into the basin. It was as if an invisible mouth was gnawing at my head, tearing bits off, ripping out the insides, and devouring the hair.

I looked at myself in the mirror, apprehensively. There were still a few bristly tufts sticking out at odd angles. I wet my scalp with water, took some of Stone's shaving cream out of the jar, and mixed it with the brush. When I'd worked up a lather, I spread it over my head. Then I got his razor out of the cabinet and started shaving my scalp, gently at first, then more firmly. The blade made a faint crackling noise as it shaved, a sound linked to the action, to the pulling of arm and hand and to the roots' resistance to the shaving. When I'd almost finished,

I looked up at the mirror, razor in one hand and brush in the other; my head was pitted with pink craters, like a battlefield after an artillery bombardment. Lighter areas of scalp were interspersed with darker ones that still had a covering of hair, islands in the sea, continents between oceans. My skull was the world.

I put the razor and the shaving brush on the edge of the basin, dried my hands and went to our bedroom. I got the illustrated Bible down from the shelf and put it on my bed. Then I knelt on the floor and flipped quickly through the pages. When I came to the Book of Prophets, I slowed down and eventually found the illustration I was looking for: Ezekiel in a blue tunic sitting on a rock, sword in hand, with white locks of his hair and beard scattered in the dust around him. God had told him to take a sharp sword and use it like a barber's razor to shave his head, then get some scales, to weigh and divide up the shaved hair. Then he was to burn a third of it, cut another third up into smaller pieces, and scatter the remainder in the wind. God was asking Ezekiel to reveal his skull to him, to give it to him by shaving it bare. By this ritual sacrifice he would be giving back all that was concealment and show.

I had no god and I was not ritualistic, so I wouldn't do anything. I was going to cup my hands and scoop up the hair that was floating in the basin and flush it down the toilet. Then I would wipe the basin with a damp cloth and wash my hands carefully to remove all traces of hair. Finally I'd lay my new skull on my pillow, feel the coolness of the pillowcase rising up into my bones and try to sleep—but there was a noise in the hall, footsteps along the corridor and Cotton was standing there staring at me with tears in his eyes, and Stone put the keys down on his desk in slow motion and made some other ominously slow movements, and String came over to me and put her hand on the skin of my skull, made me turn right around and rubbed me with her fingertips, and I felt friction and strips of heat, and she slapped me on the skull, but not hard, as though she wanted to hear what noise it made, like people do with a baby when it's born, and she said: "You're crazy, you're crazy."

•

On May 7 I explained everything. I used Scarmiglia's story, with some modifications. Stone gave me his Aqua Velva to put on my scalp to keep it soft. It was green and had a nice scent. The next morning String looked for the nearest pharmacy, bought some antiparasitic powder, and sprinkled it over me. Cotton, no longer frightened, watched TV.

I'd arranged to meet Scarmiglia and Bocca in the early afternoon to go to the Mediterranean Fair. As soon as Bocca saw my skull he became agitated and kept apologizing to me and Scarmiglia; it wasn't till we got to our destination on Via Imperatore Federico that he finally calmed down.

The Mediterranean Fair was a state of mind, one of the many forms boredom could take: walking aimlessly, just moving about, and randomly coming across the *porchetta* stall or the bumper cars.

That was what the Mediterranean Fair was, every year.

Porchetta; bumper cars; the smell of frying; cotton candy; the Italian Army stand; people constantly barging into you as you walked along; the witches' house; the roller coaster with its three parabolic curves; onion from hot dogs trampled underfoot; grimaces, leers, clowns; sweat on your chest and back; cigarette stubs and piles of plastic cups; cats rooting for food among the garbage; throwing a Ping-Pong ball into a bowl to win a goldfish; carrying the goldfish, once you'd won it, in a plastic bag full of water; the goldfish dying before you reached the exit because the water was overheated; dropping the goldfish among cigarette butts and plastic cups, or in a pot on the florists' booth; tractors; bulldozers; walking, eating, buying

things; looking for a toilet; looking at Utveggio Castle illuminated above Monte Pellegrino: tapping on your neighbor's
shoulder to draw his attention to it.

Doing all those things, every year.

We bought tickets and went in. We walked down the first
row of booths and looked people in the eye. Scarmiglia and I
were in front, with Bocca to one side and half a pace behind.
Scarmiglia and I were handsome and sensuous; we were fully
clothed but felt half-naked, riding on a thunderbolt. People returned our looks, but immediately tensed up and turned away,
made gestures, followed us out of the corner of their eyes,
turned around to watch as we walked on. Old people shook
their heads in despair, kids shouted insults in dialect.

We stopped for a drink of water at a kiosk. Bocca looked at
some shards of green glass from a broken bottle scattered among
gray chunks of asphalt. Then he looked at us, and his eyes
expressed jealousy and envy and love, and that same endless
agitation.

We walked on. We knew a dead body had been found in
the fair the night before—we'd read about it in the paper; we
wanted to see where.

We went around behind the tractor pavilion. Noise and
light came through the wall, but both were muted. We found
ourselves in a narrow space, bordered on one side by the blue
corrugated iron wall of the pavilion and on the other by the
outer wall of the fair. The person who'd died was a boy who'd
come into the fair, paid for his ticket, met someone, eaten
something, seen things and said things, then come around the
back here and shot up. The heroin had been cut with masonry
dust and he'd died. The paper said he'd been wearing jeans, a
shirt, and black Dr. Scholl's; and there'd been a string around
his wrist.

Bocca clearly wanted to say something, but he stared at our
shiny skulls and said nothing. We looked down at the asphalt,

trying to imagine the exact spot where the body had lain. Then we went back out into the crowds to flaunt the dry, living bone under our soft scalps, the pride of our hairless skin.

We were a disconcerting sight, and we were proud of it. It was everything we'd hoped for. What could be more disconcerting than a shaven-headed boy whose skull was so bare you could run your finger along the sutures between its plates? Previously I'd been nasty; now I was disconcerting. Previously I'd been hostile; now I was disconcerting. Disconcerting yet unflappable, disconcerting yet calm. People walked past, looked at me, and didn't know that in doing so they'd looked at my nimbus, my halo of light and election. They didn't know. But people know nothing.

As we walked through the crowd we saw only faces blown apart by the dialect that had exploded in their mouths—faces generated in the darkness of family ties, by daily collisions, forehead against cheekbone, mouth against temple. Palermitan faces whirled around us like the big masks at the entrance to the tunnel of horrors.

I was hot; my shirt clung to my chest. We sat down on some red-and-white steps in a quieter area. It was getting dark. Bocca's breathing was loud and fleshy; he talked but I found I couldn't listen to him; Scarmiglia looked at his fingers, rubbing them, twisting them, pulling his forefinger back till it touched his wrist. A booth in front of us had a sign displaying different types of ice cream. I stood up, went over to the booth, leaned on the metal counter, and looked at the photographs of cones and Popsicles on a sky-blue background. Their names were pathetic—Paff, Mike Blond, Dalek, Bananita. I chose an ice cream sandwich with a chocolate-and-vanilla filling. On the top and bottom cookie layers, there were little comic strips showing animals and speech balloons. I read and they talked nonsense to each other. As I nibbled and swallowed, I felt the inane sentences slip down my throat.

Meanwhile I enjoyed the cool air from a fan inside the booth. There was a full Coca-Cola bottle on the counter with a rose in it, an ornament. The stem fished in the black depths, absorbing bubbles; the corolla was broad and thick, a bulging eye. Now and then, people in Palermo would have the idea of putting a flower in a bottle. I used to see them on windowsills, on graves in the cemetery. But usually the bottle was empty or full of water. This rose had absorbed enough bubbles to make it burst; the carbon dioxide had made it neurotic.

I asked the man at the booth if I could take it. He couldn't see me clearly and didn't hear what I said; then he looked at my skull, made a downward gesture with his hand, meaning "help yourself," and turned away to serve someone. I picked up the bottle and gestured to the others that I'd be back in a minute. I went back behind the tractor pavilion. One of the tractors had been switched on and was being revved up, the furious noise pulverizing everything. I stared at the asphalt, took a step to one side, a step to the other, then one step forward, and placed the bottle almost at the exact midpoint between the blue corrugated iron and the outer wall. As I did this, I listened to the furious noise and felt that what I was doing was stupid; I wouldn't mention it to Scarmiglia and Bocca. I took a last look at the rose with its drooping head and went back to the others. When we left through the main gate I looked up at flags fluttering on tall, pointed poles that pierced the sky, among the indecipherable flights of early bats.

·

All of us should get to know our own skull sometime—touch it with our fingertips, spread out our fingers and measure it in spans, twisting our arms to complete its perimeter and compress its area, absorbing its shape, its hardness and tenderness, and locate the crack of the fontanel, the little vagina through which the silent world enters us.

And all of us, at least once, should wash our own skull, soap it, listen to the fizz of foam as it penetrates the scalp, spread it meticulously all over the skin, even behind our ears and inside our ears, and then rinse it away, by first splashing water over it with cupped hands, and then, to complete the rinse, exposing our skull to the jet of the shower, closing our eyes and feeling each thread of water bore into our brain.

On the morning of May 8, while taking my shower, I touched my whole skull with the palm of my hand, rubbed it, rinsed it, and rubbed it again. Then I washed my testicles and felt them smooth and cold, like bone or china in my hand.

When I got to school, I saw Scarmiglia; then I turned and saw Bocca coming, his rotund body surmounted by a perfectly smooth sphere with an arc of contentment etched in the middle. He came up to us and started chatting delightedly; he was a bundle of euphoria and plans. We entered the classroom, pushing our way through a thicket of questions. We told the teachers our parents had found out that we had head lice and sent us to have our heads shaved.

Sitting down, I saw Morana at his desk. When we'd walked into the classroom he'd looked at us for a moment, then averted his gaze. I kept staring at him till he turned back toward me: his expression was calm, restrained, and slightly surprised, as if welcoming me to a place where he would never have dreamed of meeting me.

During recess we sat on the steps that led out of the school, just inside the closed gate. Scarmiglia smiled at us and explained. His speech consisted of measurements in perfect sequence—meters, centimeters, millimeters. Each word marked out and had meaning. He never took his eyes off our skulls, never stopped or even hesitated for a moment.

"Violence," he said, "is not dangerous; it's neither dangerous nor bad. In fact, paradoxical though it may seem, violence is not violent. It only becomes so if it's wrongly used. When correctly used, it's an aesthetic, a style, a project."

He paused to make sure that we were following him; we nodded to indicate that we were. I wondered how and when he'd thought all this out. It was what he'd always wanted: to become the ideologue of a Red Brigade cell at its birth.

"Some actions are intrinsically violent," he went on, "and yet we don't see them as such. Eating is violent, digesting is violent; it's violent to run and it's violent to speak. On the other hand, there are other actions whose violence we tend to overestimate—such as breaking, cutting, tearing, and shattering. It's wrong to consider these things violent; they're not violent, they're life-giving. The seed *must* break, the cells *must* separate, the newborn baby's body *must* be torn from its mother's womb. Otherwise there's no life. They're life-giving and foundational. Romulus kills Remus and founds a city. Cain kills Abel and determines the course of human history. Violence is courageous because it identifies and admits the existence of pain and guilt. Violence dares to be guilty. The Red Brigades dare to be guilty and are aware of pain. The Red Brigades were born out of fear and desire—a fear of distance, and a desperate desire to be at the center of time, in the burning heart of history—not to disappear, but to be visible. Because that's the destiny for which, without realizing it, we are preparing, we are being prepared: disappearance."

Something hobbled toward us from the other end of Piazza De Saliba, to which Scarmiglia's back was turned. It came a few meters closer. It was another dog. Palermo was exploding with dogs; they came up out of the asphalted roads—dogs made of stone mixed with bitumen. This one too was a wreck; it looked as if bits of its body had been torn off. It came up to us on the other side of the gate, looked at us, and sat down. Scarmiglia didn't notice it.

"The Red Brigades's way of achieving visibility," he went

on, "is to carry out operations—exemplary operations. Power in Italy at the moment is a mass of immovable energy whose only purpose is to perpetuate itself. We must devise some exemplary operations that can break it up."

The dog, after listening patiently for about a minute, had moved closer. It looked at me and Bocca as if to ask what the hell was going on. We didn't react. It pushed his nose through the bars and sniffed at Scarmiglia's skull. But Scarmiglia was immersed in the joy of language, aware of nothing but words.

"But it's going to take time," he said, "before we get to that stage. We've begun by shaving our heads, but that's only the beginning. We need to carry out socially disruptive operations. To do that, we need to create a structure, form a strategy, and train ourselves. Only when we've done all those things will we be able to think about carrying out real operations."

The dog had pulled its head back through the gate and started licking itself. It cleaned one of its paws, then leaned back and licked its belly. It stopped, looked at Bocca and me, and then at the back of Scarmiglia's head waggling about as he talked, then thrust its nose further down and licked its penis, a red cherry.

Bocca and I didn't react, but we were distracted and missed some parts of Scarmiglia's speech.

"In Italy," he was saying, "everything is reduced to the level of posturing, appearance, fashion. The sordid charade of fashion. All such things are trivial and of no concern to us."

The dog continued to nuzzle itself greedily, licking its member, which in the meantime, through friction, had become long and taut, a thin branch quivering in the cool May breeze. It made noises, a snuffling sound and a contented, derisive whine, but Scarmiglia didn't hear.

"From now on," he said, "the only things that will concern us will be our strategy and our training. We'll have to concentrate on building up a geometrical hatred, a transparent, reticular snow crystal."

Just then the dog emitted a piercing squeak; Scarmiglia stiffened, turned around, and saw the animal's swollen, cyanotic erection. He turned back toward us, and we bit our lips. He stood up, leaned over the gate, hissed, and tried to shoo the dog away, but it cocked its head to one side, rolled its nutbrown eyes, and didn't move. Its red erection, swaying casually between its legs, was the heroic, militant erection of Red Brigade thought, sex penetrating ideology.

Scarmiglia turned away in disgust and walked off. Bocca followed him, but I went over to the gate and called out to the dog. It stared at me, put its nose through the bars, and held it there, ears lowered. It sat down, and I gently stroked its head, feeling its skull with my palm; I leaned over, stroked its chest and belly, and touched its erection; the dog nibbled two of my fingers with its gums, turned around, and walked away.

Scarmiglia said we needed to meet at the clearing after school. But before that there was the schoolyard, the other kids, the Creole girl. I squeezed between the bodies on the steps and came up behind her. In the wavy motion of her hair, in the ruffling of the demons, I saw a drop of the purest red blood. More blood, I thought, months after the last time. A tiny fraction of her distant life that I still longed to capture, a naked globule, a pulsing crimson light set off by the black of her hair. I stretched out my hand toward the blood, and was about to pick it off between my finger and thumb, but as we came down the last step into the immense curving space of Piazza De Saliba to see the blue sky streaked with clouds, the blood drop opened its wings and a ladybug flew away into the sky, leaving only the black of her hair. The Creole girl turned and saw me, and on her forehead and her other features an expression of doubt, of reproof, appeared—and it was only then, as she gazed at the curved bones above my eyes, that I became aware of my skull and *felt like* a skull and was filled with horror, real, absolute horror, and tears came to my eyes, when she pushed toward me with her chest and seemed on the point of speaking to me, but instead made a strange, angry movement, beat the back of her right hand against the palm of her left, a kind of asymmetrical, botched clap, and wrinkled her features, all of them, like you do when a bright light dazzles you, and again struck her palm, with the sound of a walnut cracking, shook her right hand twice, forming a two with her index finger and thumb, as if loosening up her arm, but again with a hint of anger, a watermark of tension and surprise that was visible through her skin, and I didn't understand as I realized that it was true, the light was too bright and was bombarding us, I felt photosynthesis happening around us, carbon dioxide degrading into oxygen, and the mass of cellular respiration hitting us, and the Creole girl's gaze moved away from me and alighted on the milling of homeward-bound bodies behind my back, on the tumult of voices and jostling, on the sky and sun and shadows—and now everything behind me and around me, and I myself, was cavity and disappearance.

•

As we sat beside the bush in the clearing, Scarmiglia christened us.

"We've changed our faces, now we must change our names," he said. "Each of us will choose a code name to replace our old ones. My name will be Flight—Comrade Flight. The word expresses our whole project, an aerial view and a dream."

Bocca hesitated; it wasn't clear whether he couldn't decide between several possibilities or whether he had no idea at all. He was pensive for a while.

"Comrade Radius," he said at last. "That's what I want to be called. It's a modest, self-effacing name. I'm just one of the radii that connect the center to the circumference."

It was my turn. My voice sounded flat and unemotional.

"Nimbus. My name's Nimbus. Comrade Nimbus."

As I said this, I drew a circle behind my head with the index and middle fingers of my right hand.

"A nimbus is a shining light," I said. "A destiny connected with struggle."

At home in the afternoon I sniffed celebrities on TV. I let my parents sprinkle my skull with parasiticide, then went into the bathroom and washed it off. The radio news said there'd been no news of Moro for several days, and that the country was holding its breath. If everyone holds their breath, I thought, the soap bubble will float down to the ground and burst.

When String went out with the saucepan to feed the cats, I accompanied her.

The natural cripple still lay against the wall, his neck curved forward, his back legs taut and hard—a question mark. He'd died in a halo of feces and now the halo was moving, teeming with cannibal ants. I tried to look at his belly and the hole, but there were too many ants and I couldn't see anything.

No more circling, no more meowing, no more degradation and anger: the natural cripple was dead, and now everything was devouring him—the cannibal ants, the midges swarming above him, even the air itself. I ought to burn him, I thought—tie a rope to one of his legs, drag him off somewhere, and set him on fire. Then I couldn't think anymore; tears trickled down my face, and I contorted my facial muscles, eating them. String gently put her hand on my head. We stood there for a while, the cripple dead, String's hand on my skull. Then she said, "You go home. I'll come up in a minute."

Back in the apartment, I went to our bedroom, undressed, and got into bed. I pulled my legs up tight against my chest, fearing what I might find at the end of the bed—dirt, bits of feces, little clumps of ants.

It was the end of the simulations, the meaningless spasms, the infection that didn't infect.

I didn't hear the front door open; I fell asleep.

CONSTRUCTION

The World Cup was on TV.

Every day we met at my home or Scarmiglia's—he had a color TV—to watch the matches—West Germany against Poland, Italy against France, Sweden against Brazil, Iran against Peru. Afterward we'd go to the park across the street from my apartment or to an empty lot near the school, put down a couple of stones to form goalposts, and reenact the goals.

It was an exercise in submission of the individual will. It meant abandoning any idea of playing freely, just for fun, and accepting an imitative, subordinate role, waiting till the event had occurred and replicating it. Playing was an experiment, the field a laboratory where we reproduced the moves we'd seen on TV in order to study them.

It took us days to replicate Rossi's goal against France. At first it seemed impossible to calibrate that chaos of rebounds—they were too fast and too random. We did a few trial runs, getting Bocca, who was playing in goal, to knock back the shot that was supposed to hit the corner of the goal frame, while Scarmiglia and I moved quickly to block our own shots. This was confusing, and we stopped. We took some sheets of paper and a pencil and marked out on them segments with dotted lines indicating trajectories from our feet to the goal. We showed how openings appeared or were closed down and calculated how the ball had rebounded, slowed, and speeded up in flight. We drew curves and arrows and estimated forces of impact and spin. Then we went and tried it all out against a wall. We lost heart, sat down, stood up, and started all over again. Eventually we were able to reenact the move that led up to the goal with an almost perfect approximation to the original: Cabrini's cross, which I hit, running down the wing and looking toward the center of the area, Bettega's deflection, made by Bocca, and Causio's header, executed by Scarmiglia, Bocca acting as the corner of the goal frame and knocking the ball back, Rossi—played by me, now back in the middle—collecting it, shooting, and accidentally hitting Causio—Scarmiglia again—so that the ball ricocheted back to Rossi in the form of my body, another shot and the goal.

It was a circuit of levers and cogs, a complicated mechanism that we gradually learned to decipher over days of study. Once the mechanism was revealed it seemed logical and inevitable, even banal. The effects narrated their causes, they described them; all we had to do was read the description. We understood that when you were studying a chain of events it was necessary to start from the end and swim upstream, like knowledge-salmons, through the generation of the parts that produced the whole episode. A retrograde itinerary—from the ball that ballooned in the net to the final pass, the penultimate one, the antepenultimate one, and so on—back to the conception of the move, the moment when what happened was not yet present but existed in embryonic form.

•

During these first days of vacation the sun was soft and the air had a fine grain that penetrated the skin of your face. Bocca, Scarmiglia, and I stayed out all morning, went home to have lunch, and watch the games, then went out again till evening. My family was staying in the city for the time being; in July, when Stone's vacation began, we'd move to Mondello.

One afternoon, as we sat on a marble bench in the park opposite my home, Scarmiglia explained what we were doing.

"In studying the formal aspects of a goal," he said, "we're analyzing two questions that are very important for our own project: chance and responsibility.

"When we repeat a move over and over again," he went on, "we're freeing an event from chance. We're saying that chance doesn't exist, that everything can be understood and controlled."

Bocca listened, sitting cross-legged, his fists between his legs. Of the three of us, he was the keenest on goal reenactments and the study of theory. He didn't see Scarmiglia's assuming the role of the ideologue, the explainer, as an abuse of power; he was perfectly happy, because he thought someone had to take the lead.

"Everything," said Scarmiglia, "must be reduced to responsibility and construction, clarity and precision."

He paused, looked at us, and went on.

"Spending hours repeating the same shot, kicking the ball in the same way, imparting this or that spin to it, knowing to the millimeter exactly where it will hit the ground, the angle of rebound, the thousandth of a second in which you have to kick it again, combining force and delicacy: all this helps to discipline instinct and marks a transition from chance to responsibility."

"Control!" exclaimed Bocca, taking his fists out of his lap. "It's a matter of control," he repeated.

"Sure," said Scarmiglia. "Even our breathing, the way our

lungs absorb and expel air while we run, must be disciplined. We must learn to breathe in unison, to coordinate our inhaling and exhaling."

We chose another goal to study. Bocca was in the goal again, while Scarmiglia and I each played several roles, taking turns to make crosses, dives, and interceptions. We concentrated on one segment of the move: a shot that took a deflection off a defender's calf, changed its original trajectory, and ended up in the goal. We had become a collective machine; we acted out the move till we lost all feeling—in the foot that kicked, the calf the ball hit, the goalkeeper's eyes that were deceived by the deflection—and were no longer aware of the game at all; we became unthinking movement.

Later, as I sat on the edge of my bed, I breathed slowly, imagining Bocca and Scarmiglia breathing at the same time, each in his own home. I breathed even more slowly, then speeded up again, coordinating myself, running a thin, imaginary thread between our bodies.

I had the World Cup mascot on my bedside table, a doll less than ten centimeters high, made of hard rubber. I'd bought it a few days before from Nunzio Morello, who in his usual jerky way had taken it down from a shelf and laid it in the palm of my hand; I'd put some coins on the counter and Nunzio Morello, pushing his arms sideways and twirling his hand with its long, knotty fingers, had grasped them and, with a series of mechanical-crane-like maneuvers, deposited them in the black tray of the cash register.

The mascot had black hair and was dressed in the light-blue-and-white striped shirt of Argentina, with a blue bandanna around his neck, and he held a gaucho's riding crop in his hand. I liked to touch him because he couldn't be bent out of shape. I hadn't yet achieved such perfection.

•

We began to train our bodies, to filter them, sieve them, and separate out their constituent parts in order to be more aware of them: we wanted them to be our tools. We knew our bodies were immature and that our muscles had yet to grow and take shape. But we were less interested in developing our muscles than in making our joints flexible and tough.

We sat in painful positions, putting our heels against our groins and forcing our knees down against the ground, pressing with our hands so we'd feel the tendons being stretched out, thin and tight. We stood up, placed the front part of one foot on the edge of a step with the heel overhanging, flexed the sole and stretched the rear muscles of the leg. Kneeling down, we sat on our heels, bent our torsos backward, and arched our spines. We held the position for as long as possible, till our bodies started to quiver.

We did hand exercises too.

Palms against a wall, we pushed with the full weight of our bodies till our wrists turned white. We held the metacarpus of one hand in the palm of the other and bent it in every direction; our wrists were pivots around which our hands revolved. We did the same with each individual finger till it became alien to us.

We spent a lot of time doing sit-ups to strengthen our abdominal muscles. We went on and on till our stomachs couldn't take anymore. Bocca found it an effort because his body was large and shapeless; for Scarmiglia and me it was easier, but the task of honing our bodies was never over.

When people passed by they saw three bald boys (we'd persuaded our parents that since it was summertime we might as well keep our heads shaved; as well as guarding against any recurrence of the head lice we'd feel cooler; after all, we weren't embarrassed about it) who played soccer, endlessly repeating the same moves, did exercises, then sat down on the ground, and studied sheets of paper. At first we noticed them and stared them down till they looked away; later we ignored them. But we felt the burning sun on our skulls: for the first time in our lives our heads were peeling, and so were the tops of our ears. The peeling skin mixed in with the sweat, and in the intervals between one exercise and another we'd run our hands over our scalps, rub them, roll the damp skin into little balls and throw them away, ridding ourselves of a thought.

•

As we sat in front of the TV at my home, waiting for the match between Holland and Italy to start, eating tomatoes and green salad with no oil or salt, Scarmiglia held forth on the history of the various teams and the different schools of thought, explaining all the possible formations and the sectors of the team. He distinguished between strategy, as architecture and planning, and tactics, as a way of adapting to circumstances.

"Some teams," said Scarmiglia, after I'd turned down the volume of the TV, "have a masterly strategy but inadequate tactics. Others have a confused strategy but manage to come up with unexpected solutions, keep their opponents at bay and sometimes even win, simply by wearing them down."

I bit into a tomato and felt the juice slip down my throat; String was in the kitchen, washing more salad, indulging our passion for vegetables.

"Italy," Scarmiglia went on, "falls into the second category. The team plays as if it was ill, with a kind of ventral bag in the middle of its body weighing it down. Like a fat, reluctant, hostile woman. A team that's completely negative right from the start of the match, never tries to create anything, and demoralizes its opponents by endlessly tapping the ball backward and forward in an intricate but meaningless tapestry of passes that never changes its atmosphere.

"At this point the game is steeped in ether. The other team

tries to attack but Italy puts up bulwarks of boredom. After a while its adversary backs off too. The game loses what little pace it had and sinks into a complete stupor. Then Italy, by pure chance, though the event has a certain statistical predictability, makes a few passes forward in spite of itself, the opposing team is taken by surprise, the ball finds its way to the feet of Paolo Rossi, a crafty little striker with hairless legs and an inane grin, and Italy scores a goal, tying the match or even winning it—either way, it's a travesty. Their whole approach is mean-spirited and cowardly, and their victory is undeserved. The only thing that can be said in their favor is that they're smart enough to have realized that results have no relation to merit, and that there's no logic or justice."

In the meantime the teams had lined up in the middle of the field for the national anthems; the music carried indistinctly— all you could hear were the strings; Mameli's anthem was a chorus of mosquitoes. Bocca was completely absorbed in watching our players; he took a lettuce leaf, brought it to his lips, and listened, forgetting to eat it.

"Over the past few days, however," said Scarmiglia, "Italy has been playing well. They're bold, not sneaky, their passing is neat, and they sweep forward from defense to attack in a single harmonious movement. You can hear a purring of turbine engines and feel an animal desire to seize their prey and tear it apart."

While he was talking, Scarmiglia didn't stop to eat for a moment. He stood with his back to the television, waving his arms about like a conductor in front of an orchestra. Lyrical flights expressing all his enjoyment of language alternated with softer, more reflective passages.

"Bettega," he said, "is playing well at the moment. Tardelli's playing well too. Causio is logic and construction. Scirea calculates with his eyes. There's a hint of black in the blue of their shirts, which makes it brighter than ever."

The game had begun. String had prepared more tomatoes and brought them in with a bottle of mineral water. She looked at us. Scarmiglia fell silent; Bocca and I crossed our arms and stared at the silent screen. String understood and left; Scarmiglia went on.

"But however good they may be, they're still Italy. The underhanded, wasteful, cowardly team: sooner or later their original ethos will come out again and they'll start knocking the ball back and forth, wasting time, spreading over the field like pearly sludge. So let's forget about them, they're of no interest to us. We're interested in strategies, shapes, archipelagoes, constellations, in seeing how thought finds a cosmos in chaos, a path through the forest."

He paused.

"Our team is Holland," he said.

Just as he said this, Italy took the lead. An own goal by Brandts.

Scarmiglia stopped talking; he went over to the television, turned up the volume, returned to his seat, bit into a tomato, and concentrated on the game.

I concentrated on the game too, and particularly on Romeo Benetti, and on his physical appearance—Northern blue eyes, thin hair, and a reddish mustache, redolent of Norway, fjords, and ice floes adrift in the Arctic.

It's true, I thought, Tardelli and Bettega are playing well, but Romeo Benetti has a spare, un-Italian, in fact anti-Italian dignity, a splendor that makes him both vertex and nucleus on the field. He's a soccer-playing version of Giuseppe Garibaldi, without the embroidered beret and the fringed poncho, the pseudo-Risorgimento rhetoric and the insignia of national identity: Giuseppe Garibaldi minus Giuseppe Garibaldi.

When he moved forward with the ball at his feet, Benetti held his head up high and surveyed the field ferociously, demanding space from it. His big blue chest shone in the sunlight, and the rest of the team stayed behind it, becoming the female defended by the male. For Romeo Benetti embodied a different ideal of masculinity—rocklike and undisputed, with no bravado, no boasting over a glass of wine, no Italian hyperbole of sexual prowess. Romeo Benetti moved across the field with his ice-cold semen within him, emanating a rugged, refractory sensuality, which was unmelodramatic, and therefore, to our eyes, incomprehensible.

One salad bowl was now empty of lettuce; in the other two bruised tomatoes lay drowning in a seedy yellow liquid. Holland had won 2-1, with Brandts tying the score, and then Haan getting the go-ahead goal.

Scarmiglia was jubilant. Holland was concrete proof of the idea he regarded as central to our militancy: the interchangeability of roles ensured the unchangeability of form. In other words, the balance of the team depended on each player's willingness to take responsibility not only for his own role but also for those of his teammates.

"Each man is every man," he said. "Mobile, responsive, alert, versatile; able to abandon his own position to cover that of a teammate. The same goes for us: we must be always ready, clear-headed, adaptable. We must abandon identity, relinquish the ego in favor of the group.

"Let me explain," he said. He stood up and beckoned us to follow him. On the way out, Bocca picked up another tomato. We went downstairs and across the street to the park. We picked a quadrangular space cornered by two scaly-barked palm trees, a bush, and a streetlight. Then, following Scarmiglia's instructions, we started walking in circles or diagonally, without stopping, going forward, turning back, moving in zigzags, going across areas we hadn't yet covered, offsetting and counterbalancing.

At first I didn't understand, then I concentrated harder and found a system and was even beginning to enjoy myself, but I

checked my feelings at once because I knew we were not supposed to be enjoying this. Bocca was hesitant and got all the
movements wrong; and when he finally succeeded in doing one
correctly he got overexcited and lost the thread. Scarmiglia, by
contrast, walked across the space as though he were observing
it from above, feeling the progressive formation of solids and
voids with his eyes, his ears, and his whole body.

"The movements," he said when we were swaying dizzily
and had lost all idea of space and proportion, "must be continuous and synchronized, as imperceptible as the vibration of
breathing."

We lay down on the lawn around the flower bed, sinking
right into the grass. It was dry and it crackled. There was a
confusion in my head that I found pleasurable. The sky, in the
distance, was full of white spirals. I listened to Scarmiglia and
Bocca still breathing deep and fast. I turned on my side and
looked at a waterless fountain a few meters away. Some mothers had lifted their children on to its circular stone rim and
were leading them around by the hand clockwise, to tame
them.

•

On the last day of school I'd seen the Creole girl asleep. I'd
been wandering around the hallways on my own, looking into
half-empty classrooms. We were leaving school early, halfway
through the morning of those frayed end-of-term days when
no one has anything more to say to the other and everything
becomes immaterial. I'd stayed in the classroom to the very
end, till even Morana had shuffled away, his body bent forward, swaying like a camel. I'd run my finger along the groove
I'd dug a month before in the surface of the desk; I'd sniffed
it, then walked around among the other desks, reading the
graffiti—swearwords, doodles, crooked phalluses, tangles of
crossings-out, signatures, a prayer, games of tic-tac-toe, the

word *tedium* written by someone who had no idea what it meant but had read it on some wall.

Bocca's desk was covered with large arabesques, curvilinear structures that intersected and multiplied their trajectories: a projection in graphic form of his wholehearted militancy. The surface in front of Scarmiglia, by contrast, had been preserved intact, as if he'd defended it, as though the physical representation of his thoughts was a blank space.

Before leaving the classroom I'd gone up to the teacher's desk, sniffed the scraped wood of the teacher's chair, then touched the blackboard with the tip of my tongue and swallowed the black taste of slate.

My light footsteps had echoed in the hallway. There was no one else around. The only sound, from outside, toward the piazza, was a muffled shouting, an exchange of goodbyes under the beating sun. I'd walked to the end of the hallway, turned left, and seen the Creole girl to my right, framed by a doorway. She was sitting alone in the middle of a classroom, her arms crossed on her desk, her head resting on them, and her hair scattered loosely around, forming a black nimbus.

I stood quite still—out of fear, I think, and respect. Whenever I looked at her I felt a religion form within me, a need for tenderness—the very need that the struggle daily excluded.

Her head rose slowly and rhythmically as she breathed, a simmering volcano. Under the lava of her hair I could make out her arms, the blue of a cotton blouse, and her dark fingers, the tip of the index slightly raised. She lay forward in limpid silence, overcome by sleep, saturated in sleep, deeply comical yet utterly serious, vulnerable, indestructible.

With astronaut-like movements I entered the classroom and approached her. I saw the little pale patch on the back of her hand and looked for a spot of red in her hair. I bent over her. I wanted to watch over her sleep—this living, honest, industrious thing—to guard it, absorb it, immerse myself in its scent. I was just about to penetrate its atmosphere, hardly able to believe that such a thing could exist, when I heard a noise by the doorway.

Scarmiglia was standing there, one hand against the jamb. His head forming a cruel silhouette, he was calmly watching me, watching us: me standing there, leaning forward, the Creole girl asleep and oblivious on the desk; chairs scattered around us; beyond the windows the shapeless blotch of the sun.

He didn't say anything. He just stared at me with a scientific, anthropological curiosity: not jealousy—he wasn't interested in the Creole girl—but a desire to read the temporal pages of the scene to the end, to discover its consequences, perhaps to see the effect it had on me, in one way or another.

I looked at her head again; from outside a twittering of voices could still be heard and somewhere, diffused in the white air, a delicate scent of jasmine bloomed.

•

On the afternoon of Sunday, June 25, the heat in Palermo stifled breathing and slowed the heart; in Buenos Aires Holland played in the final against Argentina.

We sat in front of the TV at Scarmiglia's home, with bottles of water mixed with Idrolitina fizzy powder, and a fan. Sweat etched shapes on our skulls; we rubbed them off with our forearms. We were rooting for Holland, but with restraint; you wouldn't have guessed by looking at us. And that was just what we wanted: an exercise in showing dissimulated support, silent enthusiasm.

On the field I watched Daniel Passerella. He was Argentinean; small and dark, with narrow eyes and a mass of black hair plastered down on his head; he looked like an adult version of the tournament mascot. Passerella expressed anger in everything he did: when he gruffly marshaled the defense, remonstrating loudly with his teammates; when he crossed the midfield line, his convex chest like a tearing, lacerating beak, and behind him Osvaldo Ardiles, with his gelled hair and the mournful melancholy of a tango singer, seemed even more languid; or when he was fouled in front of the opponents' penalty area and let out a roar from the ground, roughly batting away the hand that was offered to help him up, then got to his feet by himself, offended in the face of the irreparable, and without lessening his rage hit a free kick that was like an insult, a viciously swerving shot whose main purpose was to avenge the wrong that had been done him, and the outcome was often a goal.

Today the Dutch team was fragile and bewildered. It fell apart through an excess of knowledge; faced with an opposing team that attacked like a gang, it forgot itself, abandoned every principle of logic, cowered, curled up, and vanished.

Kempes scored the first goal for Argentina at the end of the first half; Holland equalized at the end of the second half, but it seemed like a fluke. We drank the carbonated water and took turns putting our skulls against the fan, which was going full blast, to absorb the coolness; then we went back to our chairs, air flooding through our lungs.

In overtime, Kempes scored another goal, and then Bertoni got a third. At the end of the match Passarella was carried on his teammates' shoulders all around the field, which was scattered with quivering, tumbling scraps of paper.

Gloomily we dried off the sweat, got out the ball, and went to work off our frustrations in the park opposite my home; for once, we allowed ourselves not to train according to our usual system but simply to play.

Despite his bulk, Bocca was a good goalkeeper. He had positional sense and was quite agile at diving. When we angled our shots toward the corner of the goal he'd throw himself full length, reach out, and parry them. The whole motivation behind his game was a desire to prove himself and prove something to us: by being extra-competitive he wanted to show us that he was up to it, that he made sense. Once, after a particularly impressive dive, he got to his feet and lifted his shirt to reveal a gash in his side; there had been a jagged stone on the ground where he'd fallen. He touched the blood, looked at it, and was happy.

Scarmiglia played the way he lived. When he ran he was direct: in accelerating he'd bend his thumb over his palm and close the other fingers to form an isosceles triangle; you could hear the sound his hand made as it sliced through the air. When he dribbled he was rational, always concentrating on what he had to do. Over the past few weeks he'd managed to reconcile discipline with his natural inclination toward ornament. He'd placed the implacable gridlines of graph paper over a sketch of a beautiful flower.

As for me, I ran as if the world was covered with a thick carpet of moss. My feet would sink in, start trudging, and come to a halt. After every sprint I had to bend down, hands on knees and mouth open, to get my breath back: not because I was short-winded or lacked stamina, but because of the way my mood affected my body. I was good at dribbling, but if after two or three attempts I didn't get through, the moss would get hold of my legs and lungs, and my shots at goal would become increasingly halfhearted.

We moved in the early evening air, with a pale swarming of lights on the facades of buildings, the mewing of cats, and the howl of sirens in the distance. I looked up at the balcony of our apartment and saw Cotton watching us. Only his head and shoulders showed above the wall; he had something in his hand that he kept putting to his mouth, but I couldn't see what.

Cotton didn't usually play with us. He wasn't the competitive type and he wasn't very skillful either. I waved to him to come down anyway. He disappeared from the balcony and two minutes later he appeared. He was eating a banana; the peel hung down in strips, concealing his hand. He sat down by the flower bed and watched us play, slowly moving his head, removing pulp from the banana in little bites like a grazing sheep. He worked his way around it, as if carving a sculpture with his teeth.

The streetlight above us had come on but it was getting harder and harder to see what we were doing. We decided to try one last move.

Scarmiglia, with the ball at his feet, went over to the side, beyond one of the two palm trees that formed our goalposts, and kicked a high, fast cross that traced an arc in the air and tempted me; with my back to the goal, I swiveled and tried an overhead kick, but mistimed it: the force of the kick wasn't absorbed by its impact against the ball, I landed on my back and lay there. Bocca approached and bent over me; I saw him upside down, his eyes where his chin should have been, his forehead in the place usually occupied by his cheeks. Scarmiglia came over too; he remonstrated with me, saying there was no need for fancy kicks like that and we shouldn't be too ambitious during this phase. I said nothing, I didn't breathe; in the background I saw Cotton upside down, still holding his unpetaled banana, with a curved piece of fruit rising out of it. I motioned to him to go, with a slow movement of my head; he turned around and left. A minute later String and Stone arrived. They sat me up gently but even so I felt a sharp pain in my back; if I tried to talk it hurt even more.

"We're going to the hospital," they said.

As we drove I watched the white center lines, the never-ending bones that held Palermo together, flow along the dark asphalt.

At the emergency room at Villa Sofia we entered the rib cage of a blind, mad whale that had swum the oceans, devouring all the horrors of the world, before beaching itself here in the Resuttana-San Lorenzo district and dying, its huge mouth agape with astonishment at this last horror. Someone had had the idea of making it into a hospital, and not removing the horrors, but leaving them forever jammed between the large, white, curved vertebrae and immersed in the creature's ventral concretions. Now they were indistinguishable from its structure and helped to support it; without them the whale's skeleton would have collapsed.

In the waiting room there were dialectal monsters with bloody faces, gashed legs, and vomit-encrusted lips; two mouths intersecting at right angles in the middle of a broken head, the blood forming a strange clot; dry and burst viscera, and the warmth of bodies, the sweat of bodies, and people fainting; and there was me, my spine arched backward to combat the pain.

We were told with a gesture to sit down and wait. Bits of chewing gum were stuck to the benches and cigarette butts littered the marble-chip floor. From the other end of the waiting room I heard a thin, continuous beam of sound at a shrill, strident pitch: the whale's blowhole, one last attempt to expel the horrors.

When we were eventually called in, the doctors thought the problem was my skull. They examined it from all sides and touched it with their fingers; I felt them fumbling coarsely in my nimbus. Then they stopped and sent me to have my chest X-rayed; an hour later, the developed photograph revealed that I had a broken rib, the seventh on the left. There was no treatment, only rest and painkillers. They gave me an injection straightaway; the drug seeped into my body and made me drowsy.

In the car I held the envelope containing the X-ray on my lap. For a couple of days it would be shown to relatives, then it would be put in the chest of drawers in the living room and get jumbled up with the other family bones.

In bed, in the hands of Stone and String, I was exhausted. Later, as I lay on my back, the jagged edge of the rib scratched the surface of my lung. In the box of Operation—the game with a patient with a pear-shaped belly and no genitals, and a red nose that lit up and buzzed if your tweezers touched the edge of the openings that contained the ailment shapes—there was a forked bone, at rib level, called the Wishbone; lifting it out with tweezers was difficult because it always swung toward one or the other of its two horns.

String turned out the light, and as I was beginning to doze off, Ezekiel was there sitting on a rock in the desert playing Operation, and he was very skillful at it: he moved the tweezers about inside the openings without ever lighting up the nose, took the bones, and put them next to one another; the bones joined up, nerves formed on the bones, then flesh formed too, and now Scarmiglia was there sitting next to Ezekiel; he was playing Operation too, but instead of the patient, I lay there, my body covered with gashes; Scarmiglia put the tweezers into the openings and took my bones out one by one till he'd completely emptied me; then, when the effect of the painkiller wore off and pain penetrated my drowsy consciousness, the Creole girl was there in front of me dressed in white, putting her hand into my chest, inserting it into my barbed-wire rib cage; she searched inside and, without cutting herself, fished out the wishbone, white, smooth and clean, then closed her hand and put it into her own chest, and just at that moment I turned on my side and the pain was so intense I felt like crying and laughing and couldn't breathe.

COMMUNICATING

We'd been on Viale Galatea, Mondello, ten kilometers from Palermo, since July 1. We had a ground–floor apartment that opened onto the street. Plane trees towered over the road, the house, and the whole area. They covered the asphalt in shade with the greedy spread of their branches, their trilobate leaves absorbing light into their globular mass and distilling it, till it dripped down, a syllabization of moving glints on car roofs.

One hot afternoon, about three o'clock, when the whole family was at home, I was lying in bed reading, massaging my chest with two fingers. I heard a noise outside, so I got up and peered through the shutters. Two boys were climbing out of the front garden over the gate, taking my bike with them. I watched them, breathing hard but not moving, with a mixture of admiration and contempt. When they were already on the other side of the gate, Stone came into the room and opened the shutters. He shouted, got his keys, went out into the street, and looked around, but there was no one there. He asked me why I hadn't called him; I didn't know what to say. String arrived; she asked me the same question and again I couldn't explain; I just let out a long groan of exasperation. String looked at me disapprovingly, as she always did, though in the past few days she'd been playing the role of the caring, sympathetic mother, not realizing that this got on my nerves. I knew I'd encouraged her fussing by playing the delicate convalescent who built castles of imaginary pain out of one little cough. But I didn't consider her behavior natural, so I rejected it, tried to expel it. She sensed this now and went out: a minute later I heard a clinking of pans and bowls in the kitchen and the fizz of Idrolitina in the bottle, the sound of maternal helplessness fading away.

Every morning String, Cotton, and I went to the beach; Stone came down later with the daily paper. I found this indestructible, old-fashioned bourgeois family set-up oppressive. Unthinking tradition governed every form and procedure, controlling every little detail of our behavior in the dining room, where we sat at table, the way we sat, the speed we walked along the street during our Saturday afternoon shopping expeditions. The bathroom curtain with its floral motifs, all four family members' hair twined into a bolus around the drain.

We shared a beach cabana with some other families; it was light blue, with a red pitched roof. When I got down to the beach I went barefoot along the wooden walkway, looking at the patterns the sand made on the wet wood. I went into the cabana and got changed, leaning against the wall, in the cool half-light, among scuba masks and folded beach umbrellas like huge sleeping bats, their multicolored wings crimped around their bodies. Before leaving, I went over to the bathing suits that were hanging up to dry and sniffed them: they had no identifiable scent; a general smell of brine covered everything.

I wouldn't be able to swim for a few days, so I sat down to read, but soon tired of it; I stood up and walked down from the cabanas toward the sea, limping a little and shaking my head, like one who knew, who had seen.

Standing with water around my ankles, I watched the shape of the waves as they formed troughs and crests through narrowed, visionary eyes. It was my way of seducing the world, of unsettling it. A twenty-year-old Cinzia and Loredana passed by, stopped, and stared at me: a boy standing engrossed among shrieking, playing children. I turned slightly away, but they kept staring at me, so to explain the situation I put my right hand to my rib and twisted my mouth into a grimace. They waved and smiled. I ignored them. Then another girl, a Patrizia, came from behind me and approached the two friends; they greeted each other and walked away laughing. I despised them.

I looked around again, waiting, showing myself, making sure I was noticed. Digging dimples in the wet sand with my big toe, I listened to the throb of pain each time I breathed. I covered my chest again and heard the world echo beneath my fingers.

•

On the afternoon of Friday, July 14, I went with my curly-haired cousin—eighteen years old, and there on vacation like us—to the apartment of a friend of hers who ran a film club in Mondello. Her friend was small and plump and wore a colored bandanna around his neck and an elephant-hair armband on his right wrist; he had a squawky voice and a rather affected way of talking. He had films sent down from Rome; he'd just received a new batch of rare, militant material. He'd cleared his parents' living room, mounted a projector on a stool, removed the pictures from the facing wall, and fixed the curtains to the wall with Scotch tape; there were a few cushions spread around on the floor, some chairs, and an armchair. Seeing my skull, he assumed this was my last summer: he urged me to sit down on the armchair and brought me a glass of orangeade. He spoke in the tones of a priest administering last rites.

My cousin sat down on a chair beside me as more people arrived, who all addressed one another as "comrade." Once everyone was there, our host stepped into the cone of light emitted by the projector. As he spoke he moved his arms and hands; his shadow behind followed suit.

He told us that *Coatti* was a film by Comrade Stàvros Tornès. He pulled out of his jeans pocket a page from a notebook on which he'd written the name STÀVROS TORNÈS in capital letters. He said Stàvros was Greek but had been living in Italy for a number of years, earning a living as an actor and factory worker; he'd made this film in Rome and played the leading role himself. The film, our host went on, was a profound and poignant meditation on modernity, defeat, and utopia. It interspersed consciously paradoxical scenes illustrating the grotesque recent developments in our country with sociological analysis and penetrating insights into reality, meaningless-ness, and death.

Before saying the word *death* he looked at me, hesitating on the brink of the word; I touched my forehead slowly and casu-ally, with one finger, and gave him an absolutory smile, my arms relaxed on the armrests, my head against a cushion, my rib calm. He continued his talk, his shadow still aping his movements behind his back. Eventually he noticed the stifled laughter around him, but couldn't understand the reason for it. He said, "We'll discuss it later," went back behind the projec-tor, turned off the light, and the film began.

We saw Tornès getting up late, not working, wandering around Rome on foot, and talking to his girlfriend. She went away and came back, then Tornès went to a bar and met a friend. There were some Formica-topped tables in a back

room, where people were eating. The people had sideburns
and wore close-fitting, high-necked sweaters. Shoulder bags
hung from their chairs, and they wore spectacles with large
square frames and tinted lenses, like Mina and Gino Paoli.
One person told Tornès he was an idiot, a fool who only cared
about the aesthetics of the proletariat, not about its ethics. Tornès said nothing; soon afterward he criticized his girlfriend:
"You read *La Repubblica*," he said to her; "I read *L'Unità*. *La
Repubblica* is hypocritical; you never know what it really means.
L'Unità is sincere; it has the words 'Organ of the Communist
Party' as the banner on the front page."

The complicated plot went on. Outside, beyond the closed
curtains, you could hear the roaring heat, and now and then a
car horn, a voice, scattered sounds of summer; I sipped at the
orangeade to make it last. Once or twice my cousin turned
toward me and asked me with her eyes what I thought of it; I
replied with my eyes that I quite liked it. And it was true, I did
like the film. Not because it was a good film—it wasn't—but
because it was an epitome of 1978, its mannerisms and its
poses: wandering around aimlessly while claiming to have a
strategy, indulging in lachrymose self-criticism, and continually regurgitating the same tired language. With his stooping
body, his wild, prophet-like gray beard and mustache, and the
nimbus of cinematic light that formed around his skull, Tornès
was me as an old man: a preacher roaming in the wilderness,
shouting meaningless sentences.

When the film ended, my cousin's friend turned off the
projector, removed the Scotch tape, pulled back the curtains,
and opened the windows. Dazzled eyes lowered their lids to
filter the light, grew accustomed to it, and reopened. Now was
the time for people to talk, and my cousin's friend waited
hopefully for that to happen, but no one had much to say; language did not proliferate, discussion of the concepts was barely
sketched out before being immediately shelved, the sea was

only a few steps away, and the sun would be up till late. So all the guests got to their feet, retrieved leathers and linen, put on espadrilles and Dr. Scholl's. There were waves, pats on the back, handshakes, jokes, and allusions, as Italian gave way to dialect; and with a lingering sense of dissatisfaction and lack of achievement, the meeting broke up.

Before leaving I needed to go to the bathroom. The friend pointed to a door and asked if I needed any help. I stared at him, and he, who was slightly taller than me, looked at my head and the light that shone on it. I opened the door and went in without answering. I took a piece of toilet paper and used it to lift the seat, then threw it in the toilet bowl, and unbuttoned my shorts. As soon as I started to urinate, a bee came in through the open window. It made two or three exploratory circuits of the room, then homed in on my penis. It circled around it, examined it, and considered it, while I watched the bee and its flight, the form of its trajectories, its circumvolutions, abrupt deviations, cutbacks, and spirals, the way it wove air around my flesh and the arching jet of pee. I wondered whether it was telling me something, or saying something to another bee which was outside my field of vision, or maybe conducting a political or existential monologue. While I cleaned my glans with another piece of paper, the bee concluded its reconnaissance with three last buzzes and flew back out through the gap between window and frame. I buttoned up my shorts, washed my hands, and went back to my cousin, who was waiting by the front door. At home I searched for a book I'd started reading the previous year, but couldn't find it anywhere; I went into the kitchen and asked String. With her back to me and her hands in the sink, she said it must be in Palermo; I asked her if she'd bring it to me next time she went into town. She nodded, her hands still closed around the drain, throttling it.

Two days later the book arrived: *The Language of Social Bees.*

I started reading it from the beginning again, on the beach, sitting on the edge of the wooden walkway, while behind me people returned from the bar holding fried calzone that drooped at the sides like ox tongues, and *arancine* soaked in yellow oil; as they passed, they brushed me with the edges of their shoes but I ignored them.

On the cover there was a photograph of three guardian bees outside the entrance to a hive: three heads with convex eyes like microscopic shields, a few pairs of legs, and double wings. Behind them everything was black; farther away, beyond the reach of the camera, inside the hive, was the queen bee.

The three guardians were Bocca, Scarmiglia, and me. Like them we were tense and alert, had an acute sense of danger, and were focused on a duty not of our choosing. For every bee has an unchallengeable, genetically determined duty, a primeval reflex that makes it constantly repeat one specific function, subdivided into specific actions: cleaning, feeding, storing, producing honey, producing beeswax, protecting, attacking, communicating.

Social bees, I read, in order to direct their comrades—yes, they too were comrades—to sources of food or suitable nesting sites, performed dances, tracing conventional paths in the air: a round dance meant that there was a food source nearby, a waggle dance indicated the direction in which it was located; the rhythm, that is the number of circuits per unit of time, communicated how far away it was. So a seemingly random phenomenon, the flight of bees, was in fact part of a strictly regulated mechanism, a system of genetically determined rules and obligations. Like the previous month, when we'd reenacted moves from the World Cup in order to study them from within.

In the evening, after supper, I read on, sitting at the living room table, while String and Stone watched a movie and

Cotton stared at the green mosquito coil burning on the sill of the French window, its metal base in an ashtray, its spiral scented.

The queen bee—I thought, as I read—was the idea. Bocca, Scarmiglia, and I had identified our queen bee. We knew it was her, that she was the right one. She was black and majestic, a double, pointed ogive at both ends, two large visionary eyes, a sting containing a poison that was both lethal and life-giving. The necessary religion, the radiant center. For her sake we had become servants, renouncing our identities and the right to make choices. No bee chose to do what it did, no bee could back out or desert. The bee fulfilled its destiny within necessity: therefore the bee was the perfect militant.

•

On the morning of July 16 I woke up late, wandered around the apartment—nobody else was home—and thought about the dream I'd had. In the dream I was having a pee, when a bee approached my glans, passed through the hole and went down inside. I could feel it buzzing but it didn't hurt, in fact the sensation was pleasurable and it seemed natural that the bee should be there; the glans was shaped like a nest. From that point on the bee lived inside me. Now and then it came out, flew around, acted as cleaner, nurse, worker, guardian, all the functions described in the book, but then in the evening it re-entered my glans and went to sleep. The next day I heard the bee rubbing its legs and wings, then its head emerged from the hole, and it flew off again. I didn't say a word to my family; the only people I told were Bocca and Scarmiglia. I boasted that I was the bee's nest. Scarmiglia told me the hole on the glans was like the fontanel on the skull, then he kicked me in the testicles, and it hurt; I unzipped my trousers, saw that the glans was red, squeezed with my fingers and out of the hole came a dry, squashed bee; it fell, and there was such silence in my dream that you could hear the sound the bee made when it hit the floor, so hard that I woke up.

In the meantime I'd continued to wander around the empty apartment.

I went into the bathroom and pulled down my pajama shorts and underpants. Everything seemed to be in order; it was just a little sore. I went over to the basin and turned on the faucet but stopped, one hand on my penis, the other collecting water in the palm, turned around, and saw Cotton standing there watching me, with a brown paper package in his arms. String arrived behind him with some shopping bags; I moved my hands to cover up but splashed water over myself; my shorts got wet, and I felt the drops on my legs. String said nothing, took the package out of Cotton's hands—I caught a whiff of sesame, of baking—and went into the kitchen. Cotton remained in the doorway, not moving, his head bent to one side: his usual broken-necked look. He didn't leave. So I turned around, shuffled over to the bidet, hampered by my shorts and my lowered pants. When I bent down to pick up the small towel, Cotton came up behind me and blew on my bottom; I turned around sharply and said to myself he was crazy.

For the rest of the morning I read and took notes in a notebook. I did some drawings too. I reproduced the flight trajectories and wrote down what they meant; I drew human bodies, put them in different poses, and jotted down more notes next to each of them. At lunchtime I phoned Scarmiglia, who'd stayed in town, and asked him if he could come to Mondello. We agreed to meet at four o'clock. I told him to bring some records and magazines; he didn't ask why but just said, "See you later." Then I phoned Bocca, who'd been staying with his grandparents for three weeks and was there in Mondello like me. I told him about the appointment, the magazines, and the records.

"We can listen to them," he said, and sounded pleased.

While I waited, I read on. I'd been hoping to finish the book but kept stopping to take notes and draw sketches and didn't get very far. At four o'clock Bocca arrived with two bags, then Scarmiglia arrived too, carrying his bundle under his arm. He hadn't spent a single day at the seaside and was completely white.

We sat down at the end of the path in the back garden, around a blue table. Not far away, Cotton was sitting at a folding table, playing Concentration on his own, while the skeleton of the rocking chair—the cats had stripped the cloth and foam rubber off the seat—rocked slowly.

The cats here hid in a hedge that ran along the low dividing wall between the back garden of our house and the next one. When nobody could see me, I used to plunge my arms into the hedge and search for kittens: I'd grope around, getting badly scratched, till I caught one; I'd pull it out and look it in the face. The kitten would contract, stiffen, hiss, and try to grab hold of the branches; I'd immobilize its front legs and watch the panic in its eyes. It would breathe fast in my hand; its eyes would breathe too—they'd explode and disappear. Almost all the kittens struggled and tried to escape, but some would go limp and let their legs hang loose. I'd sniff them—they smelled of dust and leaves—and hold them by the scruff of their necks in my teeth—just for an instant, just to know. When I put them down again, it was as if they'd suddenly been released from a magic spell and felt stunned and embarrassed. A moment before running away they'd turn and gaze at me with an expression that still expressed panic, but also gratitude.

Sitting around the table, we looked at one another. We seemed so vivid and yet so unreal. Over the past few weeks we'd continued to train, each on our own. Scarmiglia's features were gaunt, his arms ridged with brawn. Bocca had lost a lot of weight; he'd hatched out of his old body, smaller than anyone could have imagined, least of all him: I looked at his hands and read his knuckles, one by one, and the dips between the fingers where you count the months. I'd lost another two kilos and the skin around my eyes had hollowed and darkened. All three of us still had shaved skulls.

String brought us Coca-Cola and orangeade, and water for Cotton. I heard cracks of broken twigs in the hedge, a shapeless rustle of leaves; I saw a shiver of foliage as something slipped through and longed to go over and investigate, but stayed where I was. I picked up the book and showed it to them: Bocca read out the title syllable by syllable, Scarmiglia lifted it slowly out of my hands.

I described how the bees' social system worked—the castes, the different roles, and how each bee was not an individual body, but part of a larger whole. Like ants in an anthill, termites in a termitarium: the animal *was* the anthill, the termitarium. Each individual was like a cell that formed part of an organism: necessary but nameless; distinct in some respects, yet indistinguishable.

"Like us," said Scarmiglia, laying the book on the table. "We don't have identity cards," he added. "It's as if we didn't exist. We're like termites or bees—anonymous cells."

Bocca nodded in agreement, and I went on.

"But that's not all. Bees," I said, "spend their time flying, making codes, and deciphering them. We observe them and don't understand; all we see are yellow dots darting around; but if we could read the invisible lines they draw we'd know what they're saying."

"Like that game in *Puzzler's Weekly*?" asked Bocca.

"No, it's more than that," said Scarmiglia, without looking at him.

Next door someone had brought a record player out into the garden and was listening to some of the latest pop songs, full of groans, falsetto countermelodies, gasps and sighs and pathetic wails. We sat in silence listening as the yeses and nos,

the stills and the alwayses, the platitudes, pleadings, and be-
seechings mingled with the fizz of our drinks, the crackling of
gas in our glasses.

I picked up my notebook, showed them the drawings, and
explained.

On one page I'd drawn a human body. It was shown from
behind; its arms were open and its back was curved in the pose
of a predatory hawk.

"This is the 'Yuppi Du' pose," I said. "It means 'imminent
danger.'"

Bocca made a face and I explained.

"It's a question of turning our bodies into ideograms.
Choosing certain poses and assigning a meaning to them. By
doing that, we can create an alphabet and a grammar. We
won't need to say words with our voices because we'll say them
with our poses. And we'll build sentences by linking the words
together."

Bocca seemed to have understood. He was tempted to
reach out and touch me but restrained himself and just said,
"Yes, let's do it."

A lizard skittered down the garden path, crossing the paler
parts of the paving stones. Scarmiglia watched it, and I sensed
him devouring it with his eyes. Then he turned toward me
and said, "All right."

I picked up one of the bags Bocca had brought, took out
the records and magazines, and spread them across the table.

"We'll take the poses from here," I said. "From singers, ad-
vertisements; actors, too; and TV and the cinema. It'll be a
way of getting our own back: by using Celentano's hawk act
from *Yuppi Du* for our own purposes we'll be turning something pathetic into something useful."

"Let me get this straight," said Bocca. "We take a well-
known form, and leave it unchanged externally, but alter its
content. Is that what you mean?"

"That's right," I said. "We take stupid poses that everyone knows and turn them into coded messages."

Scarmiglia, who'd remained silent till now, made an expressive gesture with his hand which I couldn't decipher exactly but which I knew was his way of getting a hold of things.

"Every week," he said, "everything is renewed. There are new records, each with its own sleeve, new films, new TV characters. New issues of magazines appear on the newsstands. All these novelties combined produce a shared imagery that enables Italy to hold itself together. Because in fact it's falling apart. Every celebrity who ends up on a magazine cover or a screen becomes a center, something that ought to provide stability. And so bodies and poses accumulate. But the center is unstable; it holds for a week, then everything moves on, in a cycle of supposed revolutions that in fact serve only to preserve the status quo."

Scarmiglia stopped abruptly and stared at Cotton, who was turning up blue Concentration cards, searching for pairs; I gestured to him not to worry. He got to his feet, picked up his records from the ground, put them on the table, and selected Donatella Rettore's "Oh! Carmela." He asked me to lend him my pencil; I passed it to him, and he put on an earnest expression, bending his right arm at forty-five degrees, with the elbow pointing down to the ground and the fist holding the pencil up, so as to divide his face in two.

"This is the 'Rettore' pose," he said. "It means you're at a crossroads, from both a physical and a psychological point of view. Of course, instead of the sword," he said, pointing to the photograph of Rettore, "you could use a pencil, or a pen, a stick, or anything else you can find. Or even nothing, if necessary: the important thing is the pose."

Bocca smiled. He too got to his feet and waited till we were looking at him.

"Can the poses be really stupid?" he asked.

"They *must* be," I said. "That's the whole point."

Bocca jumped up in the air, spread his legs, one knee protruding, his right arm stretched upward, index finger pointing toward the sky, the other arm slightly arched, fist clenched.

"John Travolta," I said. "*Saturday Night Fever.*"

"Got it," said Bocca, laughing.

"What does it mean?" I asked him.

"I don't know."

"It's a danger signal," said Scarmiglia.

"No, danger's too strong," said Bocca.

"It could mean there's something wrong," I said. "Something unexpected."

"I don't know whether it's right to include a matter of chance in our alphabet," said Scarmiglia.

"Why not?" said Bocca.

"It's not consistent with our philosophy. We've spent a month eliminating chance and reducing the world to a perfect geometry. To let it in now would be an admission of defeat."

"The unexpected isn't exactly chance," said Bocca. "It's something smaller."

"That's true," I said. "I think we can include it."

Scarmiglia said nothing; he looked unconvinced, but I didn't know how much he was being serious or how much he was just putting on an act. So I pressed home the point.

"The unexpected is a ripple on the surface of order," I said. "Chance in miniature."

Then I fell silent too. All communication between us, I thought, is play and torture.

Scarmiglia waited, savoring the silence. Then, making it clear that this was not a collective decision but a concession by him to us, he nodded.

Meanwhile Cotton had dozed off, his head on the table and the glass of water on a Concentration card. His feet didn't touch the ground, his chest was slightly hollowed. Scarmiglia went over, looked at him, and drew one arm back, with his hand open, as if he was about to give him a slap. I jumped up and he stopped, open-mouthed, with a wild stare in his eyes.

"*Allegria!*" shouted Bocca, behind my back.

Cotton didn't move and went on breathing slowly, with eyes closed, even when Scarmiglia said, "That's right—Mike Bongiorno," and turned toward me with an expression of mock outrage at having been unjustly suspected.

"It looks as if you're stopping something," said Bocca.

"It could mean just that," said Scarmiglia. "Bringing things to a halt, a situation that won't move forward."

"An impasse," I said.

"Wait," said Bocca, "I've got another one."

He walked off down the garden path, swaying from side to side, his arms stretched out in front of him, his movements mechanical; I watched his shoulders quiver, muscles prevailing over inert matter. When he turned around and walked back toward us, his eyes were closed and his face taut, but he was struggling not to laugh, and when he couldn't keep it up any longer his face crumpled, he laughed, and his arms dropped.

"The zombies," Scarmiglia and I said together.

It means "to act, actions," Scarmiglia added at once.

"That's fine by me," said Bocca.

"Me too," I said.

It was like a game: one person thinking up gestures, the others trying to guess where they came from. We decided, for the sake of consistency with the Italian alphabet, but also in order to set ourselves some limits, that our alphabet would consist of twenty-one poses.

There was no stopping Bocca now: he had two more suggestions.

The first was connected with Cochi and Renato. There was something subversive about them, an unruliness that appealed to him. When they sang "Canzone intelligente"—Cochi dressed in tights and a shawl, Renato with a potbelly under his black-and-white-hooped T-shirt—they did a little march backward during the refrain and stretched one leg out even farther back, kicking out and saying, "The idiot in blue." It was an ungainly movement, yet there was something beautiful about it. The backward kick, the "Idiot in Blue" pose, would mean "hatred."

His second suggestion came from the films of Bud Spencer and Terence Hill.

"In the fight scenes," said Bocca, "there's always some character who gets punched over and over again, spins around, sways for a few seconds, and then, with a lopsided grimace and a boss-eyed stare, falls down on the ground.

"It always makes me ashamed," he went on. "I feel as if those characters who spin around and around in circles are screwing themselves into our essence as Italians, our pathetic national identity that always turns struggle into farce."

Scarmiglia and I were impressed. We'd never heard him talk in this way, with such peremptoriness and such clarity. The "Spencer-Hill" pose would of course mean "shame."

I felt that it was my turn again. I walked down the garden path, ran back up, and when I reached a point between Bocca and Scarmiglia, did an unreal, mimed jump, pretending to rest my hand on something and kicking out both legs to one side, in the sequence I'd seen a hundred times in the Cuore Olive Oil advertisement: the rustic athleticism of Nino Castelnuovo leaping over the fence was so rooted in our minds that Bocca and Scarmiglia guessed it at once.

"I'd like it to mean passing through," I said. "Crossing a border."

It was nearly evening. I woke up Cotton and told him to go inside. He looked at me in a daze, picked up the Concentration cards, collected them into a pack, and went off, clutching them in his fist. Scarmiglia got up, sat on the metal structure of the rocking chair, and started to rock, making a squeak that sounded like someone crying.

"Now that we've come this far," he said, "we must go even farther. We must be willing to make fools of ourselves. And without being ashamed of ourselves. If we can do that we'll become invulnerable."

Bocca and I looked at him uncomprehendingly. I heard more rustles in the hedge; the foliage shook for an instant and then settled.

"What I mean is," he went on, "if we really have the courage to walk along the street twisting our arms and legs about into stupid positions and not caring if anyone thinks we look stupid, we'll be ready for anything."

His voice came and went; it changed with the rocking and broke when the squeak cut through it. Then suddenly he stopped rocking the chair, lifted himself out of the seat so that he was hovering twenty centimeters above it, put his arms forward to keep his balance, pretended to fall backward and sideways, then steadied himself and started swaying about again. He smiled and laughed.

"I suggest," he said, struggling to keep his balance, his voice quavering with the effort, "that our alphabet should include the 'Fracchia' pose. The clerk Giandomenico Fracchia," he called out in the manner of an auctioneer, "and his shapeless armchair. The crisis of instability in the Italian petite bourgeoisie. Inadequacy, submissiveness, and cowardice."

He paused to get his breath back. Then he went on.

"While the tibia-tappers kneecap a new victim every day, our national television company keeps us happy with Giandomenico Fracchia, with Johnny Bassotto, with Isotta, the car that toots her horn and can do it if she tries. With 'My Name Is Potato.'"

He stopped and fell back on to the rocking chair, which lurched downward with a cracking noise. It was close to collapsing but it held.

"With 'My Name Is Potato,'" he repeated, shaking his head. "With Rita Pavone," he said again. "With her ultra-English diction. With her highfalutin' pronunciation—*po-ta-to, my name is po-ta-to.* The talking potato, the singing potato."

He fell silent for a moment, metabolizing intelligence and bitterness.

"What we have," he said, "is this. The grimaces of Rita Pavone. Edulcoration, phoney compassion. A never-ending carnival. Macario playing an old man talking to a child. We have children; one dies in every film, run over by a car or falling off a cliff, or from anemia or leukemia—every film a via crucis. But in the next film he always comes back to life, indestructible, the cinematic martyr with the blond mop of hair. Yes," he said, convulsively, "that's our idea of death.

"And we have Giumbolo," he said again. "We have Grisù. We have Obabaluba. Zigo Zago. The wizard. The chicken bone and the magic potion.

"That is what we have," he concluded feverishly. "That is what we are."

Bocca and I looked at each other; we knew he was putting on an act. We know he too sometimes yielded to the need to spread his wings, to expand in declamatory form, consuming as much language as possible.

"The 'Fracchia' pose," he said, lying back on the metal frame, "will mean 'to understand, to comprehend things.' I understand, we understand. A state of mind that's seemingly related to stability, but is in fact a precarious teetering on the edge of a precipice."

At eight o'clock we split up. Scarmiglia took the bus back to Palermo, Bocca went off on foot. We agreed to meet the next day. Each of us would suggest three new poses, which, with today's nine, would bring us up to eighteen. We would choose the last few together, to make our total twenty-nine. We'd decided that we would proceed in reverse order this time: today we had started with a gesture and found a meaning for it; tomorrow we would start from what we wanted to say and seek the most suitable poses.

•

On the morning of July 17, before going down to the beach, I shut myself in my room and did some training. Despite the difficulties—my rib still hurt—I needed it in order to feel the closeness of my body. When I finished, I had sweat around my eyes and I was breathing heavily. A sense of things disappearing.

We found a shady spot on the beach between the last cabana and the shoreline; the sand was wet and spongy. Scarmiglia wore a short-sleeved shirt and jeans cut off at the knee; Bocca and I were in swimming trunks. People around us were surprised. They'd got used to me and my skull; the sight of three of us astonished them. We didn't care: our former bodies had been interlopers; only now were we authentic.

Bocca said he'd thought up a name for our alphabet during the night. It was simple but he thought it appropriate: the alphamute. Because it consisted of silent gestures. We liked the name and decided to adopt it.

Each of us had brought some words we thought should be in the alphamute. Bocca went first.

"Stop." "Hide." "Leave."

I listened and combined them: to leave a hiding place and stop; to stop leaving one another; to hide separation; to stop hiding.

Scarmiglia had written his down on a sheet of square paper with a pencil, in capitals, going over the letters several times, making deep grooves in the paper.

"Take." "Good." "Die."

I mentally combined them: the good that dies; to die after being taken; to cause good to die by taking it; to take the good and die.

It was my turn. I too had written my words down on a piece of paper, forming a diagram shaped like an isosceles triangle.

"Go away." "Seek." "Desire."

Desire was the vertex of the triangle; go away and seek were the other corners. Desire, then, was projected upward; it was that toward which the other two sides converged. It stood at the top of a propulsion. A vanishing point. To seek desire. To go away from desire.

I'd wanted to include fear as well but wasn't sure about it.

We started to examine them, discussing each hypothesis in turn and searching for the most appropriate pose.

"Stop"—which by extension could also mean "to be still, to think"—would be the pose on the sleeve of Baglioni's *Un cantastorie dei giorni nostri*, his head against his right hand, his left arm resting in front of him: we all agreed that it was sufficiently tacky.

For "hide" we thought of "Portobello"—not Enzo Tortora's show itself but the parrot they tried to get to talk. Every week, guests would take turns to have a go: they'd approach his perch and call out to him, making mechanical or animal noises, imploring him to win them some money. No act was too demeaning if it would earn them a pot of money. Italians talked to animals in order to get rich, like a horde of venal St. Francises. But the bird said nothing; it just looked at them and said nothing, leaving everyone poor. And it made a characteristic movement with its body, retracting its spine into its feathers: as if hiding in disgust. "Hide," then, would be this movement of the back, with the head drawn into the chest.

Three meters away from us there was an abandoned Zoom Ball. The orange plastic oval—a kind of rugby ball with cords strung through it—was half-buried in the sand. Scarmiglia picked it up, untangled the cords, and passed the ends with their two handles to Bocca. Then he took a few steps backward, holding the other two handles himself, and suddenly opened his arms, driving the ball toward Bocca, who returned it. And so they went on, till the cords got twisted up and the ball stopped in the middle.

"What interests me," said Scarmiglia, retrieving the toy from Bocca's hands, "is the position you have to adopt in order to launch it."

"It's like welcoming someone with open arms," said Bocca.

"I think it looks like a crucifixion," I said.

"It's neither of those things," said Scarmiglia. "It's a gesture that means 'I give up.' It'll be the pose for 'leave.'" And with that he dropped the Zoom Ball on the sand.

We took a break and went to the drinking fountain for some water. Then we came back to our place in the shade to contemplate the Palermitans' bodies—their revolting bodies. Once, here on the beach, I'd had to get changed in a different cabana because the key to ours was bent. This second cabana was used mainly by a group of old people. Inside, the air had smelled of gauze, matted absorbent cotton, lukewarm water, and translucent skin. I'd held my breath while I got undressed and put on my swimming trunks. The Palermitans' revolting bodies had that same smell. It wasn't a matter of cleanliness—it was them, their lives. The smell was the result of their way of speaking; words aged in their bodies and rotted. The dialect was rotten to start with, and in their bodies it rotted still more. They'd wade into the sea up to their knees with their children in their arms, among the cigarette stubs and dark seaweed, and point at things and laugh. They were proud and they were ignorant. They stuck together.

For his first word, "take," Scarmiglia had thought of a film he'd seen at the movie theater with his brothers. It had been X-rated but they'd let him in anyway. It was called *Last Cannibal World*. You wouldn't have thought it, but it was an Italian film, about a man who got captured by cannibals. At one point he called some cannibal children over to his prison, stretched out his hand to the face of one little boy, and withdrew it with the tip of his thumb sticking out between his index and middle fingers, pretending to steal his nose.

The inclusion of this little game in a film that featured people getting their heads chopped off, animals being skinned, human arms being devoured, and alligators crawling through vegetation was a symptom of what Scarmiglia termed the "Italianization of the universe," the national tendency to reduce all phenomena to familiar forms, making everything provincial.

"Italy is one big metabolic machine," he said, "which can make anything plausible. It can turn an Amazonian forest into your dining room or a cannibal child into the boy you play with in the park. I wouldn't be surprised to see a pack of MS cigarettes in the alligator's stomach in that film and a soccer betting form tucked into one of the cannibals' loincloths."

When we started thinking about the pose for Scarmiglia's second word, "good," I suggested we use Sir Oliver. They weren't familiar with him—they didn't read *Alan Ford*—so I adopted a dignified, stable pose, with my arms held out slightly in front of me and my hands resting loosely, one on top of the other, over the knob of an invisible walking stick. The position you might adopt when listening calmly, steeped in the good. Listening to the good. We didn't know what it meant but we wanted it to exist.

This brought us to "die." Scarmiglia curled up on the sand, with his arm bent, his hand on his hip, and his head slightly inclined to the left: Aldo Moro dying and being born again in the metal womb of the Renault 4. Over the past two months we'd seen that photograph so many times that as far as we were concerned it was the quintessential photograph of death. To curl up like that would mean "to die."

My first word was "desire." It was similar to "good" but slightly different: a striving for goodness. We thought something complete was needed to represent this word, a spherical pose.

"No," said Bocca, getting to his feet. "Desire isn't round, it's fragmented. Look," he said.

He bent forward and touched his right knee with his left palm, then his left knee with his right palm, working his way up rhythmically, touching his sides, shoulders, and forehead in the same way, then raising his arms up like a fountain before returning to the initial pose.

The whole beach had frozen. Everyone was staring at Bocca's portrayal of Raffaella Carrà dancing the *tuca tuca*. To help us identify it, he repeated the sequence, this time rhythmically moving his feet and swaying his hips as well.

The people around us looked increasingly uneasy; Scarmiglia burst out laughing.

"See?" he said. "They don't understand. They realize there's something familiar about it, but can't figure out what it is."

"And that's not okay?" asked Bocca.

"You bet it's okay," Scarmiglia replied. "It's just what we want."

The other two words didn't take us long. On the sleeve of the single "Woobinda" there was a picture of a kangaroo in profile, its forelegs sticking out and its long fleshy tail raised. It was a simple pose and it was perfect for "go."

As for "seek," Scarmiglia thought the sleeve of the album *Nuntereggae* would do very well. If you separated Rino Gaetano's pose from the rest of the photograph, it looked as if he was rummaging around in a container with his hand, searching for something. We decided that this was the *Nunte* pose.

It was lunchtime. We walked barefoot to the little bar outside the bathing establishment, on Viale Regina Elena. We sat down at a table and ate minipizzas. We didn't talk. But now and then one of us would take out his notebook and jot something down, an addition or a modification, improve on the drawing of a pose, and memorize it as he redrew it. Then he'd close the notebook and start to eat again, still making movements—a pencil held up vertically in front of the face, then quickly lowered again, arms suddenly outspread, a hand opened in greeting with its fingers splayed, something snatched in the void, brought in toward the body, given back, and snatched again.

While we chewed and consolidated morphologies and connections, a bee arrived, then a second, and they started to trace their trajectories over the sparsely laid table. We watched the yellow gleam in the sun and listened to the faint buzzing. Bocca opened up a crumpled paper bag; there were still a few minipizzas inside. The two bees glided down, sucked the sweetness from the surface of the cheese and the tomato pulp, then rose up again, and flew off into the distance.

After lunch we decided to go for a walk along the beach, among the revolting bodies. There was a cool, industrious breeze, which blew against our backs and propelled us; I pressed my heels into the wet sand and, after each step, turned around to watch the holes fill with water.

We arrived at the public beach of Partanna, where there were no cabanas. This was where the Palermitans from the old city center and the kids from Villa Sperlinga came. At night they made bonfires and burned tires; the sand was littered with wastepaper. There were colored espadrilles scattered around, broken buckets, ripped beach towels, and cigarette stubs stuck on the incoming waves, drifting backward and forward. A few pigeons flew low, looking for food among the garbage; scuffing up sand they pecked at one another's heads and eyes. There was one with a clawless leg; he was the angriest, the one who'd fought against the dogs in April, the one I'd seen with his head in the amputee dog's mouth. He'd survived and was still fighting. Nearby, small groups of tough little boys called out to one another at the top of their lungs; they were angry too; their lips encrusted with sand and ash, eating what they could find, they were fearless.

How different from me: over time String had managed to instill in me a fear of everything, with her idea that good behavior consisted of keeping still and disappearing. You can play with the sand, but don't *move* it; if you've eaten, don't swim for another four hours; be quiet, don't breathe, but don't you dare die. The shame of being alive. Imagining you're playing and supposing you're swimming; mothers raising phobic, visionary children. The matrilineal transmission of fears.

"We must include the word 'fear,'" I said.

"No," said Bocca, then he stopped, thought about it, knew he was going out on a limb but carried on regardless.

"No," he said again, this time more quietly.

"Why not?" Scarmiglia asked him.

"Because there are some words it's better not to have."

"You didn't object to 'unexpected.'"

"'Unexpected' isn't 'fear.' 'Fear' is something else."

"I think we could use it," I said.

"Do you have any particular pose in mind?" Scarmiglia asked me.

I said nothing; I built up little dunes with the toes of one foot and then kicked them down. Meanwhile the angry pigeon was coming toward us; he hopped around our feet, poking his beak into the sand.

"Yes, I do have a suggestion."

"Do you really want to include 'fear'?" asked Bocca.

He was tense, pleading; he saw what was happening as diminishing our grand plan, tearing the membrane of the bond between us; and for him a break, now, would be unbearable.

"Why are you so against it?" Scarmiglia asked him.

"Because it hurts us."

"So?"

"It's the thing, the experience, that could ruin everything."

"So?"

"It's self-destruction."

"Don't you think it's just a word, not reality?" Scarmiglia asked, staring at him.

"Do *you* really think that?" asked Bocca.

"You tell me."

"I don't know. I don't know what it is."

"How about you?" asked Scarmiglia, turning to me.

Out of the corner of my eye I saw the movements of people around us—backs curving and lengthening out again, shoulder blades flexing like butterflies' wings, a head bending sideways, in the background a jackstraws of interlaced legs on towels.

"I think it's reality," I said.

"Of course it's reality," Scarmiglia said to Bocca, with an expression indicating that the subject was closed.

Then, after a pause to let it sink in, he asked me what pose I suggested.

I raised my hand—palm turned toward Bocca and Scarmiglia, fingers slightly apart—and slid it across an invisible wall; I tried to make the movement as dramatic as possible.

"I've seen that," said Scarmiglia.

"So have I," said Bocca, and it was as if by recognizing the pose he'd found a means of instant readmission into the group.

"It's when the Baroness of Carini dies," he added, barely able to contain his enthusiasm. "In the serial."

"I'd like to call this pose Agren," I said. "After the actress."

Before they could reply, I caught a sudden smell of mulberries, and then I saw them, black in the little basket from which the sprays protruded. A dialectal family—all with thick dark fingers and fingernails like slabs—were offering them to the Villa Sperlinga kids, who dipped their hands into the basket and took them out full and stained up to the wrist, thanking them and cracking jokes in dialect, girls as well as boys. One member of the family came over to us and held out the basket; Bocca looked inside, then stepped back; Scarmiglia shook his head. I stretched out my hand; the family smiled at me, as Bocca and Scarmiglia looked on incredulously. I smelled the damp mulberries and the odor of sweet and sour, then pulled out my hand with a little black globule between my index finger and thumb: I put it to my lips and swallowed. I said, "Thank you," and the family said something which presumably meant "You're welcome," turned, and walked off toward a tent made out of the pole of a beach umbrella with a tarpaulin spread out around it.

"Did you really take it?" Bocca asked me.

"No, he didn't," said Scarmiglia. "It was his thumb."

He looked at me; he studied me.

"He didn't take it," he repeated. "He's so squeamish, he couldn't have done that."

"Let me see," said Bocca, coming closer.

"There's nothing to see. He didn't take it, I tell you."

He studied me again. He was looking for a signal, something to remove all doubt, but I kept my lips tightly shut. I felt like laughing, but I said nothing. I watched the angry pigeon, who had approached the basket on the sand; he was after the mulberries. He was swift and slow at the same time, like a reptile. Birds are descended from dinosaurs, I thought. They're frightening like dinosaurs, because of the shape of their legs, their claws, their black eyes on the sides of their heads, the jerky, segmented way they move their heads, staring and tearing, transforming panic into existence. We had a canary at home, and I used to shut myself in the kitchen, open its cage, and take it out to examine it. Even that defenseless canary was frightening. When it cocked his head backward and rolled its dark eye, there was something ancestral about it; I felt as though I was holding the primeval world in my hand. So I locked prehistory up in its cage, put the cage back on top of the wall unit, and washed my hands.

"There's Morana," said Bocca, pointing toward the shoreline.

We peered between the bodies and walked forward and sideways, shielding our eyes from the glare with our hands.

"Yes, it's him," said Scarmiglia. He didn't express any particular emotion; he was simply registering the event.

"Let's go and say hello," said Bocca.

I didn't want to, and Scarmiglia didn't seem too keen either, but we followed Bocca, who had already set off. As we walked away, I saw the dialectal family shooing the prehistoric pigeon away from the basket; still furious, he went back to join the other foraging birds.

Morana was sitting alone on a towel with frayed edges. He wore brown swimming trunks. His poorly vascularized skin was dry and gray, like a big hematoma. Looking at his mass of thin blond hair, I thought there must be some Norman element in his blood, which had come down to him in degenerate form. He sat on the sand, leaning forward, facing the sea. He hadn't noticed us coming. He was fiddling with his fingers in the sand, burying and unburying something, listlessly moving his hands between his legs just below the surface, and breathing audibly, as if his nose was blocked.

When Bocca greeted him, he stiffened as though expecting to be punched. Then he turned: his eyes were glassy, and there were scabs on his lips. He was like the natural cripple, but without the rhinotracheitis. Or maybe he had that too. At any rate, again I felt a mixture of repulsion and respect for him.

He didn't seem to recognize us at first.

"Hi, Morana," Scarmiglia repeated, and this time the message got through.

"Hi," Morana said.

Bocca sat down beside him, with Scarmiglia opposite them. I kept in the background; I didn't even know if he'd noticed I was there.

A person like him, I thought, spanned the ages; he existed and he always would. He represented vulnerability in its most repugnant form; someone you felt you ought to defend, but you knew you'd have to get your hands dirty to do so, so you hesitated, pretended not to hear him. That was Morana. His destruction was never-ending. There would never be anything in his life—never a thought, never an intuition, nothing at all. And yet he was there; he continued to exist.

"How are you?" asked Bocca. He addressed him as we always did on the rare occasions when we talked to him at school out of embarrassment or pity, looking him in the eye and enunciating every syllable slowly. Scarmiglia just stared and smiled at Morana, while I examined his back—the moles, the dirt, the opaque spots. I said to myself that he must have a poor diet, not get the right food. I understood that I needed him and sat down between Bocca and Scarmiglia.

"How are you?" Bocca repeated.

He didn't reply. He finished burying something in the sand, without looking up.

In class Morana did his oral tests separately, during recess or after school, when no one else was around; not because he was shy—the whole concept of shyness was alien to him—but to avoid holding up the rest of the class. He spoke very slowly, in a mixture of dialect and Italian. His words were like werewolves: they'd jump out for a moment, then run away to hide.

Bocca persisted.

"Have you done the vacation homework?"

Morana didn't answer; one hand stirred the sand, the other rested motionless on his thigh. I saw the shape of his genitals under his trunks; they seemed large and you could see the pressure, but that too was inert, a tumoral formation.

Finally he nodded.

"Yes, done it."

"All of it?"

He paused to gather strength.

"All of it."

"Well done, Morana," Bocca said. "I haven't done it yet; neither have they. But there's plenty of time."

Bocca looked at us, as if urging us to participate. I didn't see any reason to—I had nothing to say to Morana. And I didn't want to hear him say anything.

"Do you come here often?" asked Bocca, lowering his head so he could look up into his eyes. Scarmiglia was losing patience; Morana noticed and was afraid.

"No."

"When *do* you come here, then?"

"I don't know."

"What do you mean, you don't know? How can you not know about something that you do? You must know."

"I don't."

"All right, Morana, you don't know. But can you at least tell me *how* you come here?"

"By bus."

At this point Scarmiglia jumped to his feet and started to kick out backward with one leg, over and over again. He straightened up, but then squatted down like a kangaroo and did three or four hops on the spot, with his arms stretched out in front of him. Then he stopped and looked at us.

"No, let's stay a bit longer," said Bocca.

"Not like that," said Scarmiglia.

"Oh yes," said Bocca. He put the side of his head against his right hand and bent his left arm across the front of his body. The Baglioni pose: think, meditate.

Again, people around us stopped talking and watched. Morana had looked up too. I smiled—I was pleased. I stood up, spread my arms, and held that position for a few seconds. I knew my gesture wasn't as clear as it might have been—our language still needed some refining—but I meant "leave," in the sense of dropping the subject.

We sat down around Morana again.

"We're tired," Bocca said to him. "We've been creating something all day, you know. It'd be hard to explain to you what we're doing, but it's something really great."

"Morana," Scarmiglia intervened, getting up onto his knees, his thin body lengthening. "I have to ask you a favor. I don't feel I can ask them," he said, indicating Bocca and me, "or anyone else. It's something I can only ask of you."

He moved his head closer, to within a few centimeters of Morana's face, becoming theatrical again.

"May I?" he said.

Morana rubbed sand between his thumb and forefinger, trying to make the grains smaller than they were. Then he nodded.

"Good. Thank you for being so helpful. And trusting. The favor I want to ask of you is this: I'd like you to say two words for me. The first two words you can think of, off the top of your head. They can be any kind of word—nouns, adjectives, verbs, adverbs, whatever you like."

Bocca and I didn't understand. Scarmiglia smiled at us.

"Come on, Morana, say two words for me."

The silence began when Scarmiglia's question ended, and it would go on, slow and tubular, until Morana, possibly, said something in reply. For the moment he kept grinding air between his fingers, looking from me to Bocca to Scarmiglia and back again, nodding his head, first regularly, then at random intervals, like a broken metronome, his ravaged face imploring us to spare him, to continue to spare him as we'd done throughout the school year, showing respect for his scabby lips and dirty hair, even if we found them disgusting. But this was our new way of showing our respect—besieging, squeezing, compelling; keeping on at Morana, to see when he exploded.

But Morana didn't explode.

"I . . . you . . ." he said, very softly.

It sounded like the beginning of a sentence, but it didn't go on; the silence had ended, but instead of an explosion all we heard were two triturated pronouns and the sound of sand between his fingers.

"Thank you," said Scarmiglia, getting to his feet and brushing the sand off his knees. "You don't know it, but you've been a great help to us. We have to go now, though; the bus will be leaving soon."

We got up too and said goodbye. Morana didn't reply; he was exhausted. Scarmiglia and Bocca walked off; I stayed a moment longer. I wanted to say something to him—not out of sympathy or solidarity: solidarity would have disgusted me. I needed to get a reaction out of his body, to understand how he could endure this continual torture, be such an uncomplaining victim. But I had nothing to say about that either; like when we'd first arrived, I examined his curved back and thin hair, and still he didn't move; he twiddled his fingers between his legs, constantly dipping them into the sand and taking them out again. I leaned over beyond his head and saw that what he'd taken out of the sand was a mulberry; he sniffed it and ate it.

When I caught up with the others, they were arguing heatedly. Bocca had demanded an explanation.

"We needed two more words," Scarmiglia answered him, "and I thought I'd get them from Morana. Or rather, from mere chance, which you two are so keen on. You ought to be pleased."

"That's not the point," said Bocca. "It's a question of method: you decided this on your own, and that's not right. You tell him," he said to me.

"It's fine with me," I said. "*I* and *you* are words that we'll need. All we have to do is decide which poses to assign them to."

Bocca was annoyed. He'd been counting on my support, but instead he found himself isolated again.

"As a matter of fact, we already have them," said Scarmiglia. "The poses, I mean. Think what Morana was doing while we were talking."

I rubbed my thumb against my fingertips. Bocca waited a few seconds, long enough to come around to our point of view, then started nodding his head. On the way back to the cabana we decided that the word I would be expressed by rubbing the thumb against the fingertips, and you by nodding.

Bocca walked home; I accompanied Scarmiglia to the bus stop. We talked about the progress we'd made and the reasons why we were doing all this—about logic and inevitability.

We walked past a former warehouse that had been converted into a games arcade. Outside was a big pool with plastic boats in it, and a man moving them from the middle toward the sides with a pole; inside there was foosball, Space Invaders, and Pong. Scarmiglia suggested we have a game; he could catch a later bus. It was cool inside, and the place was almost empty. One or two dialectal boys fired away on pinball machines, a few old men dressed in shorts and vests peered at lighted monitors; heaps of dogs dozed under Ping-Pong tables. There were also two girls a little older than us, about thirteen or fourteen, dressed in two-piece bathing costumes, with thin hips and round stomachs. They went up to all the boys, walking barefoot with painted toenails, joking, and talking in loud voices.

"Little girls make you cry," said Scarmiglia, when he saw me looking at them. I recognized the allusion but didn't know what to say.

"Especially when they're not so little," he added.

We started playing. First Pong, then we moved on to foosball. We were well matched, both clean strikers of the ball, and we never had to resort to illegal moves like spinning or hooking. The ball clicked to and fro and banged against the sides, making a hollow clunk against the wooden back of the goal when you scored.

"Did you know today's her birthday?"

The green surface of the table disappeared. He'd said it without raising his head, completely focused on the game, as if a fragment of thought had randomly found acoustic expression and a questioning intonation. I lost my grip on the rods; the ball ricocheted twice and ended up in my goal. I heard it being digested by the table, rolling along and across, gliding along rails and pathways until, with a final acceleration, it joined its fellows in the wooden lung at the center.

I bent down and looked for another ball, but the slot was empty.

"Let's go," said Scarmiglia.

As we reached the door of the warehouse the two girls came up to us; one had a mole by her navel. Seen from up close, the polish on their toenails was chipped. They asked us if we could spare some change. I was mesmerized by the way they talked and moved, by the brazen coquettishness with which one of them leaned against the other and embraced her, smiling at us as she did so; by their absolute certainty that they would get what they wanted.

Scarmiglia searched in the pocket of his cut-off jeans, found a fifty-lire coin and gave it to them. They thanked him, laughing; I knew they were mocking us. We left.

The sidewalk was covered in sand. To our left was a blue railing anchored in a wall; I ran my fingers along it.

"I didn't know," I said.

We walked on in silence for fifty meters. The bus stop was not far away now. Scarmiglia stopped and turned toward me.

"What *do* you know?" he asked me.

I stopped too. Scarmiglia made an impatient gesture, as if shaking something out of his hand, but with some restraint, forcing himself to be calm.

"I mean," he said, "what do you know about her?"

He wasn't aggressive, nor was he hostile, but I still wished I could go away.

"I don't know anything," I said.

Scarmiglia peered at me, examining the pores of my skin, the film of sweat on my forehead and temples. I'd have liked to dry myself with my hand, clean myself, wipe off the sweat; but I didn't. Around us there was nothing but squashed cicadas and their torn-off elytra.

We reached the bus stop; the bus wasn't there. We sat down on a wall; behind us was the bare earth of a parking lot with a few cars and some withered scrub. Scarmiglia sniffed; there was a dark smudge on his neck—engine grease, or an early evening shadow clinging to his throat.

"Her name's Wimbow," he said, looking straight ahead. "The name comes from Central America—the Antilles, I think. It means 'wind-rainbow.'"

Here, on this road, like every road in Palermo, the asphalt was full of cracks. They were split seams in a black fabric, gaps through which evil entered the world. My head was black and covered with split seams. Sounds entered through them: car engines roaring, children shrieking, stray dogs barking as they ran in packs toward the sea, Scarmiglia talking about the Creole girl, making her exist, transforming her into reality, giving her an origin and a name, biography coloring the raw created being. *Wimbow* didn't seem like a word. It was like a sound plucked from the outside world, from phenomena, the way water flowed at night, the way air introflexed when you moved through it. It contained the word *whimper*, the word *billow*, and the word *nimbus*. For an instant the Creole girl was the light of my nimbus, a darker, intenser light, a pale yellow dotted with corpuscles. The word *Antilles*, too, entered my head and created an image of dispersion, disgregation. I knew the Antilles were tiny islands; on the map they looked like a skin rash. The

Creole girl—Wimbow—originated from disease, dispersion, an oceanic swarming of islands. But the word *wind-rainbow* was new to me. I knew the two individual words: one of them, *wind*, I liked; the other, *rainbow*, I was less fond of—it seemed interfering, intrusive. It reminded me of children's drawings, of curved bands of color blurring into one another. Wind-rainbow was the wind of the rainbow, or the rainbow of the wind. There was a pot of gold coins at the end of the rainbow. Bees lived in the wind. Bees were the color of gold. A pot full of bees. A gold coin with a sting.

"My parents know her parents," said Scarmiglia. "They adopted her and brought her to Italy."

He spoke more words that penetrated through the gaps in my head, powdery words inside sentences that gave them existence and history, syllables that entered me, mingling with pollen and ash. Scarmiglia's voice had brought contagion: the knowledge that "Creole girl" was an insufficient name, that it was unrealistic to think of a creature separate from everything, that Wimbow existed, did things, was there.

The bus came and people got on. From outside I saw horizontal and vertical bars and hands grasping them. Scarmiglia gathered his things and stood up; I remained seated. He turned toward me, with his back to the bus, the engine roaring and black smoke pouring out of the exhaust pipe.

"She's a deaf-mute," he said.

Then he waved goodbye, stepped up on to the footboard and disappeared among the bodies; the folding doors closed, the bus departed, and I was left alone.

The wall beneath me was a mineral; like every mineral, it was mute. The cracked asphalt was mute. The tree, the streetlight. The pollen, the ash. The Creole girl was mute. Today, July 17, 1978, was her birthday. Her new father, her new mother. They would touch her head, her dark skin. They would give her presents. There'd be cousins, a cream-colored tablecloth.

Perhaps a garden, a country cottage. She would open her presents, look at them lingeringly, turn boxes over to read instructions, gently touch china eyes and nylon hair. Then she'd touch her own hair, and on the back of her hand, where the little pale patch was, she'd feel warmth and softness. Her parents, for no reason, would feel inadequate. Her mother would smooth out creases in the tablecloth, her father would take photographs. Perhaps they and her cousins would ask her questions; she would reply with cautious smiles. Then they'd bring in the cake, which would be big and contain all the cakes in the world and the cakes of lost time and millions of candles, one for each breath she'd ever taken. And Wimbow would wrap up her whole existence in breath and blow the infection of silence onto the world; flames on pink and sky-blue tips would quiver and twirl, and around them a ring of heads and voices would call out and encourage her, but no sound would come, there'd be silence, no sound at all, and with another puff the flames would go out and Wimbow would be one year older and know everything and her blood would flow calm and red, so red, inside her body and everywhere. And I would still be there, in my mineral life, with the solace of words.

ECLIPSE

(AUGUST 1978)

Bocca and Scarmiglia were away—Bocca on vacation with his parents up north, Scarmiglia staying with relatives in Castel-buono. I spent a lot of time at home, killing whatever I could find—worms, ants, everything except for bees. I had a special method for killing ants. I concocted a poison by mixing to-gether various kinds of detergent in a little bottle and adding DDT, Idrolitina, and Stone's Aqua Velva. I screwed on the top and shook the bottle. I went out into the garden and walked down to the flower bed alongside the cats' hedge, where I knew there were ant nests. I located two or three apical holes, where the softer earth was, and poured the poison into them. The ants came out, streamed across the flower bed, and swarmed over the tiles on the path. I shook the poison again and poured it into the joints between the tiles; it formed an impassable, hissing liquid wall. The ants were trapped in the poison; some managed to extricate themselves but their legs were wet and they could hardly move. When the bottle was almost empty I used up the last drops trying to hit the largest ants and drown them one by one. Then I went back inside and rinsed the bottle under the bathroom faucet for a long time—for the rest of the day, in fact.

Sometimes I switched on the television. There were always movies on in the afternoon—Don Camillo and Peppone, Franco Franchi and Ciccio Ingrassia. Italy only understood caricatures, one-dimensional figures. "Come on out, you fool." Fear of the Sarchiapone. Any character with the slightest hint of complexity was immediately suspect. One day I watched Tina Pica playing Caramella in *Bread, Love and Dreams*. I liked it when she shouted; she was always shouting, grumbling, scolding, and moralizing. I think she'd realized that this was a crucial facet of the Italian character, and one that was worth portraying. A whole republic built on people screaming at other people at the tops of their lungs, but when you blew on it you realized it was nothing but froth.

During the past few months, since Moro's death, the political picture in Italy had changed. Leone had been an implausible figure for years and now had been ousted. That smooth exterior, that thin bleating voice, those superstitious gestures to ward off students and cholera—they didn't wash anymore. The bleat needed replacing with something more substantial, something grittier. Pertini was Italy with a new tone, more suited to the times: staunch and austere, with a touch of senile bemusement that was rather endearing. He'd been a partisan in the war, fought against the Fascists, and escaped from political imprisonment, so he had all the credentials of the old-fashioned socialist. He was the right symbol at the right time, as the country was trying to put its pieces together again; national unity would be restored by ranting and rhetoric.

So Tina Pica was perfect; she was a female Sandro Pertini, with the same voice and the same gruff, fiery temperament.

But when she appeared on the screen wrapped in her cutwork shawl and I went over to the TV to sniff her, a smell of old incense flooded through my nostrils and down my throat, conjuring up the sacristy, the censer, a tabernacular atmosphere. I was used to the smell—it was the smell of Palermo and the smell of all Italy—but I still found it overpowering. It was anachronistic; it opened a door to reveal dark, grimy, rural petit-bourgeois interiors, an extension of the picture postcards that rolled by on *Intervallo*, a vast array of shawls, doilies, opaque glass ornaments, blotchy wardrobe mirrors, and drinking glasses on which I could see, as in some translucent nightmare, layer upon layer of encrusted saliva. I knew that if I put my nose to Stone's and String's skin I'd smell that same odor. I sniffed my own skin, in the crook of my arm and on the back of my hand, and tears came to my eyes.

•

In the mornings I went to the beach, sometimes alone, sometimes with String and Cotton. While I was there I kept to myself. I read and I walked. I went to the public beach and looked for Morana, but didn't see him. Once I saw the mulberry people, the dialectal family. They recognized me and asked me in gestures if I wanted a mulberry; I said no and walked on. I passed a circle of kids with two dogs who were playing and scuffing up sand. One boy was talking to another; he shouted, "*Stronzo!*" but it was just part of the game. I kept the word *stronzo* in my head for a while—it buzzed, it was a black hornet. I parted my lips and attempted to articulate the first syllable, till it rested on the *o*. That was enough. When I got back I locked myself in the cool half-light of the cabana. I took the piece of barbed wire out of my knapsack, squatted down, and carved little figures on the wooden floor with the spikes—my private hieroglyphics: thousand-pointed stars, little spirals with letters in the middle, scrawled flights of bees, postural variations on the alphamute. My fingers numb, I sat back and contemplated my work, pleased and nauseated, split in two. I sat there for a long time, alone, silent, the barbed wire on my lap, the summer shut out; then I took down a mirror that hung on a hook, wedged it between two overturned beach umbrellas and looked at myself. I rubbed the tips of my forefinger and thumb to indicate who was talking; holding my arms stretched out in front of me, I bent my legs; I touched my knees, sides, chest, and forehead with my hands; then I rested one hand on top of the other, in a dignified pose.

I. Understand. Desire. Good.

I understand that desire is a good.

I continued: I rubbed my fingers, spun around as if I was about to topple over, then slid my hand down the wall.

I. Shame. Fear.

I am ashamed of fear.

I *was* ashamed of fear, it was true, but I needed to be able to say that I was afraid. Because fear was a tool. It enabled you to know, to understand. It was necessary for fear to exist. The only trouble was, for me it was *always* there.

I left the cabana. Cotton was doing something with wet sand; behind him, String was reading under an umbrella. I walked over, stood in front of her, stared at her and rubbed my fingers, kicked out backward and nodded my head several times; then again I rubbed my fingers, kicked out backward, and nodded. String shut her book. She wasn't so much worried as embarrassed; she didn't know what to say to the people around us. And I persisted: I rubbed my fingers, gave the backward kick, and nodded, faster and faster, until the three movements overlapped—I rubbed my fingers at the same time as I was doing the backward kick and nodding my head. String got up and came toward me; I didn't know whether she was just expressing anger or whether she intended to stop me; I did another backward kick so hard I hurt my leg, while my fingertips were numb from rubbing, my head felt as if it was about to fall off my shoulders, then I lost my balance and fell on my face on the sand, in front of String. I rubbed my face in the sand, turned my head, and stared up at her.

"I hatred you, I hatred you, I hatred you," I said, with all the rage I could muster. Then I got up and walked away, brushing sand off my lips.

When I got home, overcome by the heat that had built up in me, I fell asleep. I slept for two or three hours. I woke at the end of the afternoon; the memory of a dream lingered in my head, like a taste in the mouth. Since there was still some time to go before supper, I got out the record player and listened to some songs. I put the box on the floor, lifted the lid, and inserted the plug in the socket. Setting the speed with the handle, I placed a record on the turntable and gingerly lowered the head, terrified of dropping it and scratching the record, till the needle engaged with the groove and there was a rustling, crackling noise.

I listened to Laura Luca singing "Domani, domani," another reconversion of the consecrated Host, this time into a voice, and then to the cosmetic tones of Dora Moroni. And yet when I'd seen them on TV, both singers had had a wonderful smell, full of sharpness and passion, a clinging, sensual smell that made me half-close my eyes. In the close-ups I'd examined their Red Brigade faces—Laura Luca with fashionably frizzy hair, Dora Moroni's black eyes full of ideology. The only difference between them and a true Red Brigade woman was the excessive, brazen, brick-colored rouge on their cheeks and cheekbones. The true Red Brigade woman was ideological and ravenous, her hair untidy and loose, her cheeks white with struggle. She wore no makeup or trinkets; she saw struggle wherever she looked and she shunned adornments.

I tired of them and put on another record, but didn't listen to it; I just watched the undulations of the turntable and the flow of the light between the grooves. I curled up on the cool floor. It was a pleasant feeling, gently contracting your muscles and bones. It was the "dying" pose—Moro's body in the car trunk—but it was also the position of bodies when they're born, of puppies held by the scruff of the neck, and of babies' bodies, both those that are born and those that are not.

A few years ago, in the summer, I'd gone with Stone and String to the open-air theater. The film was nothing special—rather boring, in fact. I didn't pay much attention to it; I was more interested in looking at a white gecko that clung motionless to the wall. Then the plot took a different turn; there was a clinic, and a pregnant woman crying as she took off her clothes. String, taken by surprise, tried to cover my eyes, but I wriggled out of her grip and saw an instrument expanding the woman's vagina while another one, a kind of knitting needle with a curved tip, scraped out dark pieces from inside and dropped them into a kidney-shaped metal bowl. Then the knitting needle caught hold of something, a black miniature, dry, encrusted, and curled up; that too went into the kidney-shaped bowl. The doctor laid down his instruments, took off his gloves, and washed his hands. On the way home String walked beside me and tried to speak, but she was nervous and twice failed to finish sentences. She tried to touch my head and shoulders, but I moved away. She began a third sentence but then trailed off again, and we walked on in silence.

The next day I looked up the phenomenon in the encyclopedia. I read definitions, learned about procedures, the names of instruments, and laws. I was able to get an idea of the situation, but only a vague one—I understood that a woman's body was a cave. The words were abstract and imprecise, imbued with the technical reticence of encyclopedias.

When String had what they called a spontaneous abortion, I thought spontaneous meant "authentic"—an authentic abortion.

It was early in the morning and still dark. Stone went to get the car. String was sitting on a chair in the hall and told me I couldn't come. But I wanted to be there. Before we left, we waited for our neighbor to come upstairs; she would stay with Cotton, and later take him to school, which that day, coincidentally, was taking the kids on a trip to the natural science museum. As we drove along I looked out at the street from the car; shops were opening and lights were on in apartment buildings. When we reached the hospital String couldn't get out of the car; two male nurses had to help her onto a wheelchair. They took her to another ward; we'd come to the wrong one. When we got to the right ward I waited outside the door. Some male nurses told me I couldn't stay there, but they didn't know who to inform, because Stone was inside with String. I pretended not to understand and sat down; on one side was the door of the ward, on the other a broken-down elevator, its indicator stuck on red. There was a smell of coffee. At lunchtime the door was unlocked and the mothers' relatives arrived. I got up and went in too. The mothers were in the rooms, curled up in their beds, handkerchiefs tucked into their pajama sleeves. Some looked at the ceiling, listening to babies' cries echoing along the corridors; they turned first on one side, then on the other, squashed their bosoms against the mattress and stared into the darkness, holding their breath. One of them touched her abdomen, pressing her fingers around her navel. I passed women shuffling along in slippers, dressed in light blue or bright red dressing-gowns, their lifeless hair combed back and fastened with headbands. They looked like sleepwalking elephants. Two pushed their newborn babies along in rudimentary strollers consisting of an open-topped transparent case made of hard plastic, embedded in a metal skeleton with wheels, like a shopping cart. Among the blankets there was a little duck and a Topo Gigio with a crumpled greeting card.

When I returned to the waiting room String still hadn't come out, so I sat down and waited. An hour later she emerged.

Stone was supporting her forearm, but it didn't seem necessary. The staff said we could go home and that she needed to rest. In the car String told me she'd had an operation, they'd given her an injection of hemostatic and another of anticoagulant, that all this would pass, but things would be different from now on. She cried. I didn't understand in what way things would be different, but didn't ask. For several days, whenever I went into her bedroom I'd find her crying; she sat in her chair, in her nightgown, her forearms lying along on the armrests, her hands open and her fingers trembling. She cried silently; from the other bedroom I couldn't hear a thing. She'd be looking upward, her face contorted, her eyes very white. At first she wouldn't notice me, then she'd turn toward me and make a gesture with her open hand, pushing air against me. Eventually she'd calm down and ask me about Cotton; she'd tried to explain what had happened but he'd just looked at her blankly and she'd given up. But she was sure he'd understood that something was wrong.

Something had changed in Cotton since the day of the miscarriage. He always carried a bread roll around with him. There was nothing strange about that in itself; he might have been hungry. But it was always the same roll. From time to time he'd take it out, contemplate it, and put it away again. He never took a bite from it, but left it intact. Once, when he was dozing in front of the TV with the roll on his lap, I tiptoed over and examined it. It was the size of the palm of my hand; oval, flat underneath and irregularly convex on top, with a number of whirls and swellings. The crust must once have been honey-colored, but now it was light yellow and had cracked in some places and flaked away in others. Almost all the sesame seeds had fallen off; only a few were left, in some hollows. There were some splits in the crust, which were green around the edges; the original soft part inside was green too, and dry.

Over the next few days the roll started to go moldy. Cotton looked at it and gently pressed the crust: it was brittle and his fingers broke through. I secretly watched him tend to his roll: he'd dip it in a cup that he'd filled with warm water, then put it out on the balcony to dry, and keep watch over it, getting up now and then to examine it. He would go into the kitchen and put it in the fridge for an hour, remove it and take it into the bathroom, wet it with the jet of water from the bidet, get out the hairdryer, plug it in, turn it on, and dry the roll for a quarter of an hour; then he'd take it back into the kitchen, climb up onto a chair, and put it in the freezer for a few hours. Finally he'd cover it in Saran wrap and then in toilet paper, and enfold all this in the old red wool shawl that String used for wrapping sick kittens in when she took them to the vet; he put the bundle in the hollow space under the drawer of his bedside table. He would get up at regular intervals during the night—I knew because it woke me—switch on the light on the bedside table, take out the bundle, and cuddle it.

I was frustrated by the fact that I couldn't understand why he was doing all this. But asking him was impossible. Cotton was a nonverbal organism; he would never communicate this in words—not spoken words, at any rate. But written words were a possibility. So one afternoon, when he was out, I gathered his school notebooks and leafed through them. He wrote like a tortoise, if a tortoise could write: the letters were made up of tiny segments, the *e* a near-hexagon, the *o* a dodecahedron. The pen strokes were faint, almost illegible. It took me an hour to decipher some parts, and wasn't much wiser when I did. Disheartened, I moved on to his drawings. There was a date at the top of each page, and, below, rudimentary houses, a flower with rhomboidal petals, a black cat with a huge body and a triangular head. Under the date when String had miscarried there was a drawing of a vase. It was transparent, a kind of glass cylinder. He'd drawn it very big—it filled the whole page—and inside it was a bread roll, very similar to the one he'd been guarding for a fortnight and trying to save during the past few days. Looking at the page, I wondered what this drawing meant to him, what its relevance was. Then, staring at a whirl in the crust which resembled a small, curled-up leg, I realized that Cotton hadn't drawn a roll, but the tiny body of a newborn baby; a baby immersed in a kind of dirty water, which he'd tried to render by mixing black with yellow and gray.

On the next page was the classic drawing that every school, sooner or later, crassly makes its pupils do: my family. On the left of the page Cotton had drawn Stone, short and stocky; next to Stone was String, thinner and with a big nose; then there was me, with brown hair and a mouth on which the black pencil must have broken, turning it into a chasm; next to me he'd drawn himself, arms by his sides and head bent over to one side. On the extreme right of the page, alongside his body and continuing the downward scale in size, was the vase containing the roll-baby. On the next page was an account of the school trip to the natural science museum, where I too had gone with the school a few years earlier, and where I remembered seeing, lined up on shelves, jars containing fetuses in formaldehyde. Cotton hadn't drawn a baby, he'd drawn a fetus—the shape of the thing that he didn't understand.

When he came home I wanted to speak to him but something stopped me, a kind of embarrassment; I just observed him from a distance. After watching television he went into the kitchen, opened the fridge, and took out the bundle he'd placed there two hours earlier, swathed in the red shawl. He removed the shawl and the Saran wrap. The body of the roll was completely distorted, its decay now unstoppable. The crust had been reduced to a flimsy skin, temporarily hardened by its stay in the fridge but now already damp and soggy again; at least four deep faultlines ran across it and the inside part had turned black. Cotton stood with the roll in his hand, watching it die. He went over to the sink, turned on the faucet, hesitated, turned it off again, went out on to the balcony, exposed the roll to the evening air, and came back inside. Finally, holding the roll behind his back, he said good night to Stone and String—who had noticed what was happening but tactfully had not interfered—and went to the bedroom. Two minutes later I went after him.

Cotton was sitting on the edge of his bed, leaning forward. He was holding the roll in his left hand, breaking off pieces and eating them. When he heard me, he stopped for a moment, looked at me, then went on breaking off morsels and eating them; they were green and black, and they crumbled between his fingers. Without a word I sat down beside him. I sat there with Cotton, unable to speak, united with him by our silence. Then I stretched out my hand to break off a piece from the roll, and joined him in feeding on grief.

•

After spending a few days scratching my arms by plunging them into the hedge in search of kittens to catch and sniff, I put on some long pants, dug out a chenille sweater, a plastic bag, and my piece of barbed wire, and set off toward the Addaura, just north of Mondello, where houses stood on the slopes of a mountain that turned blue in the evening.

I arrived; bougainvillea was exploding around me. I began to search, found a swarm, followed it with my eyes, and located its nest. I put on my sweater and pulled the bag over my head; it wasn't completely transparent but I could see well enough. I walked toward the nest, and the buzzing grew louder and louder. I wished I could explain to the bees what was happening, tell them not to be afraid. When I was standing in front of the nest, which was in a crack in the garden wall of a house, I bent down, took out the barbed wire, and pushed it into the crack. The cloud of bees became thicker; I felt them beat against the plastic bag and against the sweater, and kept my hands inside the sleeves. I forced myself to keep calm and kept probing in the crack. I thought of the sensual implications of what I was doing; I felt embarrassed but went on. I moved the barbed wire from top to bottom and from bottom to top, stirring up a huge swarm. I went on till I felt a violent battering against the bag and against my chest, a hail of attacks, while the oxygen thinned inside the bag, the air dampened, the plastic contracted and expanded, and I was breathing like Darth Vader, with a rasping sound, and couldn't help laughing. Eventually the cloud dispersed and the noise decreased. I walked away, took the bag off my head and went back on to the road to get a wider perspective. The bees flew in globes which lengthened out into ellipses, then condensed again as they sought the queen. They formed the shape of an upturned cone, which changed into an oval and then rose up, becoming a huge, horseshoe-shaped zucchini, which hung in the sky for almost a minute, a divine cucurbit; then in a series of pulsing movements it narrowed into bottlenecks before reverting, in a series of pulses, to the shape of an upside-down cone. The swarm was meditating on itself—a flying monologue, an introversion that, all in the space of a few seconds, generated its own extroversion, untying the knot. Following the queen, the bees settled on a bicycle chained to a pole, first encircling it in a ball about two meters in diameter, within which the bicycle was still visible, then closing ever more tightly around the frame till they swathed it completely, leaving only the stumps of the handles and the metal peduncle of the bell uncovered. I stood for a while watching the teeming bicycle, the bustling of bees, the buzzing that was really a growl.

The next day I went back to the Addaura. I walked past the wall; the scene was calm. The pole was unoccupied; the bicycle was no longer there, but the chain with its padlock lay on

the ground: during the night the bees had devoured the bicycle, frame, pedals, seat, and all. Or maybe they'd torn off the
chain, swarmed into the shape of a human body, and gone off
for a ride along the promenade.

I walked a kilometer farther uphill and felt as though I was
being watched; at every rustle I turned around with a start.
Still, I started searching among the bougainvillea; pushing
aside the branches, I explored the outer walls of the cottages. It
was quiet and there was no one around. I saw a bee pass by; I
watched its course but soon lost sight of it. Another arrived,
then a third, and others; I walked faster in the same direction.
After a while I stopped. I saw that they were flying toward
some wooden planks heaped up against a tree in the middle of
a patch of bare earth; they entered through a gap between two
planks and disappeared into the darkness. I prepared for action
again, putting on the sweater and the plastic bag, but today I
had a shovel and a plastic rake that belonged to Cotton instead
of the barbed wire; I'd also brought some gardening gloves. I
went up to the tree, knelt down in front of the planks, and
pushed the shovel between them. I couldn't see a thing; I
poked about this way and that, and a swarm flew up into the
air. Through the transparency of the bag I saw that the swarm
had formed into the shape of two thin, muscular, open wings
a few meters above my head, with a similarly thin oblong figure tapering downward like a spindle, its sharp tip above my
bagged skull. I dropped the shovel and rake, stepped back,
looked upward, and rubbed my fingers hard, not an easy thing
to do with gardening gloves on, then held my left hand out in
front of me to simulate holding something, while with my
right hand I rummaged in the something I was pretending to
hold.

"I-am-search-ing," I said from inside the bag.

"I am only searching," I repeated. I spoke syllable by syllable, as Bocca had done to Morana.

The Yuppi Du swarm didn't change its shape; so I raised my hand to tell it to wait, then squatted down like a kangaroo, and hopped three times.

"Just a little longer and I'll go," I shouted skyward. Then I bent down again, thrashing about with the shovel, between the planks.

At last, although I couldn't see her, I flushed out the queen; a hemorrhage of bees spilled out and rose up, plastically uniting with the other swarm. I walked back twenty meters, took off the bag and sweater, and breathed in the lemony smell released by the pheromonal storm. The bees had surrounded a watering can on a cottage lawn; for a few seconds I could see it orange, then it turned yellow and black.

At night I dreamed in swarms. Every figure I dreamed of was a multitude of moving particles, as if I was dreaming about the atomic structure of the dream, electrons whirling around the oneiric nucleus, bodies emitting a chemical buzz. One night I dreamed of the Creole girl as a swarm of particles, her form broken down into swirling dust, or perhaps not broken down but raised up, elevated to the primordial dimension that had preceded my discovery of her name and my knowledge of her past, as the instant when everything had begun, at the well-spring of perception: the Creole girl intact again, at last. In my dream she stood still and serene in the sky and looked at me, though I couldn't see her eyes, because her face, like her whole body, was dark pulviscular matter, but I knew she was looking toward me, and there wasn't a sound, not even a buzzing, only the mute vision of her, a marginalization of all sound, a continually recurring silence. Just before I woke up, the cloud she was formed of began to disperse, her belly burst, and silence gushed out of her bowels in the form of fire.

On the last day of August, in the late afternoon, I went back to the Addaura again. I wandered around for a long time without finding anything. Then, as evening fell, I noticed a few scout bees returning to their nest after their last mission, and I watched to see where they went. A short distance away, on an illuminated stretch of road, a swarm of comrade bees was buzzing near a tree. Before going into action I went back to the promenade and looked for a phone booth. What I found was a phone in a small, gun-metal gray parallelepiped on a pole with a quadrangular yellow base. I took a phone token out of my pocket but put it in the wrong way, and the groove didn't match; I turned it over and inserted it correctly. I dialed the number and Cotton replied; I told him I'd be staying out for dinner at a friend's house—I didn't say which friend. I told Cotton to pass on the message, hung up, and returned to the new bees' nest. This time I worked fast. I walked around the tree and inspected the area. I walked to the escarpment that sloped down from the road and found a bamboo stick. I put on my protective gear, whacked the trunk with the bamboo stick, and prodded the nest with its tip; I kept shaking it till the swarm dispersed, then condensed into a cloud. But this time the number of bees had multiplied. It was as if their anger had increased over the last few days, leading to an alliance between different nests: the cloud expanded wildly in the sky, filling it completely; the glow of evening vanished, to be replaced by a bee-made night.

In Exodus the third plague that God inflicts on the Egyptians when Pharaoh refuses to set the people of Israel free from slavery is of gnats. God orders Moses to strike the dusty ground with his staff; the dust is transformed into swarm and destruction, for the swarm covers the sky and spreads over the Earth, bringing torment to man and beast.

Standing there with the bamboo stick in my hands in that double twilight, I felt like a tiny Moses. The bees were the plague, I was the authorities; they were the Red Brigades, I was the state—a state that besieged, corroded, provoked, and, finally, by raiding its hideouts, confronted the enemy grouping.

But besieging, corroding, and provoking were also the Red Brigades' methods.

While a black magma hung over my head and the queen bee, the wandering hostage at its center, was deciding where to nest, the state and the Red Brigades merged into one. Their thought processes were the same; the language they used, if you examined it closely, was the same. We had a brigadist state, an institutionalized version of the Red Brigades, a state where production alternated with destruction, and order with disorder, where equilibrium was established, then upset, then restored again, like the changing shape of a swarm of bees or a sentence that's being constructed. Then suddenly the magma lengthened out, became liquescent, and released the dusky evening light, flooding around a streetlight, coating every inch of the pole, from the bottom all the way up, leaving only the shining light at the top uncovered. I looked at the new, luminous bees' nest and felt as though I'd been forgiven. I felt grateful to the photosensitive queen who in settling on that source of light had unwittingly created my twin, a living human body topped by a nimbus: ideology recognizing the chosen one and enveloping him with her swarm in public acclamation. I bent down to pick up my things, intending to leave, but just at that moment the swarm shifted upward and within a few seconds had covered the light at the top.

Above the Addaura, the blue mountain, and beyond, right across Palermo, the sky was saturated with bees, blotting out the light. I set off for home, wondering how I was going to survive the eclipse.

DIALOGUES

Afternoon. The air was clear. We'd left Mondello and come back into town. I had a list of textbooks for the new school year and the money to buy them; I went out. My hair was three millimeters long. I kept running my palm over my head; it hurt my scalp when I pressed. I knew that whether we grew our hair out, parted it, or kept it strategically unkempt, our skulls would always be underneath, osseous eggs harboring evil.

I passed the porn clearing, skirting the edge of it; the bookshop was about a hundred meters farther on. I touched the bills in my pants pocket, pressed them with my finger, and they crumpled. I looked around in the waning light and touched the money in my pocket again; I turned around and went back. I got to the clearing and pushed through the bushes, which gave a little, then parted, and I was inside. At first I could still hear cars, but soon I was only aware of what lay ahead.

The bush was blue, flecked with glinting yellow. I looked at it, then at my bare arms. I bent down and sniffed the plant's pith and juice, brushing the surface of the leaves with my forehead. I knelt down and pushed my arm in: my fingers touched fine thorns and embryonic branches with little dots of serum on their tips. I didn't find anything, but continued my exploration. Toward the bottom I felt something stringy and rough, something that didn't belong to the bush and felt both dry and wet. I cupped my fingers underneath it, pulled it out, and straightened up. It was a nest containing a tangle of broken shells and dead chicks surrounded by globes of feathers. There seemed to be four or five of them; it was hard to tell. Their bodies were swollen, their pink and gray skin raw; a few little hairs stuck out, as stiff as exclamation marks; their beaks were small and twisted. A black ant walked out from the tiny crater of an anus. A bird's anus is called a cloaca; its bones are hollow. Two or three ants were walking around my wrist; I blew them off. I put the nest down and as soon as it touched the ground, a pool of insects formed, which spread and dispersed, then quickly reformed and contracted again. The insects swarmed over the chicks, entered through their beaks, broke off tiny fragments of entrails, and carried them away.

Hearing a noise, I turned around and saw the prehistoric pigeon come out from the base of the bush. He took three hops toward me, stopping a few centimeters away, near the nest. His feathers were dry, hard, and blotchy, his orange eye still angry, his clawless leg loose on the ground. He hopped into the nest, among the down and dead bodies, and raised his head to stretch his vertebrae.

He looked at me, and I looked at him.

"What were you searching for just now?" he said. His voice was a rattle of nails in a box.

I didn't answer.

He tucked his head into his breast, breathed in, and turned toward me again.

"What were you searching for?"

I thought about it. Nothing could surprise me anymore.

"Comics," I said.

He looked at me, waiting.

"Sex," I said. "I was searching for sex."

He nodded, as if he knew that already and had all the time in the world.

"And instead of that you found me."

"Yes."

"You also found insects—larvae and other flesh-eating parasites."

He paused for a few seconds, then went on.

"Decay," he said.

He hopped around slightly to the right, looked away, and stared at the space in front of him.

"Your imagination produces decay," he added.

"No, it doesn't."

"Yes, it does. You're like me: you're always in search of struggle."

We were next to each other but didn't look at each other; he was in the nest, I stood by the bush.

"You're attracted by destruction," he went on.

"No, I'm not," I said.

"Then why did you never imagine that your barbed wire could generate a good infection?"

"Infection can't be good," I said at once.

He didn't reply, his scaly feathers rising and falling on his breast as he breathed. I knew I was in the wrong but that I had to stonewall, play for time.

"Nimbus," he said to me, modulating to a higher pitch. It was the first time anyone had called me that. "You came here searching for sex and struggle," he went on. "To you, sex and struggle are the only possible infection, the only way to go."

As I listened I noticed the inside of the shells; they were

calcareous and smelled of amniotic fluid. I didn't know what amniotic fluid smelled like, but I knew it was like this—a smell of cytoplasm and dying, old secretions, ammonia.

"The only thing that matters to you," the prehistoric pigeon went on, "is the thrill of militancy. The ferocious infection."

"I'd like to have a child," I interrupted him suddenly. I wasn't addressing him anymore. "I want a child."

"You're eleven years old."

I paid no attention. His objection seemed logical but it wasn't. There was no logic in it at all.

"I want a child," I said again.

"Nimbus, you can't have children. You may want them but you can't."

"Why not?"

"I've just told you: because your imagination generates only struggle and decay. And because a child is the danger."

"A danger?"

"*The* danger, Nimbus. The infection you couldn't endure."

I thought of my simulated spasms before I went to sleep, of how I longed to embody infection, of how those spasms resembled those of a mother when she gives birth, and a baby when it's born. Since the death of the natural cripple, my simulations had taken a different form.

My thoughts were interrupted by a movement at my side. The prehistoric pigeon was staring at me. He was still restraining his anger; I could hear it sizzling.

"You're incapable of perceiving anything that's fertile," he said, "or understanding that what is fertile is a responsibility. You spend your time creating distorted forms and artificial alphabets, thinking about words."

He stopped talking. He made a movement with his head, a brief shake to accompany his thoughts, like some grandfathers and some politicians.

"You're like me," he said. "You turn panic into existence."

He cocked his head at me again and seemed to open one of his wings. Then he hopped across the dust to the bush, stopped for a moment in front of it, examined an opening in the branches, and disappeared into it.

Now the breeze passed softly through the clearing, bringing little sounds with it—the elastic tremor of clotheslines stretched across balconies, the quick flash of a sheet hung out to dry.

In the evening, after dinner, I felt drowsy and lay down on my bed fully dressed, without taking my shoes off. The light was still on. I fell asleep as I measured its intensity, my eyes wet. I had no dreams.

·

The next day was still vacation. I went out, walked as far as Via Maqueda, turned along Via Vittorio Emanuele, and came to Piazza Marina—the yanked-out railing of Villa Garibaldi, the split sidewalk, and the Moreton Bay fig trees. Even the smaller ones were majestic; and one, in a corner of the gardens, was immense.

Being a father was that same monster of climbing roots, the same explosion of plant-snakes intertwining to form one upward-soaring branch, a mass of living tissue that over the centuries had built the shape of the father and his natural despair: Stone's despair when he came home at night, the despair of working day after day to put together meaning; reading the Bible every night, though nobody could believe; his square, fleshy face and compact hands, his fingernails cut neatly along the fingertips; the wedding ring on his ring finger, his fingers, his wrist; his watch with its strap and its metal case and a green blotch on the glass.

I squeezed between the climbers, clung onto them, slipped through the gaps, coiled up in the branches; I ran my hand along the spine of a root that curved away, disappearing into the dust ten meters from the main trunk; I lay down in a fork between two branches, the leaves forming a nimbus around my head.

When I got home later that morning, Crematogastra was in the kitchen, sitting on the utility sink. She'd finished cleaning and was waiting for her son to come and get her. I never talked to her because she only spoke dialect. I avoided her; a nod of the head in greeting, nothing more.

I opened the fridge; I was hungry. On the utility sink Crematogastra was regulating her breathing: she ventilated and hyperventilated, then her breathing became more regular. I got out some cheese, cut off a piece, and put it in my mouth.

"Nimbus," I heard behind my back.

I didn't turn around; I kept the cheese in my mouth, my mouth bulging.

"Nimbus," Crematogastra repeated calmly, "what are you three boys going to do?"

The voice was hers, the voice I usually listened to without understanding a word. But she was speaking Italian—clearly, without a trace of an accent.

I swallowed, put the rest of the cheese back in the fridge, and turned around.

"We're going to go on."

"Do you think that's a logical decision?"

"It's not a question of logic," I said, pulling out a chair and sitting down at the table. "It's a question of circumstances. Time."

I paused.

"There are circumstances in which logic is suspended," I added, "when it doesn't apply: other rules exist in its place."

"What rules?"

"The rules of struggle."

"Does that make you more solid?"

"In a way. But we're not stupid, we know our limitations."

"I wouldn't have thought so, from the way you express yourselves."

"We have to express ourselves like that. Those are the rules of magniloquence."

Crematogastra pushed down on the edge of the sink on one side and on the washing machine on the other. She got up and shifted her position. Then she went on:

"More rules."

"Rules are important," I said.

"Do you have a rule about time?"

"Yes, we've decided that time is short. Or rather, we've decided to look upon this period of time as something that will soon end."

"Well, 1978 *will* soon end. Time doesn't end, though."

"It doesn't matter," I said. "We think about the last things. About end times."

"About egg timers," she said, her tone turning frivolous.

"We need to be aware that we're coming to an end."

"Does Scarmiglia think that too?"

"Even more strongly than I do."

"Does Bocca?"

I nodded.

"Don't any of you worry that your anxiety might seem ridiculous?"

"Someone has to take responsibility for the ridiculous. For thinking ridiculous things. For saying them, and then doing them. Otherwise nothing happens."

I paused and gathered my breath.

"Being ridiculous is the price you pay for the tragic," I said.

"It's a political process," she said.

"A responsibility," I said.

Crematogastra stared at the floor for a few seconds; then she spoke again.

"Do you really believe that?"

"I have to."

"It's a superstition."

"It's necessary."

"But it's a superstition."

"The stories Stone reads to us from the Bible are superstition too. I listen and I don't believe them, but I like the form the Bible gives to the world: in the Bible the world is a serious thing."

"Yes, the structure holds," she said.

"It's a machine that produces meaning," I explained. "In the beginning there's disorder, sickness, and error; at the end, the cosmos, salvation, and justice."

The intercom at the main door of the apartment buzzed. Crematogastra snorted, got up, smoothed down her light-blue skirt, and bustled off; when she reached the kitchen doorway she turned around. She seemed on the point of speaking, but didn't say anything; she just stared at me, or rather, she examined me. Then she waddled out into the hallway.

In the afternoon my curly-haired cousin came to pick me up on her scooter. I got on behind her, and we went to her film-buff friend's apartment—in town this time. He'd ordered some new movies and begun a new series of showings. The setup was the same as in the summer, only with more jackets and fewer espadrilles in evidence. Since my hair was growing back, the friend didn't usher me toward the armchair or the sofa this time, but motioned to me to sit on the floor. Everyone else was older than me, in their late teens or early twenties. They said some stupid things to me, and when, to the same repeated question, I replied, "I've just finished my first year at middle school, and I'm just going to start my second," they nudged each other on the shoulder and chest, saying, "Remember the days?" and forgot about me.

After a few pleasantries our host, with the same bandanna around his neck, speaking in the same squawky voice, an-

nounced that today we were going to watch a film directed by
Cassavetes, which he pronounced with a voiced double *s*, turning it into a double *z*, in the mistaken belief that he was being
authentic. He stressed that Cassavetes, though an American,
was an independent and a comrade. Then, in his usual awk-
ward manner, he said, "Right, then, the title is *A Woman Under
the Influence*," and sat down behind the projector.

The film was about a married couple. They were in their
bedroom and couldn't sleep. The husband was a factory worker
and had been working all night; the wife was a nutcase and
had been whistling all night. Above the bed was a large window screened by Venetian blinds; light fell in fragments.

Sitting on the bristly carpet with my back against the sofa, I
watched the wife get up, comical and irritable, and walk into
the bathroom, on the door of which there was a notice saying
PRIVATE. The husband tried to get back to sleep, but the children came in and jumped on the bed to show him they'd
learned how to whistle, though when they tried to do so the
result was barely audible, a chorus of enthusiastic puffs con-
verging on the middle of the bed. At this point the husband
gave up all thoughts of sleep, gathered them on the bed, and
taught them to whistle "Jingle Bells."

The reel ended and there was a pause while the next one
was being loaded. Beer was passed around; I was given a plastic
cup full of water. I drank, bit the plastic, and checked the teeth-
marks: I was caricatural. Meanwhile my curly-headed cousin
chatted to a boy whose hair was like mine had been before I'd
shaved it off: brown and floppy, with a ridge on top. Our host
fitted the new reel onto the spindle, hooked on the end of the
film, and the projector shone its beam on the wall. The film
resumed.

In the dark, the story went on with the wife singing and going crazy. I rubbed my fingers, then straightened my torso, raised
my shoulders and spread my arms like a hawk's wings; another

rub of the fingers and a hop from a sitting position, three times; a third rub and again I spread my arms. They told me to stop it, my hands were throwing shadows on the screen; they rebuked my cousin, saying this kind of film wasn't suitable for children; she glared at me and I sat still, quiet but unrepentant.

After six months in a psychiatric clinic, the wife returned home. There was a party, to which relatives came; they were tense and drawn; they hugged the wife and clasped her hands in theirs. Then there was a quarrel and the relatives left; another quarrel, and the wife climbed up on a table in the living room and waved her arms about, mutely singing *Swan Lake*, while the husband tried to stop her. Then the children surrounded the father to keep him away from her and people started chasing one another up and down stairs; the wife ran into the bathroom and got out a bottle and some pills, and a few seconds later her hand was covered in blood—she'd cut herself with glass and picked up some razor blades and grasped one in her fist. She reminded me of String and her unhappiness with being a wife, String going crazy with blood on her palm. I looked around and saw the others pale in the glow from the projector. I rubbed my fingers again, stuck one leg out sideways, and gave a few backward kicks against the sofa, then I nodded my head, aiming the nods at my cousin's friends one after another in an arc, like a burst of machine-gun fire; I aimed another nod at my cousin, who didn't react, and two more at the wife in the film and the absent String. Finally our host turned off the projector, switched on the light, and asked, "What's he doing?" staring at my epileptic fit, this new manifestation of my spasms. He said, "He's not well." I looked at him, but my cousin grabbed my hand before I could start rubbing my fingers again; then she pulled me to my feet and said goodbye to the others, and we left. As we rode along on the scooter, she talked to me and asked questions. Sitting behind her, I smelled the scent of her hair; I was calmer now but I said nothing.

We reached Mondello, parked the scooter, and went for a stroll along the seafront. I was on the point of asking her if she wanted to go to the Addaura and see what I could do with bees, but thought better of it. I listened to her, noting her curly, bouffant hair, her String-like nose, her blue blouse, her floral skirt over her knee-length socks and clogs, and her schematic way of moving her hands as she talked.

"You're in the Red Brigades?" I asked.

She stopped short.

"What?"

"You're in the Red Brigades," I said. My intonation was no longer interrogative; I was stating a fact.

"What do you mean?"

"I mean you're a comrade; someone involved in the struggle. You let your hair hang loose. You wear those clothes. You smell nice. You don't wear rouge."

"So?"

"So you're in the Red Brigades."

She examined me. My skull was covered with a dark brown moss. The hair was still sparse, though thicker in some places, especially over the parietal bones, and the variation in density created shapes and undulations that followed the curvature of the bones. My cousin looked at the shapes, peering at them intensely, as if she could sense something, read an image of the future in them. I hoped she'd see fighting, warriors, men and women with their arms and legs interlocked in struggle and sex. I wanted her to tell me what she saw. But she said nothing and walked on.

We arrived at the public beach and went on toward Capo Gallo. We walked across a broken layer of rock, passing gingerly over jagged and slippery sections, and stopped in a little cove among the rocks, a few meters from the sea. There were still some people swimming, but we were in an open-air capsule, invisible and protected from sounds. I pulled a limpet off a rock and laid it upside down in the sun; my cousin picked it up and threw it into the water. She was right. I was sorry, because I wanted her to trust me, to tell me about the pain and pride of the struggle. When I saw a crab scuttle sideways along the greenish bed of a pool I moved my foot to allow it to reach its lair undisturbed, but it stopped halfway, hesitantly. In the meantime my cousin said nothing. As tiredness seized my lungs and I felt a slight fever of lethargy spread through me, she said she didn't understand what was happening to me—the way I reacted, the things I talked about, the way I talked—that perhaps I didn't know, or didn't remember, but I didn't use to be like this. She didn't expect me to tell her what was wrong, what was bothering me, but she wanted me to think about the embarrassment I'd caused her, how much concern I was causing to everyone. That was all she asked of me, to think about it. And not to talk about things like the ones I'd mentioned earlier, because if *she* was listening, it was one thing, but if I talked about them at other times and with other people it could be different, I might cause trouble.

That, I thought, was the problem. Needing to speak. Finding a way of translating hunger into words. If I didn't find a language, the hunger would remain hunger. I had thought my cousin might listen and tell me; but no. She sounded didactic. Not like the others—her tone wasn't indignant and censorious; but she'd chosen not to tell me anything and to resort to moderation and defensiveness.

The crab had started moving again beneath the surface of the water. It slid obliquely into its lair with wet, crackly movements. My cousin got to her feet and said, "Now let's go home."

•

The next day Scarmiglia phoned me. He said before the beginning of school, which was only five days away, it was essential that we get together. He'd already spoken to Bocca;

they'd agreed to meet at three o'clock that afternoon, at the clearing.

I arrived ten minutes early, walked into the clearing, and found myself in front of the bush. I walked around it, bent down, and searched underneath, in the gaps that were visible at the bottom. I put my ear to them; Scarmiglia caught me at my auscultation.

"What are you doing?" he asked.

I got up and said nothing, but made an embarrassed sound with my mouth; he looked at me but didn't press me. We waited a few minutes and Bocca arrived. Their heads too were covered with short, close-packed hairs; fair in the case of Bocca, dark in that of Scarmiglia. We sat down on the ground and Scarmiglia immediately explained what he'd been wanting to tell us. That we couldn't waste time. That it was vital we start doing something concrete. That the time had come, therefore, to plan some operations and carry them out. "But first of all," he said, "we must change the way we see ourselves, which is still childish, despite everything."

"When you think of me," he said, "what do you think?"

I didn't reply; I feared his analytical powers. The question seemed straightforward enough, yet I sensed the judgment implicit in it. And the judgment that would flow from my answer.

"What I mean is," he said, "when you think of me, who do you see?"

"I see you," I said.

"And who am I?"

"Scarmiglia."

"Exactly, and that's no good. The way we see each other is still dictated by habit. Since we call ourselves by our surnames at school, we do the same out of school."

"That's true," said Bocca. "I think of you both by your surnames."

"And yet," said Scarmiglia, "we chose new names for ourselves: Flight, Radius, and Nimbus. Our code names. But we
never used them. It was almost as if they were clothes too small
for our bodies. But things have changed since then. Our bodies have slimmed down, our movements have become more
precise: from now on it's essential we call each other by those
names. It's part of our metamorphosis."

"Like snakes shedding their skins," said Bocca.

"You're right," I said to Scarmiglia. "I mean, you're right,
Comrade Flight."

Comrade Flight gave me a curt, crystalline smile.

"Thank you, Comrade Nimbus."

"And now that we've adopted our names, what are we going to do?" asked Comrade Radius.

"Radicalize," said Flight.

"And what does that mean?"

"It means carry out real operations. Pathological operations. Starting with simple ones."

Comrade Radius and I listened intently. Again I sensed that
Comrade Flight's thought had greater capacity than mine;
more attention to detail, more grit.

"First of all," he said, "we must learn how to tail."

"You mean follow someone?" I asked.

"Tailing, Comrade Nimbus, is different from following."

I liked being called Comrade Nimbus; I liked mentally
translating Bocca into Radius and Scarmiglia into Flight: by
being translated they were disembodied, and became tools that
helped in the process of turning us into militant machines.
Sometimes I forgot, but I always corrected myself at once;
my mind retracted the old names and substituted the code
versions. Soon, I told myself, they would come naturally.

"Tailing," said Flight, "is not what we've seen in films.
Tailing is prayer. We don't believe in God but we can understand what prayer is: tailing is silent prayer that uses move-

ments instead of words, prayer by means of which our body appeals to another body—not a divine one but an earthly one—and to a space; this body and this space possess a secret which we must make them divulge by tailing them."

Flight stopped talking and stood up; he suggested we try an experiment. We went out on to the street, and he asked us to wait. In less than five minutes, a boy not much older than us walked by on the opposite sidewalk. He was small and wore a denim jacket, red pants, and white sneakers. Flight told Radius to tail him. At the same time we would tail Radius.

Radius closed in on the boy, who was strolling along in the direction of Viale delle Alpi, and came to within two or three meters of him. However, he failed to match his pace to that of his quarry and nearly bumped into him, so he had to drop back and start off again, but a minute later he was right up behind him again. Thirty meters farther back, Flight and I watched him lurching back and forth, his sole concern not to lose contact with his target; instead of interpreting space, he was being dominated by it.

"Look at him," said Flight. "He's like a yo-yo."

"The tailee," he went on, "can take the tailer anywhere, just as prayer can reach out an infinite distance toward a retreating, elusive god. So it's vital to keep your bearings. Instead of sticking so close to him, Radius should let him get at least fifty meters ahead and switch to the opposite sidewalk; that would give him better perspective."

We accelerated and drew even with them, on the other side of the street. Radius was concentrating so hard that he didn't notice us. Whenever the boy stopped for some reason—a traffic light, a shop window—Radius didn't know what to do; he slowed down and feigned an implausible indifference.

The tailing went on for another twenty minutes, in the direction of Viale Strasburgo and Via Belgio. Flight explained to me that it was possible to deduce your quarry's destination.

What you had to do was plot a series of variables: his physical appearance, the way he was dressed, the speed he walked at, the distance he covered, and the time of day when he did it.

"For example," he said, "this boy's middle class. You can tell that from his haircut, a compromise between fashion and tradition; from the way he wears his shirt inside his pants; and from the soles of his shoes, which are worn down to the edge of the rubber, a sign that he uses them both for gym and as normal shoes. He's someone who combines concrete goals with irrational fears, and who strides along, eager to get to his destination, but is frightened, because this isn't the district where he lives—when he comes to an intersection he always checks the street names; someone who'll be starting his first year at high school in a few days' time—a science high school, I'd guess (a classical school would be out of his league), someone who will buy his textbooks secondhand from older students, except for the religious studies ones, which he'll buy new, as a matter of respect; someone who's walking through a charmless area full of high-rise buildings, haberdasheries, and clothes shops, and who therefore, it should be obvious by now, is heading for Il Triangolo, the small but well-stocked sports shop, which is just up ahead, on Via Aquileia, and is the only shop in the area where you can get a discount, from the blond owner who winks as she purses her flame-red lips.

"So," Flight continued, still keeping up a brisk pace, "in preparation for his entry into a new class this boy is on his way to buy some sneakers, something his parents have agreed to on condition that he walk to this other district in pursuit of a discount, because nothing reassures the middle classes so much as the mirage of a bargain. Hence the confident gait of one who for the first time in his life has ten or fifteen, maybe even twenty thousand lire in his pocket, and so feels particularly alive, because an awareness of money invigorates the body and the imagination."

As Flight speeded up to overtake Radius and the boy, I thought about what was happening in his brain, about the number of silent detonations that had occurred while he'd been speaking, and about how, whatever the accuracy of his deductions, what he'd said was a remarkable exercise in controlling things.

When he was twenty meters ahead of the two boys, Flight crossed the road and started walking back along the sidewalk toward them. He walked normally for ten paces and then, without stopping, started nodding his head vigorously, then twirled around, walked on, and after three more paces, nodded and twirled again.

The boy had seen him and slowed down. Radius didn't notice in time and bumped into him; as he fell he caught a glimpse of Flight nodding and twirling—you shame, you shame. Winded by his fall, Radius lay curled up on the sidewalk, gasping and trying to draw in air through his mouth and nose. As Flight and I strolled casually past, the boy looked at Radius squirming, coughing and crying, then turned around and walked off. We helped Radius to his feet and went to buy an ice cream at Stancampiano's, across the bridge on Via Notarbartolo. Flight explained Radius's mistakes to him, point by point. I listened and agreed, but it seemed to me that in fact there was no technique, only vague intentions mingled with chance. We decided that for a few days each of us would work on our own.

The following afternoon I went out and walked around, equipped with a notebook and a pen. Comrade Flight said we needed to know everything about every space. This was our second exercise. To observe and take notes. To find out the names of the streets, where the shops were, what they sold, where the streetlights were, the phone booths, the bus stops, electricity and telephone junction boxes. We had to know everything, so that we could turn any place into a theater for our actions.

I decided to explore a street not far from my home. I knew the street—I was always walking along it—and yet, as I rested my notebook on a blue Fiat 500, I realized that I didn't know its name.

Via Di Liberto—I read the name on the street sign—was a dead end, an offshoot of Via Sciuti, soon interrupted by a dividing wall that separated it from the arterial system of the railway lines of Notarbartolo Station. About fifty meters long in all, perhaps a little less. In the dividing wall there was a door made of dark metal, a service entrance for maintenance workers, I imagined. On the left, a small brown wooden door with a glass pane protected by a metal grid; next to this, a car mechanic's workshop, small and modest, the rolling shutter not fully raised. It must have been pushed up in the morning, but, not having reached the very top, was working its way slackly down again, a fractionally slow descent which didn't prevent you from going in but forced you to bend down. Inside, on a wall of tiles that must originally have been a quaint light blue but now were invaded by cumuliform patches of sludge, there hung a 1973 calendar showing Antonello Cuccureddu in action, ball at his feet: his shoulders hunched, his skin smeared with engine grease, his face rotting. Below Cuccureddu, blurred by the electric light, was an organic sculpture of the mechanic. Blue pants streaked with engine grease and a pink-and-black Palermo shirt—that cadaverous pink which colors the cheeks at the onset of death. He was petrified in humiliation, examining the entrails of a white Alfa Giulia, like those used by the police. In his hands he held a twisted piece of metal that he contemplated in disgust. Here too there was a flower stuck in a Coca-Cola bottle; this time a tattered geranium, in incongruously yellow water. Then there were some parked cars—mostly small, low-consumption, post-oil-crisis runabouts—a pair of stray dogs that shuttled between the garage and the mouth of the street, and a swirl of scraps of crumpled paper that periodically, caught by the wind, collected together to rustle faintly against the cars' tires.

When I finished the exercise I closed my book and set off toward Via Giusti. I waited, walked on, stopped, and started again. On reaching Via Petrarca I saw a possible target. He was a man of about fifty. Light-gray hair, round head, small introflexed body. He wore a brown jacket and a crumpled white shirt—it looked as if he'd sat on it. His pants too were brown, his moccasins patent leather. Color: brown. An excrementitious little man. He was clutching to his chest a jar wrapped in light-blue cloth held in place by a triple twist of string. He walked with a light step; he put a flourish into his stride that had something noble about it; I could only see the back of his head but I was sure that when he stretched his leg forward he smiled.

He worked as a clerk. At a public counter. Or in the back office of a bank, administered through memos and directives. He was a man who thought things like "respectfully yours," "the circumstances having arisen whereby," "I have pleasure in informing you that." He thought them and wrote them. But he had a way of walking that contrasted with the stereotype of the bureaucrat. He marched briskly into the future, though in the direction, now, of the Politeama, cheerfully swerving around the puddles that a September downpour had left on the road. So I revised my first idea: the excrementitious little man was indeed a clerk, but, having nursed some grudge for years, was taking a homemade bomb to the post office on Via Roma in pursuit of his incendiary plan.

I speeded up and moved alongside him. As we walked shoulder to shoulder, with him looking ahead and smiling, I seized my chance and sniffed him. He smelled of wet, matted cloth; a dog-chewed slipper on which the saliva had solidified; and clothes that were never aired, a smell linked to the way they'd been washed, to laundry detergent dissolving in a bowl at the bottom of a bathtub, and a fading collar soaking in it, with Raffaella Carrà on TV in the next room.

I moved on ahead, turned back to walk past him, described a circle, and went around him once; I whirled around and around him; I was a bee on a scouting mission. As I circled I stared at him unashamedly; he was ugly-looking, with a narrow forehead, a bent nose, and dark, pockmarked skin covered with a film of sweat. So he was ill, the jar contained not a bomb but his feces; he was taking it to a laboratory to have it analyzed; he'd contracted a tropical disease and they needed to examine the enterococcus to establish its nature. But a man like him didn't travel to the tropics. The jar contained one of his internal organs, then, something he'd had removed; he carried it around with him everywhere, like the inhabitants of the Moon in the comics, who walked around with their heads tucked under their arms. So somewhere beneath his shirt he had a scar, there'd been suffering in his life, a presentiment of death, but all this had left him with nothing but a strange ambulatory madness. Or the jar contained a tiny baby, the child that I longed for, curled up against glass walls misted over by its breath, the air dwindling second by second, and I must hurry to free it, prevent the little man from finding a place to hide it.

This was what tailing was, I thought: a multiplication of hypotheses, a proliferation of conjectures. Leaning over someone's life, sniffing it, contemplating its horror; being bewildered.

The little man stopped on Via Cavour outside a hunting and fishing shop. Standing next to each other, we stared through the window at the twisted limbs of multipurpose penknives. Our breath formed patches on the glass. I turned sideways and looked at him; he did the same and all at once seemed to recall all the times he'd seen me during the past hour. Before he could understand I flung myself on his arms, tugged at

him; he lost his balance and fell backward, grabbed hold of me
but I managed to shake him off, wrest the jar away from him
and run off toward Via Ruggiero Settimo and then toward
Piazzale Ungheria. I didn't stop till I was under the INA sky-
scraper. I tore at the string and the cloth, hurting myself in the
process—a red welt appeared on my palm—to reveal the jar,
which slipped out of my hand, hit the ground, and smashed to
release, like a dead man's ashes or a god scattering himself, several bloodred rosebuds that scattered along the street, and I
looked at the welt on my hand, my bloodied hand—like the
wife's, like String's—closed it and opened it again and it hurt.

One rosebud had fallen into a puddle of water and engine
oil. I bent down, picked it up, pushed my nose into the crust of
petals, and smelled a fresh alcoholic scent, vegetable hydrocar-
bon. While I sniffed, someone grabbed me hard by the neck
and gave me a wrench; the rosebud slipped out of my grasp and
fell back into the puddle. A young, angry carabiniere stood
there, his eyes bloodshot, his bandolier white against his light-
blue shirt; the little man and a handful of other people stood
behind him. The carabiniere shook me again, and yet again;
he disorientated me. He'd taken me for a dialectal boy, a purse
snatcher; the fact that my hair was so short was a further sign of
nefariousness because hair that short meant disease, abuse, lo-
botomy. I tried to speak, so that he could hear my Italian, but
he shook me again and the words came out in fragments.
Meanwhile the little man had got down on all fours to gather
up his rosebuds in dismay. I wished I could ask him why he
carried them around sealed in a glass jar, whether it was a gift
for a lover or an homage to someone who'd died, but I knew
I couldn't do that, so when one rosebud rolled near my feet I
kicked it to move it closer to him, but the carabiniere noticed,
misunderstood, cuffed me on the head, and said "*Stronzo*," the
word with the buzz, the black hornet. I decided to stay quiet
and let myself be led away like Pinocchio by the gendarmes,

but while the carabiniere shook me, twisted me around, and said, "This way," I caught a glimpse of the excrementitious little man picking up his rosebuds; one of them had fallen in a puddle—not the same puddle, but another one shaped like a horse's head, and the rosebud was the horse's eye; it watched me as I left.

In the barracks, they treated the palm of my hand, and then Stone and String arrived. They were alarmed and bewildered. When they heard what had happened they apologized profusely, expressed their dismay. They knew this wasn't some little prank that could be resolved with a talking-to or some token family punishment. I'd really done something serious this time, getting myself arrested for robbery and violence; if I'd been a few years older it might have meant prison. The carabinieri advised them to keep a close eye on me, I was at a critical age; they treated us to another three minutes of cops' educational theory and let us go. In the car Stone exploded. At first I turned pale. Then I refused to accept his method and withdrew into myself; I sat there in silence, not caring what he said or did.

While Cotton watched TV in the living room, munching on cookies, in the kitchen Stone and String acted like Barbapapàs, stretching out wide and fat, and then long and thin, before finally merging together into the shape of a Sanhedrin. They put me on trial. I took the form of Christ, then that of Caiaphas, then Christ, then Caiaphas again, switching schizophrenically back and forth between roles; finally I sat down on the utility sink and lapsed into a state of familial dejection. After two hours I was dismissed, and the Sanhedrin continued its deliberations behind closed doors.

I went into the living room to watch TV with Cotton. When he started to nod off I got up and changed channels. CTS was showing "coming soon" trailers for movies that were due to open in Palermo. The names and addresses of the theaters and the showing times were given at the top and bottom of the screen, while scenes from the film were shown in the space left in between. Some scenes were uninteresting, but suddenly I found myself watching a girl stretched out on a lawn, dressed in a short tartan skirt, part of her school uniform; her thighs came together, then parted a fraction, a little more, then closed again. A flicker of light between her thighs. I turned the volume knob down to zero, blocking Cotton's view with my body, and contemplated the infinitesimal light perceptible for every new, split-second opening—a bright dot, an inner flash, a firefly shining in a black womb. I looked around to check on Cotton, turned back toward the screen, inserted the tip of my thumb between my middle and index fingers, put my hand to the glass and pulled at the screen as if I were assisting a birth, and out of the screen, out of that white photon in the darkness between the girl's legs, I extracted, one after another, broken shells, three ants, some roots, Stone's fingers, a crab, some rosebuds, and a puddle shaped like a horse's head.

The puddle shaped like a horse's head still had its rosebud eye.

"How romantic you are, Nimbus," it said. "Incorrigibly so."

The adverb irritated me; it was ostentatious.

"Why?" I asked.

"Because you're a prey to militancy."

"Does that make me romantic?"

"Certainly. To be romantic is to be feverish: to imagine with all your might."

Its voice was liquid; the words formed through a movement of water, as if there were more solid nervures, elastic ligaments, inside it. Its tone was canny and playful, dreamy.

"You're right," I said. "It's all part of the metamorphosis: being feverish, imagining. They may seem trivial to you, but they're not to me. They're not to Comrade Flight and Comrade Radius either."

"*They're not to Comrade Flight and Comrade Radius either,*" it repeated, mimicking me.

I kept calm; there was no reason to quarrel.

"Not to them either," I said.

"Scarmiglia and Bocca don't exist anymore, do they? They have other names now. Quite a change. Highly significant."

"I see you're another ironist," I said.

"No, don't worry, I won't be ironic. What I really wanted was to ask you a question."

I waited and gazed at the puddle, the flower fully open now, with broad, vulgar petals.

"You used to have language," it said. "Now you have the alphamute."

I nodded.

"Was it worth it?"

"It was necessary."

"Why *necessary*?"

"Because the language—the one we had before, that included everything—was too much."

"What do you mean?"

"It was never-ending."

"Are the twenty-one poses of the alphamute more reassuring?"

"The alphamute has an end."

"Is that better?"

"Language is a boundless existence," I replied. "But there comes a point where you start to long for a different existence. One that's more limited, but more comprehensible."

"An existence where it's easy to tell the difference between goodies and baddies?" it asked.

"A form of life that tells us who we are, and who we have been," I said.

"And who you will be," it added.

Now the puddle shaped like a horse's head fell silent. It had achieved its objective.

"I was tired of language," I said.

"And militancy is the solution," it replied.

I didn't speak; I didn't know what to say.

"If you adopt that solution you forgo pleasure, Nimbus."

I bowed my head.

"If I adopt that solution I forgo pain," I said.

The edges of the puddle started to tremble. The water rippled, dispersed, spread out till it lost its shape; it evaporated and disappeared.

I turned off the television and stood there in front of the black screen. I heard a rustle; Cotton was standing beside me. His eyes dazed with sleep, he looked at the screen, then at me, then back at the screen, then he went up to it and put his ear to it, looked at it again, sniffed it, put his ear against the glass again, and sniffed determinedly once more. Then he stepped back into line with me; we stood gazing at ourselves in the blank television, our grayish-black silhouettes hollowed out in its reflection.

FIRE

(OCTOBER 1978)

When I told them about how I'd been arrested, Comrade Flight asked me a question.

"Didn't you declare yourself a political prisoner?"

"No, I didn't."

"You should have. You were captured on active duty."

"It was a training exercise, as a matter of fact," Comrade Radius interposed.

"There's no difference between training for an operation and carrying one out," replied Flight. "We're always militant, always fighting."

"Even when we're asleep?" said Radius.

Flight looked at him sternly, trying to make out if there was irony—our bête noire—in his question, or he'd asked it in good faith, in a pardonable fit of naïveté.

"Yes, comrade, even when we're asleep."

I didn't understand what he meant. We were always fighting,

he said. *Who* were we fighting, and who was fighting us? Like Flight, I felt a need to be persecuted, and yearned for a constant and devoted—yes, devoted—enemy who would satisfy my needs by persecuting me. But I didn't have such an enemy. Nobody *was* persecuting me.

"Listen, Flight," I said. "In fact, listen, both of you. If we go on like this, just learning techniques, we'll never get anywhere. We're operating in a vacuum; we don't exist. Our enemy's imaginary, a mirage. Take our tailing operations—we've been tailing people who weren't expecting to be tailed, who weren't targets in any sense of the word."

"Those were training exercises," said Comrade Flight. "It didn't matter who we tailed."

"You just said training and carrying out operations were the same thing," I replied.

"They are. We must always be ready, always be real, even when the context we're operating in doesn't know about us."

"That's just the point," I persisted. "Nobody does know about us."

Flight said nothing for a while; he saw the blind alley.

"We've also been learning techniques," he went on at last, "for shaking off someone who's tailing us, and eluding the surveillance of someone who's spying on us. And that's a paradox, because, as you rightly say, nobody *is* spying on us; the enemy is abstract."

"The enemy's a hypothesis," said Comrade Radius.

"More than that," I said. "He's something we hope for. We hope for a concrete enemy—someone or something. Otherwise he'll remain an abstraction."

"You're right," said Flight, listening with head bowed. "We must invent our enemy. If he doesn't exist, we must create him."

"But that's crazy," said Radius. "It'd be like choosing to have hallucinations—seeing something that doesn't exist and saying that it does."

"Comrade Radius," said Flight, "listen. There's no such thing as a perfect enemy. A real enemy is always imperfect: never perfectly evil and never perfectly invincible. He has mild, even gentle characteristics. He's vulnerable. The perfect enemy is the one you create yourself."

"But why can't we have an imperfect enemy?" Radius persisted. "If evil is imperfect, if it's so weak and helpless, why should we force things and give it a perfection it doesn't possess?"

"Because *we* have to be perfect," said Flight. "It would be demeaning for us to fight against an inferior enemy, who easily gives in or slips on a banana skin when he tries to fight us. It would defeat the purpose of our apprenticeship. Therefore we must supply the enemy with the qualities he lacks."

"What you're saying is, we must be his adversaries and his accomplices at the same time."

"Exactly."

"That's ridiculous! An imperfect enemy should be an advantage, a guarantee of winning."

Flight was silent again, for a long time, without looking at us. His thoughts had been prompted by an intuition of mine, but he had the ability to transform a spark into a bonfire, whereas I stopped at the spark; I guarded the flame without making anything of it.

He stood there in silence, making us feel that silence to him was work. Then, when we were no longer expecting an answer, he raised his head and stared at us with eyes that were black yet transparent.

"Who says we want to win?" he said.

•

When school started we decided that the first thing we had to do was introduce ourselves. One morning we got to school early, long before the others. Our classroom this year was on the ground floor. We all put on yellow rubber washing-up gloves. We filled a plastic basket under the blackboard with sheets of newspaper, poured alcohol into it, and threw in a match. When students and teachers noticed smoke and came running, they found a ball of fire blazing fiercely, melting the sides of the basket. We watched from the schoolyard windows.

Another time we waited till recess, when the classroom emptied; then we took some light, summery jackets off the coatracks on the walls and stuffed them into the area below the teacher's desk, into the niche to the right of the drawer, where the grade book was usually kept, and into the drawer itself, which we'd pulled out. More alcohol, another match, and another fire. This time we hurried back in with the others and were shocked and indignant. With our rubber gloves rolled up in our pockets we gaped in wonder at the burning desk, the flames billowing out from the desk, and the hungry combustion flooding the rectangular drawer.

Fear spread through the school. We felt proud. The principal called an assembly, with parents present too. They thought someone outside the school premises had discovered a means of entry and was getting into the classrooms unobserved to wreak havoc on the furniture.

We listened. Something was still missing.

A few days passed; we waited till everyone thought the emergency was over—that these had been two cases of high jinks and nothing more. Then one day, when we knew the school would stay open in the afternoon, as soon as the last bell rang at one o'clock and the students left, we went to the gym, slashed the imitation-leather cover of the high-jump mattress with a kitchen knife, pulled out the foam-rubber filling, and scattered it around. Before setting fire to it, Flight took a black marker pen and wrote the date and time on the wall, to make the details absolutely clear, and then added our message:

YOU CAN BELIEVE IT IF YOU LIKE—WE DON'T

And underneath, the signature: WIN.

The idea of using a line from the theme song of *Di nuovo tante scuse* had been Comrade Radius's. It was an extension of the concept of the alphamute—giving a political twist to Italian trash, this time the words of a song. When people read the graffiti on the wall of the burned-out gym, they'd immediately hear the voices of Raimondo Vianello and Sandra Mondaini singing inside their heads. The notion appealed to us; it added an extra bit of spice.

As for WIN, that was the name of our viral microcell. It was an acronym of "Wild Italian Nucleus": "wild" described the present time, the only time worth living in; "Italian" was what enraged us, the essence in which we were immersed; "nucleus" expressed our solidarity as a group.

We decided to carry out a new operation and make an even more unequivocal claim of responsibility. We wanted news of our activities to spread outside our area; our aim was to get a newspaper headline.

The site we chose was a small field behind the school full of mounds, dips, and holes, a garbage-littered wasteland that the school used for PE lessons, making us run single file up and down the slopes among broken bottles, open garbage bags disgorging their contents, and scores of cockroaches and rats.

The work fell into two phases: collection and destruction. The first involved stealing, over a period of several days, a series of objects whose disappearance, taken individually, wouldn't cause any alarm; everyone would think they'd lost this pencil or that book, or perhaps forgotten it at home. We'd steal dozens of pieces of school property, piece by piece.

Applying our usual techniques, covering one another and communicating by means of the alphamute, we went around the school stealing pencil cases, erasers, rulers and squares, two maps of Italy, one physical and one political, a map of Europe and a terrestrial globe, a reproduction of a seventeenth-century town plan of Palermo that hung on the wall in one of the hall-ways, several wooden crucifixes with tarnished, warped, and blackened figurines; not to mention sheets of Formica, which we peeled off desks without much trouble, boxes of chalk and blackboard erasers, part of the frame of a blackboard, a mop from a broom closet, all the religious affairs books we could lay our hands on, the cork from the Nativity set that had been made the previous December, also stored in the broom closet, and anything else we could find that could be hidden in a knapsack and carried away. We collected kilo upon kilo of material—at least three cubic meters of school property—distraint by installments. Many of the things we hid at home; others we left in the field, in bushes between the dunes.

Next we prepared for the second phase. Every morning, before going into class, we brought our plunder from where we'd hidden it at home and took it to the field, placing it out of sight, between dunes or in crevices.

Now it was time for the last phase: destruction.

One evening, taking advantage of the fact that the glow from the streetlights didn't reach the field, we gathered the ob-jects into a space between two dunes, a point clearly visible both from the road and from the entrance to the school. It took a while to move it all, but the final effect was remarkable. The next morning we arrived very early, each bringing four cans of alcohol bought at the supermarket. We'd hidden some long thick sticks behind the dunes, and rolls of cotton gauze inter-twined with string and other flammable materials. When the school was still closed and there was no one about in Piazza De Saliba, we sprinkled the heap with alcohol, poured more alco-hol onto the rolls of cotton gauze and lit the ends. As soon as the fire had gained rhythm and strength, we stood a few meters back and threw the rolls onto the heap. At first it didn't seem to be catching, and Comrade Radius was beginning to despair, but eventually it sent up a thin column of smoke, followed by two, three, four others, then the first little flame appeared, then a second, which spread, and then yet another, which cracked like a whip, urging its companions to work harder. We poked the fire with the sticks for a few minutes; then, when we were sure it wouldn't go out, and that the blaze would be long and fierce, we put our communiqué in a hole and slipped away.

Like the others, I went home, taking a different route from my usual one to avoid meeting anyone—a strategy we'd agreed on beforehand. Then I set off for school again. My body was covered in sweat, my legs were trembling, and I smelled of smoke, but I knew that by the time I got there the wind would have blown the smoke around and everyone would smell the same.

As soon as I turned into Via Galilei I saw that a crowd had already formed outside the school, and I slowed down—not because I was afraid but from of a sense of shame that I couldn't understand. At each step I pressed my foot down on the sidewalk, so that I could feel the sole flatten out and rise up again.

Radius and Flight were standing among the crowd of students, parents, and teachers, watching the fire. They looked pale, with the innocent, troubled air of mere bystanders. They weren't pretending, the expressions on their faces weren't feigned. What was happening went beyond our direct involvement and responsibility; it was as if we were experiencing for the first time what it meant to serve a cause that surpassed us in importance and intensity. As the sweat dried on our backs and chests, we watched the spectacle of ideology burning, its flames fueled by our lives; we were stunned and mesmerized, like the bees when the queen gathered the swarm around her and with her mythical power decided, in a single movement, where the center of the world would be.

The firefighters arrived, so we moved back and spread out around the perimeter of the field. The pumps generated jets of water that entered but didn't douse the fire that was devouring the heap; in the meantime the principal walked among the dunes, while one pupil recognized a notebook that had disappeared the previous week, others a half-burned cotton sweatshirt, a textbook, a charred ruler. Finally, anger erupted. People said it must be the work of the same group that had started the other fires; some parents shouted that this couldn't go on, that it was one thing to have the Red Brigades elsewhere, in Rome, or in the universities, or at worst in the secondary schools, but that this kind of thing could not be allowed to happen in middle school, among eleven- and twelve-year-old children.

One fuse still lay among the dunes. Comrade Flight stepped out of the crowd, picked it up, and looked at it as if he'd never seen it before. I saw a line that on the one hand joined his hand to the remains of the fire, and on the other connected his life—and mine and that of Radius— with the operations we'd carried out. It was a longer fuse than the ones we'd thrown on the heap—it ran back through time, both into our social roots—our solid middle-class backgrounds—and into our biological roots, our need for sensuality, power, and impotence.

The next day two articles about the fire appeared in the *Giornale di Sicilia*. In the first the reporter described what had happened, the state of alarm that existed in the school after what he described as the "umpteenth attack" on it. Previously, he wrote, these attacks had been dismissed as childish pranks, but now the matter was getting serious, especially since, judging from the last two claims of responsibility, the culprit—or more probably, culprits—were students. In conclusion, the article supported the parents' protests and criticized the principal and the teaching staff.

The second article referred to our communiqué. We'd written it on an Olivetti Lettera 22 typewriter kept on top of a closet at Comrade Flight's home, which no one ever used. It had taken us three days to compose it, painstakingly tapping out one draft after another on a sheet of brown paper that had originally been wrapped around a loaf of bread, waiting till everyone was out and taking turns to type when the tips of our forefingers got sore, our hands sweating inside our rubber gloves. The text was chiefly my work. I'd studied the Red Brigades' communiqués, sitting alone in the porn clearing every afternoon, scissors in hand, surrounded by newspaper cuttings, analyzing them in even more detail than we had done in May. I'd tried to dismantle and reassemble them, to change the syntax and think of different vocabulary. I wanted to change their style and create a different language: one that was still technical and violent, yet distinct from that of the Red Brigades, with a quality that was entirely our own. Now, on rereading my work in the newspaper, I realized that I'd failed. Despite all my efforts I was a prisoner of the phraseology that I'd tried to remodel.

According to the text, signed by the acronym WIN,

our patience is exhausted and the time of abuses is about to end. The intensification of school repression can only increase the potency of our attack. The small group of useful idiots that still fails to understand the extent of our struggle will soon have an opportunity to form a precise idea of who we are, what methods we use, and the direction in which we are heading. First of all, let it be clear that our group is connected, not by direct affiliation but by politico-libertarian inspiration, to those that have long been conducting a campaign of organized struggle against the ganglions of the Bourgeois State, namely the Red Brigades, of which we are therefore an offshoot. The Wild Italian Nucleus endorses the popular prosecution of every kind of Fascism and the indissolubility of political and military practice. Our final objective is to construct a single armed political organization involving society at all its levels, from the factories to the universities, from the army to the prisons and ultimately the schools—not, however, as has hitherto been naively assumed, only the higher secondary schools, but also the lower ones, where the level of attention to social issues, especially at the present time, is no "lower" than anyone else's. Political avant-gardes of a critical and rational nature, at this time when there is a natural acceleration of the processes that bring an individual to full maturity, are also present in middle-school classrooms, and we recommend that they not be underestimated. Our intrinsic nonexistence makes us both impossible to distinguish from others and almost invisible to any investigation that the State may attempt. Our thought is great but our bodies are elusive, and our agility enables us to pass through the mesh of any attempt at containment. We may justly claim to be the antibody that the school system has generated in order to defend itself from itself. Forced by risible considerations of age into a subordinate social position, we react by constructing the destruction of the system itself. The very fact that we put our challenge in these terms, stating explicitly that those responsible for the recent operations are inside the school, testifies to the certainty of our intangibility.

Then the article quoted our justification for this attack:

The aforementioned useful idiots are hereby informed that the present action is in the nature only of a warning. To continue to expose the classes of the school to the risk of infection and headlong falls and cuts to the arms and legs by compelling them to do their physical education lessons on what can only be described as "a garbage dump" is an abuse that can no longer be tolerated. We therefore demand that this perverse practice cease forthwith and that the said garbage dump never again be utilized for such purposes. The school bonfire that we have staged thus represents both the destruction of a structure, namely the school, which is dilapidated in itself (as witness the ease with which we were able to detach supposedly static parts of the said structure and take them away), and the destruction of a place, the vile garbage dump, which is a disgrace and outrage to any imaginable concept of education.

There followed three slogans, three war cries, which, we realized now, as we reread them in the newspaper, we'd unintentionally made into a paradox.

CARRYING THE ATTACK TO THE IMPERIALIST SCHOOL SYSTEM

SHATTERING THE STRUCTURES AND PLANS OF THE SLAVES OF PROFIT

YOU CAN BELIEVE IT IF YOU LIKE, WE DON'T

In our revolutionary fervor we hadn't considered the order of the sentences in which we'd tried to express our thoughts. The third sentence, a line from a lighthearted song converted into a sinister threat, undermined our intended meaning and made us look stupid. It was like pointing a machine gun at someone and then firing blanks.

At the end of the article the journalist, while acknowledging the gravity of what had occurred, couldn't resist pointing out how comic the conclusion of the communiqué seemed: a lapse into farce, a parody, a wink, as if to say, "Don't worry, guys, we're only joking."

"We'll get him for this," said Comrade Radius.

We were sitting on a bench in Piazza Strauss, near Piazzetta

Chopin. Some mothers were watching their children play. They were about twenty meters away and out of earshot, so Flight didn't mind Comrade Radius speaking emphatically and raising his voice; what he couldn't accept was the content of the sentence.

"We won't get him for anything," he said. "It's our fault, not his. We should have checked the communiqué more carefully."

He stared at me as he spoke, and this time there was no doubt that he was judging me.

"If anything," he went on, "we'll have to intensify our attacks in order to restore our credibility: it's the only way of showing we're not amateurs, and raising the stakes. In the meantime we'd better be prepared for a crackdown; things are going to change at school now."

He was right: the very next day they started summoning students to the principal's office. One at a time, all the students were called, both boys and girls; at first it had been announced that only boys would be interviewed, but then the girls had protested and demanded to be summoned as well. Everyone appeared before a committee comprising the principal, a few teachers, and a man not from the school who was immediately identified as a policeman. The principal spoke calmly, the policeman wore a disgusted expression. When it was our turn, each of us was quite relaxed about facing the interview. "We did it," historical truth would have said, but historical truth bowed to myth. We didn't even have to feign innocence, because when we answered the questions put to us by the principal and the policeman, it was like when we'd watched the fire—we genuinely felt we'd been mere spectators, like everyone else. Yes, we too had been the victims of minor thefts, but we hadn't even noticed; it was only when we'd been sifting through the debris of the fire with the others that one of us had found a pencil sharpener, another a charred soccer card album, another the stump of a pencil.

They kept me a little longer than the others. Somehow they'd found out about my encounter with the excrementitious little man. They ran checks and made a couple of phone calls, but then the matter was dropped. They concluded that there was unlikely to be any connection between the two acts: the one was too impulsive and bizarre, the other too carefully planned. I felt slightly aggrieved about this on a personal level, but from the point of view of the struggle, I said to myself, it was better this way.

•

"Obviously we can't do anything more at the school," said Flight, when the three of us met that afternoon in the clearing. "But it doesn't matter," he added. "We have a large part of the city at our disposal, thanks to the descriptions and analyses we've made. We'll choose a suitable, vulnerable target and strike there."

Our choice fell on the Arab Well in Piazza Edison. It was a quarter of an hour's walk from Via Sciuti and twenty minutes' walk from the school, in a district which must originally have been working-class—living accommodation for railway workers—but had since been gentrified. Piazza Edison was a circle enclosing a square, or rather a quadrangular hole, about twelve square meters in area, surrounded by a low wall topped by a railing. A bare stairway without any handrail ran around the walls, spiraling down to a depth of some twenty meters. Tufts of scruffy grass protruded from cracks in the rotting stone, nests of rats, and huge arthropods. At the bottom, where the stairway ended, an iron gate barred access to the chthonian world beyond.

We paid several visits to scope out the land. We checked the views from the buildings, the times when people came out on to their balconies, the likelihood of their seeing us, the risks of climbing over the railing and going down the stairway, and the amount of light provided in the evening by the moon and the streetlights on Via Libertà. There were no shops, and only a few people passed by, usually on their way home. Clear yet muffled sounds came from the apartments; otherwise all was quiet.

We rummaged through drawers in our homes for all the cloth we could find. I looked up the chapter on sewing in *Fanciulle operose*, String's old schoolbook. I felt uneasy, because I accepted the stereotype that sewing was a feminine activity, but being a comrade meant abandoning prejudice in favor of a hermaphroditic willingness to do whatever the struggle demanded. So I learned what it meant to impart form to something, to shape it, by sewing—the subtle laws of stitchcraft.

Armed with this technical knowledge, I met up with Radius and Flight. We went around the shops; we needed some foam rubber. We'd ruled out the idea of stealing the foam rubber that had been bought to refill the high-jump mattress at school; too much attention was focused on the school at the moment. We found shops that sold yellow foam-rubber soccer balls; but we'd need a lot of them and we didn't have enough money. Then Comrade Radius remembered that there was a vacant lot on Via Liguria where people dumped things they didn't need. We searched there, and among disintegrating refrigerators and dead animals we found what we needed: armchairs and sofas with torn covers that were losing their stuffing. The foam rubber was soaking wet and smelly, and in places as hard as brick, but it would do for our purposes.

We took the cushions away with us and piled them up in the clearing. We broke the foam rubber up with our hands, then packed it together to make bodies, each a meter and a half long, with heads, arms and roughly modeled hands, legs, and feet. Then we began to sew. We made skin out of pieces of cloth joined together and cut around the edges to give it a body's shape. We fitted the skin onto the foam rubber and made three human dummies.

The next stage involved finding various garments and ac-
cessories. This time we avoided taking things from our homes.
We went back to the garbage dump and found some things
there. A gray jacket, too big for the dummy, and some children's corduroy pants, too small. We adapted them and dressed
him; then we put pens and pencils in his jacket pocket. We
dressed another dummy in a pair of flared pants bought at a
market; they were blue and hung limply from the knee downward. For the top part we bought—again at a market—a
white shirt, a short-sleeved sweater embroidered with flowers,
and a Tolfa bag. We made our purchases on different days, in
different areas; each of us went alone, wearing a beret or sun-
glasses. The third dummy was the one that required the most
work. But Flight knew how to go about it. One afternoon he
accompanied one of his brothers to a friend's house. The friend
was at the university, studying at the department of chemistry
on Via Divisi. While they were chatting in his bedroom Flight
kept quiet; then, as soon as his brother and his friend had left
the room, he quickly and silently opened the drawers: it took
him a while but he found what he was looking for.

When he showed us the lab coat he was very pleased with
himself.

"It's white," said Comrade Radius.

"It belongs to a chemist," replied Flight.

"We need a blue one."

"We'll color it."

We spent several afternoons, after homework, hidden away
in the clearing, felt-tip pens between our fingers, bent over the
material. We mainly used dark blue, but also light blue and
black; the important thing was the overall effect. When I was
bent over like that, my chest was compressed and I found it
hard to breathe. I went on, despite the fact that it was a needless effort. The world was a simple thing, if you wanted it to
be, but we liked obstacles—we made a cult of them; we were

attracted by impediments and complicated tasks. They helped us to *feel* the enemy, to perfect him.

When the three dummies were ready, we rustled up some nooses, some long hard nails and a hammer, waited for the first available evening and moved into action. We told our families we were going to the movies; so we'd have to be finished by eleven o'clock. Carrying the dummies from the clearing to Piazza Edison took time. It wasn't far, but Flight had only managed to find one camping backpack—the source was one of his brothers again—so we had to make three trips. When we'd finished, we sat with our backs against a tree whose resinous trunk protruded crookedly from a flower bed, and we waited for the lights in the buildings to go out one by one. It was ten o'clock, but it was a hard-working area: people went to bed early. The lights dissolved in our eyes, the resin stuck to our fingers. We waited another ten minutes and climbed over the railing, hoisted the three dummies over too, and went down into the well. Halfway down we stopped and knocked in three nails, all in a row. To do this we put a folded piece of cloth between the head of the nail and the hammer blow, so that the only sound was a dull thud. We tied one end of the nooses to the nails and hung the dummies on the other, then we pinned the communiqué to the stomach of the middle one. Before we left, Comrade Flight took something out of his backpack and a second later we heard the sound of spraying; our slogan appeared in the half-light, on the wall beneath the dummies, this time without any other phrases, but with our acronym below it. Flight put the spray can in his backpack, we walked back up the steps, and twenty minutes later we were home.

It was two days before the news appeared in the newspapers—the time it took for the residents of Piazza Edison to notice the hanged dummies and inform the police; for the event to be transformed into a news item, and so forth.

The article described the scene as ghoulish, and continued with a string of other equally clichéd adjectives, but that was not the important thing. It acknowledged that something was happening in the city; it sensed an infection spreading. The absence of an immediate claim of responsibility, it said, meant that this group was interested not so much in publicizing a single act as in making its silent presence felt.

This time we felt grateful to the journalist for making explicit through his analysis what we wanted: to be constantly present, material, perceived by everyone, but in the way that ghosts are perceived, or light, or air—to enter through the eyes, or in the air people breathed, to be absorbed without anyone noticing.

The piece went on to discuss the graffiti and the communiqué, and explain the symbolism of the action. We'd hanged—WIN had hanged—three symbols of school power: the teacher dummy with his nondescript jacket; the custodian in his blue coat—and here the journalist noted that the coat had been entirely colored by hand, proof not so much of the poverty of our resources as of our application—and lastly a representative of high-school and university students, who claimed to be the only ones who had the right to carry on the struggle. By hanging them too, the Wild Italian Nucleus absolved itself of any complicity with a subversion that had become mannered, a parody of its former self, ineffectual protest that colluded with the very power it claimed to combat. The only credible avant-garde in Palermo now was that of middle-school students. It was their task to show the way with a new wave of initiatives in which the stakes would be steadily raised, passing from human dummies to dummy humans.

The idea of ending on a threat hinting that our next objectives would be real people had been Comrade Flight's. In proposing, or rather imposing it, he'd impressed on us that this wasn't just wishful thinking, or an idle threat; our next

operations really would target real people. "We have the ability," he said. "We have the means," he said. "And the duty."

•

I had trouble sleeping at night. When I got under the covers I
stayed awake. I heard Cotton's breathing, low and long, running through his body from head to toe, cleansing him. My
own breathing, by contrast, wasn't right. I tried to discipline it,
but that was the problem—you couldn't discipline breathing.
You couldn't order breath to flow into your mouth and lungs
like soldiers on parade. My breathing, despite having served my
body for eleven years, was unaware of itself and would have to
remain so; any attempt at control made sleep unnatural. So I
got out of bed again, walked along the hallway to the foyer,
curled up on the armchair, and stayed there listening to the
sounds of the television from the living room. Then I fell
asleep, until Stone gently lifted me up, walked me along the
hallway, and put me back into bed, where again I lay awake; I
waited till I heard the sound of Stone and String's breathing
from the other room, got up again, returned to the armchair,
and fell asleep. I woke up at dawn, when the first light entered
through the frosted windowpanes of the hallway. I went back
to the bedroom and entered my bed and a state midway between sleep and waking. I saw Wimbow as she'd been at the
beginning of the month, on the first day of school, black and
red, her skin and her dark irises luminous, an unexpected smile
when she'd seen me arrive. The movement of her hand, a
glimpse of the little pale patch; I didn't know whether it was a
wave or a gesture telling me not to approach. Wimbow during
the following days, absorbed in reading, in learning the words
of history and geography, the words for describing the Antilles,
while I was stealing and smashing and burning and hanging.

Soon I'd have to get up, but in the blur of my drowsiness I
saw Wimbow again on the morning of the fire, with little

flames in her eyes, deciphering the scene and translating it into the language of silence. Then it was seven o'clock, String pulled up the blinds and woke us.

·

Our meetings in the clearing became more frequent. To Comrade Flight they were meetings of the executive, of the strategic command. Both he and Comrade Radius were increasingly concrete, constructive, clear. I stayed in the background; I found it hard to concentrate but didn't oppose any of their suggestions.

Flight said we were nearly there. One more operation directed at objects, one last step on the stairway, then we'd be ready for bodies.

This time our objective was the principal's car—setting fire to it. Not when it was parked at school, though; that would have been too dangerous, and incorrect from a strategic point of view. We had to find out where he lived and strike when it was parked outside his home. His address didn't appear in the telephone directory. We couldn't ask the teachers, and we couldn't run after his car. So we decided to adopt a progressive system that could be built up over several days—tailing in stages, you might call it.

First of all, when the last lesson finished at one o'clock we waited for the principal to come out of school and get into his car. It was an old red Simca 1000 and was in a poor state of repair, with mottling along the sides, wide scratches across the hood, and a dented fender; there was no mistaking it. Each of us took up a position at a turn that the car might take; we recorded which one he chose and compared notes the next morning; then we stationed ourselves a little farther away, always covering the alternatives. In this way, after a few days our tailing in stages was successful and we located the principal's home: Via Lo Jacono, a street parallel to Via Sciuti, near Via Nunzio Morello.

Now came the hard part: getting gas without buying it at a filling station.

Radius made a wild, and therefore plausible, suggestion. There was a scooter in the garage under the apartment building where he lived. It was a Piaggio, and it was broken. But he knew—he'd shaken it around and heard the sounds, and poked inside with a twig—that there was still fuel in the tank, a lot of it. The problem was getting it out.

We went to have a look. The scooter's tank was indeed full: we shook it and heard the fuel sloshing around. Radius suggested using a syringe—removing the needle, then sucking out the liquid, and squirting it into a container. The trouble was that once the first few liters of fuel had been sucked out, the syringe would be too short to reach the bottom, and the rest would be left inside. And it would take a long time.

"It would be better than sucking with a straw, though," said Radius.

So I discarded what would have been my first suggestion and moved on to the second, which was to find a way, I didn't yet know which, of lifting the scooter, turning it upside down, and pouring the fuel out of the tank.

Radius and Flight looked at me in silence, for a long time. I didn't feel so much mortified as tired.

Finally, after consulting *Il Modulo*, we hunted out a long, thin tube, a rag, and a bottle, and decided to apply the principle of communicating vessels.

The tank had to be on a higher level, the bottle on a lower one. We put the tube into the tank, sucked with our mouths, trying not to swallow the gas but doing it long enough to bring up the liquid; then we inserted the tube into the bottle and sealed it with the rag, and the tube filled up and channeled the gas into the bottle.

Now we were ready for action. Again we carried out our plan in the evening, telling our parents the same story as before, that we were going to the movies. We chose a Wednesday because there shouldn't be many people around. Comrade Flight had everything we needed in his backpack: the bottle full of gas, some dry rags, some cotton gauze, a thin, flexible metal rod, some thread, a sharp piece of iron, some pliers, and some matches. In the afternoon he'd checked to see where the principal had parked his car: a hundred meters away from his home, on Via Pascoli. In fact Flight had stayed there for a while, leaning casually against the side of the car, hands behind his back, trying to work the cap of the gas tank loose.

When we got there the car had gone. Flight said he was sure it had been parked in front of the printer's shop. As a rule the principal never went out in the afternoon and the car always stayed in the same place till the next morning. His wife didn't drive and they had no children.

Radius looked at Flight, stood with his legs apart and stretched his right arm upward, pointing with his forefinger: he did a John Travolta.

"Yes," said Flight, "you're right: unexpected."

There wasn't much time so we had to move fast. We decided to split up and walk around the blocks in the neighborhood. Not wanting to call to one another out loud we communicated at a distance using the alphamute. Fifteen minutes later Radius signaled to us and we joined him. The Simca was on Via Nunzio Morello, parked right in front of the shutters of the stationery shop.

"What's the matter?" Flight asked me.

"The shop belongs to someone I know," I said. "If we set fire to the car the shop will be burned down too."

"We can't help that."

"But he's got nothing to do with it."

He cocked his head as if listening to a distant sound.

"Do you think *anyone* has got nothing to do with it?" he said.

"*He* hasn't. He sells notebooks."

"We can't have any favoritism, Comrade Nimbus; it's out of the question."

"How do we justify involving someone who's completely innocent?"

"We don't have to justify it."

"Why not?"

"Because no one's completely innocent," he said. "Involvement is common to us all, and inevitable. We're born: we're involved."

Radius, crouching to the left of the car, motioned to us to be quiet. He'd already emptied the backpack. Flight stared at me and said it would be more useful if I watched the street corner. It was unlikely anyone would come, but it was better to be on the safe side. I said nothing and walked off. Flight joined Radius, and they talked for twenty seconds; there was a disagreement, the tension was palpable. Then Radius got up and moved to the other corner, in the opposite direction to mine, while Flight got down to work. He forced the cap of the gas tank open with the pliers and the piece of metal. The fact that he'd loosened it earlier made the job easier. He made two fuses out of cotton gauze with thread wound around it to bind it. He dipped the first fuse, which was about fifty centimeters long, in gas; when it was soaked he wrapped it around the metal rod and pushed it into the hole till it disappeared. Then he rolled one of the rags up tightly by twisting it, steeped it in gas, and stuffed it into the hole to block it up, leaving a corner sticking out. He picked up the second fuse—longer than the first, about three meters long—wetted it, tied one end to the protruding piece of rag, and unreeled it, moving as far as possible away from the car, to form a whitish, sinusoidal tail lying along the road.

Suddenly Comrade Radius started waving his arms. He pointed behind him and did, in quick succession, John Travolta, Celentano, and the Woobinda kangaroo: "unexpected," "imminent danger," "go away." Flight hadn't noticed him, so I did John Travolta too, thrusting my hand angrily skyward, but it was no use, Flight was intent on the last stages of priming the fuse and didn't see me. We were at an impasse for fifteen seconds, Radius and I at either end of the sidewalk miming a hawk and a kangaroo, Flight sixty meters away from us, at the vertex of an isosceles triangle, taming the white snake.

Then, finally, there was a rasp of the match against the end of the box—the sound of an animal's stomach being ripped open—an instantaneous mixing of phosphorus and oxygen, a tiny luminescence, then a pale little ball of fire that fizzed up, settled, and started marching along the snake's body.

Now Radius was no longer at his post and was running toward Flight. I wondered what I should do, whether I should do anything. The fuse was burning much more slowly than we'd expected. Flight bent down again and tried to light it farther along so that it would reach the car more quickly. Meanwhile, from the direction in which Radius had been pointing I saw four people, two boys and two girls, walking along and talking, and at the same moment Radius grabbed Flight, shook him, and pushed him away but Flight resisted, crouched down over the flame again, tended to it, encouraged it, so I ran toward them too, I heard the beats of my steps on the asphalt, my side hurt, farther up my rib throbbed and ached, I reached them and grabbed Flight by the arm but he wriggled free, I grabbed him by the neck and he fell backward as the fire devoured the fuse with a joyous, skipping rhythm, so Radius stamped on it but couldn't put it out, picked up the backpack and came toward me as I held Flight, who had turned back into Scarmiglia, and now Radius had turned back into Bocca, he had tears in his eyes and helped me drag Scarmiglia over to the other side of the road, we covered thirty, forty meters at speed and kept running and dragging; when we were some distance away I turned my head and saw that the four kids were coming around the corner into Via Nunzio Morello, I heard them laugh and a girl sang at the top of her lungs one of last summer's songs, which said there's no time to stop this endless rush that's sweeping us away, and I was filled with rage because it was absurd, there was no reason why this should happen, I left Scarmiglia with Bocca, turned back, and from the end of the road waved to the kids not to come forward, to go away, but they didn't see me, I ran another ten meters and now they raised their heads toward me, so I stood on tiptoe, opened my arms and mimed the falcon with a precise, measured, pulmonary, cardiac rhythm, raising and lowering my arms, a heartbeat shaped like danger; the kids said something to one another, called to me from afar, asked me what the matter was, was I ill, but I couldn't talk, I was forbidden to talk because I was a militant, I was a prisoner, and at that moment the fire bit the last piece of fuse, went down the pipe, spread along the second fuse inside the tank, there was a first flash, a scorching of space, a second flash, then the Simca exploded and I couldn't see a thing.

·

String and Stone were watching television; they heard the explosion and made several phone calls but couldn't find me. They asked our neighbor to stay with Cotton, then went out into the street, walked toward the lights of the sirens, toward the noise, asked questions, tried to make out what had happened. Then they saw me sitting on the steps of the church of San Michele. They approached, String hugged me, Stone touched my shoulders and my head, to see if I was real. I was real. I was dirty, my shirt was torn at the elbow, and there was a little blood. My rib was hurting again. They asked me questions. I said I'd been walking home from the Fiamma after the film and had just turned down a side street nearby when the explosion had occurred.

String asked me about the others. "Your comrades," she said.

I looked up; I saw her nose, her tears. I said they'd gone a different way home from the theater and I didn't know where they were.

Stone said we'd better leave.

I got up. To the right, where the corner of Via Nunzio Morello began, there was still a residue of flames inside the skeleton of the Simca; the firefighters were quenching it. The shop's shutter had been blown inward and there was a gash in the middle. Farther back were the police cars, an ambulance. Another ambulance had driven off with its siren squealing. There were people in bathrobes and slippers with ruffled hair; others wearing jackets over pajamas.

By the time we got home it was two in the morning. Cotton was with the neighbor, still awake; he came toward us barefoot and asked a question. I went into the bathroom; I needed a shower, I was covered in sweat and dust and I smelled of smoke. I sat down on the edge of the bath; a few minutes passed. I drank some water from the faucet and heard a faint scrabbling noise from the drain. I turned off the faucet and looked at the drain. The scrabbling continued and a few seconds later up out of the darkness came the legs of the mosquito. It crossed the metal ring that encircled the drain, then climbed up the ceramic, still hostile and determined. It avoided the droplets and sought out the dry areas; when it encountered a trickle, it twitched its legs irritably, found another route, and continued to climb. When it reached the rim of the basin I sat down on the edge of the bath. We were face to face.

"Hello, Nimbus."

I could barely hear it; my eyelids were drooping.

"No shower?"

"I'm tired," I said softly.

"Do you think it wouldn't be *decent*?"

Its voice was a nylon thread plucked by fingernails. Thin, elastic.

"You're right," it went on. "There are times when it's not decent to wash. Not hygienic. Better to leave the body soiled with struggle."

I looked at it. I should have asked it so many things. It would have been the natural thing to do. But talking was such an effort.

"Besides," it went on, "when epidermal dirt and inner chaos combine, blood becomes more appetizing. It has a richer flavor."

"Stop it."

The mosquito remained silent, like someone forcing himself to be patient. Irony hardening into sarcasm.

"All right, Nimbus," it said. "I'll stop it. In fact, I apologize. Perhaps this is not just a time for not washing; it's also a time for not talking."

"It's not a time for anything," I said.

"No, it's not a time at all," said the mosquito under its breath.

I bowed my head. Not a sound was to be heard, not even cars. Everything had vanished.

"Now," said the mosquito, "the problem is how to give form to responsibility."

I tried to look at it but couldn't bring it into focus.

"In the sense," it went on, "of establishing who is to blame for what—how much is due to the actions that were taken and how much to the intentions; how much goes beyond those intentions and how much is due to chance."

"Why do you speak of blame?" I asked.

"What do you expect me to speak of? A boy was nearly killed tonight."

"*Was* he killed?"

"No, he wasn't; he has injuries to his arms and legs. Badly

burned. The papers will report about it the day after tomorrow, the television news tomorrow. Later today."

I sat where I was for a while, leaning forward, elbows on knees. What I longed for more than anything else was to sleep.

"Do you want to know who he is?"

"No," I replied, without moving.

"Better to think of an inevitable victim, eh? Someone who was involved by the very nature of things?"

"It's not that."

"What is it, then?"

"We had no way of knowing that somebody would come along, that the fuse would burn so slowly, and that Comrade Flight would go crazy. Everything mingled together; it mingled badly."

"Was it impossible to predict your silence too?"

I straightened up again; I felt all the vertebrae that made up my backbone.

"I warned them."

"You said nothing."

"I said there was danger."

"You said nothing."

"I repeated it over and over again, as many times as I could."

"No, Nimbus: no. You made some movements that nobody except you, Bocca, and Scarmiglia understands."

"I spoke."

"That's not speaking."

I said nothing. Again I felt sleep rise powerfully up from my stomach. The mosquito moved a few centimeters along the edge of the basin. It stopped, came back and turned toward me again.

"Your white fuse was burning," it says, "first slowly and then picking up pace, on the asphalt. But there were other fuses too. Time and space, for example. And the fuse of four people in the street. Maybe they were coming home from the movies. Maybe from the Fiamma itself. Or from a pizzeria. Not many people eat out on Wednesdays and the service is quick. And those words were a fuse, words that are consumed, the knowing gestures and the stupid jokes. Then, at some point, someone stands up and says: 'Let's go.' So they walk part of the way along Via Notabartolo and enter the narrower streets—Via Petrarca, Via Leopardi. Another two hundred meters in one direction, a hundred in another—they turn, they talk—another fifty meters, they turn into Via Nunzio Morello and there's a girl with frizzy, romantic hair, the kind of hair you like, singing 'Figli delle stelle,' then she stops because at the end of the street she sees a little boy gesticulating but not saying a word; the girl and her friends look at him and walk a few meters farther on and the little boy stands up on tiptoe, spreads his arms, and arches his back. The friends think he's strange, they tell each other he's weird, they call out to him and ask him what the matter is, another word, a step, and then the explosion sweeps and erases, bodies hit cars, houses, the air turns hard, and there's fire, smoke, voices calling, shrill or deep, and roars and sirens."

The mosquito stopped and stared at me, forcing me to look at it.

"How do you calculate all that, Nimbus?"

I shook my head. Not defeatedly, but as if to banish an itch. I put my hands against the edge of the bath, on either side of my legs, to prop myself up.

"You don't calculate," I said. "You accept."

The mosquito moved thoughtfully on along the edge of the basin, walking on its spindly little legs, its stylet vibrating in front of it. Suddenly, without any comment, it turned and began to descend the white ceramic. I stood up.

"I have something to ask you," I said.

It stopped, turned its head back, and waited.

"I wanted to know about the blood."

It said nothing; its stylet continued to oscillate imperceptibly.

"My blood," I said. "And the Creole girl's. Inside you."

"What do you want to know?"

"About the mingled blood, what it was like."

"I bit you, but I didn't take your blood," it said. "There was no mingling."

It turned toward the bottom of the basin again, resumed its descent, reached the drain, and disappeared into it.

There was a knock at the door. I opened it. String asked me if I'd finished. I told her I hadn't washed, I was tired. As I came out of the bathroom she touched my head and I stopped, turned toward her, rubbed the place where she'd touched me, and walked off down the hallway. In the bedroom Cotton was asleep. I switched on my bedside lamp and got undressed, but didn't put on my pajamas. I slipped under the covers and felt as if I was slipping into a crevice. I fell asleep in the crevice, suddenly.

•

The next day I didn't go to school. I listened to the radio. They said there'd been an explosion in Palermo. They gave the name of the street. They said four young people who were passing by had been caught in the explosion and one of them had suffered severe burns. No one had claimed responsibility yet, but the incident was thought to be linked to recent events in the city, though it was far more serious than the other cases. They spoke of a Red Brigade threat, a new acronym, subversion, the armed struggle spreading rapidly even to cities that had hitherto been unaffected. As I listened, I thought it was like living in the third person, having your story told, being transformed from subject into object, existing in the perceptions of other people— something that might have seemed an abuse, a form of manipu- lation, but in fact was a pleasure.

When I spoke to Radius on the phone, he told me that after we'd split up he'd taken Flight home to Via Ugdulena, waited for him to calm down and go up to his apartment, and then he'd gone home himself. We discussed what they'd said on the radio, the boy with the burns. He told me not to read the newspapers tomorrow, and not to listen to the radio anymore, or watch television.

"It's not our fault," he said. "Sometimes harm is done without people intending it and affects someone they'd never intended to harm."

"It wasn't a matter of chance on this occasion," I said. "We went there to do harm."

"That's true, but we intended it as a symbolic gesture."

"We intended it as a symbolic gesture but we nearly killed someone."

"No, Comrade Nimbus, no. We didn't *nearly kill* anyone. We blew up a car; we destroyed some property, the property of the principal, a symbolic figure. That's what we did. The explosion belongs to the realm of the uncontrollable. It's like an earthquake: it's not out to get anyone, it doesn't hate anyone. We're responsible for lighting the fuse; from that point onward we're not involved."

He was quiet for a moment, waiting for his arguments to settle, inside the telephone wire, in my thoughts. Then he told me he'd had a call from Flight, who was calmer now. He'd apologized for last night; he shouldn't have lost control. It had been his frustration at the fuse not burning, at reality obstructing the plan. He'd thought about it during the night and now understood the nature of the problem; reality was unstable, and our plans must follow suit. He wanted us to meet that evening in the clearing, at six o'clock, to discuss it.

I heard sirens in the street. Mobilization. Grayish-green police cars, with their blue sirens and sweptback aerials. The dust lifted as they passed, forming a shell, then a ball; then the connections loosened, broke down completely, the individual particles scattered and settled in dots on the ground.

The others were already there. They were relaxed. Flight gave me a welcoming look; I returned it as I sat down by them on the matted grass. My ligaments were sore from all the running last night; on my elbow, under my shirt, were three Band-Aids covering a scrape. Flight wore a green sweater with no shirt underneath; it was made of old wool and had a musty smell. Radius wore a gray-and-black checked shirt. They both looked as if they'd been carved, excess matter pared away by the blade of a penknife; what remained was essential, the nervous system. On Flight, in particular, I could see veins and arteries, a forest of vessels branching out under his skin.

In Radius's opinion, what had happened yesterday was a crucial step along the way, a glorious one. The fact that we'd produced a serious casualty—those were his very words—was significant. In an operation still aimed at objects we'd hit a person: this proved that our power was greater than we were aware.

There was a few seconds' silence, during which Radius passed on the baton of exposition to Flight.

"The fact that the radio attributed paternity of the attack to us," he said, "means that our acronym is now so well known that we don't need to claim responsibility anymore. What's more, just as we imagined, no one suspects us, because the inquiries are carried out by adults and focus on other adults. Being eleven years old makes us invisible. It doesn't matter what we say in our communiqués. To them it's unthinkable that eleven-year-olds could be responsible for all this; we're ghosts."

The ghost, I thought, was me. Not because the others didn't give me a chance to speak—after all, I made no effort to do so—but because their analysis was already self-sufficient, spherical, complete. Any further comment would have been superfluous.

"The next step," said Radius, "is to target a person. But we'll have to take it one step at a time. It wouldn't be advisable to kidnap a major target right away; we need to refine the mechanism first."

"In other words," said Flight, "we need to master the process, its skeleton."

"Make a sculpture of a kidnapping," added Radius.

"Exactly, comrade," said Flight, supporting him. "Learn its form, take its measurements."

"As an exercise," said Radius.

"If we're going to do that," Flight went on, "it's important to choose the right person."

He paused. He'd completely regained control of the situation. And now he found in Radius something more than a mere comrade: an accomplice, into whom his theories penetrated and expanded.

"Since it's only a rehearsal," Flight went on, "albeit a very important one, the person we take on our shoulders must be an easy target. Someone vulnerable. Someone who'll help us understand what it means to collect a body, hide it, control it, and manipulate it."

Relegated to this role of a guest, an onlooker who listened and merely nodded in agreement, while Flight continued to describe our target, I thought about the nuances of his exposition. *Take on our shoulders*, the phrase he'd used a moment ago, was wonderful in its very absurdity. It expressed effort, encumberment, even suffering; a task you accepted against your will. But more importantly, it expressed a paternal sense, a consciousness of having to take care of something. When he'd discussed how responsibility for the attack had been ascribed to our group on the radio, Flight had used the word *paternity*. As if, through our actions, we were begetting children and becoming little fathers—fathers of actions, of silent alphabets, of fires and explosions.

As I pondered this I hadn't really been listening, except in snatches. I knew the person we targeted had to be manipulable, simple-minded, slow-moving, docile, physically small, free of ties, isolated; someone who wouldn't put up any resistance. I put all these individual qualities together and formed a constellation. I saw the image of our target, this son we'd have to capture and hide. It was the one technique we had yet to learn: how to guard the helpless, take care of the vulnerable. My desire.

PRESSURE

I tailed Morana. I did it alone, while Radius and Flight worked on the logistics of the kidnapping. I'd asked what point there was in tailing someone I knew and who knew me; I could simply have asked him where he lived, or walked home with him to find out which route he took, if we really needed to know. The reply was that it wouldn't be orthodox.

My tacit demotion to the status of mere factotum with no say was fine by me. I stayed in the atom but gravitated around the nucleus, a doubting, restless electron. After all, nothing specific had been said—the matter hadn't even been discussed—so I could still convince myself that this was a phase in which I did the tailing, while my two comrades, based on my reports, planned the kidnapping and subsequent imprisonment.

When Morana left school he walked across Piazza De Saliba—two hundred meters of emptiness, on non–market days.

He had an unusual way of walking; his right leg didn't line up with his left but described a semicircle to the right. Seen from behind, he moved diagonally: it was easy to keep him in sight. Moreover, he always went to the same places—his home on Via Aurispa, a drab, dark street whose name sounded to me like that of a cruel little spider; the streets around Via Aurispa, when he was sent out to buy something; and Villa Sperlinga, where he went to watch people even more often than I did, especially the kids on the lawns and the merry-go-round man, but also the pony and the dogs. He never rode the pony; with the dogs he made gloomy attempts at friendship, holding his hand out when they passed by. There was little or no response; at most a dog would slow down, look blankly at him, and move closer, only to stop, dazed by the aura he was penetrating, veer off to one side, and move away.

On Saturdays Morana changed his route. He didn't go straight home to Via Aurispa, the spider street, but walked to the station and then turned down Via Lincoln. I followed him as he went on to Villa Giulia, where he stopped outside the gate and stood there, gazing at the cast-iron pattern intertwined with climbers.

Most Palermitans went to Villa Giulia on Sunday mornings; I'd only ever been there once before. There were mutant families scattered among the flower beds; a little train that ran on an oval circuit, chugging around at a regular speed, with children crammed into its little red-and-blue cars; brutish oleanders, tall spindly palm trees, various shades of green; white statues cowering on pedestals as if trying to hide, and dusty gravel paths.

Morana walked through the gate and wandered around. He speeded up, stopped, retraced his steps, and went on again, an uncertain stutter of a walk; then he went through a gap between two flower beds and stopped in front of an iron cage on a concrete base. Inside the cage lay an old lion. It breathed with difficulty, shaking its mouth; its pendulous chops revealed pink gums; its eyes were glazed. A senile lion that never changed its position and looked at Morana through the bars.

I'd heard of the lion but had never seen it; I'd thought it was just a legend. But here it was, snorting occasionally, unable to raise a roar, and now and then tossing its head, making its whole body shake, and staring bitterly into the void beyond the hedges, the trees, and the gate, beyond the first sidewalk and the roadway of Via Lincoln, losing its anger out toward the sea.

Morana looked at the lion.

As I watched from a few meters back, hiding behind a banana leaf, I couldn't help admiring Morana. Although he was a child, he didn't behave like one; he didn't coo at the lion, go up to the cage and try to touch it, or offer it a demeaning, half-eaten crust of bread—he made no attempt at contact. The miserable, defeated animal lay there wheezing in its cage; the miserable, defeated little boy stood outside in the dust looking at it. Around them, the silence of a Saturday afternoon in early November, the air cool, the sunlight meeting few obstacles and shedding a stark, diffuse light on things.

When I showed them my notebook with the notes I'd made on routes, times, and situations, and explained the details to them, Radius and Flight listened in silence. They compared my drawings with their diagrams, spreading out piles of lists and tables on the grass of the clearing, all designed to help them calculate the ideal conditions for the "pickup"—that was the term they used.

"The biggest problem," said Radius, "is vulnerability."

I looked at him blankly; I had no idea what he meant. He'd acquired Flight's manner—the formulaic, esoteric phrase intended only for the initiate, the challenging, judgmental looks, the poses of a strategist.

"What I mean is," he went on, "because Morana is *always*

vulnerable, he presents us with a difficulty: his fragility is limitless."

"It's a provocation," Flight intervened. "Or rather, although it isn't a provocation in itself, we must regard it as one."

"What is this?" I asked. "Another step toward creating a perfect enemy?"

"You can see it that way if you want," said Radius, "but what Comrade Flight says is true: Morana provokes us with his vulnerability."

I was getting irritable; the skin of my hands itched. I knew it was tiredness, lack of sleep.

"But wasn't that why we chose Morana in the first place—because of his fragility?" I asked.

"Yes," said Comrade Radius, "but we can't let all our training go to waste just because he's always weak. We need obstacles."

"What kind of obstacles?" I asked.

"We could kidnap him when he's at school with the others, for example," replied Flight. "Or when he's with his parents. In the street, or some other crowded place."

"Or on Sunday," said Radius, "while he's having lunch with all his relatives. Or we could burst into a café in broad daylight: maybe we could even take him there ourselves, beforehand."

"We could do it crawling on all fours," I said. "Or hopping along on one leg, with one arm tied behind our backs. Zigzagging from one side to the other."

Flight stared at me.

"That's irony," he said.

I felt a bit guilty and said nothing. But there was something about the paradox we faced that made me uncomfortable.

"We need obstacles," Flight resumed imperturbably. "For afterward, for the future."

"I see," I said, and I thought about afterward, the future. I didn't ask how they intended to organize the kidnapping, whether they were thinking of demanding a ransom, or something similar. I didn't like to ask. I wanted them to tell me of their own volition, but they weren't giving anything away, only a few details about the place where they wanted to keep him. It was a small cellar, an underground concrete room, which Radius's father used for storing things. It was on Viale delle Magnolie, near my home and Flight's, and farther away from Radius's home, oddly enough. A few years ago, his family had lived on Viale delle Magnolie, then they'd moved and decided to rent their old apartment, but had kept the cellar for their own use as a storeroom.

"It's on the same level as the garages," Radius explained, "in a maze of corridors. Nobody ever goes down there. It's damp. There's enough space to build a little cell. We can find some of the materials we need around town, and use the wood from a cupboard and shelves that are stored in the cellar."

To make sure that his father couldn't get in, Radius wouldn't just make duplicates of the keys; he'd hide them. They weren't used often, so nobody would be surprised if they couldn't find them or couldn't remember where they'd put them. In an emergency, that would gain us time, while we decided what to do.

I still couldn't sleep at night. I continued the same nightly routine of walking along the hallway, trying to sleep in the armchair in the foyer, returning to the bedroom, going back along the hallway and settling down in the armchair again. I dozed for a few hours, hunched on a small, lumpy cushion, my knees pulled up to my chest, my back leaning uncomfortably against the armrest.

The school was still on high alert. In fact, since the boy's injury—about which I and the others feigned ignorance—the tension had increased. The policeman with the disgusted expression spent more and more time in the principal's office and we were all questioned again, one by one. They couldn't believe, when they looked at us, that the epicenter could be here, among desks, history books, the sweat of the gym, and preadolescence blooming in bodies.

In class, during lessons, I tried to focus my attention on the bridge of a nose, an ear, or anything that might distract my thoughts and give them respite. Next to me, Radius and Flight behaved like Bocca and Scarmiglia, two generally quiet, polite, and attentive pupils. I'd been told to follow their example—to be attentive and work hard; even a slight drop in performance might arouse suspicion, in the present circumstances. I did my best, but when I tried to read I couldn't concentrate. Once I caught myself writing in pencil in the margin of my math textbook, "You can believe it if you like, we don't"; and on another page, "Death to the dead." As soon as I realized what I'd done, I looked around and erased it, but the impression of the letters still seemed to be legible, so I tore out those parts of the pages and destroyed them.

For much of the time I looked at Morana as he listened limply, mouth half-open, head still, hair thin, and the joints of his fingers as large as knots. When the last class finished at one o'clock, I followed him home. He went in through the wooden wicket door, beyond which I could just see a narrow staircase. I stood outside, a short distance away, for another half an hour, examining the dark facades of buildings, while people swerved around me on the sidewalk. I hoped Morana would come out—I liked the idea of another trip to see the lion. He didn't, so I went home.

Then one day Morana went in and closed the wicket door behind him, only to come out five minutes later. He saw me and I said hello. He looked at me and rubbed his fingers together. I told him I was looking for a shoe shop, because I had to buy a pair of sneakers. It was two o'clock in the afternoon and all the shops were closed; I said I'd been waiting for them to open, but had felt thirsty and was looking for a snack bar. He still didn't say anything; there were scabs around his mouth and on his forehead and temples; they looked like bread crumbs. I felt embarrassed and tried not to stare at him. I took the piece of barbed wire out of my pocket and held it out.

"Look," I said.

Morana took it. For a moment my eyes closed; the air was cool but not cold, and the sun was out; it would have been good to sleep.

The barbed wire in his hands looked like a grasshopper. He touched it, turned it over, brought it to his nose, and sniffed it. I forced myself to keep a straight face.

"You use it to make those cuts," he said in a low voice, "at school."

He turned it over and over, looking for a top and a bottom, an inside and an outside. Then he stopped.

"We've got some water in my apartment," he said, giving it back to me. He turned around and walked away.

I hesitated for a few seconds, then accepted the apparent invitation. After all, it would be useful to know the layout of the place he lived in. Such a reconnaissance hadn't been planned, or even discussed at a meeting, but it could prove important if we decided to kidnap him when he was at home.

We went through the wicket door, climbed the narrow staircase, and came to an open door, which we entered. The apartment had a certain dignity. It conveyed a sense of what it must be like to carry on a constant battle against the impulse to abandon decency altogether. It was reasonably clean, and not untidy. The ornaments were tawdry, but this was a simple family; that was the way such people liked things and you had to accept it. Fancy glass trinkets on all horizontal surfaces; small pictures on the walls, painted by artists who held their brushes in their mouths, noses, or ears, exhibitions of deformed minor art; a predictable plump doll on the sofa, with her legs open and the edge of her satin skirt raised to reveal a mass of petticoats and gauze, her lips parted and dark marks on her forehead, looking as if she'd been abused every day for years by the entire family; two sprigs of bougainvillea in a Coca-Cola bottle, sparkling green and purple above the TV set; and an incredible number of doilies scattered everywhere, attempts to fill domestic emptiness.

Morana went into the kitchen and came back with a glass of water. I took it and examined it; the rim was wet: it had been drying on the rack. I tried to breathe on it and wipe it with my sleeve, aware of all the other mouths that had drunk from it; to put my lips to the glass would have been like kissing Morana, his family, and his whole life. I held it in my hand and waited for a chance to put it down on a doily where it could be forgotten. In the meantime Morana had crossed the living room and opened a French window that led to a terrace overlooking the courtyard; it was at least ten meters square and covered by a roof. The floor was scattered with grape stalks, fruitless twigs that twitched in the breeze, nervous movements of vegetal insects. They gave me a feeling of dirtiness, but delicate dirtiness. I didn't ask any questions but saw that each stalk had a different degree of dryness, a kind of patience, an ability to lie there and wait. In one corner there was a large red plastic washtub with handles, and beside it a wooden cage with an opening in the center. I imagined a dog's crate but I saw a goose. Morana noticed my surprise and was pleased.

"We got her at the Mediterranean Fair," he said.

He sounded embarrassed, whether about what he'd said or about the way he'd said it I couldn't tell. He spoke almost in a whisper, perhaps self-conscious about his dialectal accent.

"That was last year," he said. "She was small then."

She wasn't small now, I thought; she was a full-size goose, tall, white, and plump. She stood between the washtub and her

cage and looked at me, making it clear that, unlike me, she had
every right to be there, and to exist: she was one of the Mora-
nas, she lived on their terrace, she was their pet, their guard,
and their goose, and when we drew near I smelled the strong
but pleasant smell of her droppings. She moved toward me
puffing out her big breast, then swerved to one side, and started
waddling around crazily, tracing the symbol of infinity on the
floor, then a series of others overlapping one another, till she
released a first inch of excrement, then a second, and a third, as
if what she'd been doing until then had been a propitiatory
dance and she was now completing the ritual; only it wasn't
complete—she continued to trace the symbol of infinity; so
Morana got some sheets of newspaper from a corner and started
to follow her helicoidal movement, collecting clayey excreta
flecked with black and green membranes, rubbing and crum-
pling and putting each ball of paper into a plastic bag that hung
from his forearm.

A voice called out from inside. A woman appeared, eating
grapes. She took one last grape and threw the stalk, with a few
squashed dark pieces of fruit, onto the floor of the terrace: the
goose abandoned infinity and started feeding.

Morana's mother looked like a mournful iguana; rheu-
matic, to judge from the way she moved. She wore a checked
blouse and a light-blue skirt—that anonymous blue typical of
cheap skirts. When I went over to shake her hand I caught a
smell of half-dried crockery. She said something to her son
in dialect that I didn't understand. Correcting herself, she
switched to labored Italian; she told him she had time now, but
later she'd have to go out. Morana asked me to excuse him and
went back inside. I followed him as he collected a chair, a
towel, and a pair of scissors. He put the chair in the middle of
the living room, handed the scissors to his mother, and draped
the towel over his shoulders and chest.

A sacrifice, I thought: Morana as a disgusting Isaac, his

mother as Abraham slaughtering him, no angel to stop the stabbing hand.

The iguana started cutting and for ten minutes the only sounds were the snip of the scissors and the tap of the goose's beak against the closed French window—her feathery breast against the glass, her webbed feet spread into triangles, a chewed grape in her beak, and a wonderful expression in her eyes.

Morana was eating grapes too. He held a bunch in his lap under the towel; now and then his hand would come out and bring a grape up to his mouth.

Neither of them said a word to me—not, I thought, because they were relaxed about having strangers in their home, but owing to an atrophy of perception: they'd both reached the stage where nothing mattered anymore. As tufts of fair hair slid down neck, shoulders, and the deflated form of the towel, landing softly on the floor, I said goodbye, thanked them for the water, took one last look at the goose against the window-pane, and left.

•

We went into action on Saturday, the day the cold decided to emerge from its shell of molecules: it cracked it open and began to rage. We wore warm windproof jackets and scarves and stuffed ski masks in our pockets—they were superfluous, as we'd have to show our faces, but they lent us strength and comfort: self-mythification needs ornaments. Since we couldn't drive, we wouldn't be able to collect Morana in one part of the city and take him to Viale delle Magnolie: absurd as it might seem, he'd have to walk to Viale delle Magnolie on his own two feet.

After school, at one o'clock, I set off behind him. When he reached the end of Via Galilei I moved up alongside him and said hello. I suggested we go for a stroll in the direction of Villa Sperlinga. He said he couldn't, he had to go home. I knew he was lying, because this time on Saturdays was when he went to see the lion. I repeated my invitation. Again he turned me down, but he was beginning to waver; the need to deal with conflict disorientated him. I looked at his fresh haircut—the electric ends, softly sharp. I invited him again, he refused again, and Comrade Radius appeared at his side. He said the bus was coming and told us to get on. There was tension and bewilderment in Morana's eyes, but he quickened his pace and got on with us. We went to the back and contrived to get Morana into a corner, with Radius and me next to him.

"Why did we get on the bus?" I whispered to Radius. "This wasn't part of the plan."

"It's an obstacle," he replied, pulling up the collar of his jacket and wrapping his scarf around his face.

"We were supposed to walk there," I persisted. "It's dangerous going by bus."

"That's the whole point. We must be able to take risks," he said. "It increases our target's value too."

We turned toward Morana. He looked at us, then lowered his eyes. There weren't many people on the bus, and in any case, they could hardly have imagined that a consenting victim was being kidnapped and carried off on public transport.

We got off on Via Libertà, some way short of Viale delle Magnolie; we'd have to walk the last stretch. Morana said he had to be going. We said, "Sure, you can go in a minute. But let's go to Villa Sperlinga first, and have a ride on the pony."

He said nothing and kept walking. We ought to have walked at a normal pace, so as not to attract attention, but whenever Radius saw anyone up ahead he'd set off in pursuit, move up alongside, and steer in close to them, relishing the chance of a new obstacle.

Finally we reached Villa Sperlinga, where we turned right along Viale Campania. Morana followed us, looking at the pony, which was walking away between the flower beds.

"We'll go there later," Radius said to him quietly.

A hundred meters farther on we turned left, into Viale delle Magnolie. We walked another forty meters and stopped outside a wicket door. Radius looked around; there was no one in sight. It was two o'clock in the afternoon; people would be finishing lunch or taking a nap. Radius got out the keys and opened the door. We went down two flights of stairs; the walls lost their plaster and became bare cement. We went along a few corridors, passed what sounded like the boiler room, and shortly afterward Radius opened a small wooden door. Flight was waiting for us, with a dog leash in his hands. As soon as Morana was inside, he grabbed his arms and tied him up with the leash; the leather cut into his jacket and sweater and the skin below. Now Morana was helpless, though he wouldn't have put up any resistance anyway. We were slaves to orthodoxy, carrying out needless actions.

It was the first time I'd been in the cellar. I'd been excluded from the work of readying the prison during the past few days—to reduce the risk, they'd told me. I looked around: there were no windows; the only light was provided by a bulb protruding from a socket in the wall. Just as they'd said, the room was very small—each wall was about three and a half meters long—and not very high either. Anything that didn't serve our purposes had been removed. The walls had been lined with cardboard egg boxes—to soundproof them, Radius and Flight explained, implying a technical knowledge of which they intended to impart only a small fraction to me. I wondered, but didn't ask, where they'd gotten all the boxes. I imagined them eating eggs, nothing but eggs, day after day: focused, determined, their stomachs processing yolk and albumen, the boxes piling up in heaps. Against one of the walls was a cubicle within the cubicle: Morana's prison. It had been stoutly constructed, by nailing doors and pieces of plywood together and leaving a gap in the middle that could be closed by a shutter and locked with a bolt. It was like the goose cage, but with a starker, more violent form: a cage raised, or lowered, to the status of a bunker. The walls of the little cell had again been lined on the inside with egg boxes—more yolk, more albumen—and there was a blanket on the floor. There was a small cardboard box just outside the opening. It contained some cookies and a bottle, Radius explained. Near the box, a meter above the ground, a faucet protruded from the wall. It worked; this would be our source of water.

Flight made Morana crawl backward into the cell, so that his legs stuck out. Taking another leash, he tied his legs up too, pulling the leather so tight that the calves slipped out of alignment. Speaking quietly and articulating the words clearly, he told him to turn around and stick his head out. He asked him if he was thirsty, if he wanted some water. Morana shook his head, so Flight picked up a piece of rag, stuffed it into his mouth, took some brown adhesive packing tape, made him bend forward, and wound it around his head to hold the cloth in place. He checked that the tape hadn't covered his nose, and then told him to pull his knees up against his chest and put his head between his legs. Finally, helped by Radius, he pushed him in, closed the shutter, and slid home the bolt. He told him not to worry, we'd be back later.

We went out one after another, at twenty-minute intervals. First Flight, then me, then Radius. It was three o'clock when we split up. We agreed to be back by seven. Flight would come first on his own and unlock the door with his duplicate key. Radius and I would come later, after meeting up at Villa Sperlinga.

When I got home I went to bed. I felt no pity. I should have, but I didn't. I felt that things were falling into place. Although I was tired—in fact, *because* I was tired—everything seemed clearer: the nature of my relationships with the other two and with myself.

I fell into a deep sleep, and slept for a couple of hours. I woke up at five thirty; something was moving between my calves. I raised my head from the pillow; the natural cripple sniffed my pants, put his paw on my thigh, and walked up on to my chest, where he sat down.

"Nimbus," he said.

His coat was dry, still a grayish color, his eyes covered with hardened mucous, his legs spindly, his tail singed; yet he was breathtakingly beautiful.

"Hello," I said, laying my head back on the pillow.

"How are you?" he asked me.

"I've been taking a nap."

"It's been a quiet afternoon, then."

I nodded.

"You're pregnant," he said to me.

I was puzzled but didn't ask what he meant. Then I understood: yes, perhaps I was pregnant.

"Well, you did want a baby, didn't you?"

His voice was a mush of hair and scabs, disease and wounds. It poured dark and twisted out of his mouth; sometimes it hoarsened and broke, but almost instantly recovered its form and stretched out again, skeletal, arborescent.

"You have an external womb," he went on. "An incubator for premature infants. Cement on the outside, wood on the inside, and lined with egg boxes. I wonder where all those eggs went."

"I wondered about that too," I said.

He inspected me carefully. Someone else judging me. He got to the end of his thought and went on.

"And inside that double womb," he said, "cocooned in blankets and excrement, is the baby."

"Why *excrement*?"

"What do you think's going to happen in there, Nimbus? Do you think butterflies will come fluttering out of Morana's bowels? His shit turn into jasmine?"

I winced at the word he used. I always mentally corrected the word when I heard it. I said feces, I said excrement. I said poop. Or I found some other expression. Not shit.

"He was all right when we left," I said.

"A person doesn't have to be ill to generate excrement: *you* generate it every day and you're all right."

I thought of my womb generating a child that generated excrement. I saw he was leading me down a blind alley.

"And so the gestation proceeds," he went on: "the baby sleeps, shits himself, and waits to be born."

"I'll be seeing him in a minute," I said.

"And what are you going to do?"

"I don't know. He's been kidnapped. We'll have to wait and see."

"What do you mean, *wait and see*? What's the matter—is the strategic command cutting you out of things?"

"No. I'm *part of* the strategic command. I may disagree with some contingent choices, but as far as the fundamental ones are concerned there's complete agreement."

"What elegant prose, Nimbus! Truly elegant!"

I couldn't decipher the tone of his jibe, but I understood that it *was* one. I felt its sarcasm and cringed.

"You're not trying to distance yourself from anything, are you?" he asked.

"I told you, there are some decisions I don't entirely agree with, that's all."

"You go along with them."

"I go along with them. But I have confidence in my comrades."

"But you're not responsible for their decisions, is that what you're saying?"

"I know I'm involved."

"But only passively," he said. "Somebody else tips up the plank and you slide down it."

A gurgle rose through his mangy throat, a liquid anger that bubbled and pressed. His voice became fuller and richer.

"It won't wash," he said, thrusting his face forward and staring at me with his blind eyes. "You can't pass yourself off as a victim."

I felt the weight of his body pressing on my chest, suffocating me.

"You're not a victim, Nimbus. You're with them—not *like* them, perhaps, for what that's worth—but you're *with* them."

He was so close to me that my eyes swiveled and I went squinty-eyed.

"You're not active," he said again. "You don't do a thing that's not in the rules, you don't say a word that's not in the alphamute."

I said nothing and sniffed him. He smelled of damp earth and urine and excrement. Not excrement—shit; not urine—I didn't know what. He seemed pleased to be so close, pushing his smell into my face.

"Do you know why you can't be a victim?" he asked me.

He clearly didn't expect an answer.

"Because even now," he went on, bitterly, "you keep making claims and distinctions and high-sounding statements. You're just playing at being a victim. You're not a victim, Nimbus: you're the caricature of one."

My head sank farther into the pillow and my eyes closed. The natural cripple gave a deep sigh, turned around, and walked down from my chest and along my legs.

"Go on with your nap," he said.

I didn't hear him jump down from the bed; I was already asleep.

When I woke up it was twenty past seven and dark outside. I quickly rinsed my face and drank a few sips from the faucet. I went down to the street and set off at a brisk pace. When I reached Villa Sperlinga I saw Radius sitting on a bench. He came to meet me and reproached me for being late. I apologized and we started walking. We didn't speak for most of the way, but on Viale delle Magnolie, shortly before we reached the door, he said I had to be more workmanlike, more professional. He stared at the ground as he said it, in a clipped, mechanical tone.

We went down the stairs and along the corridors till we reached the cellar door. Radius knocked softly, in a coded sequence. There were more knocks from the other side. One more knock from Radius—I presumed it meant yes—and Flight opened the door. As soon as we entered I smelled the stink: barely four hours had passed and the air was already foul.

The electric light was on, but was dimmed and absorbed by the egg boxes. Flight ignored me and demanded an explanation for our late arrival from Radius. They argued tensely in low voices. Neither of them seemed to notice the smell. They weren't worried about me but about whether or not Morana's family was likely to have informed someone yet. Flight reckoned they wouldn't tell anyone for a while. In a family like that, he argued, people were slow to understand, and even slower to react. They agreed that this was to our advantage, because even when it dawned on Morana's family that he'd disappeared, they would hesitate before contacting the school, let alone the police.

While they talked, not a sound came from inside the cubicle, not so much as a grunt or a rustle. The only other noise was the buzz of the electric light.

"Time to feed him," said Radius.

They bent over the little cell, drew back the bolt, and opened the shutter. The smell became stronger. Flight reached in, shook one of Morana's legs and told him to come out. I heard him slide along on his bottom while Flight pulled him by his feet. He bent forward and put his head out; one last pull to extract him and he raised his head. Flight gripped one end of the packing tape, stripped it off, and removed the rag from his mouth.

"Don't say a word," he ordered.

Once again, the order was superfluous. Morana wasn't saying, and wouldn't have said, anything. He was waiting. No, not even waiting. He was existing, he was being. He was an organism made up of cells. It was as if everything about him was telling us that he didn't exist, except as a small body with no perception of the present and no imagination of the future. Like the kittens I'd held by the scruff of the neck in the summer, he was suspended not so much trustingly as helplessly, aware that his existence couldn't be any different.

Flight opened the box and took out some cookies and an empty bottle, which he filled with water from the faucet. He told Morana to open his mouth; Morana opened his mouth. Flight pushed into his mouth, a bit at a time—leaving time for the slow mastication—four cookies. Then he told him to put his head back. Morana put his head back. Flight opened the bottle and poured the water slowly down his throat. It overflowed a little but Morana didn't react. Flight wiped his face with the edge of the blanket, then told him to get back into the cell. I wanted to say that there was a smell, that he must have shit his pants, but I kept quiet. Flight stuffed the rag back into his mouth and put on the packing tape. The cell was closed again and we prepared to leave.

At nine o'clock in the evening we met outside a *rosticceria* on Via Notarbartolo. To get there I went along Via Nunzio Morello. There were some black marks on the wall of the building, in line with the explosion. Nunzio Morello's roll-down shutter had been replaced; the metal looked like tin foil.

We bought some food, walked a little way, and sat down on the benches in Piazza Campolo. There was sparse Saturday evening traffic around us; a few lights, a few voices.

Radius and Flight discussed the kidnap. Morana, they said,

was kidnapping degree zero—perfect for our needs: to analyze the phenomenology of the action. Partly for this reason—so that we'd only have to concern ourselves with essentials—we wouldn't be demanding a ransom. Later, things would change, they said.

As I listened to them I felt soft. My hands felt soft, so did my eyes; my mouth melted. I turned, made a nest of my arms on the back of the bench and laid my head on top, sideways, in the middle—the skull, the egg in the nest.

•

The next day was Sunday. Instead of sleeping late, I got up early and went out. It was the time of day when most people were attending mass or visiting relatives. I went to visit the kidnapped Morana, but I wasn't bringing him communion wafers or fancy pastries. When all three of us were in the cellar Flight opened the cell, got Morana out and made him stand up, but without removing the packing tape. He made him shuffle backward to the wall, made him put his back against it, and told him to stand up straight. Then, without violence, he pressed his hand against his chest. Hard, harder. As if he wanted to smash his way through it, not by hitting him, but by concentrating all his strength on one point. Morana didn't move, but his eyes became wet and glowed in the electric light. Flight stopped to get his breath back, then repeated the same action, this time pressing on his forehead. Silent and bloodless. He wasn't venting emotion, he gave no outward sign of aggression; he wasn't roughing him up. It was all a question of intensity, concentration.

The forehead was deformed by the pressure. Morana didn't resist. The world, now, wanted this. It wanted pressure, and Morana didn't contradict the world. After three minutes Flight stopped to get his breath back. He made him bend forward, at an angle of ninety degrees, then stood beside him and pressed on his neck and his back. He tried to bend him, to close him up. He continued to press for several minutes, till he noticed that Morana's legs were trembling, that he couldn't hold the position any longer and couldn't breathe because of the constriction of his chest and stomach. Flight increased the pressure, pushing the head farther and farther down. I saw his open hand on the back of Morana's head, his fingers splayed, his palm adhering to the curvature of the bones; the corresponding vibration of the compressed body. I stepped forward and checked his arm.

"That's enough," I said.

Flight turned and looked at me. He reduced the pressure and stopped. He stepped back; his forehead was wet.

"What are we doing?" I asked.

"What do you mean?" Flight replied.

"What are we doing to him?"

"We're interrogating him."

"But we're not asking him anything."

"With our bodies."

"What?"

"We're interrogating him with our bodies."

"But what do we want him to tell us?"

"Nothing."

He dried the sweat off his face with his forearm; his skin gleamed in the light from the bulb.

"We don't want him to tell us anything," he repeated.

Meanwhile Morana had straightened up. The skin of his face was red. Not reddened: red. Radius made him sit down, stripped off the packing tape and removed the rag from his mouth, fed him and gave him water. Morana swallowed, gasped for breath, bent over to one side, and vomited. Radius got some sheets of newspaper from the box and cleaned up. Morana straightened up again and took in air, without effusions or histrionics. Radius replaced the rag and the tape, backed him into the cell, tucked his feet in, and closed the shutter.

We left at twenty-minute intervals, as before. We met at Villa Sperlinga and walked on to the English Garden. We went up a little slope, passed the first fountain, which had water in it, and came to the second, which was empty and deep, so no one could see into it from the paths. We climbed over and sat down in the bowl, invisible among the dry leaves and the dirt, near the nests of snakes that drank the rancid water and ate the crumbled orts of leaves. Now we should talk, now we should try to understand, or else sit still and wait for snakes. I picked up a dry leaf and pressed on the central nervure, trying not to break it, then dropped it among the other leaves again.

The liturgy of destruction I'd witnessed consisted not of kicks and punches but of pressure and density. It was a black column that pushed down, bent and compressed—soft violence, gentle violence, concentration as destruction. Morana's body and the tenderness of his unknowing pain; our capacity for doing evil.

Nobody talked; our meeting unfolded silently in the dry belly of the basin, among the snakes that invisibly innervated the space.

The following day in class we contemplated Morana's empty seat and his bare desk: for the time being he was simply absent. Over the next few afternoons we let him out of the cell, laid him on one side, made him curl up, and pressed on both sides: two of us on his back, one against his legs—always in silence. We instinctively understood the order in which the actions had to be performed. In addition to the simultaneous pressure on his back and legs, we made him assume other postures, always intensifying them. Afterward we'd give him something to eat and clean up the vomit and excrement, but only superficially, without ever washing him thoroughly. He put up no resistance; each time he'd just look at us, and his look had no meaning.

After a few days Morana's absence became a void. Not an emotional void—that would have been implausible—but a physical one. Usually, though opaque and insubstantial, he was always in class. The teachers asked; nobody knew. Another day passed and the whole class was summoned to the principal's office. They told us they'd phoned Morana's home. For several days—his parents weren't sure how many, the principal said— Morana hadn't returned home. The police had been informed and would now begin searching. They asked us, his classmates, if we could provide any useful information. But no one knew anything; Morana didn't exist, he'd never existed. For a year he'd embodied a deprivation from which we averted our gazes. He'd been part of the class, yes, but nobody had his phone number, nobody had ever met him outside school to hang out or play soccer with him. A burn on the school photograph: instead of his head, a little hole.

•

We realized that we couldn't let too much time pass, that we had to be careful. For two days Flight went to Viale delle Magnolie alone. We knew he stayed for two or three hours; when we met in the morning in class he only made brief allusions to his visits. On Saturday, a week after the kidnapping, choosing our routes carefully and each arriving separately, we met again in the cellar. There were flies, and when Flight opened the cell a cloud of midges came out. Morana was thinner than ever. Flight removed the tape and rag and fed him. He raised his arms and cleaned his stomach and back with a wet rag. He lifted his sweater higher and washed him up to his chest and armpits. He dried him and cleaned his face too. The scabs had multiplied; at each rub they broke up and came off; little patches, some darker, some lighter, remained around his lips and on his forehead; the flies and midges settled on the lighter ones. Flight made him lie down on the floor and got to work.

He pressed his forehead against his legs, for a long time. He made him crouch down with his head between his knees, sat on his back, and squashed his head even further down. He made him sit with his side against the wall, so that the outside of one leg adhered to the wall; then he made him put his head between his knees, his ankles tied down with the dog's leash, and pressed against the knee of his outer leg, crushing the bones of his head, and Morana couldn't breathe. When he jerked backward and inhaled, in that movement which for an instant disturbed the swarm that hung permanently in the air, there was no rebellion: only the snatching of one more morsel of oxygen, like a drowning animal.

When I got home I stepped out of the elevator and came to a standstill. A large slab of wood, a flat, wide, dark-brown, coffin-like object, lay on the floor in the doorway. Protruding from one of its two longer sides were some small metal cylinders of varying lengths, like the pipes of a miniature organ. Kneeling around the coffin were two men wearing blue dungarees over clammy sweatshirts. They ran the palms of their hands over the surface, put one ear to it and listened attentively, studied the cylinders, adjusted them, clicked them open, fine-tuned the mechanism. When, with huge effort, they lifted the structure and moved it between the jambs to its correct anchorage on the hinges, Stone was on the other side of the threshold, gratefully contemplating his new purchase.

The security door was his way of rationally measuring danger, of giving a pragmatic response to it, in pursuit of the ideal of responsibility and safety. Stone reacted to dangerous times by putting sheets of galvanized steel between thick layers of solid wood and shooting bolts in all down its length; offering up, in the form of a door, a prayer against all intrusion.

After a few trial openings and shuttings, during which Stone responded to every silent draft produced by the door's movement by inhaling this good air, this honest air, this responsible, safe air, the two technicians handed over two pages of instructions, took their leave in dialect squeezed through their lips, hoisted the discarded coffin onto their shoulders, and, moving cautiously, still guttural, started to descend the stairs.

The next day, Sunday, I watched TV with Stone after lunch. String was helping Cotton with his homework in the other room. Outside it was a beautiful sunny day. Without approaching the screen I sniffed Corrado's skin till a full smell formed in my mouth. The smell of an Italian Sunday afternoon, the smell that was generated underneath clothes worn since early morning, when the molecules were beginning to disperse but still preserved some cohesion. I sniffed the odor of justice, then Stone asked me how I was.

I turned around. He was sitting on the sofa, his pack of MS lying nearby. He played with his wedding ring, running it up to his fingernail, then sliding it back down into the hollow between his fingers. He didn't know what to do. I thought of the fig tree in Piazza Marina, its climbing roots, its branches. I looked at the twig of flesh along which Stone threaded his wedding ring.

"I'm fine," I said.

"Do you want to talk?"

That's certainly the right question, I thought. Because yes, sure, I want to talk, I always want to talk, and go on talking forever, because by talking I construct something, but more than that, by talking I *prevent* something. The problem is my interlocutor. I don't want to talk to you—either of you.

"Okay," I replied. "Let's talk."

"Go ahead."

"What do you mean?"

He was drifting helplessly, but he couldn't stop.

"Is everything all right at school?" he asked.

I made a movement with my shoulders, as if to shake something off. I knew he wanted to get me to tell him what was happening, to find out what I thought about it, understand what I wanted, support me, reassure me, maybe provide me with armor—clasps, steel cladding, bolts—giving me exactly the right degree of protection; to drive me around in the car, and defend me. But there was nothing he had to do or that he could do.

"There's a bit of a commotion," I said, "but it'll pass."

"Does it bother you?"

"No, not at all," I replied.

"That's the main thing," he said.

"I'm okay."

"We're here, you know that."

"Sure," I said, thinking that at this point there couldn't be anyone, but only a principle of inertia, regulating all that happened.

"Remember that," Stone said again.

"Don't worry," I said.

We sat for a few minutes longer in front of Corrado introducing his guests, while the early afternoon sun crept across the floor and began to glint on the screen.

"I'm going to do my homework," I said, getting up, as a dance routine began on TV and Stone was left alone in the middle of the living room, his wedding ring between his fingers, floating on the raft of his security door.

•

At six o'clock we were back on Viale delle Magnolie. This time when Flight took Morana out of the little cell he also took the blanket. He made him eat—a lot. Even when he didn't want any more. He'd brought some bread; it must have been old because it was hard. He broke it up and pushed it between his lips.

Grinding his teeth, Morana split the crust, chewed, and swallowed. Then Flight made him drink water, this too in excess. More bread, more water. While he was still chewing, he shut his mouth with the rag and the packing tape, pressed him forward and held him still, squeezing hard downward, with steady determination, till he hiccuped, and was seized by increasingly violent convulsions: as soon as Flight moved away and Morana's chest rose, vomit oozed out from the tape and the rag. It was in his throat, he couldn't breathe. I approached to remove the tape but Radius stopped me and gestured to leave things be. The process went on.

Flight made him lie down on his back, sat on his belly and pressed on the lower part and on his chest, digging his knees into his breastbone. He beckoned to Radius and got him to climb up on his back; he held Radius's legs up so that all his weight rested on him, and below that, on Morana's chest. More hiccups, more vomit. Then he made him lie prone and pressed down on his neck, squashing his throat against the floor. He did the same with his back, sitting on it, first on his own and then with Radius.

He concentrated on his head. First he made him bend it to one side and sat on the parietal bone. He'd put a rag between Morana's ear and the cement, to prevent any cuts. He repeated the process, making him bend his head to the other side. He uncovered his mouth and made him drink again. A first bottle, a second one, half of a third. With the damp rag he wiped away the tear streaks below his eyes. He covered his mouth and began again. A precise itinerary, codified stages, mineral postures: a solidified via crucis. After two hours, at eight o'clock in the evening, another pause for bread. Again lots of it, again dry. Another full cycle of compression. While Flight and Radius squashed his head against the cement with all their strength, I leaned over and looked into Morana's eyes: inside them there was only an illiterate fear.

Flight lifted him up and made him sit with his back against the wall; the egg boxes were deformed. Morana was only half-conscious, his eyes were almost closed. Flight told him to open them, then got the newspaper that he'd bought that morning, spread it out in front of Morana and tried to get him to hold it, but his fingers couldn't grip and it slipped down into his lap; so Flight told Radius to stretch out his arm and hold the newspaper open in front of him. He took a Polaroid, focused, and pressed; when it formed, the picture was dark but recognizable, Morana's head slightly bowed to his chest. Radius laid the photograph aside, filled another bottle with water, and made him drink it. Morana breathed with difficulty; he no longer reacted to what Flight said to him, he was losing consciousness. The water gurgled in his throat, trickled down onto his chin and his neck. Flight dragged him into the middle of the room, got the blanket, put it on top of him and covered him completely. Identifying his form with his hands he knelt with one leg on his throat, the bone in the hollow between the breastbone and chin; he held that position, pressing him with his knee, for ten minutes. Then he got up. He put his ear to the blanket and listened for a whole minute; he moved the body again, shifted its position, moved the arms: the blanket rippled with little puffs of air. So Flight pressed down again on Morana's throat, this time with both knees. After a while a movement came from the body: it was disjointed, unconscious. Flight gestured to Radius, indicated that he should sit behind him; Radius came forward, sought out Morana's chest with his hands and got on top of it. I stood watching them: in the struggle there was no struggle. We struck at the heart but the heart was not there. The body put up no resistance; striking at the heart was a turn of phrase. Flight and Radius pressed Morana's body, locked it up in itself again. They deformed it silently.

Morana's body gave way.

I responded to Flight's gesture and sat on his stomach; I

squashed it right down. I noticed in the immobility a residue
of abdominal respiration: I increased the pressure and elimi-
nated it. We held our positions for a length of time I couldn't
determine. I smelled our smells mingling. They were strong,
good. Now and then one of us would stiffen and increase the
pressure: then as the muscles would hurt, that one would ease
off. Mingled with one another, we were a knot. Within the
knot we brooded on a dead body. A simple dead body. *The*
simple dead body. We don't brood on it, we gave birth to it:
Morana's dead body came out of our living bodies. If the reserve
imposed by militancy hadn't forbidden it, we would and should
have wept with emotion, with joy, and grief. We'd found the
place where everything was concentrated and revealed. We
killed; we knew how to kill.

When we got up, everything had shrunk. My hands had
become tiny. With tiny hands Flight lifted one edge of the
blanket, held it there for a few seconds, then lowered it again.
With tiny hands Radius started to dismantle the little cell; he
laid aside the rag, the packing tape, the bottle, the leftover
bread, the cookies. He collected and cleaned. When he left he
would throw them all onto the empty lot on Via Brigata Ve-
rona. I would leave after Radius; then, I didn't know when,
Flight would leave too. He'd dispose of the body. Before leaving the cellar I approached and, as he'd done, I raised the edge
of the blanket. One eye was closed, one half-open. His features
were calm. There were irregular blotches around his lips. Ezekiel wouldn't be coming here to prophesy. I dropped the blanket, stood up, and knew that, whatever happened, Morana's
death was what would nourish the rest of my life.

•

During the night, sleeping askew on the armchair, I dreamed
that String and Stone made me assume the poses of the alphamute. They changed from one pose to another disjointedly,

without fluency—the alphamute of a stammerer. Stone moved away and String continued to manipulate me on her own. With her hand behind my head she made me nod, she took my arm and extended it forward, half-closed my fingers and made them fumble in the void, then opened my hand, made me rub it against a wall of air, and again, making me bend my knees, curving my shoulders gently backward. I tried to decipher the meaning but couldn't.

The next day, at school, Flight said we must talk. We waited till recess and went to Piazza De Saliba. He told us that yesterday he'd waited for night to fall. He'd crammed Morana's body into a large carryall, put the blanket in as well, and hoisted the load onto his shoulders. There'd been no one about on the streets. He'd arrived at Villa Sperlinga. He'd taken the bag off his back and pulled out the body and the blanket. He'd poured alcohol over them and tried to set fire to it, but the body wouldn't burn. He'd tried again, and then yet again. It still wouldn't burn. It was four thirty. He was in the dark and well away from the road, but more and more cars were passing. He'd made one more attempt, but the body just wouldn't burn—maybe because of the damp, or maybe there was something wrong with the alcohol. So he'd pushed the body behind a flower bed and hid it under some bushes, then he'd taken the blanket and gone away. This, he said, meant that the news would come out very soon.

His words were prophetic. We went back into class and the principal and several teachers arrived. There was a disturbance; a female teacher started crying, then a male teacher did too. We went out into the hallway, the doors of the other classrooms opened and there was confusion, despair.

In the afternoon we had to go back to school; they wanted to talk to us. When we arrived, the teachers were arguing among themselves. We were told that Morana had died of cardio-circulatory failure. He had strange lesions all over his body; strange—as if he'd been run over, but he hadn't been. There would be a funeral, but not for a while; first they'd have to establish what had happened, and where and how. Undoubtedly he'd been killed. There was thought to be some connection with events at school over the past few months. No member of Morana's family could be considered a target, from a political point of view, let alone a financial one. So Morana had probably discovered something—perhaps unintentionally and unwittingly.

It was essential that we talk, they said, addressing us with voices of glass; we must tell them what we remembered. Any information we could give them, even the tiniest detail, might be important.

On my way home, instead of stopping on Via Sciuti I walked on to Viale delle Magnolie. I reached the front door and stood on the sidewalk across the street. It was dark when I set off home again, except for a few small lights from the lower floors of buildings. I had to keep stepping off the sidewalk because the roots of the magnolias had split the cement in many places and come through. Shortly before turning down Via Sciuti again, I recognized, in a pool of pale light at the base of a magnolia, among the tangle of roots, the shape of a pregnant woman's body.

At home Cotton was sitting on the sofa in the living room playing with modeling clay; he made little colored dolls and lined them up on the arm of the sofa. On TV, *Almanacco del giorno dopo* began: a slow ballad played by flutes and a wheel on which pictures of monstrous men went around; one held a lobster by its tail, one was putting a bunch of grapes into his mouth, one carried a sheaf of hay on his back; they were followed by a dwarf dancer, a decapitator of animals, and a half-naked old man with a white beard, like Ezekiel, with open white wings and an hourglass in his hand. When the *Almanacco* started, the television became a seventeenth-century mechanism; its internal workings were organic, a concatenation of rack rails, wooden prisms, cog wheels, and sprockets. The *Almanacco* played a tune like a maleficent musical box; inside it the devil was at work.

The speaker was blond and stern. Sternly she said what day it was tomorrow, gave the saint's name and the times when the sun and moon would rise and set. She said 1978 was the last lunar year in the century with thirteen lunations, and that there were no more than six such years in any century. Thirteen moons meant emotional instability, the collapse of thought. Human sensibility was devastated: perceptions became visions, premonitions nightmares. As the sun and moon's stony faces followed each other behind the speaker's back, Cotton lined his dolls up on the arm of the sofa: a battered black cat, a bird with a missing claw, a fat woman with an apron and a face like an ant, a horse's head with a red eye, and a brown insect with six thin legs and a stylet.

Now he was making an old blue man with a white beard; while I slept Cotton rummaged through my head.

"I want to give them as Christmas presents," he said.

"Who to?"

"Our cousins."

Behind him was a half-eaten piece of bread. Or maybe that was clay too.

"What's going to happen now?" he asked.

I sat down on the sofa beside him.

"I don't know," I said. "We'll go on."

"What lies ahead of you?"

"More bodies."

"Are bodies important?"

"Bodies embody. They represent."

"Bodies are bodies," he said.

"They're symbols."

"What's Morana's body a symbol of?"

"A discovery."

I paused. I hadn't planned to; I was just searching for the right expression, one that rendered the meaning. Then I said it.

"It was wonderful."

Cotton had finished making the old man with the beard and put him next to the others. From the little lumps of clay lying in front of him on the newspaper, he took some green and some red.

"What was wonderful?" he asked me calmly.

"Being guilty."

"You feel such a strong need to be guilty that you think everyone is," he said, looking at me.

"What do you mean?"

"As far as the three of you are concerned, Morana was guilty."

"He had to be."

"Being guilty is contagious," he said. "Maybe it's a disease."

"Yes. It's an infection."

"And the three of you make it your business to spread the infection."

Using the green and red, to which he'd added a bit of blue, he'd made a tree. He corrected the curvature of a branch, then looked at the palms of his hands, sprinkled with colored dust.

"Do you know when pain will come?" he asked.

Now that, I said to myself, was the question. The only real question.

"No, I don't know that," I replied.

"Are you waiting for it?"

I didn't answer. He put the finishing touches to the roots and, holding the tree up with two fingers, handed it to me.

"There you are," he said.

I took it and stood it on my palm.

"It's a present," he said.

"Even though we're not cousins?"

"Yes."

"Even though it's not Christmas yet?"

"It's for your birthday."

"That's a month away yet," I said.

"It doesn't matter."

He put the other dolls on the newspaper, taking care not to let them get stuck together. He stood up, lifted the newspaper, holding it taut from the edges, a paper stretcher, and walked slowly out.

I stayed there, the TV still on, the sounds of String cooking, the tree taking root in my hand.

•

A few days passed. I didn't sleep much and I was losing weight. On the way to school I watched this opaque world. I rubbed my eyes; it remained opaque. Saturday came, and after the last class Comrade Flight said we must talk. At four o'clock we were at the clearing.

"I was called in," he said. "Yesterday afternoon, with my parents. They asked me a lot of questions. The principal was there, and two policemen. They asked me about the hangings—the dummies and the clothes. They didn't let on what they know exactly; they said I'll have to go in again."

Comrade Radius looked at the lank grass. A few ants appeared between the blades. He flicked the grass with the tip of his shoe and made them disappear.

"Maybe it's because of the chemist's lab coat," he said, "the one that belonged to your brother's friend."

"I thought of that," said Flight.

"That's how."

I too looked at the grass; I had a sense of something becoming brittle. But I wasn't worried. There was no fear in Flight's voice either; there was concentration. An awareness that some of the connections, inevitably, wouldn't hold, but that this didn't contradict the meaning of what was happening. On the contrary, it developed it and strengthened it.

"I must go away," said Flight.

That's what he had to say, I thought.

"What are you going to do?" asked Radius.

"Go underground. It's the right time. I've been planning it for a while; I've got it all worked out."

Radius and I looked at each other. Comrade Flight, the ideologue, the boy murderer, geometry and obsession, the extinction of the human, the transformation of every centimeter of flesh into discipline. And hence, now, the dematerialization of the flesh; life in hiding as the ultimate form of life.

"When?" Radius asked again.

"Today. Now. I know where to go."

We looked at him. We felt the seduction, we envied him; we'd have liked to do what he was doing. Go underground, move into the permeable word beyond which the body disappeared.

"How will we communicate?" I asked.

"Don't worry, I'll contact you. I'll be around."

"We must carry out more operations," said Radius.

"We certainly must. Now we'll raise the stakes."

The light in the clearing was increasing. It came down from above, entered the vertical tunnel of vegetation, spread through the grass, and flowed down into the earth.

We got to our feet; soon we'd say our goodbyes and agree on a few details—places, times, the creation of a new code. We'd feel the sweetness and melancholy of parting, the bewilderment of another ending and another beginning. Then each of us would set off for home or toward the point of disappearance, recognizing the November sun that came up in glimmers from the cement of the road, from under the dust and sand.

MATERIAL

(DECEMBER 1978)

In December the street was underground, the facades of the buildings were underground, the metal railings, the streetlights, the garbage heaped up on the sidewalk—all were underground. An entire topography, a new concept of space. Even the densest surfaces, those which seemed to me solid and thick, in fact concealed false bottoms, and secret passages connecting the outside to the inside.

During classes at school I looked at the blackboard: the deep black slate and the quantity of matter that emanated from it; the wastepaper basket and the patch of wall blackened by the fire of our first callow act of terrorism; the grooves on the surfaces of the desks, the political map of Italy, underground Italy; Morana's empty desk, on the other side of the room, intact and virginal; and his death, life inventing death; and the inquiries which now also involved, to widespread astonishment and disapproval, the disappearance of Comrade

Flight, of Dario Scarmiglia. His family was alarmed and the school was dismayed; all the pupils were summoned to the principal's office again, particularly Comrade Radius and I. We were questioned firmly but not unsympathetically. They wrote down our answers to their questions, having identified us as possible keys to the understanding of an abnormal phenomenon. Because their inquiries were taking a different tack: they now knew that evil could be generated from below, by us. The focus was gradually sharpening, but this, far from worrying me, gave me pleasure. I felt the joy of legitimization: being perceived through invisibility—our original ambition.

At the beginning of the month the Christmas market opened on Via Mariano Stabile. Cartloads of model shepherds piled up on shelves, pieces of cork, acorn-shaped flashing lights, silvery braids festooned around everything, boxes full of little ornamental balls, some of them broken, shards of glass left to be crushed into even smaller shards in the middle of the heap. Christmas trees in pots, their green needles spilling onto the asphalt, decorative spires stuck on the tops of trees or arranged in a row like weapons, the varied and intricate jumble of objects. I'd stand there every afternoon, poking my fingers between shepherds' bodies, stirring up little legs and lighted torches, cardboard lakes, sheep and pigs and an inexplicable rhinoceros with a pointed horn.

One afternoon I came home and String told me Comrade Radius had phoned. She didn't say Radius, she didn't even say Bocca; she said Massimo. I called him back and he asked if we could meet. We fixed a rendezvous in the clearing in half an hour.

He was excited. Comrade Flight had made contact. For a few days, he'd told Radius, he'd fended for himself, living on the street and buying food with money he'd stolen at home, but he didn't feel safe doing that anymore, so he'd asked him for the keys to the cellar; he wanted to use it as a base and disguise himself when he went out onto the streets. He'd gotten hold of some old clothes and learned how to change his appearance. During Carnival at the beginning of the year, Scarmiglia and I had been the only ones not to wear fancy dress. Now Comrade Flight would put on a costume, dab charcoal under his nose, and roam Palermo like a metropolitan Zorro.

He wanted us to join him the following day after school, Radius said—at the cellar. He'd planned the next action and wanted to carry it out before the year ended. We met the next day at two o'clock in the afternoon on Viale delle Magnolie.

Flight was a sculpture in coal, a piece of thin, veined, twisted lignite extracted from a mine, his body leaner from living outdoors. In a short space of time he'd become antique, and now, in the harsh serenity of his features, he revealed a capacity for knowledge that was still beyond Radius and me. His metamorphosis was complete; there was a combustible power in his eyes.

He'd made some alterations to the cellar. The egg boxes were still there, but where the little cell had been there was now a mattress on a blue metal cot. The blanket was the one we'd used for Morana; I instantly noticed the faint smell of his body and of the splashes of alcohol on the fabric. There were some provisions, which it would be Radius's task to replenish, and cardboard boxes containing heaps of clothes. On one of the heaps there was a camera, and hidden between the boxes and the wall were some sticks of wood. There were also a few books, several notebooks, and some pens and pencils. From one notebook the edge of a Polaroid stuck out: I recognized Morana.

We greeted each other with a handshake, and for a moment our heads, now covered with hair, were skulls again. Flight sat down on the edge of the cot, Radius behind him on a closed box; I squatted down with my back against the wall. The air was constantly pierced by a faint buzz of flies.

Flight said he was fine. He knew they were looking for him. They must have guessed there was a connection between his disappearance and Morana's death. They were probably weighing two hypotheses: that either both he and Morana were victims, or the second boy to disappear was responsible for the death of the first or was in some way involved. He didn't know if the investigators were capable of imagining that he'd gone into hiding, but the possibility might well occur to them before long. He said he'd thought for a long time about the next step, about how to put the experience—especially the psychological experience—of Morana's kidnapping to good use.

"Our next action," he explained, "will perfect everything we've done so far, and take it to even greater extremes."

He stopped and looked at us. He wanted to understand if we'd grasped his words.

"After this," he said slowly, "the whole country will take notice."

Another pause, during which he scrutinized us to see how far we'd be prepared to go.

"We'll be invisible," he said, weighing every syllable, "radical and perfect."

Radius's eyes were shining. To take my mind off my own excitement I watched his. It was immense and childlike, sending out little waves that flowed through his flesh and his thoughts.

"A few days ago," Flight resumed, "I started doing some tailing. Then I had to stop; it was getting too dangerous. You guys will have to take over."

He turned toward me.

"*You* will have to take over, Comrade Nimbus," he said, with a smile.

For the past month and a half I'd often felt left out, demoted to the rank of a handyman who carried out secondary tasks, but now, seeing Flight's eyes welcome me and his smile acknowledge me, I lost all my misgivings and felt part of the project again.

"The person we're going to kidnap," said Flight, "is Wimbow."

Wimbow, I thought. I thought nothing. I saw black and red. Wimbow's body.

"But why?" said Radius. "Why her?"

He stood up; his voice was like an excoriation.

"She hasn't done anything to us," he said. "She can't be a target. She isn't a target."

He broke off; he wanted to walk about, to change his position, but there was no room. Comrade Flight hadn't moved; he'd merely suspended the flow of his argument.

"No one," he resumed, "has done anything to us. No one has ever acted against us, directly. But if we'd applied that criterion we'd never have done anything right from the start."

"No, comrade," said Radius, "that's not true. In each case we identified targets that were our adversaries, in one way or another."

"Morana wasn't our adversary," said Flight.

"But Morana was necessary," Radius replied, "educatory. He was our original sin."

"In the struggle, comrade," said Flight, "there are *only* original sins."

His stark words entered the air.

"The Red Brigades have never targeted a woman," Radius said. "Even they haven't done that."

Solid and nervy at the same time, he moved his hands, piling little bricks of air one on top of the other, building himself a logical structure that would serve as a barrier. I was still squatting on my haunches, pressing the back of my head against the wall, like when I dug out my nimbus. As if I was trying to stop the wall from collapsing.

"The gender objection is baseless," Flight said calmly.

"Why is it baseless?" said Radius. "She's a female. A girl."

"She's also a deaf-mute," said Flight. "She's a half-caste. She's beautiful. She's everything she should be."

Radius hesitated. He was frustrated, but he realized that the direction in which he was heading led nowhere. With Comrade Flight logic was an unpredictable path.

"What good will it do us to hurt her?" he asked.

"I never said we were going to hurt her."

"What good will it do us to kidnap her?" Radius modified his question.

Comrade Flight rubbed his head with his hand, in one particular place, hard; then he was composed again.

"We'll be able to study her. Find out who she is."

Which is the exact opposite of what I want to do, I thought. Originally I'd had the Creole girl, and that had been enough for me. I'd wanted to enjoy her as a phenomenon unsullied by history. Since she'd become Wimbow I'd been faced with the uncontainable. Comrade Flight, by contrast, sought understanding, knowledge. He wanted to trap her in the amber of our little cell, immobilize her, turn her into a fossil.

"But we've already done that with Morana," Radius objected. "We kidnapped him for precisely that purpose. There's no point in doing the same thing again."

"It's not the same thing," said Flight. "Wimbow is not Morana. Morana was alone, completely alone. Wimbow is not. Wimbow is a link."

I thought of the electrostatic forces that held the atoms together in a molecule, all the invisible forces that gave things cohesion. Wimbow was that—an invisible force, a link.

"I don't understand you, Comrade Flight," said Radius, shifting about jerkily.

"Wimbow generates links," explained Flight. "She does that on her own, simply by existing. Morana was the opposite: he rejected. With him everything was simple, there was nothing to break. Wimbow attracts. She links things together."

As Flight now slowly massaged his neck, Radius turned toward me. He wanted me to intervene, to join him in his fight. But I didn't move; I said nothing, because what disoriented me, even more than the idea of carrying out an operation against Wimbow, even more than what Comrade Flight was saying, was the discovery that others were aware of her existence, of her name and her life; the sense that she could, and did, exist outside my imagination.

"We, comrades," Flight suddenly resumed, "must be able to do without links. We must learn to forgo things."

Radius said nothing. He was exhausted. Until a few moments ago he'd still had the strength to slice the air with abrupt, impatient movements; now he bowed his head.

"Why?" he asked, but it was a residual question.

"Because little girls make you cry," said Flight, turning to glance at me.

I raised my head, gazed at him, and again recognized his submerged discourse, the anger and provocation crystallized within him.

Minutes passed.

Radius had sat down again, his temples between his fists; Flight ran the forefinger of one hand over the back of the other, following the line of his veins. Suddenly he looked up. We're nearly there, he told me with his eyes. A little more effort, a little more courage. Flight knew my silence had nothing to do with Radius's objections. It had nothing to do with logic or with a concept of justice—those brittle ramparts. To me Wimbow was where euphoria and melancholy merged, the firmament of my imagination, its origin. To imagine the destruction of all that was a kind of death, and Comrade Flight was a student of death, so he looked at me and said nothing. Then he nodded and I nodded back. Radius intercepted the gesture and got to his feet, his body noticeably thin; some-where or other he too had found a sufficient degree of despair.

We remained in silence among the flies, and only later, much later, when all the buzzing had stopped, did we start to map out the plan.

•

The next few days sleep disappeared altogether. I went to the swimming pool, as I did every autumn. The instructor moved me about, making me lie on the water, telling me to lower my abdomen (he pushed the small of my back downward with one hand) and hold my shoulders higher (he pushed them up with his other hand), how to bend my head, how to kick with alter-nate feet. For the first twenty minutes I swam with my fore-arms supported by a little cork board, so that my legs did all the work; clutching this vegetal piece of flotsam I thrashed back and forth, length after length, pushing my head down into the water, seeking liquid sleep.

I was so tired, I saw school differently. When I raised my head from my desk and looked around I always felt a great anguish, a need for tenderness and tears. During recess, alone in the hallways, I wanted to bite the walls, to go into the toi-lets and eat the ceramic basins, to drink the water from the faucets, all of it, right down into the pipes, to enter every class-room and devour the desks, the backpacks, the books, the stu-dents. Then I tried to calm myself because I could feel that I was staggering; I repressed my hunger, aware that this hunger was nostalgia for everything, the desire to go back and the pain of doing so.

I began to tail Wimbow. The first few times I lost her at once; I'd start tailing her name and forget about her. Then I found the right degree of concentration and succeeded in fol-lowing her. But she was rarely alone—a short walk outside school, in Piazza De Saliba with a classmate, a goodbye, a few more steps, a greeting, her parents, getting into the car and driving off.

At one of our meetings Flight, sitting on the edge of the cot, told me where she lived: Viale Lazio, a street of white buildings and small shadows. He asked me to explore the area and find out what her routine was. I stood on the sidewalk across from her front door and waited. I spent entire afternoons fruitlessly studying lighted windows on the various floors, not knowing which was the right one, and imagining her doing her homework.

Then one afternoon she came out through the door, wearing a red coat and black gloves, with her hair tied in a ponytail. She walked in the direction of Via Libertà and looked around. I followed her, staying on the sidewalk across the street. She slowed down beneath a row of balconies, stopped, and looked up; I waited till she walked on, then crossed the street, and looked where she had looked and saw lumps of black clay in the corners under the stone balconies. Swallows that had survived the autumn flew mazily above our heads—wings curved and pointed, tails forked—cutting the bright halo of the streetlights.

I crossed over to the other side of the street again. In the meantime Wimbow had stopped and was waiting. I stopped too, in the dark; I turned up the collar of my windproof jacket, feeling rather foolish. A few minutes later another little girl arrived; she wore a green coat, had blond hair, and was not much taller than Wimbow. They smiled at each other, exchanged greetings, and started walking. After a while I saw Wimbow slow down, stop, walk on, and stop again, as if there was something wrong with the street, or with her feet, trying to work out some concept of harmony but failing and growing increasingly frustrated and annoyed because she couldn't understand where she'd gone wrong. She stuck to her task, staring first at her own feet, then at her friend's, watching the way they walked and rebuking them; then she made a sudden movement, a little skip that brought her into step with her friend and walked on more briskly, happy now and reassured by the symmetry.

They stopped outside an ice cream shop, and I took advantage of their absorption to cross the street and move closer. I hid behind a hedge, where I smelled the strong, chaotic odor of moldy leaves and damp earth. The little girl in the green coat ordered a cone. She was going to order one for Wimbow too, but Wimbow stopped her, got up on tiptoe and made a sign through the glass to the ice cream man, who had already taken another cone, that no, she didn't want that; then she touched her chest with one finger, lifted her arm, the fingers half-closed to grasp a globe of air, and immediately brought both hands forward, the tips of her fingers touching, and parted them smoothly and quickly as though flattening out a strip of pastry.

The ice cream man turned toward the girl in the green coat, who again made to intervene, but again Wimbow stopped her, stared at the ice cream man, and more slowly, spacing out her movements, repeated the sequence. Then she stood with her arms folded, looking at him; at first he didn't move, then he stirred himself into action and pointed quizzically at a display case containing croissants; Wimbow nodded to say yes, he was forgiven, she pointed to the flavor she wanted, took her croissant, and held out the coins. When they set off again Wimbow moved her lips, arms, and hands, and the little girl nodded— she too spoke in sign language; green and red blended together as I tried to read the movements, to understand what they meant, but the street was dimly lit, each gesture was multiplied and blurred by shadows. After walking for twenty minutes, briskly but aimlessly, like dogs, like everyone—Wimbow and her friend bade each other goodbye and parted. I stopped behind an electrical junction box; I sniffed the myriad copper wires knotted together inside. Wimbow waited till her friend had walked into the distance, then turned back. I crossed the street and speeded up to get closer to her. I sniffed the air, sure that I could recognize the smell of her body spreading through the air around her as she walked, determined to intercept its molecules suspended there in sediments, and deeply moved to be passing through her breath.

She went into a baker's shop, and I watched from outside. The baker knew her. He said something to her; she shook her head, took a step backward, so as to be more visible from the other side of the counter, and with an earnest expression on her face drew semicircles and wavy lines with her fingers, conducting a silent orchestra; then she pointed to a loaf of bread behind the glass and with her hands formed an invisible vase, a tapering, cone-like shape in the air; when the baker bent down and stood up again holding a bottle of Stelat milk, she melted and forgave him.

I knew there was no great significance in all this, it was an everyday event to her, but still it pierced my heart: the thing that I'd hoped would always remain immovable, primal, and creatural moved and existed outside my imagination.

I watched her come out carrying the bread and milk in a plastic bag. She passed the greengrocer's, where the goods were displayed in their crates. She stopped and I moved in close again; the greengrocer greeted her. She returned his greeting, smiled at him, and pointed to some small tomatoes, lettuce, and yellow apples. While the greengrocer served her, speaking in dialect, but politely, Wimbow leaned over a big black pot that stood on a rotting wooden bench. Three more steps and I found myself standing beside her; oblivious to everything else, we contemplated the murmur of the simmering water and the immersed potatoes, from which a column of little bubbles rose up to sputter on the surface. Then, when I sensed her body, I tried to move away and, without meaning to, knocked hard against her shoulder, the plastic bag fell out of her hand, I saw the glass smash, white liquid flow out of the bag first quickly, then more slowly, soaking the bread. Wimbow jumped backward to save her shoes, looked around, and my eyes met hers as I stood there at a loss, then leaned over a wooden crate of tomatoes, took one, and squashed it between my fingers.

The greengrocer left his packages on the scales and came toward us. I hid my tomato-bloodied hand in my pocket. The greengrocer said something to us in dialect; I didn't understand him, but Wimbow nodded and talked to him with her hands, pointing at the white on the ground and then molding a shape in the air, and like the baker before him, the greengrocer went away, came back, and handed her a bottle of milk.

Exiled by language, I, the mythopoetic one, went over to Wimbow. I wanted to say sorry, but the word didn't exist in the alphamute, so I took my hand out of my pocket and made a vague, crippled movement with my fingers covered in red pulp and yellow seeds, but she didn't understand, so I spun around in circles, hoping an admission of shame would be enough. But Wimbow just watched me impassively, then took the plastic bag that the greengrocer handed her, put the bottle of milk into it, waved goodbye, and left. Disconsolately, I watched the red of her coat move away and the white of the milk lengthen out in geometrical streams along the joints between the tiles, as the greengrocer's words swirled around me.

•

When I told Flight and Radius about my attempts at tailing Wimbow I said she was unassailable. She followed a regular route from home to school and from school to home, and was always accompanied every step of the way.

"You've tailed her yourself," I said to Flight. "You know it's true."

Flight said nothing. Since he'd taken to spending most of his time in the cellar, reading and thinking and slowly planning the project, while Comrade Radius and I went out on scouting missions, going back and forth between our underground base and the world outside, he'd become our queen bee, an embodiment of ideology. Radius and I were the workers who untiringly connected the heart of the hive with the outside world, and vice versa.

He ventured out only at night, each time in a different disguise. Sometimes I went with him, telling my family I'd be spending the night at a friend's house. Stone would always offer to drive me there and pick me up afterward, but I'd tell him there was no need, everything was fine, and I could look after myself. As we walked around the streets, Flight explained to me, without making any explicit reference to Wimbow and her kidnapping, the underlying reasons for the struggle, this magnificent, unpredictable coexistence of the political and the private.

"The reason we've gotten this far," he said to me, "is that we've understood that fear and desire are not antithetical, but intertwined, inseparable experiences. Other people don't understand; they don't realize that that is the case. They've got it into their heads that they're faced with an external social phenomenon; they've embalmed it and rejected it. But we know that the struggle is in everyone's body, inside the veins."

Eventually, after several days of incubation, he told us that if there were no natural chinks in Wimbow's everyday life, we'd have to create one artificially. We'd force her to change her route home, taking her somewhere where it would be easier for us to strike.

"I've already thought of a method," he said. "I just need to perfect it. For the moment," he added, to me, "keep tailing her."

I took up my position opposite her apartment again. For

hours I waited for her to come out, but she didn't. I leaned against a railing on the other side of the street. I looked down from the lighted windows to an illustration in the science textbook that I'd brought with me. It showed a cross-section of a human bone—calcium minerals, spongy tissue, lymph, bone marrow. In the space of two months a bone self-destructed and regenerated completely.

Wimbow's bones immersed in her flesh.

The spine was also called the rachis. It had between thirty-two and thirty-five vertebrae. Between the vertebrae there were intervertebral discs made of fibrocartilage.

I couldn't put the bones inside the Creole girl's body, couldn't think of her as matter—bones, flesh, tissue, internal organs, a spine; that she disappeared and reappeared every two months. I couldn't do it.

Her eyes were ocular globes. They were situated in the orbital cavities. Inside them was the vitreous humor, which was a transparent jelly; on the outside was the sclera, which was fibrous and opaque. The hair and nails were keratin; keratin was a protein containing sulphur. Inside the ear was the cochlea, which was a bony spiral; it contained the perilymph and the endolymph. The heart consisted of striated muscular tissue and was surrounded by the pericardium.

The reduction of one's love to an organism. Or perhaps the opposite—the elevation. Loving a body that was primarily an organism. Loving it despite this, *because* of this: because it was also an organism, an anatamophysiological machine. The body that had existed before my imagination had taken possession of it, the body that generated the movements, the beauty of the movements; the splendor of her dark skin, the luminous darkness; the mouth that breathed and didn't say words; the cavities, the anus out of which excrement came every day; the vagina about which I knew nothing, which was a millimeter away from the unimaginable, but which I tried to imagine anyway, and which was terrible to imagine; the way the celestial and the infernal combined to give rise to an existence—love filtered through biology.

The hours passed, the book in my hands, the bones in my hands, the Creole girl in her apartment, and the idea of bodies expanding in my head.

•

Then everything converged toward a vanishing point.

Comrade Flight's plan for kidnapping Wimbow was so lucidly unreal that Radius and I listened to him without argument, without even interposing minor corrective objections: seduced by the improbable, we accepted everything.

"We must create an exposed area where we can strike," he said. "A vacuum."

Comrade Radius and I sat on the floor of the cellar, the electric light making the flies' bodies into sparks. We nodded.

"That void," said Flight, looking at me, "is your birthday."

My birthday, I thought, was in a few days' time. December 21, a Thursday. The day after that, the Christmas holidays began.

"You're going to invite her to your party," explained Flight. "Only her."

Only her, I thought, is what has been on my mind for more than a year.

"Only there won't be any party," he went on. "We need Wimbow to go to your home on the evening of December 21 and to buzz the intercom after the doorman's office has closed: we'll be there waiting for her. We'll grab her, keep her quiet, and take her away. It'll be two or three hours before her parents come to pick her up, so we'll have plenty of time to get away."

"How can Comrade Nimbus be with us," Radius interrupted, "if Wimbow buzzes for the door to be opened and there's no party? We can't have his parents answering the inter-com; it's essential that he does it."

"Of course. Nimbus will wait in his apartment till Wim-bow buzzes. He'll answer and open the door. He'll tell his parents some friends have dropped by and run down the three flights of stairs to the doorman's office. From that point all three of us will work together."

"But if we do that," Radius objected again, "Nimbus's cover will be blown. The police will never believe the kidnapping was a spur-of-the-moment decision; they'll realize it must have been planned and that he's in on it."

I said nothing and listened. The others both looked at me, at my caution and my inertia.

"Yes," said Flight. "You're right: after this operation, Nim-bus will have to go into hiding."

That's it, I thought: I disappear. At last I disappear. I too become a little hole in the photograph, something missing, perhaps something missed.

"Okay," I said. "I've got time to prepare for it, and it's fair enough. But I want to know about Wimbow—where and how we're going to look after her."

I realized the phrase I'd used was completely inappropriate. We didn't look after anyone. We kidnapped people, then we imprisoned them, then we deformed them.

"Don't worry, comrade," Flight said to me in a tone that was both friendly and tense. "We'll *look after* Wimbow in here."

I imagined the little cell being rebuilt, with its shutter and bolt. The blanket was already there. The two dog leashes, wa-ter, cookies, sheets of newspaper. Cleaning her skin, rubbing it. The exposed physiology. The ritual of compression.

"How can we be sure," asked Radius, "that Wimbow won't tell anyone else about the party? She might talk about it, es-pecially if she thinks other kids from the school have been invited. Then she'd find out that she'll be the only one there."

"She would indeed, comrade," said Flight. "Only Wimbow is a deaf-mute. Most people just look at her or ask her questions, which she reads on their lips and answers with a nod or a shake of the head. It's true that some of her friends, and even some of the teachers, understand her sign language. But she won't tell the teachers; nobody talks to them about invitations to parties. As for her friends, we'll have to tell her not to spread it around."

"*You'll* have to tell her that," he continued, addressing me alone. "Write her an invitation, specifying that you're inviting only a few people."

He paused and smiled.

"The ones you like best," he said. "That should do it."

Sure it'll do it, I said to myself. Thinking up intricate schemes for deceiving people has become a way of life to us.

●

Days passed, dross thrown up by the workings of time. Everything that happened was intermediate and conducive to a final outcome; it prepared the way for it, like the complex of phenomena that occurs when cells create a body inside a womb. The time that passes in preparation for dying is of the same nature.

I bought a card and tried to write an invitation. My first attempt was unsatisfactory; I crossed it out and went to buy several more cards. I tried again but made a mistake, so I picked up my science textbook and went out. I walked from Via Sciuti to Viale delle Alpi, then went on and turned down Viale Lazio. I stopped on the sidewalk across from Wimbow's apartment and looked up. It was seven o'clock, dusk had fallen but people's shutters and curtains were still open, and Christmas tree lights glittered in chorus all over the building's facade.

I leaned against the railing, expecting to spend a couple of hours with my attention divided between the chemistry of bones and the contemplation of windows, but all at once something red materialized in the doorway: Wimbow came out and turned left. I shut the book and followed her. She walked slowly along Viale Lazio. More Christmas trees stood outside the shops; the chromatic psychosis of their flashes reverberated on her coat and penetrated deep inside to light up the infinitesimal catastrophes that were happening in her body— dark-blue meiosis, bright-red mitosis, phosphorescent white streams of cells which breathed within the yellow cytoplasm, moving and changing shape and producing a ruby-red flash at each metamorphosis, then the acid-green indentations of the mitochondrial crests, the dark grains of the ribosomes, the blue nuclei that split up as they multiplied: a pyrotechnic metabolism, the invisible becoming vision.

After turning right and walking another fifty meters, Wimbow stopped in front of a florist's, an open-air stall with flowerpots displayed on a stepped green metal structure. The flower vendor was a young boy of about twelve or thirteen. Wimbow looked at the flowers, leaned over, and was about to lift one up by its stem; the boy warned her off in dialect but she picked it up anyway. The flower was violet and orange, its petals threadlike. The boy continued to remonstrate with her and gestured to her to put it down. Wimbow plucked a flake of air between her thumb and forefinger, brought it to her chin, and embroidered a little spiral; then she pointed to the flower and slowly, earnestly, stroked her cheek.

The boy said something exclamatory. I thought I recognized in the dialectal mess the words *deaf and dumb*. He was asking her. Wimbow again mimed the flake and spiral and took some coins out of a purse. Suspicious, and deciphering only the financial code, he approached and selected three from her extended palm; he took some tin foil out of a drawer and wrapped it around the stem. Holding the flower in her fist like a vegetal scepter, the Creole girl passed close by me but without seeing me. I waited for her to move away and now, as I tailed her, saw light crystallize inside her in buds that opened out violently, some globular, some radial, others calycoid, eruptive or flabellate, followed by clusters of efflorescences that contracted and expanded in time with her breathing, corollas of campanulas that blazed white for an instant, then turned into ox-eye daisies and snapdragons, mimosas and hyacinths, mallow and mighty hibiscus, the ferocious blooming of life in her body.

I saw her go back in through the front door of her building and disappear. I returned to my post on the sidewalk and looked up, and thirty seconds later a light lit up on the first floor, then another; a fragment of living room, its walls dark yellow, whether the color was paint or the glare from the light I couldn't tell. A red lampshade, a dark-brown wooden bookcase, another lampshade, this time green.

I stood on tiptoe; it wasn't enough. I stood on the wall and clung to the railing; people passed by below and glared up at me disapprovingly. I saw, or imagined seeing, the beginning of a hallway, a white kitchen, its tiles decorated with little light-blue sails, and then, as I stretched and twisted my body, her bedroom with a bed, a closet for clothes, and a corner for games; the flower in a thin transparent vase on the pale surface of the desk.

Clutching the railing, I searched for her life behind the window, and the form of that life, feeling proud of her body but also pitying it, this body that today was silence, tumult, and glory but in time would change, its cells growing inhospitable, its tissues merciless; even then I'd still be able to imagine it and wouldn't abandon it, and I'd still be able to love it; because it's a wonderful thing to love a body's slow decay.

•

That evening I told String and Stone I'd be sleeping over at a friend's house. I was firm but reassuring, as before; neither of them raised any objections. Then I joined Flight.

It had become a regular routine, the ghostly student being taken on educational excursions by his ghostly teacher. While we waited for darkness to fall, we made our preparations. When Flight had his back to me and was busy rummaging through the old clothes for a suitable disguise, I reached out toward the notebook I'd seen, slipped the Polaroid photo of Morana out of its pages, and put it in my pocket.

My disguise was a black wig of tangled hair and a dark-gray herringbone coat, instead of my usual windproof jacket. Flight stuffed a small cushion under his sweater to make him look plumper and put on a trench coat and fedora, so that he looked like a nocturnal, portly Bogart.

As we plodded heavy-legged along Via Principe di Paternò on the way to Via Libertà, I understood that we weren't so much realistic as hyperrealistic; we strove to exist in the real world by radicalizing its features. Walking the streets at night in our overcoat and trench coat, our wig and fedora, it wasn't just us who were overblown, it was the air, our entire lives. Then there was our way of talking: we were prima donnas of the dumb show, melodramatic and languescent. We looked at each other with blazing eyes that stared out of white lead, our features taut. When we spoke, a speech balloon appeared, the words written in white on a black background in curlicued letters. After each sentence we should have fallen into a valedictory swoon that would be our comment on proceedings.

On Via Libertà we turned left and walked back up toward the Statue. No cars passed, though it was a mid-December evening and there was already a festive atmosphere. We turned left again and climbed the steps that led to Piazza Edison. We sat down beside the Arab Well. Flight took off his fedora and laid it on the wall. We listened to the wind emulsifying on the floor of the well and coming back out to breathe.

"Comrade Nimbus," he said, looking down, "did you

know that when a bee stings, its sting stays in its victim, and the bee dies?"

I thought of the book about bees, and the fact that I'd never finished it.

"No, I didn't know that," I said.

"The bee injects the poison, its body is torn apart and it dies."

Comrade Flight was building now; I could see the faint outline of yet another thought cathedral taking shape in the darkness.

"It's the same with the drones," he said. "Their only function is to fertilize the queen. They leave their genitals in her body and die immediately afterward."

"Yes," I said, "I see."

He looked at me and waited.

"So?" I added.

"So they always die: the workers, the drones, the queen. All bees die."

"And we too have to find our own way of dying," I said.

"Exactly, Comrade Nimbus."

"How can we do it?"

"Each of us will find a way. That's why we're here—you, Comrade Radius, and I."

Although we were out in the open air, I could smell on him the rancid, half-washed odor of someone who took water from the faucet in the cellar and rubbed his body in patches, foam turning cold on his skin.

"Do you know how *you* are going to die?"

"By means of a sentence."

"Which one?"

"The one that separates one world from another and yet joins them together at the same time. The zip, the magic formula."

"What is this sentence?"

"I declare myself a political prisoner."

Out on the road I saw early car headlights, heralding dawn.

"In the brigadist code," he said, "there's a vertex that supports everything."

His false stomach bulged under his trench coat, incongruous next to his thin hands. The implacability of his thinking was perfect; I couldn't have asked more of these times of ours.

"Imagine an inverted pyramid," he explained. "The vertex of the pyramid is the sentence, 'I declare myself a political prisoner.' Everything rests on that sentence."

The wind shook the hat on the wall, shifting it a few centimeters.

It was true, I thought. From the beginning we'd dreamed of becoming three Socrateses of the armed struggle—inevitably defeated but proudly defeated, and therefore invincible even in our defeat.

"Do you understand?" Flight went on. "It's the ultimate tribute to the words of militancy, the sentence by means of which you can break free of your own narrow, personal history and enter the infinite time of revolutionary mythology, where the labor of language—the language of communiqués, initiatives, meetings—no longer has any value."

He paused and bowed his head.

"No longer exists," he said.

He made a longer pause, drained of strength, as if it was unbearable to continue to understand what he'd understood.

"You go into the silence of myth," he added then, "into dying."

His head still bowed on his chest, he sought me out with his eyes in the dense gloom, meaning it was my turn to speak.

"And for that to happen," I said, "you have to be captured."

"Yes," he said, without moving. "Capture is what separates us from time and space."

He was ever more weary, an exile in history who would soon be free at last.

"Remember," he enunciated slowly, "that the purpose of all this is defeat."

He'd said it. It was an idea he'd understood and whose seeds he'd sown, the idea of not being able, not even wanting, to win; contemplating victory only in linguistic rhetoric, as a mirage, and all the time striving for perfect defeat—perfect. And for our defeat to be perfect, our enemy must be perfect. We'd made him perfect; now we could lose.

"When will the capture take place?" I asked.

He raised his head, picked up his fedora, and put it on.

"There's no hurry, comrade. There's still a little time; enough for this operation, at any rate."

He got up from the wall and came close to me; we looked down at the blackness at the bottom of the well, into which the dawn light was slowly sinking. The holes we'd made two months earlier were still visible on the wall. As the glow revealed furtive movements among the weeds, and the sound of car engines grew increasingly noticeable, Flight put his mouth to my ear.

"It's 1978 and reality is already exhausted," he said in a barely audible whisper. Then he gestured that it was time to go back.

Along the road we said nothing. Inside my skull, however, I repeated at every step, "I declare myself a political prisoner," the sentence in which everything ended, and beyond which the freedom of the captured militant began; beyond which we'd finally be free.

We arrived on Viale delle Magnolie and went down to the cellar in silence. Still without speaking I got undressed, put my clothes on the floor, and lay down on top of them. I meant to sleep for a while, then at eight o'clock I'd go to school. In my drowsy state, while Flight's body drifted through space in slow motion, I kept repeating in my head, "I declare myself a political prisoner," and each sentence was one rung of a ladder; I climbed up the sentences, rising higher and higher but never reaching the top. Then, after the umpteenth repetition, I tried to grasp the next rung but I couldn't—it wasn't there; the other rungs were in place but where I wanted to put my hand now, there was nothing. As I sank into sleep, I knew that that void was the Creole girl, the silence between sentences, the space between words, stillness, a pause in my language, something that wasn't language, a perfect place where I didn't exist.

I woke up with a start. The light was on. I couldn't tell whether I'd slept for a few minutes or for hours. Flight was sitting up on the cot, his trench coat folded on the floor, his pillow and fedora on top of it. He wasn't asleep. He took a cookie out of a box and put it in his mouth, long green veins running down his forearm. He turned toward me, a patient look on his face. I found the question between my lips without having formulated it.

"What are we going to do with the Creole girl?" I said.

Flight dropped the cookie he held between his fingers into the box, moved over so that he was sitting on the edge of the bed, and leaned forward.

"Who?" he asked.

"Wimbow," I said. "What are we going to do with Wimbow?"

He straightened up again, relaxed and alert, all trace of tiredness gone.

"Are we going to demand a ransom?" I said.

He wiped his fingers on his pants to remove the crumbs.

"We're going to *look after* her," he said.

I didn't react to his tone and took his words at face value.

"How long?"

"As long as we need."

"Comrade: how long?"

He picked up the cookie box, closed the lid, and laid it aside; by the order of his movements he described the way things should go. Then he leaned forward again; he looked at me, examined me; he wanted to absorb me, assimilate me entirely.

"Nimbus," he asked me in the tone of one who wouldn't listen to any reply, "How long would you say a link can last?"

•

In the afternoon I was due to have a lesson at the swimming pool; I went, even though I felt drained. After the warm-up out of the water there was free swimming; I didn't go in but stood on the edge, at the end of the pool, watching the traffic in the lanes, the mechanism that governed the flow of bodies, the rhythm, the different speeds and slownesses. I estimated averages and noted exceptions—the lane of the swimmers who could keep going for an hour without stopping, with organically perfect lungs, little industries of respiration, and an ever-clean armstroke that sliced through the surface without raising any spray, the articular movement of shoulder in capsule, a hundred and eighty degrees of full water cleanly cut, the resurfacing, the head turning sideways, the mouth sucking in air.

The lane of the flounderers and the spluttering.

In the echoes of muffled noise I worked out the rules of the game I had to play. When I thought I understood them I looked for the right lane, the emptiest one, waited a few seconds longer, then did something I'd only ever imagined doing.

The dive was clean, the entry into the water sharp. I went straight down, as far as I could, exploiting the momentum, my chest skimming the bottom of the pool, and when the first impulse was exhausted I did breaststroke, turning my head to look up at the streaky light blue and the shapes of bodies. I took care to avoid any superfluous movements, drawing breath from my whole body, turning liquid into silence, meters of silence that I had to pass through, eking out air. Three-quarters of the way along I felt that I couldn't go on anymore, that the pressure of the water on my temples was too great and that I had to go up, but I forced myself to keep calm and to go on swimming slowly, low down, my eyes closed, the skin of my thorax compressing and expanding. The moment my head exploded above the surface, two meters from the end, and I took back air through my mouth, nose, and eyes, I knew that for a short time, down there, I'd been Morana, I'd been the Creole girl, and I knew that for me, today, to understand the rules of the game was to change them.

•

I spent another day writing my invitation. I touched it all over, feeling its texture, and ran the edges along my lips, wondering what I could write.

In the evening, after several attempts, I decided and wrote it.

I used simple words, "my birthday," "I'd be very pleased," the day, the time, and the address, abandoning magniloquence in favor of precision, though I did allow myself, with some embarrassment, two little twirls, one red and one black, in the top corners of the card. I slipped the card into its envelope and put it on the table. Then I went into the bathroom and locked myself in. I searched behind the radiator and pulled out Morana's photograph; I'd always looked at it whenever I could, questioning the dead and Death. I examined his pale, lopsided face, and the involuntarily bold eyes that stared into the camera, judging the person photographing them. With Morana's face fixed in my mind, I went to bed.

The next day, at school, I waited till classes were over and the bustle had died down, then I went to look for Wimbow.

She was standing by a tall hedge, wearing her red coat and a colored scarf that framed the dark skin of her face. I stopped and examined her features, my pupils visiting each of them one by one, traveling along the curved grooves that marked the outline of her cheeks, down into the faint, paler hollows below her eyes, into the double arc of her silent lips, and into that tiny vertical line on her forehead, so small it seemed like a dot emanating puzzlement about who I was, what I wanted, and why I'd been standing in front of her for a minute without saying a word, staring at her face and her silent throat.

I took the envelope out of my pocket and handed it to her. She took it, opened it, pulled out the card, and read. The dot on her forehead introflexed even further till it disappeared into a primal, personal, genetic pain, then suddenly it calmed and relaxed, the forehead rose again and filled with December light, Wimbow nodded a decisive yes, raised her hand, and twice pushed it hard with its back toward me.

I didn't move; I wished everything would end now.

Then a grown-up called from behind my back and her face broke away from the confusion of leaves, which were now budding, green and red, all together.

LANDER

In the year of the thirteen moons, when the most visionary psyche imploded with images, on December 21 a Soviet space probe landed gently on the surface of Venus. It was the winter solstice, the shortest day of the year, a brief interval of sunshine in the long Northern Hemisphere night. As it landed, the probe stirred up little radial puffs of ferrous dust. Its name was Venera 11, and it had little time to carry out its mission, because the clouds that sweep rapidly across Venus are composed of sulphuric acid, and when they turn into rain they corrode and volatilize everything. It had an hour and a half—of terrestrial time: Cytherean time is different; the rotation there is slow and retrograde, and one day lasts two hundred and forty-three Earth days. After that hour and a half, the probe would dissolve and turn into a basalt plateau, an immense planitia the size of a continent, one of those snakelike veins that can be seen from Earth with the naked eye at dawn or just after sunset.

About three hundred kilometers above the surface, the two modules that made up the probe—the orbiter and the lander—separated, and the lander went into free fall, slowed by the airbrakes and slightly rocked by the thunder and lightning.

Venera 11's lander had come to gather data: its aim was to discover what substances the soil was composed of and the exact nature of the clouds, to investigate the chemical structure of the atmosphere and study the effects of the solar wind on the planet.

But that was only the ostensible reason.

The real reason Venera 11 had touched down on Venusian soil on December 21, 1978, at the end of a year from which there were no escape routes, was a different one: to observe the Earth from afar.

Or rather, to be more precise, not the whole of Earth but just Italy. To examine its geology, its individual phenomena, its glory, and its squalor.

But that was still not enough: the core sample had to be more narrowly circumscribed.

A single city: Palermo.

Prehistory.

In order to make the analysis more accurate, this space was to be traversed by a cursor, a moving body which, through its perceptions, made it possible to accumulate data—an unsuitable, incongruous body, that of a boy whose twelfth birthday it was today and whose name was Nimbus.

About three minutes after the lander had touched down, the last iron corpuscles stirred by contact having settled and sunk back into their mineral sleep, the hatch opened, a small mechanical stairway extended and several small figures walked down the metal steps to sit down, one beside the other, on a ridge darker than the predominant dull yellow, an outcrop of bronze-colored rock, a fragment of a solidified stream of lava.

From there the Earth, Italy, Palermo, and Nimbus were perfectly visible.

Without saying a word, the natural cripple, Ezekiel, the mosquito, the prehistoric pigeon, Crematogastra, the puddle shaped like a horse's head, Morana, String, Stone, and Cotton watched. Just as they needed the human probe Nimbus in order to acquire a knowledge of space and time and their collapse, so Nimbus needed their perception.

I needed it.

In order to finish.

•

December 21 began just before dawn. From an immense distance, as the light rose, I felt under observation.

I got out of bed, after nocturnal sojourns on the armchair, and looked out of the hall window. Below, in the alley where the bakery was, a little light filtered out from under the half-lowered shutter. There was a smell of bread. The air was fresh and clean, and looking up, for the first time I caught sight of Venus, ochre and pulsing, a tiny dot in the Palermo sky. It was hard to keep it in focus—my eyes grew sore after a while—so I looked down again, saw the light from the bakery, and rested. Then I looked up again, and so I went on until Venus disappeared and the bakery light was switched off; dawn had passed, the smell of bread remained.

I went into the bathroom; the others were still asleep. I undressed, turned on the shower, soaped myself and rinsed off, swathing my skinny body with my hands. I cranked the cold water up high and took the icy jet on my face and chest. While I was getting dressed, from my bedroom in the half-light I saw a sleepy String glide past the doorway in her bathrobe and head for the kitchen; near me, on the other side, I could hear Cotton's faint breathing. When I went into the kitchen String was cleaning out the canary's cage with her back to me. On the table were her bowl and mine, full of milk, with the inevitable seven Atene cookies soaking in it, as always. I sat down.

"Pass me the panic, please," she said to me.

I didn't understand the sentence; it was meaningless. I didn't move.

"The panic," she repeated, "give me the panic; my hands are busy."

I knew the word, but had no idea what she meant. As she said it she'd gestured toward the shelf where the canary's food was. I went across, picked up some lettuce, and took it to her.

"The panic," she said impatiently. "The seeds up there, next to the millet: the ear."

I went back to the shelf, replaced the lettuce and surveyed the row of different kinds of bird food. There were two big brown spikes, like ears of corn; I took one and brought it across to her.

"Thank you," she said.

I sat down again, picked up my spoon, and ate.

"Didn't you know it was called that?" she asked me after a while, still fiddling with the cage.

"No, I didn't."

"They're called panic seeds. It's a cereal. He likes it," she said, gesturing with her head toward the canary.

I went on eating; I still felt cold from the shower. String put the cage back on the top of the wall unit and sat down.

"So there *are* still some things you don't know," she said, picking up her spoon.

There are some things you don't know either, I thought inwardly—inside my chest, and deeper down. The thought gave me no satisfaction; it was painful.

She started to eat, slowly moving her hand, with its chapped knuckles. As she brought the spoon to her mouth I knew that even in her, somewhere deep inside, there must be bewilderment and desire, a daily longing to be in the world; I knew I should clear the air with her, too, but I couldn't, not today.

"Today," she said, sliding her spoon into the bowl.

"Oh, I'm so sorry," she added at once, and looked at me and changing her expression, making it more melancholy. "I'd forgotten, I'm sorry. Happy birthday."

I looked up at her in surprise. To me, today, my birthday wasn't my birthday. It was the context of a plan.

"It doesn't matter," I said, sensing that I'd accumulated a little power. I finished my milk and stood up.

"Can I take it?" I asked, pointing at the ear that was still on the shelf.

"Of course. Are you going to school already?"

"No, I'm going to do a bit more reading. I have to finish my homework."

"All right."

She paused and looked at me, trying to seem affectionate.

"Shall we celebrate, later on?" she asked.

"School vacation starts tomorrow," I said. "This evening I'm going out with my friends."

"Your comrades," she said.

I put the ear of panic in my pocket and didn't answer.

"That'll be nice," she added.

"Yes," I said, as I left the kitchen.

"Hey," she called me back.

I turned around; I knew she'd remain there forever, half of her body visible above the table, the other half out of sight below, her thin nose constantly searching for molecules in the air, with the same impulse to sniff the world in vain that had come down through blood to me.

"I'm sorry," she said.

"It doesn't matter, really."

Just then Stone came into the kitchen. We passed in the doorway. String and Stone. And Cotton in the other room, still asleep. I left them behind, I abandoned them, because I'd reached a point beyond which they couldn't go with me.

•

The morning in class passed normally. The emotional temperature was slightly higher than usual because the end of school was looming. But no one got carried away: everyone's thoughts were haunted by the classmate who'd died and the other who'd disappeared. People would burst out laughing about something but then suddenly remember and check themselves, turning the laugh into a cough or a clearing of the throat. After the fifth period, as I left school—the ear of panic in my jacket pocket, my hand clasped around it—my gaze met that of Wimbow. She smiled at me and again made a sign to me with her head, a yes, like when she'd read the invitation. I smiled back from a distance, then looked around to see if anyone had noticed.

In the early afternoon I joined the others in the cellar, and we went over our plan. Radius would arrive on Via Sciuti at half past eight in the evening. I'd given him a copy of the keys, so he'd be able to let himself in. He'd hide in the triangular space under the stairs, behind the entrance to the doorman's office. Even when the light was on, the recess was always in shadow; anyone hiding there would be invisible. At eight forty-five Flight would arrive; he too had a duplicate of the key. Together they'd wait under the stairs till nine o'clock, when Wimbow was due to arrive. I'd be upstairs, by the intercom, ready to answer it; as soon as I'd done so, I'd hurry downstairs to join them.

During the past few evenings we'd checked how many people went past the doorman's office between eight o'clock and half past nine. The answer was very few; anyone arriving home from work usually got in around seven at the latest. There was a theoretical chance of someone going out for a game of cards later—it was not uncommon at that time of year—but most of the residents of the building were elderly. In any case, both Radius and Flight, in their hiding place under the stairs, would be armed with broomsticks—the kind that are fitted with sorghum bristles. I imagined the two of them chasing residents around the doorman's office, brandishing their weapons; the idea that we, our hands, had killed someone, killed anyone at all, was almost incredible.

As we parted I looked at them carefully—not so much their eyes but the area around the eyes, the skin that encircled them and more subtly registered all the changes; the shadows, the creases, the slow transformation of the facial expression into a wound.

Then, later that afternoon, for the first time I went into action.

When it was dark I spent two hours writing. I filled about ten pages torn out of a notebook, writing as clearly as possible. When I'd finished I put the pages into an envelope and went out. Outside it was almost too dark to see, because the streetlights were still off. I saw one that was trying to come on; it buzzed, gave a few orange flashes, and gave up. People found their way about with the help of the Christmas tree lights that shone out from windows onto the street. When I reached Piazza Edison I looked around and waited for a man to enter the front door of a building. Then I went over to the Arab Well, and dropped the envelope inside and watched till the pale rectangle came to rest at the bottom. Then I walked back home.

No one was in, so I could move freely. I opened the broom closet, got some boxes down off the shelf and started rummaging through them. I picked out unused Christmas decorations—a few strings of lights, some colored garlands, discarded cork from last year's Nativity scene, little balls, shepherd figurines, paper hats, Carnival masks, a luminous Baby Jesus, the spare one—in case the best one got lost: a constant obsession of the ever-prudent, visionary String—and stuffed them all into a capacious backpack. I got the box where Stone kept the keys, found the ones I needed, and put them in my pocket. I went into the kitchen, wrote a note, and left it under an ashtray. Finally I took a bottle of milk from the fridge, put that into the backpack too, lifted the backpack onto my shoulders, and went out.

It was six o'clock in the afternoon and the streetlights still hadn't come on. I walked to the patisserie on the corner, looked at the window display, chose the smallest and most beautiful cake, and had it gift-wrapped. I walked down Via Principe di Paternò, arrived on Via Libertà, and waited for the bus. It was dark there too; there'd been a partial power cut, affecting only the streetlights. I waited for a while, then the bus came. I got on. It was crowded; I staggered, trying to keep my balance, then grabbed hold of the rail, and gripped it tightly, feeling the molecules of bodies pass into the flesh of my palm. When the bus entered La Favorita park, which links the city to Mondello, the darkness became total because there were no longer any houses but only woodland, the vault of the high bushes and trees blocking the view of the sky. A fine drizzle began to fall. I sat down at the back, my knapsack under the seat, the cake on my knees. Not thinking about what I was doing, I rested my temples against the window; then I realized what I'd done but still didn't move. Nothing disgusted me anymore.

By the time I got off it was six-forty. The rain had stopped. Along the road I kicked at the heaps of wet leaves and they whispered; I splashed my shoes in the puddles and repeated over and over again, in my head and between my lips, "I declare myself a political prisoner I declare myself a political prisoner," clicking the words like the beads of a rosary, walking in time to their rhythm. I reached the beginning of Viale Galatea, where I stopped and waited. A minute passed; I looked behind me: there was nobody there, nothing to wait for. In front of me the road was silvery—sad plane trees with raindrops trickling down off the backs of their leaves; above, the sky was black.

I wished I didn't have to move another step. I wished I could stand there, my shoes happily immersed in one of the countless puddles, motionless and purely sensory, to cure myself of the infection of words. I'd realized that while Comrade Flight had been striving to turn himself into a political prisoner, all my efforts had been directed toward the moment, now, when I could call myself a mythopoetic prisoner, the pleasure of being inside sentences, the effort, the fear of leaving the world of sentences. For the past year I'd been fashioning language—proclaiming, declaiming, threatening. I'd progressed through language step by step and word by word to find myself here and now, just before seven o'clock in the evening on December 21, 1978, a subverter of subversion.

I looked back again; the road was empty. Ahead it was the same. I set off again, the cake beginning to weigh heavy, the shoulder straps of the backpack chafing. I arrived, got out the keys, and unlocked the back gate. The garden path was carpeted with leaves. There were scraps of wastepaper, and noises from the end of the garden behind the house, where, months ago, I'd begun to invent the alphamute with the others—the reawakening of the invisible life that inhabited the space where we didn't live.

I sniffed; the air smelled good. I shut the gate and walked through the darkness toward the backdoor. As I walked along the path I started repeating my chant again, with different words. "I declare myself a mythopoetic prisoner," I murmured, "I declare myself a mythopoetic prisoner."

I opened up the house and took the sheets off the furniture to let the space breathe. I switched on the indoor lights and then those in the garden too: for a moment, the foliage of the hedge shivered in the gloom with the rapid passage of kittens. Then I turned on the faucets in the kitchen and ran the water till it lost its rusty color and turned clear. I did the same in the bathroom: this evening I wanted the house to be alive, its body awake, its lungs full of air, and its blood transparent.

I emptied out the backpack and started putting up the decorations. I stood on a chair and draped red and silver garlands around the curved arms of the chandelier; I scattered pinecones around, put a shepherd figurine on the edge of the table and fixed the elastic of a clown's mask around a vase so that his face was cupped on the bulge. I went out into the garden and tied bows everywhere, two strings of lights around the medlar tree and one around a bush; I put the plugs in the sockets and the lights came on at random, two red ones on one side, none on the other, then three green ones and one yellow, then one blue one, then nothing for twenty seconds: I had no idea how to correct it and went back inside.

I took the segments of cork and put one on the table but dropped another. I bent down to pick it up but instead turned it over onto its convex side, arranged others in a line behind it and more alongside them, a meter away, in a parallel line, forming a pathway along the floor. Then I twined more lights around the chairs, the rocking chair, the television set, and the big valve radio that stood on top of a cupboard.

A sudden doubt crossed my mind; I picked up the phone and dialed for the official time: it was nearly half past seven, there was still a little time. I worked faster, scattering a few more red berries around, sticking bouquets of dried flowers in vases and glasses, putting the luminous Baby Jesus in a corner on the floor, hanging paper hats on nails, arranging the Zorro mask between the wires of the lights and the television screen so that one green light and one red one shone out of the eyeholes, tying the ribbons to door handles and, outside, to the branches of trees.

I filled my arms with little colored balls and strewed them around the room, both on the furniture and on the floor. Almost all of them were made of plastic but one was glass; not noticing this, I dropped it along with the others beside the rocking chair and it smashed. I gathered the pieces with the edge of my shoe and started pushing them into the corner but then stopped—it didn't matter. I took a polystyrene composition with a smoke-eater candle in the shape of a candle on top and some leathery mistletoe glued all around and put it on the table, then picked up the house keys, half-opened the shutters that gave onto the street, went out, and walked quickly down the street to the phone booth halfway along Viale Galatea. I put in some tokens, took out the scrap of paper I'd written the number on, and made a call. It was quick and to the point. I tried to disguise my voice and make it sound grown-up, but I couldn't keep up the pretense and went on in my own voice. When I'd finished I walked back to the apartment. I checked the time again; it was a quarter to eight. I went into the kitchen, carried the cake, still in its gift wrapping, into the living room, went back to get a glass, filled it with milk, and put it beside the cake. I looked for some matches and candles, lit the candles, and stood them on the furniture and on the floor, along the little cork path; I lit the smoke-eater candle too and switched off the light. Then I turned the radio to a moderate volume, searched for a station that was playing some songs, placed a chair in front of the shutters, sat down, and waited. Minutes passed, I couldn't calculate how many. Now and then I looked out through the gaps between the louvers. No one passed by; I saw only the wet road gleaming with light. From where I sat I could see the sky too.

Soon, I thought, the police would arrive on Viale delle Magnolie to arrest Dario Scarmiglia. They'd catch him in the cellar, or maybe already in the street on his way to Via Sciuti. At any rate, I was sure, Scarmiglia would smile like someone crossing a threshold. He'd request three seconds' silence, look them all in the eye and then, spacing out the words, utter his magical, capitalized sentence: "I Declare Myself A Political Prisoner."

After that, if they followed up all the information they found at the bottom of the well, they'd soon find Massimo Bocca too. They'd find him hiding under the stairs in the dark, clutching a broomstick. Maybe Bocca would misunderstand the situation and put up a fight, but broomsticks are only good for chasing off bats.

The fact that, along with my account of the past few months, I'd put the photograph of Morana in the envelope would have convinced them that the person who'd phoned telling them who to look for and where was a credible witness, and they needed to act quickly and intervene at once.

The confession mentioned me too, but in any case by that stage everything would be straightforward. The police would go upstairs to our apartment and speak to String and Stone. String and Stone wouldn't understand, because there were some things they didn't know. They didn't know they'd been harboring a militant day after day for the past few months, they didn't know what a world of horror could live, quite naturally, inside a skull. They didn't know anything about ideology or sex. They'd sit with their hands clasped together and their feet in slippers, asking questions and answering the ones that they were asked in monosyllables.

A car stopped outside the gate at the address written on my invitation, and I saw Wimbow get out, say goodbye, and turn toward the house. I increased the volume of the radio, opened the shutters and went out, pulling them closed behind me. While she waited outside the gate, bundled up in her overcoat, looking beautiful and serene, the cold air crinkling her skin, I remembered that I'd said in my confession that they'd soon find me. That was true, but I needed more time: I needed Venus to alter time, to disarrange chronology.

I opened the gate and let her in. The car drove off and we

were left under the black sky, with the strains of Italian music coming from indoors. She looked around at the ribbons and the strings of lights festooned around the medlar. She was holding a small white and light-blue package tied with a red ribbon; she handed it to me. I took it, opened it without tearing the paper or creasing the ribbon, and found myself holding a piece of smooth white wire interspersed with spikes.

Now Wimbow smiled—how she smiled! She pointed at the little package with her eyes, formed an intangible rectangle with her forefingers and thumbs and presented it to me, then closed her fingers to make two little bunches and rubbed the tips together. I understood that she'd made it, that it was her work. My sentence—one of my two sentences, clean, and no longer rusty, and painted white.

"And now?" I thought. Now it had to end.

But it didn't end, not yet.

I took two steps forward; I wasn't sure whether to speak or try to communicate in gestures—I didn't know what people usually did. I said, "Come in," or something like that. She gestured to show that she'd understood and to urge me to speak, that it was all right for me to speak, then she walked toward the shutters. I opened them first a little, then completely, and there was nothing there, Wimbow entered and there was no one inside, only a cavern reddened by candles, a dimly lit room, and in the half-light scattered ornaments and a jumble of other objects and the blare of the radio, although that, inside her, was silence. I turned the radio off, while Wimbow looked at the Zorro mask tied to the television screen with green and red flashes in its eyeholes, the colored pinecones, the smoke-eater candle, the festoons and hats.

She turned toward me. I avoided her gaze and tore off the wrapping of the cake, the paper rustling between my fingers. I showed her the cake, with its topping of candied apples and small strawberries, and its delicious smell. She looked at me, then turned toward the half-open shutters beyond which lay the street, the world outside, her father's car that had driven away, everything that wasn't there. I walked toward her and told her not to worry, the others hadn't arrived yet, there was nothing wrong, but she didn't believe me. She put her forefinger on her chest and then brusquely cut the air with her fingers extended. She froze for a moment, then again sliced space with her hand. I felt sick. I took the disintegrating ear of panic out of my jacket pocket and showed it to her. I told her it was called panic, like fear. I explained that it was a funny coincidence. I told her panic soon passed—it melted away and turned into existence. But the little wrinkle of concern in the middle of her forehead had reappeared: not so much fear as anger at having been tricked.

I gestured to her to wait, to trust me. I took the piece of rusty barbed wire out of my backpack and stuck it in the middle of the cake: tarnished and twisted, it looked like a hunchbacked monster. Then I picked up the white piece of wire and planted it next to the other—the bride. The bride and her hunchbacked monster. I tried to light them with a match, but they didn't catch fire. Undeterred, I kept trying, dipping the tip of the barbed wire into the flame, but only burned my fingers. One after another the matches died in my hand. Dejected, I sat down on a chair and bowed my head. I watched my arms glow red in wind-like gusts in the shadowy room, while nothing happened. Then Wimbow touched her chest again. She formed the roof of a house with her hands and made a gesture indicating something going away, and finally, after a pause, brushed her chin with the middle and ring fingers of her right hand.

I didn't understand, but I did understand. This was not where she wanted to be.

While I was thinking, Wimbow moved a chair aside and came to stand in front of me. She put the fingers of her right hand to her cheek and stroked it gently, twice, three times. Beside us, on the table, was the cake with the two unlightable pieces of barbed wire sticking out of it, surrounded by match stubs, curved and blackened.

How old are we now, I wondered, as the little pale patch flickered on the back of her hand, and where are we? What has become of the deep time that I imagined, the soft, liquid time, the material time that would quench my thirst? Why in its stead are there words, thousands of sentences, this orderly slaughter of insects? Why does language keep flashing, when all I want is to enter silence, your silence, and cry—stop just feeling the need to and cry?

I got up from my chair, stepped forward, and started shaking her. I shook harder and harder, brutally. At first she was astonished, then she was terrified. As I shook her I thought of Morana's body, of the pressing, the crushing, the breath disappearing, the silence. For an instant a bonfire blazed between Wimbow's lips, and a sound came out of her mouth, a hoarse, feeble, animal cry, her first voice. I let go of her. She ran to the other end of the room and crouched down in the corner between the sofa and the rocking chair. I sank down again on the chair and hours seemed to pass in a minute—our whole lives in a coagulum.

We were twenty, we were in love, and that evening we'd eaten a slice of pizza, scorched brown, the tomato sweet and frothy, sitting on the steps of an apartment building, under the shelter of the eaves, while the rain teemed down on the street and crumbs and raindrops pulverized on our fingers.

We were thirty, we lived together, and one day, while I was having a bath, there was a power outage and the hot water system broke down, so you heated up water in the kitchen and brought it in a saucepan; you saw me naked, and, though we knew each other naked, I was embarrassed and looked at the bones of my legs.

Thirty-five, and early one morning, while we were in the last phase of sleep, you lying on your stomach with your arm along your body, I on my side, turned toward you, you opened your hand and took me between your fingers, gentle, unconscious, and in my somnolescence I felt that your hand was asleep and I was your dream; later, awake, we went out onto the balcony to smell the jasmine.

We were fifty and had forgotten so many things. We were no longer together and never met. Now and then something would remind us of a gesture or a word, and, separately, we'd do archaeology.

We were a thousand years old, and we were biology. Our bodies no longer existed and were something else. One of your feet was a rock, my nose was sand, your ears had become apples, one of my eyes was a sea urchin on the seabed. Your mouth was now flesh in a man's hand, my lungs had become a pencil. Matter changed, and we changed with it. Without consciousness, the man's hand, in which you were, picked up the pencil, in which I was, and wrote sentences, and we still lived on in the movement and the writing.

I thought half an hour had passed, I thought it was the dead of night. There was the sound of rain. I got up and walked toward her: she was still crouching behind the rocking chair, wrapped up in her overcoat, among the fragments of the glass ball; in the gloom I saw the white of her eyes, the animal light that absorbed. She had the gentle, feral pride of the hunted.

I don't know why, Creole girl, I'd decided that you were the link. I don't know why, without knowing you, without having you, I missed you so much. You were where the sentence crumbled and flaked away, one layer of skin after another, till only a void was left.

Again I sought the white of her eyes in the dark cocoon of her body. Staring at her, I rubbed my fingers and stretched out my arm toward her, but didn't touch her and withdrew it with my thumb between my middle and index fingers, then nodded my head. Wimbow retreated till her back was against the wall. I rubbed, opened my arms in the crucifixion, and nodded again.

She didn't move.

I rubbed my fingers, gave several nods, then squatted down sideways on, in the pose of a kangaroo, and hopped up and down on the spot, three, four, ten times. I stopped, panting hard, and turned toward her to glimpse the light of her face. I rubbed my fingers once more, spread out my arms, bent forward, and loomed over her, then rubbed my fingers again, spun around and around like a pin in a bowling alley, nodded my head, straightened up, and, trying not to tremble, put one hand over the other, in a dignified pose, then bent down and touched my knees, hips, shoulders, and forehead crosswise with my fingertips, then repeated the sequence, knees, hips, shoulders, and forehead, doing my best to remain compact and not scatter myself, then I kicked backward angrily, more and more angrily, because Wimbow gazed at me uncomprehendingly, and as I did so, my foot hit a piece of cork, knocking it against the wall with a bang, which was followed by silence, and in the silence, once more, my arms shaking, I frantically jumbled up all the forms of the alphamute, yet another desperate language in which there was no pose for me to say love, to say it was only love, till I was exhausted and spinning around disjointedly, out of control. Wimbow stood up, stepped toward me and touched my neck, my cheeks, and my cheekbones, then put her fingers around my head like a crown, with her thumbs on my forehead and the other fingers splayed; I felt the warmth of her fingertips, felt it soothing me. Then she lifted her hands (and my nimbus disappeared, and I asked my nimbus, as it disappeared, "Isn't it me?" "It's not you," it replied), and she looked at me, and there was calm time in her eyes; then she left me and went back into the shadows behind the rocking chair.

Without realizing what I was doing, I slid slowly down onto the floor, on the other side of the semidarkness; behind us the candlelight had almost completely died down: the tiniest of flames still flickered against the walls.

Time passed.

On Venus, eyes began to get sore. In single file, the same way they'd come down, the figures trooped back up into the lander, then they squeezed up together till each body merged into the next, and waited, immersed in the sky, for the final corrosion.

I was there too, immersed in the sky. And the bodies—my bending body and the Creole girl's body—were there.

My despair, her silence.

When I touched my forehead, there was something wet on my fingertips.

I sniffed them and smelled blood.

While the lines of time and space converged and the vanishing point of 1978, the moment when it would end forever, was reached, I knew that now what remained was the sense of pain.

Like a nocturnal animal, taking care not to erase the blood from my fingers, I approached the Creole girl's body.

The floor beneath my palms was cool.

The Creole girl's body was in silence. The white of her eyes was no longer there. She'd fallen asleep. The white, the light of her body, the depth of the organs. The breathing. The Creole skin. The word *Creole*, which means to create and bring up. The word that created silence, that brought it up.

I moved closer and bent over her.

The shoulder, the hollow of the neck. The forearm, the back of the hand resting in her lap—the little pale patch. And the half-open palm. On the little cheek of the palm, below the thumb, another small patch: dark, of unconscious blood; on the floor the shards of the glass ball.

I came within a millimeter of her hand: in that interstice between my perception and her existence, I concentrated the imagination of what I'd lost.

Then, reaching after so long something that was source and estuary, for the first time I smelled her smell. Brown, earthly, firm, and eternal. The vision that didn't disappear.

In one breath I sniffed her life.

I straightened up and knelt there, watching the world sink meekly into her body.

The world and the sky.

All need, desire, and fear, in the light modulations of breathing.

I looked around. The line of the furniture half-erased by the darkness, the things, the remains. I heard that the rain outside had stopped too.

A meter away from me, on the floor, in a rarefied pale halo, there was something that glowed. Sliding across the tiles, I reached out, and picked up the tiny light in both hands. Through the phosphorescence I recognized the slightly curled body, the arms already parted to bless, a small plastic nimbus stuck behind the head.

I imagined a Nativity scene.

The Nativity scene of biology, made with the sidereal darkness that filled the female cavity and with the stellar matter shattered in the male sperm that, when it entered the cavity, disintegrated in the blackness and created the white swarm, the stria of glittering constellations, and in the body and the cosmos, in the sweetness of every conflagration, gave birth to night—and every child was night and conflagration and bewilderment, time incarnate, and for millennia the generations had bent over the body of time and gazed at it and imagined it and worshipped its star-defended darkness, imagining that there was a purpose in things, beyond the infinite impulse to remain, and so had mingled language and the destruction of bodies with time, and in darkness had created and disintegrated words, the fragmentation of lights.

In the silence of that last minute, crouching in front of the crouching body of my love, my oblivious love, my real and invented love, my Creole, created love, I listened to the future roar of matter mingling—in me and in her—stars with bones and blood with light, the sound of the infinite transformation of matter into pain and of pain into time.

And it was only then, when in the making of our night stars exploded in blackness, that at the end of words the crying began.

AUTHOR'S NOTE

In this book the real chronology of the events of 1978 has been to some extent changed in accordance with the needs of the story. Also, the nature of some TV shows and the order in which they were broadcast, as well as the times when the public became aware of certain scientific discoveries, have been adapted to the requirements of the narrative. I take full responsibility for these conscious inaccuracies.